Rachel Hore worked in London publishing for many years before moving with her family to Norwich, where she teaches publishing and creative writing at the University of East Anglia. She is married to the writer D. J. Taylor and they have three sons.

Her previous novels are *The Dream House*, *The Memory Garden*, *The Glass Painter's Daughter*, which was shortlisted for the 2010 Romantic Novel of the Year award, *A Place of Secrets*, which was picked by Richard and Judy for their book club, *A Gathering Storm*, which was shortlisted for the RONA Historical Novel of the Year 2012, and the latest bestseller, *The Silent Tide*.

Praise for *The Silent Tide*
'Compelling, engrossing and moving;
a perfect holiday indulgence'
Santa Montefiore

'Engrossing and romantic, it's a wonderful story of family secrets and the choices women make'
Jane Thynne, author of *Black Roses*

Praise for *A Gathering Storm*
'With a serious eye for exquisite detail, Hore's latest, brilliantly crafted novel aptly follows a photographer, Lucy. She takes a journey to capture past, life-changing family secrets, embracing three generations along the way, across Cornwall, London, East Anglia and Occupied France'
Mirror

Praise for *A Place of Secrets*
'A fascinating, hugely readable book ...
Rachel Hore's research and her mastery
of the subject is deeply impressive'
Judy Finnigan

A Week in Paris

RACHEL HORE

**SIMON &
SCHUSTER**

London · New York · Sydney · Toronto · New Delhi

A CBS COMPANY

First published in Great Britain by Simon & Schuster UK Ltd, 2014
A CBS COMPANY

3 5 7 9 10 8 6 4

Simon & Schuster UK Ltd
1st Floor
222 Gray's Inn Road
London WC1X 8HB

www.simonandschuster.co.uk

Simon & Schuster Australia, Sydney
Simon & Schuster India, New Delhi

A CIP catalogue record for this book
is available from the British Library

PB ISBN: 978-1-47113-076-2
EBOOK ISBN: 978-1-47113-077-9

Typeset by M Rules
Printed and bound by CPI Group (UK) Ltd, Croydon, CR0 4YY

For Juliet and Victoria

November 1944
Derbyshire, England

She was a scrappy wisp of a girl who lived with forty-three other children in a large ugly house on the edge of a country town. The meagre grounds of Blackdyke House were covered not with grass, but with gravel, and enclosed by a wooden paling fence because the original wrought iron had gone for scrap. The orphanage had been evacuated here from London, but that was long before the girl had arrived. Her mind refused to contemplate the past. She'd blotted it out. So far as she was concerned, she might always have lived at Blackdyke House. Perhaps she always would.

The dark-panelled walls inside were studded with gloomy portraits whose eyes seemed to follow her as she walked in line with the other children from dormitory to refectory, from refectory to schoolroom. In the entrance hall hung the painting she feared most of all. It showed a row of dead rabbits and birds nailed to a beam. The glazed eyes and the trickles of dried blood that ran down their bodies had been executed with deft brushstrokes, as though the artist had taken pleasure in the task. She would hurry past it without looking, but still she could sense it there.

The town was near an airfield, and whenever planes roared overhead she would run to hide in a cupboard or under a bed, where she lay curled up, her small body taut with terror, until they'd passed. Some of the older children teased her about being afraid of their own planes, but she couldn't help her reaction. And she didn't explain because she couldn't speak.

The nurses at the orphanage were not uncaring. They simply did as Matron said: 'Treat the children equally, be kind but firm, don't get too close.' Some of their charges were grieving, several had lost both parents in terrible circumstances, but Matron believed that a strict routine should settle them: good plain food, fresh air, church twice on Sundays. A list of rules was displayed on a board outside Matron's office, opposite the picture of the dead creatures. At five years old the girl could not read all the words, but she knew each rule began with the same instruction: *Don't.*

The number of children in the orphanage wasn't always forty-four. Sometimes a relative would come to claim one. Sometimes there would be a new face: sad and bewildered, or angry and desperate. Never anything to cause Matron to deviate from her routine.

And every now and then there would be a viewing. A married couple might come to inspect the children and perhaps pick one out. For adoption, was the awed whisper. The children knew about adoption – it meant being given a new mother and father to replace the old ones. Most of the children longed to be adopted, to have somewhere to belong. Yet she noticed the doubtful expressions of some who were chosen. Not all the prospective parents looked kind.

She wanted to belong somewhere, but nobody ever chose her. Most of the couples picked babies or toddlers, and those willing to take an older child certainly didn't want a girl who couldn't – or wouldn't – speak. That might be storing up all kinds of trouble.

So she lived her life day by day, unable to mourn the past she'd suppressed or to hope for the future. She wasn't unhappy, exactly. Rather, her heart had frozen up inside. Only in sleep did she know deep happiness or sorrow. Sometimes her dreams were full of noise or fear or simply laced with loneliness.

There were some nights, however, that she dreamed of someone singing to her in a soft low voice, a woman's voice. A woman with a lovely face and gentle hands. And after such a dream she would wake to find her pillow streaked with tears.

Chapter 1

March 1956
Paris

Fay pushed open the heavy door and followed the other girls into the soft gloom of the interior. The air hung heavy with incense and it took a moment to adjust to the whispering darkness and the vastness of the space. On either side of the nave, a line of arches undulated towards a light-filled area before the altar. High overhead soared a vaulted ceiling. It was all breathtakingly beautiful.

'Gather round, girls!' Miss Edwards' well-bred English tones summoning her sixth-formers sounded distant and dreamlike. Fay crossed the chequered floor, and lingered at the edge of the group in time to hear her say, 'Notre Dame is French for what? Our Lady, that's right, Evelyn. A masterpiece of gothic architecture, and the heart and soul of Paris for centuries. The cathedral is built on the site of . . .' but Fay was hardly listening.

Her attention was attracted instead by a row of stained-glass windows. She edged sideways to contemplate them more clearly. Each was a patchwork of glowing colours with rich, sensuous names. *Crimson*, she said to herself. *Imperial purple, indigo, lapis lazuli.* Far from being overwhelmed by the darkness of the church, the colours shone out, their beauty enhanced by it. She was pondering the significance of light shining out of darkness when Miss Edwards said, 'Fay, dear, are you still with us?' which brought her out of her reverie.

'Sorry,' she mumbled. After that she did her best to keep up.

When they reached the open space before the choir stalls and the altar, the girls loitered, pointing in wonder at the great rose windows floating high above the transepts on either side, bathing everything in jewelled light. Even Margaret, usually bored by sightseeing and culture, spread her arms to admire the rainbow on her coat. 'Golly,' she managed to muster, her bold eyes softened with delight. '*Golly*.'

Fay smiled at this, but as she glanced about, half-listening to Miss Edwards, she felt troubled. The more she tried to catch at her unease, the stronger it became. It meant something to her, this place – and yet how could it? She'd never been here before. This school trip was her first time in Paris. She knew it was.

Later they explored the aisle that curved round behind the altar, and stopped to peep into some of the prayer chapels that fringed the outside walls. Fay and Evelyn liked an altar where there was a carving of the Virgin Mary cradling the dearest Baby Jesus, who reached out a dimpled hand. Evelyn insisted on lighting a votive candle there, but Margaret hung back, more interested in a group of boys in striped blazers who were milling about outside.

'Aren't they with us?' she whispered to Fay.

'I think so.' She recognized one, a tall slender lad with butter-coloured hair that gleamed like a choirboy's in the dimness, remembering him from the Channel ferry. She'd been going up on deck to get some air and had met him coming the other way down the narrow stairway. He'd smiled as he'd held back to let her pass.

The girls were leaving the chapel when it happened. From somewhere high in the building a bell began to toll with a sound so deep and grave that the very air vibrated. Fay clapped her hands over her ears to shut out the sound, but on and on it rang. She couldn't breathe. She needed to get out. Turning, she ran blindly. And barged straight into someone. A hand gripped her arm. 'Whoa!' the someone said softly.

She looked up to see the blond boy. 'Sorry,' she gasped wildly, but allowed him to steady her.

As suddenly as it had begun, the ringing stopped. As the echoes died, her panic, too, ebbed away.

'Are you all right?' the boy asked in his clear, cultured voice. He released her and she stepped back, hardly daring to look at him properly. His forehead was crinkled in a frown. Such an expressive face he had, the dark eyes full of concern.

'Thank you, I'm fine now.' She could not stop the shame rising in her cheeks. Evelyn came across to claim her whilst Margaret set off with her funny loping run to fetch Miss Edwards. The boy remained quietly by. His companions hung about in the background, cuffing each other and laughing.

Eventually the graceful figure of Miss Edwards hurried up and Fay was glad to hear her light tones: 'Fay! That'll do, everyone. It's all over now.' And she steered Fay away with gentle firmness.

They sat together in the chapel before the Virgin and the

entreating baby. 'What on earth was the matter, Fay?' her teacher murmured. 'It was only a bell. Summoning people to a service, I expect.'

'I don't know,' Fay answered with a shiver. 'It frightened me, that's all. I'm all right now, really.' She was struggling to capture a formless memory. No, whatever it was had gone.

That evening, the chatter of English voices rose to the roof of a huge reception room in the Hôtel de Ville. It was like the twittering of starlings in the trees of Place de la Concorde at twilight. At the sound of a car backfiring, the birds would lift together in a great cloud, its shape forming and reforming against the purpling sky.

These were gaudier birds than starlings – several hundred sixth-formers and their teachers from fifteen English schools gathered under one roof for the final night of a spring trip to Paris organized by the League of Friendship. The girls were awkward and self-conscious in their first evening gowns, the boys hot and uncomfortable in formal suits with stiff collars. Earlier there had been lengthy speeches by stuffy French dignitaries, then a buffet supper of strange meats in aspic and an oily salad. Rumours of a skiffle band had been dismissed, but now that the string quartet was tuning up beside the area cleared for dancing, excitement was mounting all the same.

From her place of safety by the wall, Fay scanned the crowd, wondering where Evelyn and Margaret could have gone while she'd been in the powder room. They'd all been talking to two boys from Winchester a moment ago; or rather Evelyn and Margaret had. Fay hung back, unpractised in the flirtatious banter the occasion demanded, and worried that her neckline was sinking too low. She'd muttered an excuse and slipped away.

In the ladies' she'd repinned the dress then stared at her fragile features in the ornate looking-glass. She tried not to notice how the garment's murky shade of green made her skin look bleached, and dulled the blue of her eyes. Her mother, reluctant to let her come on this trip at all, had not been able to afford a new dress to be made up for a single night, so Fay had borrowed one from a neighbour's daughter.

Mummy had done her best to alter it, Fay conceded, and had shown her a pretty way of wearing her dark hair – she tucked a stray wave back into the slide – but they both recognized that the dress would no more than 'do'. Certainly she felt dreary next to striking, chestnut-haired Margaret, sheathed in full-length ivory, or fair Evelyn, pretty as a doll in gauzy blue. She frowned at her reflection, scooped up her homemade evening bag and set off back to the hall. There must be some boy, she thought grimly, who would save her pride by claiming her for a dance.

Standing by the wall, watching the crowd, she eventually spotted a statuesque white figure that could only be Margaret. As she started to weave her way towards her, someone touched her arm and a clear voice said, 'Hello, again.' She turned and found herself looking into the face of the blond boy from that morning.

'Adam Warner,' he said rather shyly, putting out his hand. 'You remember ... from Notre Dame?'

'Of course I do,' she said, shaking it. 'I'm Fay – Fay Knox.' She added, 'I should apologize for my ridiculous behaviour.'

'Nothing to apologize for,' he said quickly. His forehead wrinkled in that nice way he had, as though he was really listening to her. 'Are you all right now?'

'Yes,' she nodded, a little too enthusiastically. 'Completely all right.'

'Good, I'm glad.'

'I'm not usually so silly.'

'The bell was very loud,' he said with a grave expression.

'It was, wasn't it?' She was relieved to be taken seriously. 'And it was the urgency of it.' She'd puzzled about the incident for the rest of the day, remembering how the sound had cut into her, unmade her. Margaret had snorted with laughter afterwards, of course. Their school lives were ordered by bells. Why make a fuss about this one? Fay still had no answer.

Just then, the musicians struck into a lively foxtrot and all around them people started pairing off. Fay glimpsed Margaret taking the floor with the taller and cockier of the boys from Winchester, but couldn't see Evelyn.

'I say, do you like dancing?' Adam asked.

'I'm not very good at it,' she said cautiously. She'd hated dance classes at school, the stupidity of being paired with other girls, nobody wanting to lead.

'Nor am I.' It was his turn to look relieved. 'Shall we try? Perhaps we wouldn't tread on each other's toes very much.'

He offered her his hand and she took it, and followed him through the crowd. She'd feared being a wallflower this evening, but here she was, asked for the first dance by this, not handsome exactly, but certainly very nice-looking boy. Margaret raised an eyebrow as she sailed by in the arms of her partner and Fay couldn't help giving her a smug smile.

She found dancing with Adam delightful and her toes were quite safe. It was much more natural than having to lead Evelyn in lessons. They seemed to float along, she giving him little glances that took in the rich brown of his eyes, his fair skin with its light dusting of freckles. He'd only just started needing to shave and his mouth still had a boyish tenderness.

They weren't able to hear easily above the music, but she learned that he was at one of the older grammar schools somewhere near the Welsh border. A couple of hundred miles then from Little Barton in Norfolk, where Fay lived with her mother, and the girls' high school she attended in Norwich. This League of Friendship trip was a one-off, so realistically, they were hardly likely to bump into one another again. For her this lent the occasion a certain poignancy.

The foxtrot ended and a waltz began. They kept passing Evelyn, dancing with another boy from Adam's school, a boy who rather gauchely kept addressing comments to Adam instead of talking to his partner. Then that dance, too, ended and Fay and Adam found themselves standing awkwardly on the edge of the dance floor, neither sure what to do next.

'It's awfully hot, isn't it?' she said, fanning herself. She didn't want him to think he had to stay with her out of politeness – that would be mortifying.

'Would you like a drink?' he asked and she nodded gratefully.

They found a small side room with a bar from which Adam fetched lemonade. As they edged their way through the crowds with their glasses, looking for a place to sit, someone knocked into Fay, splashing her drink over her dress. Adam solemnly produced a handkerchief and they stood together in the cool air by an open window whilst she mopped up. Then they looked out at the silvery river, the soft lights on the bridges, each searching for something to say.

'It is lovely, isn't it?' Fay said. 'Have you enjoyed Paris?' She cursed herself for such an obvious question, but he didn't seem to mind.

'Very much. It's so sophisticated compared to London, isn't it? Not that I don't like London,' he added hastily, 'but when you read writers like Camus and Sartre you realize how stuck we English are in our old-fashioned ways.'

'We've not really read them, I'm afraid. Our teacher Miss Edwards pointed out that café where they're supposed to go – what's it called, Les Deux Magots? But I think she finds what she calls their "irregular lives" a little shocking.'

Adam laughed. 'She seemed rather a brick today, your Miss Edwards, but I can well imagine.'

'What do you make of Existentialism?' she asked, genuinely curious. Miss Edwards had at least explained the philosophy, but made it sound grim.

Adam glanced to where, nearby, a strapping boy was gesticulating as he told some funny story very loudly to an admiring circle. 'It's a bit difficult to explain in a nutshell,' he said and she felt sorry that she'd asked. Perhaps he thought her too serious. People often did.

The music changed to another waltz. 'Oh, this is Strauss,' she said, changing the subject. 'Our orchestra played this last year.' She listened to the joyous swing of it.

'You're a musician, obviously,' he said, watching her fingers move to the music.

'I play the violin. And the piano, too, though I gave that up.'

Fay's mother was a pianist. She taught music at the village school and took in pupils at home. For a long while she'd taught Fay, but Fay had come to prefer the passionate voice of the violin. It expressed so many things she couldn't put into words so that it became her voice too.

It was when Fay outgrew the violin teacher in Little Barton that her mother had found Signor Bertelli. Long ago, before running off with his conductor's young English wife, Signor Bertelli had been Leader of the most prestigious orchestra in Milan. Fay visited their flat in Norwich near the cathedral twice a week after school for lessons, painstakingly saved for by her mother. If she played well he closed his eyes and listened with an expression of dreamy pleasure, but if she hadn't put enough work in, he would slap his brilliantined head in despair and groan, 'No, no, no,' as though grievously wounded.

'I'm fond of listening to music,' Adam was saying, 'but a duffer when it comes to playing. I admire anyone who can scrape the catgut and get a few notes out of it.'

'It's not made of cat,' she said, laughing. 'I love it. It's all I want to do.'

'Good for you.' He sighed. 'I haven't the faintest clue what I want to do. University, I expect. I'm thinking about languages – my French isn't too bad. After that, I'll see what turns up. Your glass is empty. Would you like another?'

'No, thanks. I ought to see if my friends are looking for me.'

'Yes, of course you must.' He sounded disappointed.

She was still clutching his handkerchief. 'I'm sorry, it's quite sticky,' she said, holding it out to him.

'Keep it,' he said. 'I've plenty. I was given some of my father's.' A cloud of unhappiness passed over his face and was gone.

'Oh. Well, thank you. I enjoyed dancing.'

'So did I. Very much.'

She didn't see him alone for the rest of the evening, though they smiled complicity if they passed, dancing with other partners.

Very early the next morning, Fay saw Adam arrive on the platform with the rest of his school group at the Gare du Nord as she was about to board the train. She gave him a tentative wave and his face lit up. '*Bon voyage*,' he said.

'Thanks. *Vous aussi*.'

When she was sitting with the other girls she felt another pang of sadness, knowing that after today she'd probably never see him again. There was something about him that echoed a call inside her, though she couldn't say what this something was.

She'd stuffed his handkerchief in her coat pocket and her hand closed over it now. What was it that he'd said? That he'd inherited a lot of handkerchiefs from his father. The implication struck her. Perhaps he, like her, was fatherless.

Fay's father had died when she was a toddler and she had no memory of him. He was American, Mummy had told her. A doctor, dedicated to helping people, and he'd been killed in the war, in an air raid. Fay couldn't recall the house that Mummy said they'd lived in, either. It had been in a leafy part of London, apparently, near an old walled park stocked with deer that kings had once loved to hunt. Mummy had shown her a picture of the house. It was pretty, part of a Georgian terrace, painted white and with a tiny front garden full of roses, which her mother adored. Two years after Fay's father's death a stray doodlebug had dropped on that house in broad daylight, destroying it and most of its contents. 'It was lucky that we were out,' her mother said. Fay thought this sounded wrong. Why should they have been lucky and her father unlucky? Luck, it seemed, was very capricious. The piano had also survived. That, apparently, was lucky, too.

Fay's clearest early memories were of Primrose Cottage in Little Barton, which Miss Dunne, a much older friend of her mother's, had lent them after the bomb, when her mother decided they should leave London for the relative safety of rural Norfolk. Since then, family life had always been her and her mother. They rarely heard from Daddy's family in America, just a card from his sister at Christmas. Miss Dunne had lived twenty miles away on the Norfolk coast, where they visited her occasionally, but she died when Fay was ten, leaving them the cottage.

Fay knew by now not to ask too many questions about her father and her early life, because when her mother was made to think about the past a glazed, unhappy look crossed her face. Fay hated making her mother feel sad. Occasionally, not often, there were bad days when Kitty Knox was so sad she didn't leave her bed and Fay had to manage for herself.

*

That evening, safe at home after the long journey, Fay laid the kitchen table for supper and told her mother about the trip. 'From the Eiffel Tower, we could see right across to Sacré-Coeur. It looks like a Russian Palace, with turrets, and its dome shines golden in the sunset. That's funny, though, because up close it's white.'

Kitty set down the shepherd's pie on a mat. It was piping hot and the browned forked pattern of the potato glistened with melted cheese, the way Fay liked it. She smiled across the table at her daughter's rapturous face. 'It must have been marvellous,' she remarked, pulling up her chair. She remembered the thrill of that view of Paris spread out below her, the Seine like a silver ribbon striped by bridges, glinting between the buildings.

'After that we walked along by the river. Oh, I *adore* those little stalls. Honestly, though, Margaret bought a postcard of that naked statue, *David*. It's a good thing Miss Edwards didn't see. It's not even in Paris, is it? Mags couldn't have claimed it was a souvenir.'

Kitty tried to look stern. 'Certainly not.' She dished up a generous plate of pie for her daughter, then served herself. No, she was being greedy. She scraped some back. Lately she'd had difficulty doing up her skirts. It was to do with being forty, she supposed. Or the new nerve pills the doctor had given her, which were definitely making her sluggish. She pushed the bowl of home-grown greens across to Fay, who wrinkled up her nose and transferred a single soggy leaf to her plate.

'Where else did you go?'

'Notre Dame.' To her dismay Kitty saw her daughter's happy expression grow troubled. 'Do you know,' Fay said, 'something peculiar happened to me there?'

'What was that?' Kitty held her breath.

'I made an awful fool of myself. A bell started to strike. It was dreadfully loud and went on and on, and the noise frightened me. Miss Edwards had to calm me down. There was a boy . . .' She stopped, because her mother was giving her such a worried look.

'A bell?' her mother frowned.

'Yes,' Fay said, a little hesitant. 'It reminded me of something.' She looked at her mother for a reaction.

'And what did it remind you of?' Those huge blue eyes, Kitty thought as she helped herself to greens. She felt a moth-like flutter inside, of fear. Had she looked as vulnerable as Fay at that age? She wanted to reach out and reassure her daughter, to fold her close and smooth her hair as she always had, but perhaps, in her seventeenth year, Fay was getting too old for that. There was, after all, a new maturity about her. The trip had been beneficial, she supposed, but Kitty hadn't wanted her to go.

'I know I'd never been to Paris,' Fay said as she picked up her knife and fork, 'but sometimes it felt as though I had. Don't you find that odd?'

Kitty's fear spread its wings and she placed a hand over her heart. 'Very odd,' she echoed. She then reached for her fork and took a mouthful of food, but despite the cheesy topping and the rich gravy, found it without real taste.

'Perhaps it was in a previous life,' Fay said. 'Do you remember that book about reincarnation I found in the library? The people in it all said they were once someone famous and that can't be right. Some had to be ordinary, a peasant or a street musician. I wonder if in my past life I lived in Paris?'

'Not in the Revolution, I hope. That would have been a bit *too* exciting.'

Fay laughed and Kitty sipped some water, daring to relax. Her daughter had always been prone to these flights of fancy. She was still so young and innocent in many ways, her darling daughter. Kitty had tried to keep it that way, to give her a proper childhood. Girls grew up so quickly nowadays. They wore too much make-up and exuded a sort of knowingness. Take Fay's friend Margaret. *Her* mother had her hands full there.

But don't let Fay turn out like that, please, she breathed, *not my dear little Fay*. Yet she had to face the fact that Fay was a young woman now. And pretty, too. She was developing a lovely figure, which even that awful gymslip couldn't conceal.

No, Kitty hadn't wanted Fay to go to Paris, she had to admit that. The girl was young for her year. Most of the others were already seventeen. The trip had only been for four nights, but Fay had never been on a school trip away before and, well, why did it have to be *Paris*?

In the end she hadn't been able to resist Fay's pleading. Margaret and Evelyn were going and that meant Fay simply *must* go or she wouldn't have been able to *bear* it, so Kitty had given in and scraped together the money.

Fay would be all right, she had comforted herself. Margaret was a menace, self-centred, too aware of her fresh-faced good looks, but Evelyn was a nice girl, as you'd expect of a vicar's daughter. So silly of Kitty to panic really. Of course Fay would come back safe. But when four days ago she'd watched the train depart it was as though the invisible cord that connected her to her daughter had been stretched to breaking point.

'A bit of peace and quiet for us then,' Evelyn's gentle mother had sighed as the train disappeared into the distance.

'That poor Miss Edwards. I hope our Marge behaves herself.' Margaret's handsome mother gave a sardonic little laugh. Five children, the woman had, and the youngest one not her husband's, or so people said.

Kitty couldn't speak for the lump of sadness in her throat.

She remembered how she'd left the two women and walked back to the bus stop, wrapping her arms round herself as though the spring breeze had turned cold. Fay's departure had been like the past repeating itself. And the worst thing was that there'd be more of it from now on. Her precious only child would grow up and leave home. What would she do then? Why did it have to be this hard?

She knew why. Because of what had happened. The past was always with her, it simply would not lie down. It made her over-protective.

Fay's next question broke upon her thoughts.

'Seriously, Mummy, are you sure I've never been to Paris before? Not when I was little?'

For a moment Kitty was dumbfounded. Her instinct was to lie. She'd told so many lies, what harm would one more do? But those hadn't been proper lies, she argued with herself, only white ones, the sort you tell to soothe someone you love. Her daughter's limpid gaze implored her for an answer. She opened her mouth to say 'no', but Fay got there first.

'I suppose we couldn't have done. The war would have been on.' She'd answered the question herself.

'Yes, the war was on,' Kitty said, relieved. 'No one could

travel to Paris then. Most of France was cut off when the Nazis occupied it in 1940. Like so much of Europe.'

Fay looked thoughtful then said, 'So why did the city feel so familiar? Why?'

'I don't know, my love.' But she did. She remembered all right. It was impossible to forget the things that had scarred her for a lifetime.

Some day she would have to explain everything to her daughter. There had been times she nearly had, when Fay had asked probing questions. But then Kitty would look into those trusting blue eyes and the words just wouldn't come. She simply hadn't been able to speak of the terrible things that had happened. She couldn't have borne to see her daughter's face fall, to have her turn away, to reject her.

One day she would have to tell her – but not yet, please God. Not yet.

Chapter 2

Fay was humming to herself as she tripped up the dingy stairs to her flat, violin case in hand. The hum was a snatch of a song that had been haunting her all afternoon, very melancholy, very French, the sort sung by some waif on a street corner in a husky voice that caught at the heart. She couldn't think where the tune had come from, it had just popped into her head and made itself at home. Perhaps it had something to do with the piece of news she'd received that morning.

It was the middle of March, sunny, with that clear light that made grimy old London look washed clean. On her way back from her rehearsal she'd noticed with pleasure the daffodils in Kensington Gardens opening into flower. The evenings were still chilly. She'd have a bath later if Lois hadn't hogged all the hot water. First she'd grill some Welsh rarebit for supper. *If* her flatmate hadn't finished off the cheese.

The flat was on the first floor of a cream-coloured building near Whiteleys department store in Bayswater and it had two principal advantages. Firstly, it was only a short step from here to the Albert Hall, where the orchestra Fay currently played for was based; secondly, the flat on the other side of their living-room wall was empty and the elderly man living above very deaf, so no one ever complained about her practising. Downstairs was *Jean-Paul's*, a hairdressing salon, and Fay enjoyed catching glimpses of the clientele emerging with fashionable crops or elegant updos. Jean-Paul, who was a sweetie and had asked the girls to call him by his real name, which was Derek, said he couldn't hear her violin over the noise of the dryers but wished he could, so there were no problems there either.

There had never been any question as to what Fay would do after she left school four years before. With rigorous coaching from Signor Bertelli and the determined support of her mother, she had secured a place at the Royal College of Music, from which she'd graduated six months ago. She played wherever she could get work but hoped that a permanent position with the West London Philharmonic Orchestra might open up soon. It was because one of the second violins had injured himself that she was practising with them at the moment.

On the landing, she stopped mid-hum, hearing the jangling tones of Cliff Richard and The Shadows, Lois's passion of the moment. She opened the door of the flat to find her flatmate in housecoat and slippers, lounging on the sofa, fair hair in rollers, painting her fingernails Oyster White.

'Hello, darling.' Lois's plummy tones rang above the music. 'I'll be out of your way in two shakes. Simon's fetching me at half-past. How was your day?'

'Lovely, thanks.' Fay put down her instrument and

shrugged off her coat, looping it over a hook. 'What about you?'

'Oh, mad as ever. Rescue that, will you?' The Shadows had faded, to be succeeded by an irritating scratching sound. Fay went and lifted the stylus then stopped the turntable. The sudden silence was blissful.

Despite their different tastes in music, it was hard to be annoyed with Lois, a bright, cheerful girl employed as a secretary in an advertising agency and currently dating one of the account managers. Fay had answered her newspaper ad for a flatmate a few months before and they'd taken to one another at once. She liked sharing with Lois because she was even-tempered and didn't penny-pinch, and also because she was out most of the time. The downsides were few, but principally derived from Lois's inability to do anything quietly at any time of day or night, and her somewhat erratic approach to housekeeping.

Fay started to say, 'I had a bit of good news actually,' but was too late. Lois had jumped up, blowing on her nails, and was flying to her room. 'There are chocolate eclairs in the kitchen,' she called behind her. 'Help yourself,' and bang went her bedroom door.

In the shabby kitchenette Fay explored the pantry and was relieved to find both bread and cheese for her rarebit. There was even a scraping of mustard left in the pot. An éclair would finish supper off nicely, she decided, as she lit the grill and laid a plate on the chipped Formica. Lois, who didn't like cooking and often ate out, rarely bought proper food, only treats.

As she settled on the sofa with her supper, Lois, now dressed, emerged from her bedroom in a cloud of Worth's *Je Reviens* and started to stuff the contents of one handbag

into another. 'Heck, I nearly forgot,' she said, examining a
scrap of paper. 'Somebody left this downstairs by the
phone.'

'Thanks,' Fay said, taking the paper. Written on it in
spindly Biro was *Miss Knox to ring Mrs Gloria Ambler,
Norwich 51423*. Her mother's neighbour in Little Barton.
Why would she be calling?

'Anything wrong?' asked Lois.

'I hope not.'

Just then the doorbell rang. 'Oh, lor', that must be
Simon!' Lois said. 'I'll be right down!' she called into the
intercom and started shuffling into her shoes.

'Lois,' Fay said, swallowing a mouthful too quickly.
'Listen. I'll be away for a week in April. You'll never guess.
I'm going to Paris with the orchestra!'

'Paris?' Lois swung round, one arm in her coat. 'You
jammy devil! How did you wangle that?'

'That second violin who's hurt his wrist won't be fit
enough. It'll be hard work, mind you, there are three concerts, but just think – a whole week in Paris!'

'In the spring,' breathed Lois, looking wistful. 'Simon
has never taken me further than Brighton.'

Fay couldn't help smiling. It wasn't often that Lois
envied her.

The doorbell rang again, this time more urgently.
'Coming!' Lois sang into the intercom. In the doorway she
turned dramatically and said, 'Paris. You lucky, lucky
thing,' before going out, slamming the door behind her.

Fay grinned. She was delighted at this chance, but as
she ate her supper, thinking about the trip, part of her was
troubled. It was five years since her schoolgirl visit to
Paris – how young and naïve she'd been then, as green as

salad. Certain memories from that time lingered The strange feeling she'd had of déjà vu in Notre Dame, the shock of the bell tolling. And Adam. She still thought about him sometimes. A boy she'd met at sixteen and only talked to for part of an evening, but had liked very much. She'd never heard from him again, but then she hadn't expected to.

Since she'd moved to London she'd been out with several men. One of them, a young solicitor whom she'd first met when a friend brought him to a concert, had, after a few months of them seeing one another, asked her to get engaged. Jim had been a charming, classically handsome man, if a little staid. She'd been rather flattered by his attention and found him good company, but when she considered the prospect of spending the rest of her life with him, it felt as though a heavy weight was pressing down on her. He talked about buying a house in Surrey and his ambition to be a partner of the firm, and the underlying assumption was that she would be a housewife and support him in all this. She couldn't see how there would be room for her music. In fact, she couldn't see herself at all in this picture of suburban bliss.

No man had really breached her reserve. Some found her aloof, though Jim seemed to have liked that about her. She had thought she loved him, but she can't have loved him enough. She should have put him out of his misery earlier. In the end he'd got fed up with waiting and found somebody else. Fay had cried for a whole day then quickly recovered.

It was strange how her life was turning out differently to that of her old friends, Fay thought as she licked delicious cream from the chocolate éclair. She rarely saw

Evelyn and Margaret now. Despite their talk about getting glamorous jobs in London, they had both been happy to stay in Norfolk. Evelyn had trained as a bank clerk, but had recently left work to become a farmer's wife. Margaret had got herself into trouble at eighteen with a fresh-faced lad who sold insurance. He was no one special but she married him anyway, to her mother's obvious relief. Now she was tired and shrill-voiced from running around after two lively small boys, and spoke of her husband as though he was a wayward third.

Fay knew that she needed more for herself than that. She wanted the kind of love her mother had had for her father, a deep, eternal love, and there was no sign of anything like that at the moment.

These days she went home to Little Barton as often as she could, but felt guilty that it wasn't more. She rang her mother once or twice a week from the coin box downstairs, and though Kitty never complained, Fay sensed her growing loneliness and sadness. The truth was that as Fay's life was opening out with new opportunities to explore, her mother's had stagnated, for Kitty no longer had her beloved daughter to look after. It was as though everything she did had been for Fay, and now that Fay had left home she'd lost all purpose in life.

If it had been only that, however, Fay would have understood, but there was something else that created a barrier between them. It was silence. Fay sensed that there were things she needed to know, things that her mother perhaps wanted to tell her, but had not quite managed to do so yet. Once, early last summer, during a weekend visit home, she'd found Kitty gathering roses in the garden and saw with alarm that she'd been crying. When she asked her what was wrong, Kitty had wiped her eyes with a weary movement and murmured, 'It's just I miss ... oh Fay, I can't – I'm only being silly ...' before reaching for the trug and starting back to the house. 'I must put these in water before that boy comes for his lesson,' she'd called behind her in a strange, hoarse voice.

Later that evening, as they finished supper, Fay asked, 'What was wrong this afternoon?'

'I was only thinking of your father,' Kitty replied, 'I still miss him, you know.'

When Fay took courage and asked about the air raid that killed him, an expression of pain crossed Kitty's face, to be succeeded by that familiar blank look. Then her chair grated on the wooden floor as she stood up and carried their plates to the sink where she started washing up noisily.

'It isn't fair of you not to tell me anything!' Fay had cried out, throwing her napkin down.

Kitty turned and glared at her. 'Nothing's fair in this life. You'll learn that soon enough, my girl.'

Fay was shocked. Her mother rarely spoke to her so cruelly. She said no more. They were both too upset and they'd never liked to hurt one another. Each was too aware that the other was all they had. It had always been Fay and Kitty, playing music together, going on spur-of-the-moment picnics on sunny days, making fudge and peppermint creams from carefully hoarded sugar. But now she was grown up Fay was all too aware that her mother kept secrets from her. And so although they loved each other as much as ever, the silence between them spread and deepened. And with it came frustration. And for Fay, a feeling that was much much worse.

It took bravery to admit it and she was ashamed of her feelings, but Fay was *furious* with her mother.

She dabbed at the last crumbs of chocolate on the éclair wrapping and glanced again at the scrap of paper lying on the coffee table. Her mother's neighbour had only telephoned her once before, and she remembered with a dragging sensation what that had been about. She reached into her handbag for her purse. She'd best do what she was dreading and ring Mrs Ambler.

Chapter 3

Norfolk

'I've come to see my mother, Katherine Knox.' Fay didn't know the middle-aged nurse with wary eyes who answered the door at St Edda's Hospital. It was a Friday morning, two weeks after Gloria Ambler's telephone call. 'I spoke to Dr Russell's secretary yesterday to arrange it.'

'Ah yes, you're Fay, aren't you? Doctor said he'd like a word with you first.' The woman spoke into a telephone and after a minute or two, Dr Russell, a fatherly-looking man with untidy iron-grey hair, appeared, his white coat flapping open to reveal his stocky, suited figure. He shook Fay's hand with a hearty grip.

'Your mother's in the garden today, it being so warm.' This was her third visit to the hospital and she'd liked Dr Russell from the start. The sympathy in his hazel eyes had drawn her trust. 'I'll take Miss Knox out there myself, Nurse,' he said. 'We'll have our chat on the way.'

Fay walked with the doctor down a high-ceilinged corridor painted a drab green and lined with radiators. She knew this to be the old, secure wing of the hospital. The closed doors they passed had viewing hatches set into them, which imparted the feel of a prison. Behind the doors she could only guess what was happening. At least her mother didn't need to stay in this part of the building.

'How is Mum?' Fay asked.

'Calmer. She's settled in, I'd say.' They had to stop to hold open a door for an orderly pushing an elderly man in a wheelchair, then the doctor spoke briefly to a nurse accompanying an unkempt young woman with a shuffling walk. None of the patients Fay had ever seen in here looked mad, exactly, she thought as she waited, just pitiful and helpless. It was sad that they had to live in this austere Victorian building, away from the rest of the world, but perhaps it was a haven of sorts. At least there was every hope that her mother would be sent home sometime.

'How much longer must she be here?' she asked when they set off again.

'It's hard to say at the moment.' Dr Russell was hesitant and Fay's spirits fell.

When Fay had returned Gloria Ambler's telephone call the woman had had a distressing tale to tell. A ten-year-old pupil had arrived at Kitty's house for her usual piano lesson the afternoon before, but no one had answered her knock. Finding the door on the latch, the girl had ventured in and discovered Mrs Knox in the kitchen, slumped at the wooden table weeping, a bottle of pills spilled out in front of her. The child had fled in alarm and fetched her mother who, with the help of Mrs Ambler, had taken charge. Kitty hadn't swallowed many pills this time, thank goodness, but since it was the second time in three years that something like this had happened, the family doctor had arranged for her to be admitted to St Edda's Hospital on the edge of Norwich, a place which local people still referred to by its old name, the Asylum.

'Her progress is slower than I'd like,' the doctor went on.

'Oh,' Fay said mournfully. 'I had hoped ...'

'I think this has been building up for many years,' the doctor went on. 'We mustn't expect any overnight miracles.'

'No, but still ... Doctor, can I ask your advice? You know I'm supposed to go away on tour on Monday – do you think I still should go?'

'How long did you say it was for?'

'A week. We leave first thing Monday morning and come home on the Sunday afternoon.' She explained to him about the concerts they were giving in Paris and what an opportunity it might be for her workwise.

'It sounds wonderful, Fay, and to be honest I think you should go. Your mother is unlikely to be aware of a longer gap between visits at the moment.'

'Poor Mummy.' Fay sighed. 'I've been thinking, perhaps I should come home to Norfolk altogether. Then I could look after her.'

'And give up your music?' The doctor slowed his stride and studied her with an expression of concern. 'Personally I would regard that as a terrible mistake. In fact, if I had any say in the matter, which of course I don't, I would forbid it. What good would it do for you to give up the life you have before you? You're so young still, and we should be able to help your mother through these difficulties without sacrificing your future. I know you have no other family to speak of, but she has friends in your village, I believe?'

'Oh yes, lots. And many of them have been very kind.' She thought of Mrs Ambler and the vicar's wife – Evelyn's mother – both of whom would do anything for Kitty. She sensed, however, that others steered clear and she worried about the effect of the illness – that was what the doctor called it, an illness – on her mother's work.

'Well then, don't do anything silly for now. As for going away for a week, although your mother enjoys your visits, she is not always aware of the passing of time. It's an effect of the medication, I'm afraid. Anyway, it doesn't sound as though you will be leaving her for more than a few days longer than usual, so my advice would certainly be to go to Paris. She will be perfectly well looked after here.'

'Oh, I have no doubts about that,' Fay said. She felt relieved, though still guilty. 'Thank you.'

They came to a heavy metal door which Dr Russell unlocked, relocking it behind them. They were now in a newer, less forbidding part of the building. 'Perhaps we could stop here for a moment,' he said.

He drew her to sit on a bench by one of a row of big windows. Despite the bars across it, the window gave a pleasant view of the grounds. Warm sunshine was pouring in and soon a cheerful aroma of oranges rose from the bag she'd brought for her mother.

'I was glad that you had asked to see me,' Dr Russell said, regarding her in his fatherly way, 'because there's a matter I wanted to consult you about.' He paused briefly. 'I believe there's something important that your mother isn't telling me and I don't know what it is. I hoped you might be able to shed some light.'

Fay thought for a moment and then said, 'No, I'm sorry, Doctor, I don't think I can. My mother . . . I believe there's a great deal that she's never told me. About my father and my early childhood.'

Dr Russell rubbed his jaw and frowned, thinking for a moment. 'Well, perhaps you could clear up a small point for me. Do you know of a woman named Jean?'

'A woman? Not a woman, no. She probably means *Gene* with a G, short for Eugene. He was my father.'

'Ah, that makes perfect sense in the circumstances. Thank you.'

'What did she say about him?' Fay asked, full of hope.

'I'm afraid I'm not at liberty to tell you.'

'Oh, of course not.' It was disappointing.

They set off once more, then the doctor showed Fay out into a high-walled garden. Here, several female patients were walking about in the sunshine or sitting quietly under the eye of two nurses. Fay's gaze was immediately drawn to a lonely figure sitting in a chair on the other side of the garden, by a magnolia tree that was coming into flower. It was her mother. She hadn't seen Fay yet. Her arms were folded in her lap and her head was bowed as though in sorrow. Fay's heart twisted with pity.

'I'll say goodbye to you here,' Dr Russell said quietly. 'I'm sure one of the nurses will show you out when you're ready.' Fay took the hand he offered. 'I do hope the tour goes well,' he said. 'And please *don't worry.*'

'It's hard not to, but thank you, Doctor,' Fay said. As she set off across the light-filled garden she glanced back and caught him watching her, a thoughtful expression on his face.

'Mummy?'

'Fay, darling!' Kitty raised her head and smiled, a spark of life leaping into her eyes. 'This is a lovely surprise,' she said, as Fay bent to kiss her. 'Did I know you were coming?'

'Yes, I told you on Sunday.' So the doctor was right about her mother's loss of awareness of the passing of time. Fay pulled up another chair and sat beside her, clasping her hand in hers. 'You look better,' she lied, studying her. In fact, her mother's face was drawn, and the skin round her eyes was puffy. 'How do you feel today?'

'Brighter for seeing you.' Then Kitty's bravado faded and she leaned back in her chair looking weary, older suddenly than her forties.

'I brought you oranges,' Fay said, passing her the paper bag. 'I know how you love them.'

'What a treat, thank you, darling,' her mother said, holding the bag on her lap without looking inside. 'The stodge they give us in this place is awful. I'm sure I'm piling on the pounds.'

Her mother didn't look any fatter, Fay thought, just sort of blurred round the edges. Still pretty, though. Her normally curly hair was lank, but at least it had been brushed and she even wore a touch of the lipstick that Mrs Ambler had taken in last week. This gave Fay hope. If her mother was able to take care of her appearance, then surely she was improving.

'Have you come to take me home?' Her mother sounded confused and Fay's hopes were dashed again.

'No,' she said gently. 'But soon, I'm sure. You must get properly better first.' Fay had only the vaguest idea of the treatment that her mother was receiving. Dr Russell, for all his kindness, had betrayed very little and she was too inexperienced to know what to ask. For now it was enough that Kitty was in a safe place and that Fay was able to visit regularly. She rarely glimpsed any visitors for the other patients when she was here, which was odd. Were their relatives not allowed to come, or didn't they want to?

Fay stayed with her mother for the best part of an hour, trying to engage her attention on a variety of subjects, among them the famous moodiness of her orchestra's conductor, Colin Maxwell, and her flatmate Lois's racy stories about life at the advertising agency, all the time avoiding telling her the really big thing, which was about going away. After a while, though, she sensed Kitty wasn't really listening. Instead her mother stared across the garden, unseeing, brooding on her own thoughts. The doctor was right: something *was* troubling her.

'What's wrong, Mummy?' she tried asking. Her mother's gaze met hers and Fay saw the anguish there. She waited, hoping her mother would say what was in her heart. Kitty's lips parted as though about to speak – then instead, she lowered her face and began to fiddle with a loose thread on her skirt.

'Mum?' Fay said again, and when her mother looked up her eyes seemed to plead with her. Yet still she said nothing. 'Mum, I hate seeing you like this. I feel it's my fault. For moving away.'

'How can it be your fault?' her mother whispered. 'It's what I always wanted for you, to do well with your music. You love it so.'

'I do, but it's meant leaving you alone. We've always had good times together, haven't we? Do you remember the upside-down days we used to have?'

Kitty gave a slow smile. 'Pudding for breakfast and cornflakes for tea.'

'Yes. And going skating that winter?'

'You were eight,' Kitty sighed. 'So excited by the snow.'

'The river was so beautiful with all the frosted trees, I remember. It was like an enchanted world. That was one of the best days of all.'

'Was it? Was it really?' Her mother's eyes were shining now – not with tears, surely?

'Mum?'

'I'm not crying. I'm just . . . so glad. That you have such happy memories.'

'I do, though sometimes . . . there's still that other one.'

'What other one?' Her mother looked at her almost sharply.

'Oh, you remember. That time at Starbrough Hall.'

'Oh, that.'

'You said it must have been something I dreamed.'

'Yes,' her mother said, but hestitantly.

'But I'm not so sure.' She thought back to that dreary winter's day when she was eleven. She and her mother had visited a stately home in the countryside where Fay was to play a violin solo in a children's charity concert. During the afternoon rehearsal she had left the drawing room in search of the lavatory, but muddled the directions. She'd wandered the corridors and fetched up in a great dark room at the back of the house where her footsteps echoed on bare floorboards. Suddenly a sense had come to her of being in another such space, one full of people, but she had been lonely. Her mind rang with ghostly voices. She turned in distress and fled.

'I suppose,' Fay said carefully, 'it was a bit like what

happened to me in Paris – that time in Notre Dame. Which reminds me, there's something I need to tell you.'

Now she'd plucked up the courage she delivered her news quickly. Her mother reacted strongly, but not with the fears of abandonment that Fay had predicted.

'You're going to Paris again?' Her attention was certainly on Fay now.

'Yes, I've only played with the orchestra since Christmas, and I've been asked to go on tour! Isn't that marvellous?'

'I suppose so.'

'It's only a short time, Mummy. No more than a week. I know I won't be able to visit you, but I'll come as soon as I'm back.'

'A week,' her mother echoed. She was staring at Fay now, her eyes full of urgency. Then she muttered something unexpected. 'It might be long enough.'

'Long enough for what?'

'To visit somebody,' her mother said, impatient.

A shadow fell across the grass and they glanced up to see an orderly approach. She stood before them, a stout, sour-faced woman, her stolid demeanour and the set of keys hanging at her belt giving her the air of a jailer. 'You must be goin' now, miss,' she addressed Fay. 'Her hev to go for her dinner.'

'Goodness. Lunch already?' Fay was disconcerted by this lack of charm. She got to her feet, but her mother hung on to her hand.

'Wait, Fay. Please listen. Before you go to Paris, go home and look in the trunk. There's a box in the bottom there ... you'll see—'

'Come along now, Kitty,' the orderly interrupted, the keys at her belt clinking with an urgent sound.

'It's Mrs Knox, not Kitty,' her mother said with some of her old spark.

'The trunk in your room, you mean?' Fay said. 'I can do that. I was going home to fetch a few things for Paris.' The house was ten miles away, but instead of taking the train today she had managed to borrow Lois's boyfriend's car. 'What is it you need?'

'I don't need anything. Just look inside the box in the trunk.' The orderly was helping Kitty out of her chair.

'Where's the key to the trunk?'

'The Wedgwood pot. Fay, promise me you'll do it.'

'Yes, of course.'

The orderly was leading her mother away, but Kitty was twisting round and saying something Fay didn't quite catch.

'What?' Fay called back, hurrying behind.

'By the church. Ask for Maremarry,' her mother said, or something like it.

It made no sense. Fay's mother was being led through the French windows. Fay saw her clutch the doorframe for support before she was dragged from view, and wondered who or what Maremarry might be.

She knew what Kitty meant by the trunk. Her mother used it as a storage chest. It was the only thing inside the house apart from the medicine cupboard in the bathroom that had ever been kept locked. Fay had seen it open once or twice when her mother wanted a spare tablecloth or the summer curtains. It was full of such stuff, all very dull and smelling faintly of camphor. It had to be kept locked, Kitty explained once, or the lid didn't stay shut properly. Fay hadn't felt remotely curious about the trunk after that, but now it appeared that she should have done. It must contain something important, something her mother hadn't wanted her to find. Until now.

Again, that rush of irritation with her mother; again, that feeling of guilt. Yet there was also something else. A low, but growing thrum of excitement.

Chapter 4

It had only been a fortnight since Kitty had gone into hospital, but Primrose Cottage already wore a desolate look. The daffodils in the tiny front garden needed tying back and the grass was overgrown. Fay unlocked the front door with a sense of trepidation. It was the first time she'd been home since her mother's illness and it was sad knowing Kitty wouldn't be there to welcome her. Mrs Ambler from across the road had been taking care of everything. It was she who had packed Kitty's suitcase for the hospital; she was also good enough to pop by occasionally when anything extra was needed. Fay gathered up the morning's post from the mat and went inside, leaving the door open to the sunshine.

In the kitchen a pile of letters lay on the table. Bills mostly, by the look of them. She slit open the envelopes and sorted them out, slipping the most urgent in her handbag for payment. Otherwise there was a picture postcard of a Welsh castle from Evelyn's mother and a rose catalogue, both of which she put to one side before glancing about for anything else that wanted doing. The kitchen was tidy, but the old clock on the wall needed winding and there was something poignant about the single cup and saucer propped upside down on the draining board so she put them away.

She started to wander about the house, sharing its loneliness. The sitting room was neat, the fireplace brushed and bare. There was little reminder of her mother in here. She straightened one of the paintings on the wall before going out.

Entering the music room at the front of the house was worse. Here she missed her mother most. It was a lovely airy space, where on a day like today the sunshine falling through the garden trees danced restlessly on the walls. Generations of local children had played the beautiful old upright piano set in its shaded alcove. The room was normally orderly, the music filed away in the tall corner cupboard, but today the cupboard door wasn't quite closed. She went to investigate and found the piles all higgledy-piggledy, as though her mother had been frantically searching for something. Fay tidied everything and managed to get the door shut. Then she turned her attention to the piano. The lid was up and a sheet of music spread open on the ledge. She slid onto the bench, where she'd sat so many times before, and arranged a hand on the ivory keys to play a broken chord. She hesitated, her attention caught by the title of the pages in front of her, surprised to see that it was Beethoven's 'Moonlight' Sonata.

Her mother had been playing the Moonlight! Kitty always gave the impression she disliked it. She simply wouldn't listen to it. Once when it came on the portable wireless in the kitchen, she had reached across and switched it off. 'But I love it,' Fay protested. Her mother turned the wireless back on then marched out into the garden where she started weeding the rosebed with fast, furious movements. Fay watched through the window bemused, wondering what she'd done to upset her.

She hadn't even known that her mother possessed the music to the Sonata, yet here it was. Fay studied it for a moment, then picked out the open chords of the first few bars using the pedals to sustain the long notes of the left hand. The mournful beauty of the music was unbearable in her present mood so she stopped. As the notes died away she was visited by an overwhelming sense of loss.

Going upstairs, she found her bedroom was as always, though the china animals on her chest-of-drawers were frosted with dust. It had always been dusty, this cottage, the ancient plaster flaking off the walls. House martins scrabbled under the thatch to make their nests, occasionally a mouse would run across the floor, which needed sweeping most days. It was a living house, Fay always felt, not like those sterile red-brick boxes that had recently sprung up down the road, where the horses' field had been. She opened the wardrobe and looked in vain for something suitable to wear in Paris, then caught an unexpected glimpse of herself in the inside mirror. Her hair badly needed cutting, she saw with dismay, and her skirt and blouse were impossibly dowdy for Paris. She must go shopping for clothes tomorrow, though maybe her mother had something she could borrow.

Kitty's bedroom was peaceful in the afternoon sun, the bed made, the trunk in its place by the wall, a lace cloth spread over it. Fay picked up the familiar photograph in a tortoiseshell frame, from the dressing table. It was of her father, taken on her parents' honeymoon, which must be why he looked so happy in it. There was a deep crease across one corner of the print, and the right-hand edge had suffered water damage, but Eugene Knox's open round face with its broad smile, his fair curly hair blowing in the breeze, was still clear to see, looking out across the years. As a child, Fay would sometimes sneak in here and study his face, trying to remember something about him. The timbre of his voice, the warmth and scent of him, his laugh even. But nothing suggested itself. It was the only photograph of him her mother had. Now Fay looked deep into those smiling eyes. 'Who are you?' she whispered and remembered with a pang what the doctor had said: her mother had been talking about him. Fay wondered again what she'd said.

She laid the photo down carefully, because its hardboard stand was rickety, then opened the Wedgwood pot next to it and fished out a small key. Kneeling by the trunk, she swept off the lace cloth and worked the key until the rusty lock sprang open. She lifted the lid and began to remove the piles of material within. Some were familiar. The winter curtains for the sitting room. Bright scraps left over from a pair of yellow brushed cotton pyjamas Kitty had made Fay once. She stacked spare sheets and pillowcases up around her. Then, near the bottom, she pushed aside a worn eiderdown to reveal a cardboard shoe box with the name of a local department store printed on the lid. She brought it out onto her lap, surprised by how light it was. Inside was a layer of tissue paper. She peeled it away. And stared, uncomprehending, at what lay underneath.

Folded up in the box was a small canvas rucksack. She took it out, put the box aside and laid the rucksack flat. It was worn and travel-stained, the canvas straps frayed and the leather fasteners in their buckles cracked and twisted with age. She knew this rucksack, but she couldn't think from where. Had it been hers, or perhaps her mother's? Her own, she thought. Her fingers remembered how to open it and when she put her hand inside, she felt rough cloth. She knew what it was before she drew it out and unfolded it. A child's dress, greenish-brown, of a simple shape. She contemplated it for a moment, remembering how, when she'd worn it, the material had scratched her neck, only that. Her hand slipped back into the rucksack, as if hoping to find something else, but it was empty. She felt a frisson of panic because she had expected something, something precious. She looked again into the rucksack, and again it was empty. There had only been the dress.

She was folding the dress back when she saw a torn piece of card sticking out of a pocket inside the rucksack, so grubby and curled up that she'd almost missed it. She smoothed it out. It was a label. On one side was written in a black sloping hand, *Fay Knox, Southampton*. The other side read, *Couvent Ste-Cécile, Paris*. St Cecilia's Convent. The name meant nothing to her and yet she sensed it should. A convent. In Paris. And she was going to Paris!

She sat staring at the label for some time, while the faintest glimmer of a memory rose in her mind. Sunshine falling on flagstones, the blue robes of a statuette, and ... but no, it was gone. It was as though a door had opened, just a chink, in her mind, before it shut again. She knew now that her mother had been trying to tell her something, something to do with Paris. Since the rucksack was her own, it suggested that they'd both been in Paris, she and her mother. But surely that couldn't be right. When she was little there had been the war, and Paris was occupied by the Nazis – and her mother had never spoken of that. Instead she'd talked of living in the whitewashed house at Richmond.

Fay put the rucksack aside to take with her, then replaced everything else in the trunk and locked it. But when she returned the key to its pot she accidentally knocked the photograph frame, which slipped forward and fell to the floor. She bent to pick it up and saw to her relief that the glass hadn't broken. It was coming apart, though. She tried to fit the backing board into place but it wouldn't go. Something was in the way. She prised up the metal tabs to investigate.

A postcard had been inserted between the photograph and the back, the same size as the frame. She turned it over. It was a sepia-coloured shot of a battleship, its prow carving through the water. It was just possible to read the name on the bow: HMS *Marina*.

The *Marina*. It meant nothing to her, but it was a beautiful craft and staring at it she could sense vividly how it might feel to be standing on deck with the wind in her hair, the smell of tar, the taste of salt on her tongue. For a moment it felt as though she was there, feeling the low throb of the engines and the sea spray on her cheeks. How funny. As far as she knew she'd never been on a ship. This card, she thought, must be there to hold the photograph firm in the frame, for its reverse was not written on and she could see no further significance. She fitted everything back together and stood the frame in its place next to the pot.

Over the next few days she often took up the canvas rucksack and examined it, smoothing out the small dress it contained and wondering what it meant. *Maremarry*, her mother had said – Maremarry by a church. Ste-Cécile's convent might be by a church, and Maremarry might be Mère Marie. She would try to find out when she got to Paris.

Fay borrowed from her mother's wardrobe an ivory blouse, a black cardigan and an evening stole that Kitty wore to concerts. In London the next morning she dipped into her savings to buy a coat of sky blue, a pair of black patent court shoes, an evening dress and two skirts, an unusually fashionable choice for her. Then returning to the flat at lunchtime, laden with bags, she walked into Jean-Paul's salon to ask for an appointment.

It was busy as usual, but to her surprise Derek said in his faux-French accent, 'Give me ten minutes, *chérie*,' and before she could change her mind, he whisked a gown round her shoulders and sat her in a chair with a magazine to look at.

When he was ready, she explained where she was going and, very tentatively, what she wanted. He nodded and stared hard at her face in the mirror, arranging her hair this way and that, frowning. Then without further ado he dampened her hair with a spray, took up his scissors and began to cut. She shut her eyes, unable to bear the sight of her dark brown locks falling to the floor, and listening to the confident snip snip snip.

'*Voilà!*' Derek said. She dared finally to look in the mirror and her eyes widened with astonishment.

'*Très chic*, don't you think? *Très gamine.*' Derek pulled a frond across her cheek, ruffled the new fringe and beamed at her reflection. And indeed he had worked a miracle. With her hair shorn into a short wavy bob and layered to give it lightness, her eyes appeared even larger in her serious oval face.

'Thank you, that's wonderful,' she breathed. Derek helped her out of her gown. 'How much do I owe?' She reached for her bag.

'Don't you worry about zat,' Derek said, with a wave of his ringed hand, and when she argued he told her, 'Do a little spying for me. Ze latest Paris styles, you know? Zat'll be enough.'

'You are so kind,' Fay said.

'It eez my playzhure. Give my love to Paree, won't you?'

Upstairs, Lois was out. As Fay whisked about packing, she kept meeting her new self in the dressing-table mirror or the one on the bathroom cabinet. The transformation she saw made her feel different, braver.

On Sunday night, in her overheated hospital ward, Kitty lay awake and anxious, waiting for the sleeping pills to take effect. She hoped her daughter had found the canvas rucksack, that somehow she'd pick up the threads of the past that Kitty had cut, that now at last, Fay would learn the truth Kitty could never bring herself to tell. What would happen when she did, Kitty didn't dare to imagine. That would be for her daughter to judge and decide.

She knew she should have spoken to Fay long ago about the secrets of the past, the things she'd suppressed. It was the heavy burden of them, and her untapped grief, that had made her ill. Fay was right, Kitty *hadn't* been fair to her – but how did one tell a beloved daughter that because of her mother's negligence, because Kitty had put

her husband first, their little family had endured so much
suffering? That, worst of all, her little girl had become the
cause of the most terrible thing ... No, she mustn't think
about that, she couldn't bear it.

She'd done her best over the years to make up for all
this: she'd put Fay first ever since. She must think of the
good times they'd had together, but now Fay was old
enough to know the truth. She must learn it. Well, maybe
not everything. The Reverend Mother could be relied on to
be discreet. She was one of the few who had not betrayed
them, one of the few who would remember Eugene. Gene,
her darling Gene, she thought drowsily. Tomorrow she
would tell the doctor about him. Maybe she'd tell him the
whole story. She needed to, in order to get better, she saw
that now. At the thought her heart grew light.

When she finally slept, her dreams were of Paris. Paris
in that glorious autumn of 1937, when she'd first met
Eugene.

Chapter 5

Early one Tuesday morning in Paris's Latin Quarter, Dr Eugene Knox was sitting outside a café in the Rue St Jacques reading the *Paris Herald Tribune*, when his attention was drawn by a slender young woman with a suitcase crossing the road towards him. There was something about her appearance that piqued his interest – the litheness of her walk, perhaps, or the determined set of her small head with its crop of dark curly hair. She had a round face with a serious expression, and large brown eyes, and her gaze rested on him for the briefest of moments, as though he was someone she thought she knew. After she'd passed on her way Eugene returned to his newspaper, but found that he could no longer concentrate.

Kitty Travers quickly forgot the burly, fresh-faced young man who'd stared at her so openly. Weary from her overnight journey, she was intent on finding St Cecilia's Convent, which she knew to be somewhere in the maze of streets between Notre Dame and the Panthéon. In the end, she stopped an elderly gentleman to ask directions and he sent her down a narrow cobbled alley she'd failed to notice before, though she must have passed it twice already in her search. The alley displayed no name and hugged the wall of a church before opening out into a tiny tranquil square, empty but for several sparrows squabbling over a crust of bread. They flew off into a hedge as she crossed the square towards a broad mansion of crumbling yellow stone on the far side, which being the only building with an entrance must be the convent. Her heart lifted, for it looked so welcoming. Its brown-painted shutters were thrown open to the autumn light and in the paved garden a cherry tree with leaves flushed magenta and gold spread its branches wide.

As Kitty peered between the bars of a black wrought-iron gate, plucking up courage to enter, the front door of the convent opened and a young nun stepped out. She was carrying a large jug of water which she proceeded to upend over several pots of geraniums by the wall of the house. Kitty called out, *'Bonjour'* as she turned to go back inside and, seeing her for the first time, the girl came down the path to meet her. Kitty, who expected nuns to be old and black-clad like crows, was taken by the youth and grace of this one. Her habit was black, yes, but its lawn collar was white, as was her coif, its starched edges curled up in a way that reminded Kitty of a ship in full sail.

'Je peux vous aider, mam'selle?' the girl asked in her light voice, viewing Kitty with interest as she opened the gate. The friendly sparkle of her deep-set eyes made Kitty warm to her. The girl wasn't pretty, exactly, but her smile lit up her serene face in a way that made it so. She must be nineteen or twenty, the same age as herself.

'Je m'appelle Katherine Travers,' Kitty replied, trying to

recall how to say in French that she was expected, but it appeared she didn't need to.

'*Ah, la petite Anglaise,*' the young nun said with enthusiasm, and stepped aside to let her come in.

'*Merci,*' Kitty murmured, following the girl up the path. She wasn't sure how to address a French nun. *Sister*, she supposed, though it seemed odd to call a stranger that when she had no real sister of her own. The fact that Uncle Pepper had arranged for her to stay in a Catholic convent at all when the family were staunch Anglicans was unnerving. It was actually the fault of her old headmaster's wife who, being half-Parisian, had given her uncle all sorts of old-fashioned advice, most of it designed to protect well-brought-up English girls from predatory Frenchmen. Kitty was perfectly sure she could save herself, if need be.

Inside, she found herself in a sparsely furnished hall with bare floorboards and ochre walls.

'My name is Sister Thérèse,' the young nun said in French. 'I'll show you to your room.' She insisted on taking Kitty's case and went ahead of her up a graceful staircase to a gallery, then along a landing with doors on either side. She stopped and opened one towards the front of the building, and Kitty walked into a tiny bedroom, where she was pleased to see her trunk, which had been sent ahead. The room was bare but for a narrow bed, a chest of drawers with a shelf above, and a small wardrobe, all in dark-stained wood. A wooden crucifix on the wall above the bed was the sole ornament, a woven blue mat on the floor the only scrap of colour. Sister Thérèse explained where the bathroom was and left her to unpack, bidding her to come downstairs for something to eat when she was ready.

The room looked out over the garden with the cherry tree and Kitty stood at the open window for a while, watching a large white cat which was sitting licking its paws in the middle of the square whilst the sparrows chattered in consternation from the hedge. The church clock softly struck the half-hour and she thought how peaceful everything was after the noise of the streets. A few minutes ago she'd been a stranger, alone in Paris, full of doubts and trepidation about her new life, but already she was beginning to feel at home. An aroma of fresh-baked bread wafted up from below, reminding her she was hungry. She set about unfolding the clothes from her case, tucking her nightgown under the pillow, hanging her dresses in the wardrobe. The contents of the trunk she would see to later.

On the chest of drawers lay an envelope addressed to her in a florid hand that had recently become familiar to her. She opened it and read it quickly. *Monsieur Xavier Deschamps*, the writing in his over-formal English, *requests the pleasure of Miss Katherine Travers' attendance at his apartment at eleven tomorrow morning for her first lesson.* Kitty knew where to go, since her uncle had shown her the street on a map and the headmaster's wife had explained that it would be ten minutes' walk away. She refolded the letter, pleased to have heard from the great man, but decided not to worry about the lesson until tomorrow. There was too much else to get used to today.

When she went downstairs, she followed the sounds of activity and found Sister Thérèse sweeping the floor of a room that must be the refectory, for it was set with four generous-sized tables, benches on either side. The girl told her to sit down and brought her warm bread wrapped in a napkin, a dish of butter, and a bowl filled with milky coffee.

'Breakfast is at half-past seven, after Matins,' she explained. She went on to say that luncheon was at twelve thirty for guests who wanted it, and supper at seven. She was a cheerful girl, and showed a shy interest in Kitty. In her hesitant French Kitty explained that her old piano teacher in London had recommended she come to Paris to study with the once-famous concert pianist Xavier Deschamps, who now taught for the Conservatoire, Paris's famous music college.

In turn she asked polite questions about the convent. 'How many nuns live here?'

'There are thirteen, including myself. Mère Marie-François is our Mother Superior, and the curé is Père Paul. You will meet them soon, I am sure.' Kitty gauged from Thérèse that she was the youngest, still a novice, and that most of the others were at work either in the convent somewhere or – here the girl waved a hand towards the alley – teaching at the church school nearby.

Kitty had finished breakfast and was brushing crumbs into the napkin when a woman of about sixty with a plain, calm face entered the room. Kitty rose politely, guessing who she was from her air of authority and the ornate wooden rosary she wore.

'Reverend Mother,' Sister Thérèse murmured, 'this is the girl from England.'

The Reverend Mother inclined her head to Kitty and greeted her in a quiet but sonorous voice. 'You are most welcome.' She spoke good English. 'Thérèse has been looking after you well, I trust? Are you feeling refreshed after your journey?'

'Very well,' and, 'Yes, thank you,' Kitty replied, feeling shy under the woman's scrutiny, though she saw kindness in the aging face, a touch of amusement in the hooded eyes.

'We are delighted to have *une jeune Anglaise* to stay, especially a pianist. Saint Cecilia, you must know, is the Patron Saint of Musicians! You have been shown your room? Good.' They spoke for a while longer about Kitty's journey and about Uncle Pepper, and then Mère Marie-François said, 'My dear, if you have a moment, I should like to show you something you might find interesting.'

'Of course,' Kitty replied, wondering what it could be.

She thanked Sister Thérèse for breakfast and followed the Reverend Mother out along a corridor to an oak door set in a stone arch which opened to reveal a short, dimly lit passage. When the nun opened the door at the far end, Kitty found herself in an ancient church of a modest size, but filled with light. She liked its quiet atmosphere, its round arches and stone-flagged floor. Most importantly, before her stood one of the loveliest grand pianos Kitty had ever seen. Its lid was open and the sun pouring in from the high windows reflected off the polished black surfaces.

'It's beautiful, isn't it? We made it ready for you. The piano-tuner came last week.' The Reverend Mother pulled out the stool for Kitty to sit on. The girl tried a few notes and was rewarded by a rich, mellifluous tone.

'It was given to the church by a benefactress, but there has been no one to play it until now,' the nun said wistfully. 'Father Paul, who is the curé here, is of the same mind as me. You are free to play whenever you like between services. Dear Sister Clare is our organist, but she is old and her sight is poor. She plays the hymns from memory.'

'Thank you,' Kitty breathed, touching the beautiful carved music-rest. She was overwhelmed by this offer.

She explained that it had already been arranged that she should practise at the Conservatoire itself, where she would also attend classes in theory and composition, but the Conservatoire was some distance away, on the opposite bank of the Seine. It would be wonderful also to have this opportunity here.

'Perhaps you'd play a little now,' the woman said eagerly. 'Bach, perhaps, I've always loved Bach.' And so Kitty played a Gavotte that she remembered by heart, and the nun listened to the simple dance tune with closed eyes and an expression of rapturous concentration. The music seemed to fill the small building, making the air ring with happiness. It was such a beautiful instrument that she went on to play another piece from the same suite.

Later, after they retraced their steps to the convent, Mère Marie-François made her excuses and went about her business. It was still only mid-morning, so Kitty fetched her coat and hat and went out to investigate her surroundings.

It was a splendid day for early autumn, the air cool but still, and with the music in the church fresh in her mind Kitty felt a bubble of joy rise in her. The city seemed to shimmer in a pearly grey light. She wandered along the quays of the Seine, under the plane trees, past the stalls selling old books and prints, then considered sitting outside one of the many cafés to sip a cold drink and view the façade of Notre Dame. However, she decided against it. Her uncle, though generous in his ambitions for her, had old-fashioned ideas when it came to a monthly allowance and she didn't know yet how much things might cost. It would also involve her speaking more French.

She found a bench to sit on instead, which cost her nothing, and watched Parisian life go to and fro. There were impossibly chic ladies with toy dogs on leads, little girls dressed as fashion plates, their brothers in sailor suits, bent old women in black, equally dark expressions on their faces, sharp-suited office clerks, a studious young man with his nose in a book. A sinister-looking senior priest in full regalia hurried out of the cathedral and got into the back of a waiting car. When, however, a soldier in a short cape and a box-like cap tried to engage Kitty in conversation, she was forced to get up and walk away.

Returning to the convent and finding no signs of lunch being underway, she retired to her room to lie down. She was exhausted, having slept little on the journey, not to speak of the emotional strain of leaving England to come alone to a strange foreign city. The crisp linen pillow beneath her cheek smelled comfortingly of lavender, reminding her of home.

Kitty's parents had both died soon after the Great War, when she was nearly three, too young to remember them clearly. They'd been sailing to India to start a new life, but had contracted typhoid on the voyage, died within hours of one another, and been buried at sea. By some miracle Kitty did not catch the disease, and on arrival in India had been taken back on the next available passage by a family who were returning to England. She'd been brought up in

Hampshire, in sight of the sea, at first by her grandmother, who died suddenly when Kitty was six. After that, Uncle Pepper, Kitty's mother's much older brother (his real name was Anthony, the nickname Pepper conferred on him as a child for a reason everybody had forgotten) had made it his duty to become her guardian. The duty had become a pleasure when he realized that not only did she share his passion for classical music but that she also had a talent for the piano, which he became determined to nurture. There was a great affection between her uncle and herself, but he was a man of reserve – he had never married – and conducted their relationship with a grave formality and a high degree of protection.

Dear Uncle Pepper, Kitty thought as she drifted into a doze. She wanted to do well for him here. The last thing she heard was the church clock beginning to strike. By the time it reached twelve she was fast asleep. She didn't wake until Sister Thérèse knocked on her door after Vespers and summoned her to supper.

At eleven the following morning, Kitty presented herself at the concierge's desk of an imposing apartment block on the Boulevard St-Germain, near the Quai d'Orsay, and took the lift to the fourth floor. She was nervous. Though she had met Monsieur Deschamps once before, when he'd been on a visit to London and her teacher had arranged for her to play for him, now she was here she wondered if he would think he'd made a mistake agreeing to teach her. What would happen if she wasn't good enough, after all?

She thought of the copy of Debussy's Clair de Lune in her music case and hoped it was the right choice. When

he'd first written to her, Monsieur Deschamps had asked
her to bring to the first lesson a piece of music that she
loved – and she did love Debussy. His free-flowing and
dreamlike compositions made her believe the composer
had been eternally yearning for a happiness beyond his
reach, and something in her heart responded to that. She
also hoped M. Deschamps would look more kindly on her
because she'd paid him the compliment of choosing a
French composer.

As it turned out, she need not have been alarmed. The
plump little maid who answered the door showed her into
a splendid drawing room decorated in Second Empire
style. Here, M. Deschamps had just finished with his previous pupil, a sallow-skinned young man with a nervous,
clever face and neatly cropped black hair, whom the
teacher introduced as M. Ramond. The youth gave a nod
of acknowledgement without meeting her eye, dropping
a sheaf of music in the process, which Kitty helped pick
up, whereupon he muttered a quick *merci* and fled the
room.

'A young man who is in an 'urry,' M. Deschamps said in
heavily accented English, his sad brown eyes twinkling,
and she warmed to him all over again. He was tall and
long-limbed, like a species of large bird. A heron, perhaps,
or one of those comical Malibu storks she'd seen pictured
in the *National Geographic* magazine in the dentist's waiting
room at home. Yes – a Malibu stork in an old-fashioned
black suit and stiff-collared white shirt. He bowed low to
her as though she were royalty and asked politely if she
was well, and whether she liked her home at the convent,
then moved straight to the business at hand.

'What do you have to play for me?' He gestured for her

to sit on the stool, then flicked up his coat-tails as he took a wooden chair beside her.

She brought the music from its bag and opened it out on the piano with shaking fingers, calming herself by silently counting down from five as her previous teacher had taught her. Then she began to play. She stumbled at first, but the music quickly cast its enchantment and she closed her eyes and allowed her fingers to take over. The room and M. Deschamps beside her, turning the pages, seemed far away. There was only the music. So it was a shock when her teacher's voice broke in: 'Stop, please.'

She withdrew her fingers from the keys, wounded.

'Start again,' he said briskly, 'and while you play, listen to the tune in the top line. See – here, and here – you go too quickly and do not allow it to sing. We will spend a little time on this, then I'll find you some Mozart. Your left hand is not strong, but I have exercises for that.' The hard work had begun.

The time passed quickly and before she knew it, it was one o'clock and the maid was knocking at the door to call her master to luncheon.

'Very well,' he said to Kitty, consulting a pocket diary. 'Thursday at the same time. And in the meantime, prac- tise, practise, practise.'

'I wondered ... was I all right?'

'All right? No, of course you were not all right. That is why you have come – to learn. Whether you succeed or not, Mademoiselle, is down to you. What you are made of. We will see. We will see.'

He smiled in a kindly enough way, and with that she had to be content.

Chapter 6

April 1961
Paris

Lois had given Fay her Oyster White nail varnish for Paris, and Fay loved the way it gleamed on her fingers as she played her violin. It was Tuesday, the West London Philharmonic Orchestra's first morning in the city, and they were rehearsing in an Art Deco concert hall, their base for the tour.

At lunchtime they were set free with a stern warning from their conductor, Colin, to be back by seven for the concert that evening. Fay laid her precious old violin carefully in its case, the wood still warm and vibrant from hours of playing. The practice had gone well; she was alive with the pleasure of the music, the soaring theme of Schubert's 'Unfinished' Symphony resounding in her mind.

As she loosened the bow and wiped the violin strings, she was brought back to earth by a nasal voice saying, 'What about you, Miss Knox?' She looked up to see Frank Sowden, one of the older first violinists, his barrel chest thrust out importantly, as though compensating for his shortness. His sensuous lips, small bright eyes and greying goatish beard reminded her of a satyr. 'Might we be graced with your company, young lady?' She was used, now, to the pompous way in which he spoke. 'A few of us are partaking of lunch at a restaurant on the Boulevard Haussmann.' Perhaps he was being friendly, but it was disconcerting the way he didn't quite meet her eye, his gaze instead sliding down her body.

'It's nice of you to ask,' she replied, trying her best to look regretful, 'but I'm going sightseeing. I hardly know Paris, you see, and I don't want to waste a moment.' This was half the truth. The other half was that she only had a little money, her fee as a stand-in and the allowance for daily expenses being very small, and she didn't want to find herself in a situation where Frank insisted on paying for what was likely to be an expensive meal. He'd brushed against her on the stairs of the hotel the night before in a not-quite accidental way that made her wary of him.

'Fair enough,' Frank said bluntly and turned away.

Anyway, it's not quite a lie, Fay told herself as she stowed her instrument in one of the Green Room cupboards. Her still-surprising new reflection looked back at her from a wall mirror and she wrinkled her nose at it. She was only in Paris a short time, and planned to make the most of it. It was with a sense of freedom that she pushed open a door at the back of the theatre and found herself outside on a busy street.

She'd felt an excitement as soon as she arrived at the Gare du Nord late the previous afternoon, clutching her violin and a suitcase, while the others in the party were tired and tetchy from a choppy Channel crossing. So much was instantly familiar from her school trip five years before. Even in the Métro, the oil-and-rubber smell, the hot blasts of air from the tunnels, the squeal of brakes from the approaching train were somehow different from the London Underground, and peculiar to itself. She recognized the kiosks selling newspapers and magazines, the advertising columns covered with bright posters of Miles Davis playing the Olympia music hall and a film by François Truffaut, the precise Parisian French in her ears, spoken too quickly to follow.

It wasn't simply sightseeing, there was something else she had to do this afternoon, something important. She must begin her search for the convent whose name she'd found on the label in the little rucksack. She'd no idea where to start. The hotel might tell her, perhaps.

L'Hôtel Marguerite, a modest establishment with no restaurant, only a bar where they served tartines and coffee for breakfast, was situated nearby in one of the side streets behind the Madeleine. Fay was sharing a room with a flautist, Sandra, a willowy blonde who was one of the few other female members of the orchestra. She consulted the tourist map they'd each been given and found her way easily. However, there was nobody in reception when she arrived, and although a notice invited her to ring a miniature hand-bell for service, no one responded to the high tinkling.

Where now? she wondered, going back out into the sunshine. A post office, she supposed – they would have some kind of directory. She walked over to the Place de la Madeleine, past the great Roman columns of the church and down a road beyond on the other side of the square lined with market stalls. The post office she came to had its blinds drawn down, closed no doubt for the long lunch-hour.

She was quite hungry herself by now, so she bought a length of crusty baguette with ham and sat on a bench in the Tuileries Gardens to eat, throwing the crumbs to some scruffy-looking pigeons. A solemn-faced boy of three or four trotted by, one hand pulled by a woman wearing an elegant short white boxy coat, the other clutching a toy windmill. Fay smiled at him, but he merely stared back incuriously and this made her feel unwanted.

To throw off the mood she consulted the map again. The Louvre was nearby, but she'd visited it last time and didn't feel a pressing need to go again. Instead, she set off along the Rue de Rivoli, looking at the fashions in the shop windows. She stopped at a kiosk to buy a copy of *Mademoiselle* with the latest hairstyles for Derek, before deciding to turn down a road that led to the river. On the Pont Neuf she loitered to watch the motor launches pass underneath, enjoying the breeze and the clear spring light, before crossing onto the Île de la Cité and following a narrow street that wound its way to Notre Dame. She caught her breath at the sight of the great west face of the cathedral, and remembered what had happened to her the last time she was there. This momentarily brought Adam to mind. Adam. It was odd that she sometimes thought of him. She considered going inside, but the memory of her fear put her off. Instead she bought a postcard of a gargoyle, which she wrote to Lois.

On her way to the hotel, she saw that the post office by the Place de la Madeleine was open so she joined the short queue inside. When it was her turn at the counter, she stumbled out her request to a stern woman in black-framed spectacles who sat behind a grille. The woman fetched a crisp new directory and thumbed the pages till she came to the one she wanted, running a practised finger down the columns. Eventually she looked up at Fay and shook her head. *'Non,'* she said, closing the book. *'Cela n'existe pas,'* in a tone that brooked no argument. Fay thanked her and retreated in embarrassment. The implication was clearly that not only did St Cecilia's not exist, it never *had* existed – and Fay was a fool for asking. It felt a significant defeat. She bought a stamp for Lois's postcard and hurried out.

Her spirits had recovered by the evening performance. Her attention was firmly on the music, on making her instrument sing, her eyes partly on the score, partly on the conductor, so that the song of her violin became subsumed in the great swell of sound that filled the concert hall. It felt better with an audience. Not only were the acoustics different in a room full of people, richer and warmer, but the air was vibrant with their expectation. The applause when it came made Fay feel part of something huge and important.

'They seem very appreciative,' said James Davenport, the second violin who sat to her right and with whom she shared a music stand. He gave her a thin smile that somehow went with his sparse white hair and greyish complexion. She knew he'd played in the orchestra for many years, but had hardly said anything to her until now. She'd thought him rude, but now she wondered if it was a natural reserve rather than dislike that kept him aloof.

Afterwards, she walked with Sandra to a dinner given by the orchestra's generous sponsor in a grand hotel on the nearby Rue du Faubourg St-Honoré. First, though, there was a drinks reception and they were shown into a room furnished with antiques where chandeliers glittered overhead and there was champagne. The bubbles slipped down easily, making her feel light and happy.

'Where's Colin, do you think?' she asked Sandra, looking round at the crowds. She hadn't seen their conductor since the performance.

'No idea.'

'Who are all these people anyway?'

'Friends of the Foundation, I suppose. Hello,' Sandra murmured, 'here comes our Frank.'

Frank was full of the news that the colourful, womanizing Minister for Culture was there. Fay drifted off to speak to some of the other musicians, then found herself being introduced to the Head of the cultural foundation that supported them – an austere older man who was extremely complimentary about the performance that evening. This made Fay's heart glow with pride to be a part of it all.

When she bumped into her again a few minutes later, Sandra whispered, 'Frank thinks that blonde in the Dior dress over by the window is the Minister's mistress.' Her blue eyes sparkled with intrigue. 'I think that can't be true because I was introduced to the woman she's talking to as his *wife*.'

'No, surely not!' Fay replied, staring in fascination at the two expensively dressed women in apparent intimate conversation. She was about to say how Parisian this was but when she turned back, Sandra had vanished again.

'*Encore du champagne, mademoiselle?*' A waiter hovered at her elbow.

'*Non, merci.*' She'd already had her glass topped up at

least twice and without anything to eat was beginning to feel hot and dizzy. She made her way over to some French windows spread open to the night air and stepped out onto a narrow balcony. There she delved into her gold evening bag for cologne which she dabbed on her temples and leaned over the balustrade to look down the street.

Now that the shops were shut the traffic had died down. Several doors along on the opposite side of the street was a café, its tables spilling out onto the street. Fay listened to the ring of plates and cutlery, the quick French voices and sudden bursts of laughter. From somewhere inside wafted the notes of an accordion and a woman singing. It was a tune she knew, she realized with surprise, a tune that she'd been humming – when was it? Only the other day. She closed her eyes, and as she listened to the music a scene came to mind unbidden. A girl in a dress the colour of cornflowers singing this same song. '*Il ne m'aime plus, ni moi non plus.*' Where had that come from?

'Fay? Hello, are you all right?' A man's voice spoke beside her.

She opened her eyes and straightened. 'Yes, yes – of course.' His voice was familiar, but she couldn't see him clearly at first, then he came into focus. He was about her age with smooth fair hair in a side parting, and kind blue eyes. He was holding a reporter's notebook with a Biro clipped to the coiled wire binding. She gazed at him in amazement. It couldn't be, it really couldn't. She must still be in her daydream. But it was him.

'I've been looking for you since the concert. Do you remember me, Fay?'

'Of course I do, but I'm not sure I believe it.' She took

his outstretched hand and he bent and kissed her cheek. It really was him. It was Adam.

'This might seem the most extraordinary coincidence, but it isn't, not really,' Adam said, tucking his notebook into his jacket pocket. 'A prestigious English orchestra comes to Paris, it's the most natural thing in the world for the *Chronicle* to send their local stringer to cover it. It'll only be a paragraph at the bottom of page sixteen, mind you, they're mean that way.'

'The *Chronicle*? You're a *journalist*?'

'Yes.' He smiled. 'Of course, I didn't know that you'd be playing. Though I do remember your passion for music. Seeing you there at the concert, well, it was a shock, I'll admit that much – but a pleasant one,' he added hurriedly. 'You looked so intent during the Schubert, almost rapturous. I recognized you at once, you know.'

'Did you really?' A few days on a school trip and they could hardly be said to have got to know one another. A couple of dances and a glass of lemonade; that had been the sum of it. But then *she* had recognized him instantly, as though a part of her had been looking for him.

'I hope I look a little different. The last time we met I was in that awful school uniform at the Gare du Nord with my hair in bunches.' She grimaced at the thought of how she must have looked. 'Well, maybe not the bunches, but still, it was ... how many years ago?'

'Four or five? Ages, anyway. And of course you look different. So ... grown up.' His eyes showed his appreciation. 'And yet the same.'

As they talked of what they'd been doing since then, she was struck by how easily they conversed. There was none of the teenage tongue-tied awkwardness of that evening at the Hôtel de Ville. After leaving school, Adam told her, he had studied French and German at Manchester University, then landed a position as a cub reporter. When he'd heard about the job in Paris he'd applied like a shot. She remembered how he claimed to have fallen in love with the city.

'You must speak French very well by now,' she sighed. ' I'm afraid I'm still hopeless.'

'Je me débrouille assez bien,' he said, in what sounded like a perfect accent.

'Un jolly sight plus que moi,' was her quick reply and he laughed. He offered her a cigarette, a Gitane, but she declined, watching as he lit it for himself and finding she liked the sweet aroma. She studied him covertly as he talked, thinking how he'd grown into himself, filled out from the gangly boyishness. The way he rested one hand on the railing of the balcony, holding his cigarette in the other as he regarded her, was graceful and confident.

'What were you smiling at?' he said, his forehead crinkling in that endearing way she remembered.

'Was I smiling? I'm sorry, I was thinking, despite everything, how very English you look. Does that sound awfully rude?'

'Not at all. In fact, I'll take it as a compliment, though that might offend our hosts.' He pretended to glance back into the room as if checking whether anyone had overheard, and they both laughed, two conspiratorial English people abroad.

'I was worried when I first glimpsed you out here,' he said, his face suddenly serious, 'half-hanging over the balcony like that. I thought you were going to pass out. I'm not used to dealing with swooning damsels, you know.

What should I have done if you'd fainted? Thrown champagne over you?'

'I wasn't swooning,' Fay said, indignant. 'I was listening to some music down in the street. But I did feel odd a moment ago,' she admitted. 'That's why I came out for some air.' She wasn't sure enough of him to describe her fancies about what she'd heard, how she'd had another of those unexpected déjà vu memories. After what had happened the last time they'd met, he'd think her really peculiar.

They idled against the balustrade for a while, looking down at the people passing in the silvery evening, young men riding noisy scooters, a sleek car disgorging two women in gorgeous evening dresses and fur stoles, some brightly dressed teenagers, the girls with fringed hair and false eyelashes. Their infectious laughter rose from the street.

'I can still hear music,' she said. The tune had changed now, to something lighter and lilting. Another song that Edith Piaf liked to sing.

He heard it too, a distant smile passing across his mobile features. '*Sous le ciel de Paris, dum de dum,*' he sang.

'You're out of tune,' she teased.

'I'll have you know I was a church choirboy before my voice broke.'

'I believe you.' She gave him a sideways smile. 'This might sound corny, but I think Paris tonight is exactly as it should be. This reception, the music, the chandeliers.'

'I know what you mean. The sense of fun and mystery, the *allure.*'

'I didn't see you here earlier. Had you just arrived?'

'No. There was a press call with your conductor I had to

attend. When it finished I came to look for you. I was terrified you'd gone.'

'I'm glad you spotted me. '

'I'm afraid I'm not able to stay for the dinner tonight,
but you're here for a few days, aren't you? You must let
me show you around. There's quite a lot more to Paris
than Notre Dame and the Eiffel Tower, you know. I might
not be as knowledgeable as your teacher was ...'

'Oh, I'm sure you are. We're here until Sunday afternoon, so thank you, I'd like that.' She felt herself grow
light with happiness. 'We're rehearsing most mornings for
the concerts, but otherwise ...'

'Would tomorrow be suitable for you? I'll see if I can
wangle the afternoon off. It shouldn't be a problem unless
some crisis strikes.'

'Tomorrow, why not?'

'Where are you staying? I could telephone and leave a
message.'

She told him about the Hôtel Marguerite, which he
didn't seem to know, then she felt the warm firmness of
his hand in hers, and met his smiling eyes, before his
graceful figure vanished into the crowd.

She could hardly believe that they'd come across one
another again like this. It felt like a tremendous coincidence, but she also accepted his rational explanation. By
luck or logic, the magic of Paris had drawn them both, and
once he'd known she was there he'd come to seek her out.
The fact that he was living here made her feel less of a
stranger herself. It gave her a solid connection that
strengthened the fanciful one she felt. She was already
looking forward to seeing him again tomorrow.

Perhaps, her thoughts ran on, he'd be able to help her in

her search. Even if she found the convent and this Mère Marie, what would she ask? Whether there was someone who knew her as a child, who could tell her the story of the little rucksack and the label with her name on it. Or even remember her mother.

She was still puzzling about this when the soft boom of a gong sounded for dinner.

Chapter 7

Wednesday

Before stepping out after breakfast the following morning, Fay asked the matronly hotel receptionist with hair in a perfect pleat if there were any messages, but on being told no, reassured herself that it was too early to have heard from Adam. She then asked in her hesitant French about the other matter on her mind, how she might find the whereabouts of the convent. 'I have tried the post office,' she explained.

The woman arched her painted eyebrows then shrugged. *'L'église?'* she suggested. 'Ask at the Madeleine?' and pointed a manicured finger.

'Merci,' Fay replied, thinking this as good an idea as any. Surely the priests there would know about convents in the city. There wouldn't be time before the rehearsal to ask now, but she'd call there later.

The morning's rehearsal did not go well. The musicians were all tired from the late night before. Dinner had involved five courses and there had been three kinds of wine with the meal, which some members hadn't been able to resist enjoying to the full. The conductor was in a bad mood and snapped at a clarinettist for playing too loudly in a quiet passage of Mozart, and at the second violins for bungling an entry. Everyone was relieved when lunchtime arrived and he dismissed them for the day.

Fay joined a group from the orchestra at a nearby café, choosing a delicious *omelette aux fines herbes* and sharing the moans about the morning, before presenting her excuses and slipping away on her quest.

She took a different route back towards the hotel this time, approaching the Church of the Madeleine from the front to appreciate its full glory. From the outside it looked more like a Roman temple than a church, but this impression was dispelled when she entered and saw the high altar, with its stone statue of the church's saint, Mary Magdalene, being swept up to heaven by two angels. The classical lines gave the church a very different atmosphere from the gothic drama of Notre Dame. Fay studied the ornate marble plaques to long-dead dignitaries and gazed up at the historical scene painted inside the dome. Everything here spoke of Napoleon's triumphalism and his obsession with the glories of Imperial Rome.

There was hardly anyone else in the church, but the organ was playing softly and beautifully. Fay hung about near the altar, hoping to spot someone to ask about the convent. She felt a little frivolous in her pale blue coat and woollen hat amidst all this formal elegance, the heels of her court shoes tapping too loudly on the marble.

She was about to give up and return to the hotel to see if Adam had called when the sound of a door shutting echoed around, and a youngish, plain-faced man in the simple black robe of a priest came down the central aisle towards her bearing a packet of small candles. She watched his quiet approach and would have lost courage to ask her question altogether had he not looked straight at her and smiled. *'Bonjour, mademoiselle, je peux vous aider?'*

He listened to her request with a patient frown and studied the piece of paper she showed him, then nodded and said in English, 'I do not know of it myself, but I may be able to find out if you will wait, mademoiselle.'

'Thank you,' she replied, and watched him go to a votary near the altar and empty the candles into a tray kept beneath for the purpose, before returning the way he had come. Five minutes became ten before he reappeared, carrying a dog-eared reference book.

'Sit down here, please, we can look together,' he said, gesturing to the front row of chairs. There was something humble and reassuring about him so she was happy to do this.

'I asked the Monseigneur,' the priest said, 'and he found it for me.' He opened the tome at a marker, smoothed the pages, and held it so she could see. His slender forefinger pointed to an entry near the bottom. 'The convent – it's attached to the Church of Sainte Cécile.'

'Place des Moineaux?' She could only just read it in the gloom. *'Moineaux* are sparrows, aren't they? Where is it, do you know?'

'Sparrows, yes,' he said. 'Here, the book definitely says *l'Eglise de Sainte Cécile*. Near the Rue St-Jacques, you'll understand. The Left Bank, by the Sorbonne. You have a map?' Fay retrieved her tourist plan from her bag and unfolded it and he showed her where the church was.

'Merci,' she said. 'Ah, I was near there yesterday!' It was close to the Seine by Notre Dame. 'Thank you so much.'

'De rien. This handbook is 1959. The convent is not in

the most recent one, only the church, I don't know why. Is there anything else I can help you with, mademoiselle?'

She hesitated, seeing the sympathy in his eyes. She wondered how old he was. Still young, in his early thirties perhaps, but old enough. 'There is something. May I ask, were you in Paris during the war? I . . . I wondered what it was like, living here then.'

A look of wariness crossed his face and she cursed herself for being so thoughtless. The organ had suddenly stopped playing and for a moment there was complete stillness.

'I was a boy of ten when the Nazis marched into Paris.' The priest was silent for a moment then added, 'It was not so bad. The worst thing was feeling hungry all the time. There was no milk sometimes for the children.'

It was not so bad. He didn't wish to speak about it, Fay saw at once. These events of twenty years ago might appear to have been forgotten in the life going on gaily around her in this beautiful city, but what if she could see below the surface? So many people must have stories to tell of the war, had to live with memories they could never forget, but which they were forced to suppress in order to go on with their lives.

As she thanked the priest and went on her way, it occurred to Fay that her mother might have been like them.

Chapter 8

1937

Kitty's new life fell into a pattern of sorts. There was a two-hour lesson with Monsieur Deschamps on Tuesday and Thursday mornings, then she attended classes at the imposing Conservatoire building on the Right Bank, but for the rest of the working week she was expected to practise. Usually she would take her music to the Conservatoire, where she would be allocated one of the small bare practice rooms, typically with an upright piano and a single window looking out onto a featureless courtyard. Here she would shut the door, adjust the height of the seat, arrange her books on the music-rest and begin.

Monsieur Deschamps had issued strict instructions about practice methods. Kitty must devote half an hour to scales and other technical exercises, before turning her attention to the pieces he'd given her, the Clair de Lune, a Mozart Sonata and a Bach Prelude, which he'd prescribed to train evenness in fingerwork. Her use of the pedals had caused him consternation. 'You utilize the sustain pedal too much,' he told her and pointed out how she was doing so to compensate for the weakness in her left hand. But

'*Écoutez*' was the piece of advice he most frequently repeated. '*Listen* to yourself play. It is the most important thing of all.' And so for hours at a time she would be alone at her practice, absorbed in the music, playing and replaying the most difficult phrases of the pieces. 'Thirty times,' she remembered her previous teacher used to say. 'After thirty it will become a habit. The fingers won't forget it.'

M. Deschamps agreed about the playing of passages many times, but disagreed that it was the hands that should know the piece. 'You should feel *une affinité intime avec la musique* in here,' he said, rapping his temple sharply, 'then your fingers will obey.' Sometimes he would make her deconstruct the harmonies on the page. 'This chord here, the D sharp is yearning, stretching itself like, how you say, a climber of mountains, to reach this E here, but in the left hand, see, he holds back from the G, so satisfaction is denied. And that is the sound Debussy makes you feel *ici*.' He pressed his fist to his chest, above where his heart might be. '*Vous voyez?*' And she would nod that yes, she did see. She had never been taught to learn the music from the inside like this, and found that listening closely to the sound of her own playing helped immeasurably. She could hear how much she was improving from day to day.

What she hadn't expected in Paris was to feel quite so alone. Practising, by its very nature, is a solitary affair, she had never minded that, but even when she was with other people – at the harmony class on Saturday mornings, for instance, where she struggled as it was taught in French – hardly anyone spoke to her. Being naturally reserved and not fluent in the language, she did not dare start up any conversation. There were very few women at the

Conservatoire, that was part of the problem, and the ones she glimpsed seemed horribly sophisticated; she felt plainly dressed next to them. They stuck with each other, too, chattering nineteen to the dozen in a way that made her feel excluded.

It was Monday morning of the second week, while approaching the building, that she encountered someone she recognized – the young man with cropped dark hair she'd met on her first visit to M. Deschamps' apartment. He was slouched against a wall lighting a cigarette and looking nervy and intense. His surname, she remembered, was Ramond. He recognized her too, for he watched her approach and muttered, '*Bonjour*,' but though she returned the greeting he seemed indisposed to continue the conversation, instead looking away, so she passed on into the building feeling a little hurt and putting his charmlessness down to arrogance. The next day, when M. Deschamps' little maid showed her into the apartment she listened to the tempestuous sounds of Beethoven coming from the drawing room, but again, when the young man emerged, he passed her with barely a nod.

The very same afternoon, however, after the slow-moving old man on reception at the Conservatoire had given her the key to her practice room, he reached into a pigeonhole and passed her an envelope with her name on it. The note inside on cheap writing paper was signed *Serge Ramond* and asked her to meet him at a café nearby at four o'clock on Wednesday afternoon. Kitty sighed, still feeling put out by Ramond's offhand manner and fearing that he'd be hard work as a companion. On the other hand, beggars couldn't be choosers and she didn't know anyone else at the Conservatoire, so she turned the paper over and wrote a painstaking couple of lines in French thanking him and agreeing to the rendezvous.

The café was on a corner near the front entrance of the Conservatoire and turned out to be popular with the music students. It was a cheerful place hung with baskets of late geraniums outside, noisy with chattering groups within. Kitty spotted Ramond sitting by himself at a round table near the bar, smoking furiously and staring into space with his usual intense expression. When he finally saw her, he leaped up, rocking the table in his eagerness.

'*Kitty – comment allez-vous?*' He shook her hand then pulled out a chair for her to sit down, and she saw at once that he was doing his best to be friendly.

'I haven't been here before,' she told him, looking round at the polished brass bar, the rows of bottles on the dresser behind, the dark varnished wood floor, seeing their reflections in the ornate mirrors on the walls.

'It's all right – not expensive, that's the best thing.' He was studying her but still he didn't smile.

The waiter brought them coffee and glasses of water and they conversed in a halting mixture of French and English. He'd been in Paris a year, Serge said. His family lived further south, in Orléans, and she sensed it had been something of a struggle financially for them to send him to be taught by M. Deschamps and to attend classes at the Conservatoire. He was currently boarding with a Jewish family in Le Marais, in a flat above their wholesale jewellery business. He spoke rapidly, so she sometimes had to ask him to repeat himself, but the gleam in his quick dark eyes and the passion in his voice betrayed both his love for the piano and an over-anxiety to succeed. Sensing that his previous standoffish behaviour had been due to shyness, she began to feel sorry for him, and even to like him a little. When after half an hour she rose to go, explaining that she had some shopping to do, she was touched when he refused to take the coins she pushed across the table.

'I can't allow it,' she said. 'We are both students living on a budget.'

'Next time we pay for ourselves, but today, no, I invited you,' he insisted. 'I hope there will be a next time? We have the same teacher – it makes sense to be friends, not rivals, no?' She didn't recognize *rivales* from his pronunciation at first, but when finally she understood, she was indignant.

'Of course we're not rivals! I don't think like that.' It was then, finally, that he permitted himself to relax and give the slightest of smiles.

She thought about what he'd said after she stopped at a tiny shop near the convent to buy needles and thread, 'to mend stockings,' as she explained to the dumpling-shaped woman in widow's black who served her. It had never occurred to her that she should feel in competition with other students. She played for the delight of the music, because it pleased others to listen, because she wanted to do well for Uncle Pepper. She had hoped too that it would somehow provide her with a living and an interesting life – but fame? Success as a concert pianist? That was for the few, surely. And perhaps she didn't have the drive that Serge had. No, they were not rivals. She had learned that much about herself through their conversation.

*

Because board was included in the cost of her lodging, Kitty had so far eaten dinner at the convent every evening, immediately after one of the several church services the nuns attended each day. If Father Paul wasn't there, the Reverend Mother said Grace, and they ate for the most part in silence along the trestle tables in the dining room.

It was not an uncomfortable silence, Kitty decided, and although the food was plain it was flavoursome: meat stews with herbs, soft fresh bread, followed by fruit and various mild sorts of cheeses, but there was no wine, only water to drink. There were fourteen nuns in all, counting Mère Marie-François and the only novice amongst them, Sister Thérèse. In addition to Kitty there were three other paying guests – an elderly woman and her middle-aged daughter who had apparently come to Paris from Toulouse to visit some relative in hospital, and an Englishwoman in her late forties named Miss Dunne.

Adele Dunne was from Norfolk, Kitty discovered in the course of a conversation at dinner one evening, and following the deaths of both her parents, had come to Paris to work with a children's charity in the city. She was a tall, squarish woman with a penchant for tweed, but the expression on her plain face was lively, and she liked to sit and draw in a sketchbook she often carried. It was Miss Dunne who pointed out to Kitty the trickle of Jewish and other refugees passing through the city from Germany. It all meant a greater pressure on the resources of the charity, she told her.

One evening, a few days after Kitty had arrived, she found Miss Dunne's open sketchbook left for a moment, with her spectacle case, on a table in the hall and was moved to see, rendered very skilfully, a drawing of a dark-eyed woman in a headscarf with an anguished expression in her eyes. Kitty would have liked to turn the pages to see what else Miss Dunne had captured, but didn't dare and instead passed on her way.

She was going for the first time on her own to the church to play the piano there. She'd felt self-conscious about doing so before, given that the building was a public place, and someone might come in, but Mère Marie-François had repeated the invitation and she thought it rude not to try. In the event, she became so caught up in her playing that she stopped worrying. It really was a most beautiful piano with a lovely touch, and the acoustics of the building were perfect. She played for an hour until Father Paul came in to ask whether he should light the candles for her.

If Kitty had been like many other young women, with a family and many friends her own age, she might have found her life in those first two weeks unbearably lonely, but she was used to spending time by herself, and though she longed to find friends and to feel at home, it didn't drag her down. There was someone in the convent to whom she felt drawn and that was Sister Thérèse. It was strange, because their lives were worlds apart, yet fate had thrown them together and the fact that they were the same age, but had made such different choices in life, had evoked a curiosity in each about the other.

Once, Kitty forgot to wind her travel clock and got up too early in a panic that she was late. Downstairs, she found the novice had just returned from buying baguettes for breakfast and she helped her lay the tables. At first they worked in silent companionship, then Kitty caught

Thérèse giving her shy glances and she asked the girl if she had always lived in Paris.

'*Oui*,' Sister Thérèse said promptly, 'but on the other side of the city, in Saint-Denis.' She had been educated at a school run by nuns, she told Kitty, and for her it had been a natural step to become one. She hadn't realized it would mean coming all the way here to the centre of Paris, but it had been God's will, and the priest's at Saint-Denis, so ... Here she made a gesture of acceptance. Despite the expression of intelligence in her eyes there was something delightfully unsophisticated about her, Kitty found, and she wondered at the calm sense of purpose in someone so young.

'*Et tu?*' Thérèse addressed her informally, as though they were already friends. 'Your mother and father allowed you to come to Paris on your own? They must worry that you are safe.'

Kitty explained her circumstances briefly and Thérèse regarded her with a mixture of dismay and compassion. 'That is indeed very hard for you,' she said, and Kitty felt a great rush of warmth for her. She would have liked to have asked the other girl how she could bear to have accepted her vocation before her grown-up life had really begun, to have denied herself hope of a husband and children of her own. It was too soon in their acquaintance, though, to ask such a probing question.

In fact, it might upset her, Kitty decided, for when she asked her if she missed her home the girl said a little wistfully, 'They say I must try not to think of my home much, though we are not a closed order and my family are allowed to visit.' Her face lit up. 'My sister and her husband have a baby boy I have never seen. Maybe they will bring him when they next come.'

Now she knew Thérèse a little, Kitty thought her beautiful. Her flattish round face and too-generous mouth were offset by fine dark eyes with thick lashes, and the dimple in one cheek gave her an appealing demeanour. Kitty liked her calm but friendly manner and the luminous quality about her she'd noticed on the first day.

After that morning at the convent, she often rose early to help the young novice with her chores in the first quiet moments of the day. On one occasion, out of a sense of curiosity rather than spiritual duty, she attended the service in the church beforehand, but not knowing Latin and there being no book to follow, she felt merely an observer and did not go again.

Miss Dunne, it appeared, liked to go to Notre Dame. She had a weakness for stained glass, she told Kitty. Kitty tried the American Cathedral near the Arc de Triomphe one Sunday, but there was a christening and finding there to be a great number of people who all appeared to know one another she slipped away quickly afterwards. She didn't notice the well-built young man with curly fair hair shooting her furtive glances from the other side of the aisle, nor did she have any inkling of his moment of disappointment when he looked in vain for her later.

Eugene Knox didn't often attend Divine Service because he was either working – he had recently started his internship as a doctor at the American Hospital off Boulevard Victor Hugo – or sleeping in after a late night out, but he'd decided to go that morning as his mother had written to say that a close friend of hers in Paris was having a grandchild christened, and would he attend to represent the family? Being a sunny sort of young man who liked to please his mother if it didn't put him out too much, he'd gone. The baby admittedly was very sweet and during the service he spotted some friends to speak to afterwards. There was to be a lunch reception in the George V Hotel after the christening so on the whole it wouldn't be too much of a sacrifice of his time.

Halfway through the prayers when everyone else had their eyes closed, Eugene looked around at the congregation and caught her face in profile. She was sitting on her own, two rows behind, on the other side of the aisle. He knew her at once, but it took him a moment to remember where from. Last time she'd been carrying a suitcase and her face had been pale with tiredness, that straight-off-the-night-train look, but today, with her eyes respectfully closed, a slight frown as though she was concentrating on the prayers, her cheeks were rosy. He noticed again the charming way her hair fell in corkscrew waves on either side of her sturdy face, the dark line of her brows and eyelashes, as though they'd been smudged with charcoal. His hopes were dashed when, after the blessing, he looked round only to see her pick up her handbag and hurry from the building.

His automatic response was to start off after her, but a man's voice said, 'Didn't think I'd see you here, Gene,' and he turned to find himself shaking hands with a man he knew slightly, Bill Delaney, a young Irish-American journalist and the baby's godfather. By the time he'd extricated himself and got outside, the girl had all but vanished. No, there she was, some way ahead of him, walking towards the river. He set off after her, though not too quickly as he wasn't sure how he would explain himself if he caught her up. The necessity of this did not present itself, for when they'd crossed the Seine he kept losing her, then when he eventually reached the Rue St Jacques, it was to see her turn down one of the many side streets near the café. Then a bus blocked his view so that by the time he was able to follow, she'd gone. He turned on his heel with a sigh, and made his way thoughtfully back to the christening party, where he presented the baby with a teddy bear and passed a most enjoyable afternoon. But from time to time he thought of the girl. At least, he thought, since he'd seen her in his neighbourhood twice now, he knew roughly where she lived.

Late September brought cooler weather, and by the first week in October, keen winds were blowing the dead leaves down dusty streets. The nights were starting to draw in, and Kitty chose to return earlier from the Conservatoire each day while the twilit skies above Notre Dame turned soft mauve and grey. She took to practising in the church in the late afternoon. On occasion a passer-by might be drawn in to listen and at first this bothered her, but after it happened a couple of times it ceased to worry her and once she'd registered their presence she'd lose herself again in the music.

It was on such an afternoon, about a month after her arrival in Paris, that she sat at the piano in a patch of candlelight amid the encircling gloom. The priest had not yet been in to switch on the lights, but she'd lit the great candles set on wrought-iron stands to either side of the piano and liked to sit in the aura of their hot smoky flames. Stirred by the feeling of mystery and calm, she turned the pages of her book of Beethoven sonatas and found a piece to suit. She knew it well, the beginning she'd learned to play when she was twelve, but only now did she have the technique and the maturity to convey the deep feeling of it. She played with her eyes half-closed, letting the music tell the story.

The screech of wood on stone brought her to a sudden stop. 'Damn,' someone said, out in the darkness. 'Sorry, didn't see that chair.' The voice was a man's, with a lazy transatlantic burr.

'Who's there?' She half-rose, alarmed.

'Only me, ma'am.' American, definitely. A tall, bulky figure separated itself from the shadows. He was a young man dressed in a soft brown suit, a little older than her – mid-twenties, perhaps – with clipped fair curls, and a round face with a pleasant grin. 'Please, don't stop, I was enjoying that. What was it? I know it from somewhere.'

'It was Beethoven. His Moonlight Sonata.' Her fear of him had faded.

'That's the one! I'm sure my big sister used to play it back home. Me, I was never any use at the piano. Or any other instrument, come to that. I guess God made some folks to play and others to listen. I'm of the listening variety.' He stopped, but seeing she still sat, hands resting on her lap, added in a humble tone, 'It would make me very happy if you continued.'

She said nothing.

'I'll go away again if it helps,' he offered. 'Should probably never have come in, in the first instance. Only I was passing, on my way home, and I heard beautiful music and since it was a church I figured maybe nobody would worry if I listened in.'

What he did not say was that he had made it his business to pass this way at various times over the previous fortnight, had even attended morning service again at the cathedral, in the desperate hope of seeing her. He didn't know what had got into him; he'd never been this way before about a girl. And it was the plaintive beauty of her music floating out on the early-evening air that, in the end, had led him to her.

Kitty smiled, beguiled by the easy run of his talk. 'You're right,' she said, 'anybody may come in, but I was only playing for myself, I'm afraid – it isn't a performance. The curé here is kind enough to let me practise. You don't have to go, but I'm worried I'll disappoint you if you stay.'

'Disappoint me? No, I don't think you would do that!' the young man said, then, 'May I?' before plumping himself down on a chair in the front row and placing his hat on the one next to it. 'My apologies, I spoiled the mood, didn't I? But go on, try again. I won't interrupt. I'll be silent as a mouse, I promise.'

She laughed. 'The mice in here can be extremely noisy. They scamper about shamelessly and gnaw the candles, but . . . all right. I'd better start again.'

She turned to the music once more and, true to his word, he was so still that she quickly immersed herself in the sublime languor of the broken chords of the first movement, as sad and ethereal as moonlight, music which built in passion and intensity to a state of rapture, before returning once more to the peaceful chords of the beginning.

The last notes echoed away in the darkness of the church. There was a long silence.

'Bravo,' he whispered eventually. 'That was . . . that was quite something. Beautiful. The Moonlight, I'll remember that.'

'Thank you,' she said, touched by his wonder.

'Somebody told me Beethoven didn't give it the name, but after his death a critic said that it reminded him of moonlight falling on the Lake of Lucerne and the name stuck.'

He nodded. 'I see why he thought that. It reminds me of when I was a child and we stayed one summer in a house by a lake. The night skies were so clear you could sit and count the stars of heaven and never get them all.' He spoke slowly and the low timbre of his voice was like music to her, so that she could see the scene he painted. 'My father took me fishing in the moonlight and I trailed my fingers in the water – and you know what? I believed him when he said it was liquid silver.' He chuckled. There was a faraway look in his eyes and she saw that the memory was a happy one. She liked his face, which was guileless and friendly, and the thought came to her that she'd been denied the chance to do anything at all with her father, and she envied him. Uncle Pepper had not known how to behave with children. He'd always treated her as another adult, with a serious formality.

'You must think me rude, not to have introduced myself,' the young man said, standing and putting out his hand. I'm Dr Eugene Knox – Gene to most people.'

'And I'm Kitty Travers. Are you a medical doctor?' She found him easy to talk to, did not feel shy with him in the least.

'They've seen fit to let me loose on the unsuspecting sick just recently, yes. I've started work at the American Hospital, if you know it.' Kitty didn't, so he explained. It had been established by his countrymen as a charitable trust, principally to look after the many Americans who were living in Paris, though it treated people of other nationalities from time to time. 'And you, you're English, of course – but what brings you to Paris, if you don't mind me asking?'

'I'm here to study the piano,' Kitty told him. 'You could say that I'm attached to the Conservatoire – that is, I go to classes there, but I'm not properly part of their system. I'm being taught privately by Xavier Deschamps. Have you heard of him? They say he was a famous concert pianist in his day.'

Eugene shook his head, a regretful expression on his face. 'As I say, I enjoy listening, but I don't know much about your kind of music. I'm more of a jazz man myself. Duke Ellington's a favourite. You ever heard him play?'

Now it was her turn to say no. She didn't even know the name. 'I haven't ever heard much jazz.'

'You haven't? Then may I respectfully suggest that you haven't lived, Miss Travers.' He paused for the slightest of moments, then said, almost casually, 'Perhaps we can remedy that. I'd be honoured to take you to hear some one evening, if you'd allow it.'

'Oh, I'm not sure . . .' she started to say, dismayed, then it came to her, why shouldn't she? Who would stop her? She was her own person here and she liked this young man, liked him very much and felt him trustworthy. 'Well, yes, I'd like that, thank you.' She was surprised at the heady sense of freedom the answer gave her. She was still getting over the fact of him sitting here, a complete stranger, and yet somehow so utterly familiar. It made sense to her that he was a healer for his was a soothing presence. There was something about him that was comfortable, comforting, and she found herself flying to him like a bird to a safe nesting place.

*

The following Friday, Kitty told Sister Thérèse that she wouldn't be eating dinner at the convent and asked if it mattered that she'd be back a little late. The young novice's response was to fetch a spare key, which she slipped into Kitty's hand with a complicit smile.

That evening found Kitty puzzling between the two long dresses she owned, rejecting the formal black silk she'd brought in the event of concert performances in favour of one in soft apricot organdie she'd had made up in London, sleeveless with a fashionably pleated skirt and a matching jacket. There seemed to be no full-length looking-glass in the convent, so she was forced to position the adjustable face mirror in the bathroom as best she could to view bits of herself from different angles and trust all was well. Her shoulder-length hair with its natural curls needed little more than to be parted in the middle and clipped back with a pair of mother-of-pearl slides. Some russet lipstick and a touch of powder were all it took for a palely glamorous face to reflect back at her, eyes bright with excitement. As a final touch she fastened round her neck the delicate sapphire pendant she'd inherited from her mother and clipped on matching earrings. It struck her that it was her first proper night out in Paris.

At the stroke of eight she slipped out unseen to meet Gene, and found his cab already waiting. He took her first to Harry's Bar near the Opéra, where she viewed the glamorous clientele, mostly English and American, through a golden haze of champagne. 'I don't come here often,' he whispered. 'Tonight is a treat for us both.'

In a cosy back-street restaurant nearby, where the walls were hung with scenes of Paris nightlife, they ate *sole meunière* by candlelight. A gypsy violinist came to serenade them, but sensing Kitty's bashfulness, Gene gave him some coins to go away.

Kitty was touched that Gene seemed to want to know all about her. She told him how she was an orphan and couldn't imagine what it must be like to be part of a proper family, as he was. She was here, she said, because her uncle wanted so much for her to do well, but she was worried about leaving him alone. 'What about you?' she asked Gene, curious. 'Why did you come so far from home to train in Paris?'

'My grandma on my mother's side was French,' he explained as they ate. 'I came here to stay with her once or twice and sort of fell into the place, like I was born here. You need to walk down a main street in Alabama to appreciate what I'm saying. Here folks are discreet, don't interfere in one another's business so much. Not that I've anything to hide, you understand.' He gave one of those friendly smiles she was quickly learning was a part of him.

'I've not found it easy to get to know people here,' Kitty confessed. 'They speak so quickly, that's part of the trouble. I should try harder, I suppose.'

'Do you know, I saw you at the cathedral,' he said quietly, between mouthfuls. 'A couple of weeks back.'

'Did you?' she said in surprise. 'I didn't see you.'

'You looked a little lonely. I'd have come across and said hello, but you ran off before I had a chance.'

'Everybody seemed to know one another – it was like a big party for that pretty baby. I'm ashamed to say I funked it.'

'Oh, I see. Well, we all do that sometimes.'

'I don't believe that you would.'

'I can assure you that you're wrong,' he said. 'Though

perhaps I wouldn't tell that to any patient of mine.' And she smiled up at him.

A waiter came to refill their glasses with red wine.

'It's such a coincidence the way you found me,' she said, and was genuinely surprised when he turned bashful.

'All right, I'll have to admit it. It wasn't exactly luck.' And he told her how he'd followed her from the cathedral out of concern, that he'd passed the spot where he'd last seen her several times since that Sunday, for he still attended the odd lecture at the École de Médecine and anyway was working out his notice on an apartment near the Panthéon. It was easy for him to walk near where he'd last seen her.

'I suppose I should feel flattered that you went to so much trouble,' she said, but he heard the disapproval in her voice.

'Now, darn it, I've offended you. I should have kept my big mouth shut.'

'No, I'm not offended, ' she said in a soft voice, her fingers stroking the stem of her glass. She looked up to meet his steady gaze and couldn't help smiling. His was a face of such honesty and friendliness it was difficult to believe he would ever do anything underhand. Slowly he smiled back at her and his eyes lit up. Soon they were both laughing.

She'd been in love, really in love, once before, painfully and hopelessly, with the headmaster's son, a golden-haired athletic boy a year or two older, whose eyes had never even rested on the quiet seventeen-year-old girl who came to tea sometimes with her uncle. But nobody had ever warned her that love could spring up as suddenly as this. That two people could see instantly that all they needed was there in the other.

'Come on,' he said, breaking the spell. 'I promised you jazz, and you shall have it.'

A cab dropped them in Montmartre where the steps up to Sacré-Coeur gleamed in the moonlight. Kitty took Gene's arm and they walked together down a steep side street, then in through the door of a building so nondescript that nobody would have noticed it unless they knew it was there. Instantly they could hear a wonderful swell of music. She followed Gene up a rackety flight of stairs. The music grew louder as they climbed. At the top Gene thrust aside a velvet curtain and drew her into a large square room swirling with smoke. It was noisy and packed with people, and the windows had been thrown open to the night, God help the neighbours. There was a bar in one corner and a makeshift stage draped with crimson in another, where three Negro musicians were playing to a swinging rhythm. The smudged, dancing notes of the piano and the rich, lilting sound of the trumpet snaked inside her in a way that was thrilling and strange, and yet at the same time felt perfectly natural.

Gene guided her to the bar and bought her more champagne. He seemed utterly at home here, and soon they were joined by friends of his – a slight, dapper fellow American whom Gene introduced as 'the renowned writer Jack Miles', and a charming, sandy-haired Irish-American by the name of Bill Delaney, who was a journalist on the Paris *Herald Tribune*. The third was a woman, a girlfriend of Bill's. Claudine was a thin, elegant Frenchwoman in her thirties with a feather in her headdress. She contributed very little to the conversation, simply smoked a cigarette through an ivory holder, but there was a mysterious air about her that fascinated Kitty.

Later, much later, in the cab home, Gene held her hand and she leaned against him, half-drunk on the champagne, the music, and happiness.

'I enjoyed myself so much, thank you, but I'll never get up for my class in the morning,' she murmured.

'You must, or I'll blame myself,' Gene said, squeezing her hand. 'I can't have you cutting your lessons. Your uncle would never forgive me.'

'He wouldn't approve of jazz. "Music of the gutter", I once heard him call it.'

'Oh, don't spoil it, I was liking what I heard about your Uncle Pepper.'

'He'd like you, I'm sure,' Kitty said, laughing. 'It's in matters such as music and painting that he has strong old-fashioned views.'

'I hope to meet him one day then,' Gene said as the cab drew up outside her alleyway. '*Attendez un petit moment s'il vous plaît*,' he instructed the driver.

She was glad to have his arm to cling to in the silent darkness of the alley. Where it opened out into the square, all bathed in moonlight, he stopped and turned to her. 'It's been the most wonderful evening,' he murmured. 'May I see you again?'

'Yes,' she whispered, while glancing anxiously at the shuttered mansion, 'but you'd better go now in case we're seen. I don't want to get thrown out of my lodgings.'

At the gate of the convent he waited while she stole in through the front door using the key Sister Thérèse had given her. Upstairs, safe in bed, she fell asleep at once, but her dreams were full of the sinuous, caressing music of the evening and Gene's soft lazy voice.

They saw each other as often as they could after that, and on his days off Gene made it his business to show Kitty Paris. It wasn't always the main tourist sights, but the out-of-the-way places, the secret nooks he took her to – a shabby theatre showing Grand Guignol melodrama, the Jardin des Plantes by the School of Botany, Chopin's tomb in the cemetery of Père-Lachaise. Best of all, Kitty loved a little piano shop in St Germain, where she roamed about marvelling at the beautiful old instruments whilst Gene chatted easily to the proprietor, learning the stories about the pianos and the people who'd owned them. In the evening he might accompany her to a concert, or they'd dine together and visit one of the *boîtes* to listen to some woman in black with a smoky 4 a.m. voice, singing heartbreaking love songs that left Kitty with the melancholy sense of how time effaced everything. Not this, she thought, not this, as she sensed the warmth of Gene sitting close, the fair hairs on the backs of his strong hands gleaming in the candlelight, and he would catch her eye and smile his open smile.

Then came a rainy November Friday afternoon when they'd arranged to meet in the foyer of the Louvre and she waited and waited with a mixture of annoyance and concern because he didn't come. Eventually she went into the maze of galleries by herself, but tired quickly of the frivolity of eighteenth-century girls in swings. She tried the sombre sensibilities of Dutch landscapes, finding them more in keeping with her mood, but really, she didn't enjoy them either. It would have been fun with Gene. All the time she worried whether she'd come at the wrong time or if something had happened to him.

She heard nothing from him until the next day, when she arrived downstairs, her face pale and puffy after a night of anxious wakefulness, to find a letter by her place at the breakfast table addressed in his loopy scrawl. She opened it eagerly. It was full of apologies. There had been an emergency admission, the child of a family he faintly knew, suffering from meningitis; he'd felt it important to stay with her – the mother had begged – and he'd no way of contacting Kitty. He hoped she would forgive him.

She did, of course she did. Her first feelings were relief, and she quashed the mean little selfish voice inside that said, *but you abandoned me*, and told herself instead how good he was, that he'd put a sick child first.

There were other times. He had to cry off a day trip to the Palace of Fontainebleau in December because of staff shortages at the hospital. Kitty managed to hide her disappointment, but grudgingly, because the outing had been long-planned and she'd excused herself from a class to go. Though she recognized the importance of his work she secretly felt sometimes that it always seemed to be him who volunteered for an extra shift and a resentment grew, though she hated herself for it.

Matters came to a head during the week before Christmas. She'd arranged to meet Gene one Thursday evening at a favourite auberge in St-Germain, where they liked to go for the traditional cooking and often met two of Gene's American friends, Jack and his girlfriend Milly. Gene hadn't arrived when she walked in, but the patron, a pleasant man with a fleshy, creased-up face, like a friendly bulldog, knew her and took her to a table, bringing her a complimentary glass of wine whilst she waited. Everyone liked Gene and this kind of reception was not unusual.

Ten minutes ticked by. Kitty pulled a novel out of her bag written by a Frenchwoman who Milly said was the latest thing, and tried to read, but her French, though much improved, wasn't up to it and she couldn't concentrate anyway. Twenty minutes, still no Gene, and by now, some of the other diners were glancing at her curiously. After three-quarters of an hour she'd had enough. She put her book away and caught the eye of the patron.

'I think I've come to the wrong place,' she told him. 'If Dr Knox does come looking for me, perhaps you'd explain.'

Outside, sleet was coming down fast and hardly anyone was about. She pulled her collar up tight against a biting wind and set off to walk back to the convent through the back streets. She'd never felt so miserable. When she was with Gene she felt happy and loved. He was completely present for her. When they were apart she thought of him all the time, as though, if her life were a piece of music, he was the bass note underpinning it.

But what if it wasn't the case for Gene? Kitty knew how important his work was to him. Did he forget her when she wasn't there? And what if he did? Would it mean he didn't care deeply enough for her? Should she go on seeing him, or was there no future? These thoughts chased round and around in her mind as she trudged on, her shoulders hunched against the weather.

When she came to the piano shop, she stopped to look in the window. The grille was down, but through the latticework in the light of the streetlamp she could see the miniature model of a grand piano, perfect down to the tiny painted man in evening dress, tails flying, bent over the keyboard, and the music spread before him, pages fluttering in some imagined breeze. She was struck by the thought that she'd never be able to visit this place again without thinking of Gene. He had coloured her whole life in Paris. Without him it would be monotone.

She turned to go and only then registered the sound of a man's hurried footsteps somewhere behind. In response she hastened her pace, but found herself slipping in the slush. The footsteps gained on her. Then, 'Kitty,' came a voice and joy flooded through her.

'Gene,' she whispered, swinging round, and found herself clasped in his bear-like hug. Her face was buried in his shoulder and the wet wool of his coat tickled her nose.

'I am so sorry,' he puffed, when he set her upright. 'They said I'd missed you by only a minute, but I didn't know which way you'd gone.'

'Something must have told you it was this way,' she said quietly.

'You were looking in the window of our shop,' he said, light dawning. He drew her into the shelter of a doorway. They stood, hardly touching, both sensing a distance between them.

His face was in shadow and she glanced up at him, unsure. The initial joy at seeing him was fading now and misery taking hold once more. The fact remained that she felt he'd abandoned her again. What excuse would he come up with this time?

'You were late,' she said tightly. 'Gene, you don't know what it feels like. The other customers stared at me, it was so public and humiliating. And it made me feel as though you don't care.'

'I am truly sorry,' he said very humbly.

'You were sorry last time. And the time before that.'

'Kitty, look, someone hadn't turned up for their shift. I couldn't just leave, surely you understand? I am sorry, but it's what happens in my job. It's my life, Kitty.' She was hurt by the stubborn tone in his voice.

'If it's more important than me, than us,' she started to say, and then caught the expression on his face. It was neither the look of abject apology she hoped for nor the stern coldness she feared. Instead it was an expression of immense calm and compassion, as though she were a struggling child failing to understand why its behaviour was unreasonable. Like a child's, too, her gloved hands were coiled into fists, beating the air.

'Hey, hey, Kitty,' he said, grasping them, unfolding the fingers, holding them firm in his. 'What I am doing with my life is not something I have chosen. It is as though doctoring has chosen me, it's my calling. To say it is more important than you, though, is to compare two things that are incomparable. It is my duty to tend the sick and I must do it.'

She turned her face to hide the tears that threatened.

'Kitty, darling Kitty, are you listening?' She nodded miserably. His voice was gentle. 'Kitty, how important is your music to you?'

'I cannot imagine my life without it,' she said after a moment. 'It's such a part of me, I—'

'And the time you devote to it, all those hours of practice?'

'That's different!' she cried, seeing what he was getting

at. 'I wouldn't devote the time to the exclusion of people I love.'

'You wouldn't?' he said, sounding surprised, then his tone lightened as he said, 'Some would though. Your friend Ramond, for instance.'

'Yes, for Serge music is everything,' she sighed. 'I can't imagine him allowing anything or anyone to come between him and his playing.' Gene had met Serge at a concert at the Conservatoire. They'd all had tea together afterwards. The two men had little in common and conversation did not flow. Serge had been in one of his moods and had scowled throughout, and Gene confessed to her afterwards that he had found him intense and very prickly, but he'd been impressed, too, by Serge's ambition.

'Kitty.' And now he drew her to him. 'I've never met anyone like you before. Someone I want to share my life with. Kitty, I love you so much. Will you marry me? Do you think you could put up with being a doctor's wife?'

'Oh, Gene, I can't imagine anything I'd like more.' She craved his love, felt she couldn't live without it. 'Yes – the answer's yes.'

'My darling.' And for the first time his lips sought hers in a kiss that was passionate but tender. They stood together for a long time in the shelter of the doorway. The sleet was still coming down hard, and a vicious wind blew, but Kitty could not remember feeling warmer or more cared for in her life.

Chapter 9

1961
Wednesday afternoon

Fay found the church of Sainte-Cécile almost by accident, and followed the narrow alley down one side of it to see where it went. When it opened out into Place des Moineaux she stopped, uncertain. The only building that could be the convent – a wide-fronted mansion attached at one end to the church – was shabby and desolate, with patches of plaster missing from the walls. Some of the shutters were hanging loose or missing altogether. The paved garden in front, where a gnarled old cherry tree was coming into leaf, had recently been swept, but appeared otherwise unloved. Only weeds grew in the cracked pots lined up against the wall. The whole place gave the appearance of being shut up and abandoned. However, the wrought-iron gate was unlocked, so with a little hope but not much expectation, she approached the front door, pressed the bell and waited.

For a long time nothing happened, and as she watched the sparrows flying about the square Fay struggled with the dark thought that perhaps this whole search was in vain. Her only real clue that she'd been in Paris as a child was the name of the convent on the tatty old label she'd found in the rucksack. With a sense of desperation she pushed the bell again, harder, and this time heard it sound inside. Yet still the mansion stood silent before her.

Just as she was turning to go, she heard footsteps within, then a man's voice calling, '*Attendez, attendez,*' and the rattle of bolts being drawn. Finally the door juddered open to reveal a priest with a neat, lean figure and thinning, colourless hair. He had a narrow, sweet-natured face and wore a pair of wire spectacles that had dug a ridge above his hawkish nose. If he was surprised to see a pretty foreign girl on his doorstep he didn't betray it.

'*Bonjour, mademoiselle,*' he said, with a polite dip of his head.

'*Bonjour,*' she replied. '*Je m'appelle Fay Knox. Ici le couvent*? Is this the convent?'

'*Oui, mademoiselle,*' he told her, 'but it has been closed for over a year now. I am the curé at the church here. How may I help you?' His English was heavily accented, but clear.

'I – I don't know exactly. It's hard to explain. Is there perhaps a Mère Marie here?'

'Not any longer, unfortunately.' She must have looked as desolate as she felt, for he then said, 'Come in – please, come in. I have left the kettle boiling on the stove. Perhaps you would like some coffee?'

She followed him through a dowdy hall with a flagstoned floor and in an instant, it happened. She knew for sure that she'd been here before. She could make out the pounding of heavy boots on the stairs, harsh voices shouting. She spun round, but there was only the curé and everything was quiet again. She blinked at him, bemused.

'Are you well, mademoiselle?' The priest was looking at her curiously.

'Yes – I mean no,' she whispered. 'Perhaps I need to sit down. I've walked rather a long way.' This place was significant, she sensed it. It had once been a place of safety, but then something had happened, something that teased the edges of her memory.

The man showed her into a dusty kitchen at the back of the building, where the open window looked out on to a courtyard and a kettle murmured over a gas flame. He pulled her out a wooden chair from the table and glanced at her with concern as he filled a glass at the sink. She drank the water slowly and watched him make coffee in a jug.

'I am using one of the rooms here as an office because of builders,' he explained. 'Too much noise at my house.' When she sipped the tiny cup of black coffee that he placed on the table in front of her she found it stronger and sweeter than she was used to, but after a moment she felt better.

'Thank you,' she said. 'I don't know what happened just then, I'm so sorry.'

'There is nothing to apologize for. But how can I help you, mademoiselle?'

She took a breath and said, 'I think this place has something to do with my mother, and I need to find out what.' She went on to explain haltingly about her own experiences in Paris, how she had flashes of memory that she'd been there before, but that according to her mother's account she hadn't. She told him about Kitty's depression and the secret that she was brooding over, about her mother's continuing grief for her father, and finally about the little rucksack that Kitty had kept hidden away and the label Fay had found inside it. And now that she'd unburdened herself, Fay felt lighter. It was a terrific relief. She'd been scared that it would sound like nonsense, but instead, the telling of it made it seem more real. At one level it still made little sense, and yet now she had put all the elements together in some sort of narrative it sounded plausible. Fay fumbled in her handbag, brought out the label and handed it to the curé. He smoothed it out on the table and studied the writing, first one side, then the other.

'Fay Knox,' he said. 'The K is silent, then?'

'Yes, that's right.'

'Well, Mademoiselle Knox, yours is a strange story, but I am not sure how I can help you. I have only been priest here for ten years, and in that time I do not remember any Englishwoman named Kitty. There were only two nuns left here after Mère Marie-François died over a year ago. Not so many young girls today feel called to this life. One of them is also now at peace, and the other is sadly wandering in her mind. She lives in another convent in the city where they have a hospice.'

'Do you think it would be worth me going to see her anyway?' Fay said doubtfully. The certainty she'd felt just now was melting away again. But then she glanced at a crucifix hanging above the door and remembered what she'd felt in the hall just now, that this place was somehow significant, and her resolve strengthened.

'It could, but I don't think it would be much use,' the priest said. 'I wish you could have met Marie-François. She was Mother Superior here for many years. Certainly through the Occupation. I wonder if there is anybody else who might remember ... Wait! No.' He seemed to be talking to himself rather than to Fay. But then suddenly he became quite animated. 'Well, maybe I've thought of something, after all,' he said, putting down his coffee. 'There was a woman who came to visit the Reverend Mother once, quite close to the end. She was at her funeral, too.' He pushed back his chair. 'Perhaps you would wait a moment, mademoiselle. I'm sure she left her telephone number.'

He departed the room and she heard a door open and close and then there was silence for what felt like a long time. Eventually she got up and walked out of the kitchen and peered into some of the other rooms. They appeared neglected and forlorn, any furniture covered in dust sheets. It felt peaceful this time, but again she was haunted by a sense of the familiar. She entered the dining room with its bare, dusty tables by one door and when she exited by another there was a shallow step down into the hall that she negotiated instinctively, as though she had known it was there.

By the front door was a narrow arched niche in the wall, about twelve inches high and four deep, in which lay a set of keys. Somehow she knew there had been a statuette there once. She could see it clearly in her mind: it was of a woman in a deep-blue robe, her hair covered in a white coif, standing with her hands folded in prayer. Fay remembered the smooth cold glaze under her own fingers. She looked about the hall, but there was no sign of it, nor of any ornament or picture, come to that. How sad it was that the place had closed. She was wondering what would become of it, when she heard the priest returning and quickly made her way back to the kitchen.

The priest greeted her with a smile. 'My papers are in a mess. I couldn't find it at first. The woman's name is

Madame Nathalie Ramond.' He held out a scrap of paper which Fay took, seeing he'd written on it a telephone number. 'As I told you, she came to visit Mère Marie-François in her last illness. She was an old friend come back after being abroad. She asked to be kept informed of the Reverend Mother's progress. It may be that she will be able to help you, I don't know.'

'Thank you,' Fay said, slipping the paper into her handbag. She didn't know why, but she sensed there was something the man was not telling her. But then a priest must be full of other people's secrets.

'Answers often bring new questions,' he said mysteriously as he showed her out. 'However, I wish you God's blessing, my child. As for your poor mother, I will pray for her.'

'Thank you so much,' she said, touched at his sincerity. His eyes through the thick spectacles were kind and concerned, but when she glanced back as she went through the gate, the door was already closed, and the building assumed the same abandoned appearance as before.

Fay made her way to the nearest Métro to go and meet Adam, but first she had to find a phone box to ring this Mme Ramond. At the top of the steps down to the station though, she encountered a hungry-looking North African man selling newspapers with headlines in angry black print. He tried to press one upon her, speaking French in an accent she didn't understand, and there was something desperate about his manner that intimidated her, so she shook her head and ducked past him down the stairs. In the station she bought tokens for the telephone, then when a booth became free dialled the number on the slip of paper the priest had given her. Finally a woman's voice answered.

'*Hello, je voudrais parler avec Madame Ramond.*' Fay had to repeat it before she was understood.

'*C'est bien moi.*'

Fay introduced herself and said what she'd rehearsed on the way from the convent, that the priest had suggested she speak to Mme Ramond about an important matter. She'd decided deliberately to keep it vague. The station was noisy and, anyway, it would be easier to explain everything properly face to face.

There was a short silence, then Mme Ramond said, '*Vous êtes qui?*'

'Fay Knox,' Fay said, more clearly.

'Fay Knox. You are Fay Knox?' the woman asked, moving from French to English.

'Yes. I am just staying in Paris for a few days. I'm sorry if it's short notice.'

'Short notice? No, no,' the woman said. 'That is not the problem. It is . . .' Fay couldn't hear for a moment as a group of loud youths was passing. She adjusted her position, pressing the receiver closer to her ear, just in time to catch something about 'the surprise of hearing from you.'

'I'm sorry if this is a surprise,' Fay said, while wondering what she meant, but the woman was continuing.

'Do you know Place des Vosges in the fourth arrondissement? My apartment is close by. Tell me when you are free to come.'

'Would sometime tomorrow afternoon suit you?' There was to be a rehearsal in the morning.

'Yes. Can you come soon after lunch, at half-past two perhaps?'

Fay managed to scribble down the address then thanked her and replaced the receiver. She was pushing pencil and paper back into her handbag when she was distracted by a commotion. On the steps going up to the street a gendarme was tussling with the newspaper-seller, whose papers spilled from his shoulder bag across the steps. She watched in horror and disbelief as the policeman struck the man on the side of his head with his baton, then wrestled him into an armlock. He proceeded to haul his dazed victim back up the steps and out of sight. Fay glanced about, sure that someone somewhere would react and protest, but the passing crowds, though briefly halted by this altercation, merely continued about their business as though nothing had occurred. All around, the papers lay forgotten, trampled underfoot. It seemed that she was the only one even remotely bothered.

When she set off through the ticket barrier to go and meet Adam, Fay found that she was trembling.

Père André Blanc relocked the door of the convent, a troubled look on his face. He'd been moved by the girl's story. What a lovely child she was, he thought. There was something pure about her, but wistful, too. Those eyes had seemed to search his soul. Fay Knox. For some reason the name written on the label she'd showed him stirred something in him. Where had he come across it before? He couldn't think for the life of him.

It was still bothering him as he returned to the small room he'd made his study. Then the matter of the homily he was writing once more occupied his mind. It was about forgiveness – the most difficult subject of all, he sometimes thought. Only last week he'd buried a man who'd died full of hatred to his last breath for the soldiers who'd killed his family. That hatred had eaten him up inside until there was nothing left. No one had come to his funeral.

Chapter 10

At Place de la Concorde Fay found Adam sitting on a bench in the Tuileries Gardens reading *Le Monde*. When he saw her, he folded the newspaper and tucked it under his arm, then came to greet her.

'Is there something the matter?' he asked, seeing her agitation.

'Oh, Adam, I suppose the man was breaking the law, but ...' and she told him about what she'd seen at the Métro. 'It was the way everyone pretended it wasn't happening that was so awful. As though a policeman attacking someone was normal and nothing to do with them.'

For a moment Adam didn't say anything. He lit a cigarette and drew on it, staring into the distance with narrowed eyes. This silence troubled her even more. Finally, he spoke. 'I'm afraid a great many people here would think that it wasn't their business – that the gendarme was merely doing his job. They'd say the man was an activist, out to stir up trouble.'

'But was he? He was selling papers when I saw him. I don't know what he did to annoy the policeman as I was down in the station. He was trying to run away so he must have done something.'

'The police don't necessarily wait for an excuse.' Fay sensed Adam's suppressed anger. 'Or if they need one they'll make one up.'

'Who do you think the man was?'

'An Algerian. They're refugees here from the fighting in their country. Algeria is not merely a French colony, it's a formal part of France, but many there want independence like everybody else. There has been dreadful violence on both sides, but the French authorities' repression in the country has been brutal, and many Algerians have escaped here – where they're not wanted, of course. Not least because they've brought the struggle with them.'

To Fay, Algeria was little more than a large country in North Africa that she'd seen on a map in geography lessons. It wasn't coloured red for the British Empire so the teacher hadn't shown much interest. She must have read about the war in the papers, but can't have paid much attention. It was someone else's war, nothing to do with her or her life. Yet now, suddenly it was. She remembered the intensity of the man's expression.

'He must have done something to annoy the gendarme,' she repeated stubbornly. 'There's no smoke without fire. A French policeman wouldn't simply have attacked an innocent man, not without cause.'

Adam threw away his cigarette. 'If that's what you'd like to believe, go ahead. I should try to forget about it, if I were you. I'm supposed to be helping you enjoy yourself. Now, where shall we go? The Orangerie is just over there. Have you seen Claude Monet's *Water Lilies* series?'

'No, but I'd like to. Let's do that.'

She fell into step beside him, feeling upset. He seemed distant with her and she realized that she'd annoyed him by her attitude, but also that he didn't wish to discuss the matter further. Did Adam know more about the situation than he'd told her? She sensed that he'd thought her naïve. Yet nothing she'd ever known had prepared her for the violence she'd witnessed just now. She wished that he'd explained properly, but the moment seemed to have gone.

Surrounded by Monet's huge canvases, Fay felt bathed in blue-green light. It was a curious feeling, peaceful, contemplative, and her troubled mind was soothed. She imagined the many hours and days and seasons the artist must have spent in that garden at Giverny, brooding on the colours of the plants and the changing effects of light on the water until the place became a part of him. She imagined the sounds of a garden, too, which an artist couldn't paint, the sigh of the wind in the trees, birdsong, the ripple of the water from a fish's tail. All these could be captured by music. Music, too, could paint a scene.

Adam smiled and sauntered across. 'Marvellous, isn't it?' he said, turning back to look at a lily from a distance. 'Those petals look white from here, but they're actually made up of many colours. Must have driven the old man mad though, painting the same thing over and over like that.'

'Or perhaps it kept him sane.' With sudden heartache Fay thought of her mother. Music had always been Kitty's way of expressing herself. Perhaps it gave her solace.

Adam considered this for a moment. 'I hadn't thought of it that way. I suppose you could be right. Well,' he continued, 'one could look at these for ever, but perhaps you've had enough?'

'I wish I could live with these around me,' she said fervently. 'I suppose you've seen them dozens of times.'

'Only once before, actually. It's surprising how little sightseeing you do when you live in a place.' He laughed. 'Of course, I'm privileged. I have more than my share of invitations to openings of shows and exhibitions, but there's hardly any time for what you might call contemplation. There are always people I have to talk to, then I rush off to write it all down before the deadline.'

He smiled at her as they left the gallery and stepped out into the late-afternoon sunshine, and offered her his arm. She took it gratefully, relieved that he seemed his usual attentive self again.

How very different from yesterday it was, walking with Adam under the filigree shadows of the trees in the Tuileries Gardens. Paris wasn't a place to be alone, Fay decided. It surprised her how at ease she felt with Adam. Although she had only met him that once, several years before when they were teenagers, it felt natural to be with him. Of course, she hardly knew him, hardly knew anything about him – there was the thrill of all that to come – but she must stop her mind rushing ahead. They found themselves talking about all sorts of things as they crossed Place de la Concorde towards the Champs-Élysées. Her work with the orchestra, the bedsit he occupied in Montmartre, whether the English-looking couple poring over a map together by the fountain might be on their honeymoon . . .

There was an air of gaiety about the gardens along the Champs-Élysées, in the bright music and flying horses of the merry-go-round, the colourful bobbing clouds of balloons for sale, the children riding donkeys, the kiosks festooned with postcards and magazines. They stopped at a café under the trees to drink a *citron pressé* and watched a model in a figure-hugging dress pose in front of a shiny red sports car for her photographer. Her stylish bob was not unlike Fay's own, she noted – something to tell Derek. They continued their walk up to the roundabout, after which the expensive shops began. And there was the Arc de Triomphe ahead, glowing sublimely golden in the late-afternoon light. On they went towards it.

Maybe it was the sight of the arch, the sun glinting off the shop windows, or a traffic policeman's urgent whistle – maybe, she thought afterwards, it was all these things combined, but suddenly Fay felt like a little child again, her ears full of the smash of breaking glass and young men shouting ugly words, and in her terror the world began to tilt. She threw her arms out to her mother . . .

'*Fay!*' she heard Adam's voice as he caught her. She opened her eyes to look straight into his anxious face. 'What's wrong?'

Gradually the world stopped spinning. 'I'm sorry,' she whispered, horrified. All around people were glancing at her warily. Everything was tranquil and normal. Nearby, a man was sweeping broken glass into the gutter with his foot. Red wine spread across the pavement like blood.

'Are you all right?' Adam asked.

'Yes, I think so. No.'

He shepherded her gently into the back of a nearby bar, to a table in a private corner inside, hidden from curious eyes. When a waiter arrived Adam ordered two glasses of cognac, which were brought right away. Fay drank a mouthful and felt calmer.

'What happened out there?' he asked, his arm around the back of her chair, leaning in.

'I don't know,' she said with a catch in her voice. 'I don't know what's the matter with me. It's like ... Adam, do you remember that time in Notre Dame?'

'Of course – the bell,' he said, his face serious. 'I've never forgotten it.'

'It was like that again. You know, I'd never been in Paris before that, but now I'm not so sure. Frightening things keep happening. Here, a moment ago, I thought they were smashing the shop windows.'

'They? Who is they?'

'I don't know – that's just it. I thought I was with my mother, and people were smashing windows and shouting. Adam, I must have been here once and she was too. When I was very small.'

'I'm not saying I don't believe you,' Adam said carefully, 'but it seems unlikely, doesn't it, if you'd never heard about it. That would have meant during the war.'

'Yes, during the war,' she said slowly. That would explain her fear, but what things might she have witnessed? The urgent tolling of a bell, the smashing of glass, then in the convent earlier, the thud of boots on the stairs. And yet she had experienced peaceful feelings too. She thought of stroking the smooth surface of the statuette in its niche. And the lovely voice of the singer she'd heard from the balcony last night – why had that seemed significant?

'You're right though,' she said, crestfallen. 'My mother wasn't here in the war. She was in England, I'm sure she was.' And then: 'At least, I always *have* been sure ... until recently.'

She explained about her mother, how she had had a nervous breakdown and was in hospital. That Kitty had tried to give her a clue, something she was to find out in Paris.

'It's possible that she hasn't told me the whole truth about my childhood.'

'I don't know your mother and, Fay, I hardly know you, so it's difficult for me to comment.'

'Of course,' she said. She felt the same rush of loneliness she'd felt the day before, while sitting in the Tuileries Gardens. He was being so kind, considering she was a near stranger, but there was a limit to how much she should expect from him. She shouldn't cast her burdens on him. She must work things out herself. She must be strong.

She sipped the cognac gratefully and thought about her life, everything she knew about herself. Adam watched her quietly.

'I don't remember much before I was five,' she said eventually. 'My father was killed when I was two or three, I believe, then our house in London was destroyed by a bomb, but I don't even recall that. Surely I would, something as important as that.'

'You might have blotted out the memory – and the other memories that are coming back to you now, if they *are* memories. Look, to be honest, I don't remember much about the time when I was five either, but what I do fits in with what I know about the rest of my life. Chasing our old tabby cat under my bed, for instance, and my mother scolding me for getting covered in dust. Rather than for cruelty to the cat, note.' He smiled, and she sensed that he was trying to make things normal.

'Then there was the famous occasion when I was four and rescued my baby sister from a pond. I remember that because people treated me like a little hero. What I told no one was that I hadn't stopped Tina falling in the first place. There – no one else knows how wicked I was and now I've told you. I'll have to swear you to secrecy or kill you.'

'At least you rescued her.'

'I did, at considerable risk to my own safety, I must add, though it wasn't much of a pond, more of a garden pool. There were goldfish and she wanted to touch one. I should have grabbed her but there was something fascinating about the idea of her falling.'

Fay laughed. His ruse had worked, she felt brighter now. The bar was a cheerful one, with red and white raffia chairs. The paper faces of Toulouse-Lautrec's poster girls gazed up from under the glass tops of the tables, glamorous, beguiling.

'I always worried that I couldn't remember.' She started to tell Adam everything, about her father's photo and the little rucksack with its label, which she took out and showed him, about visiting the convent and how she was seeing Nathalie Ramond the very next day. 'I've no idea who she might be, but there's a chance, just a chance that she can help me.'

Adam was as interested as she hoped he would be. 'It'll do no harm to try, anyway,' he said. 'I hope you're lucky. What are you doing tonight, by the way? Perhaps you'd have dinner with me?'

She bit her lip. 'Oh Adam, I can't, what a bore. There's a reception at the British Embassy. The whole orchestra is expected to go. In fact, I ought to go back to the hotel now to change.'

'Of course,' he said smoothly, but obviously disappointed. 'Perhaps tomorrow night. You're here such a short time. I'd like us to make the most of it.'

She beamed at him. 'That would be lovely.' The musicians were to be left to their own devices the following evening, and perhaps the others wouldn't mind if she didn't join them.

Adam hailed a waiter and paid the bill. 'I'm not certain what time I can get away tomorrow, but I'll leave a message at your hotel.'

As he put her in the taxi, she said, 'Thank you for everything.'

'It's my absolute pleasure.'

In the cab she gently touched the place on her cheek where he'd kissed her goodbye.

Chapter 11

The next morning after the short rehearsal, Fay and Sandra sailed forth to explore the boutiques of the Rue du Faubourg St-Honoré. 'Strictly window shopping,' Sandra said firmly. Neither had cash to spare for Parisian *haute couture*, but it was lovely to pretend. Tall and slim with good bone structure, Sandra would have been an ideal mannequin. Under the appreciative eye of the corseted saleswoman in Pierre Cardin, she dared to try on a suit in black and white hound's-tooth check with fashionably large buttons and a Peter Pan collar, but in the end managed to escape the woman's persuasive murmurings with purse intact. Around the corner they visited a department store where Fay pounced on a blue and white Hermès headscarf of whispering silk, whilst Sandra tried on shoes without success, bemoaning the tiny feet of Frenchwomen.

'*C'est un cadeau?*' the chic shop girl asked in crisp tones when Fay paid for the scarf.

'*Oui, c'est pour ma mère.*'

'*Ah, bon. Pour votre mère,*' the girl said, her voice softening, and as Fay watched her wrap the scarf with pretty paper, she breathed a prayer that her mother would be well enough to want to wear it soon.

Outside the shop, a woman with a face as wrinkled as a prune was selling violets and they each bought a posy, breathing in the delicate fragrance. They browsed for somewhere inexpensive for lunch, choosing in the end a family-run café in a back street where they ate hearty helpings of boeuf bourguignon. Sandra confided, eyes dancing, that she had a date with the dapper French film-maker Fay had seen her flirting with at the reception the night before.

'Georges is *very* attentive,' Sandra said. 'He's taking me to Maxim's tonight and there's a chance Alain Delon will come. He was in *Purple Noon* – did you see it?' Fay shook her head. 'What about you?' Sandra went on. 'There was that nice-looking English boy I saw you with on the first night after the concert.'

'Adam?' Fay said, as nonchalantly as she could manage. She didn't know Sandra had seen them together. 'Oh, he's only an old friend. I'm sure he doesn't know Alain Delon.'

'Never mind that. You're seeing him again while you're here?'

'I'm having dinner with him tonight,' Fay replied, trying to speak lightly. She didn't want to talk about Adam to Sandra. Perhaps she feared that the special feeling of exhilaration she had in his company was as delicate as the scent of the violets and might disappear if she laid it open to another's scrutiny. And Sandra, who always had such a casual way with boyfriends, might make fun of her. No, she would keep the secret of Adam close.

At just before two-thirty Fay waited in the cool of the marble-floored lobby of an elegant Second Empire apartment block for the grim-faced, grey-haired concierge to finish berating someone on the other end of her telephone. This gave her time to be nervous. Mme Ramond must be reasonably well-heeled to live somewhere solid and respectable like this, but otherwise she knew nothing about her. It occurred to her now that the priest she'd met at the convent had merely been trying to be helpful and the whole thing could turn out to be a red herring. Mme Ramond might not even have heard of her mother. What then? The thought of failure was terrible.

Still, she remembered the woman's reaction on the telephone. Fay's name *had* meant something to her, or so it had seemed. There came unbidden the vision of her mother's anxious face and this gave her resolve.

The concierge ended her call with a weary, '*D'accord, d'accord,*' and gave a gesture of exasperation as she replaced the receiver. She frowned as Fay asked where to find Mme Ramond's apartment.

'*Vous êtes anglaise?*' The woman looked her up and down critically, but decided that she passed muster and instructed her to take the lift to the second floor.

The name *Ramond* was written in italics on a card in a small brass frame screwed to the door of Apartment #12. Fay pushed the bell and tucked the violets more securely under the lavish red bow on the box of chocolate truffles she'd bought. The gift had somehow felt in order.

After a moment the door opened. The short bony woman with neat greying hair who stood there might have been in her late forties, but it was difficult to tell, because she moved so stiffly, and her face, despite make-up, was pale and etched with lines of pain. Her expression was anxious, the dark brown eyes filled with uncertainty as she stared out at Fay.

'Fay? Is it really little Fay?' she breathed.

'Yes. Madame Ramond?' Fay didn't recognize this woman at all.

'You don't remember me, do you, I can tell. Well, never mind. I can hardly believe it. Last time I saw you, ah, you were such a sweet child.' Her mouth trembled but then she straightened her shoulders and said, 'I'm sorry, it is something of a shock. I forget myself. Come in, please.' She beckoned Fay inside and showed her where to hang her coat on a carved mahogany hat-stand. She leaned on a stick, and Fay noticed that the joints of her fingers were swollen and misshapen.

'Oh, you naughty girl,' she said, laughing, when Fay handed over the truffles, 'and what pretty violets.' She looked down at the gifts in wonder as though she wasn't used to having them, then set them down on a console table.

Half a dozen doors led off the narrow hallway, and Mme Ramond showed Fay through one into a large light drawing room that looked out at the buildings across the street. It was lined with shelves full of books and records, but Fay's attention was caught by the grand piano that stood in the window, its black surface glossy in the after-noon sunshine. Its lid was raised, and a music book was spread open above the keyboard as if someone had recently been playing. Not her hostess, surely, with her poor crooked fingers ...

'No, I've never learned,' the woman said, echoing her thoughts. 'It's beautiful though, isn't it? It's very old, but it still has a lovely tone. I sometimes tell my husband that he values it more than he does me. As a joke, of course.'

'Of course,' Fay murmured, though the woman's dry humour left her not quite sure. 'It is lovely.'

'I should put those flowers in water. They don't last long, poor things.'

Whilst the woman was gone, Fay glanced round the room. On the shelves were several framed photographs of a dark-eyed, dark-haired man with a pale face and an intense expression. One was a close-up of him playing the piano, but the others were dramatic studio portraits, such as might feature in a concert programme. She was studying one of these when Mme Ramond returned with the posy in a small crystal vase, setting it on the mantelpiece and indicating that Fay should sit down with her on a stiff striped sofa with scrolled arms – the sort of thing made for an ambassador, Fay thought.

'My husband is away in Vienna until Monday,' the woman said. 'Since we moved back here from America two years ago he often tours, though I am no longer well enough to go with him. This time it is a Mozart festival. Serge is passionate about Mozart. But enough of him. You must tell me news of your mother. '

'You know my mother?' Fay's relief was immense, but she was horrified to see hurt spring into the other woman's eyes

'She has not spoken of me to you, then?'

'I'm afraid not, no. I only found you because of the priest at the convent. Please, madame, I'm sorry, but there is so much I need to ask.'

'How much do you already know?' Mme Ramond said in a quiet voice.

'Know about what?' Fay cried. 'I'm so confused!'

'Ah.' For a while Mme Ramond was lost in thought, her expression immeasurably sad. Finally she stirred and said, 'Fay, I have had no correspondence with your mother for years. I do not even know where she lives.' She stopped and gave Fay a searching look. 'What has she told you of your early life? About your father, for instance?'

'She doesn't talk about him. It upsets her.'

'She grieves still, after all these years,' Mme Ramond murmured. 'She loved him so very much.'

'I don't remember him at all,' Fay burst out. 'I don't remember our house in London or feeding the ducks in the park or any of the ordinary things she says we did. Madame Ramond, my mother is unwell and I need your help.' She described her mother's deep sadness, and how she had directed Fay to the little rucksack hidden in the trunk.

'And that's all I know,' she finished.

'That's all you know,' the other woman echoed. She massaged the joints of her hands and flexed them gently. 'I had no children of my own,' she said, almost conversationally. 'My health has not been good. But sometimes I wish . . . no, what is the use.' She did not sound bitter, Fay thought, just sad, but she didn't know what to say to this woman who, though a stranger to her, seemed, she sensed, to know so much about her.

'How did you meet my mother?' she ventured. 'Was it here in Paris?'

'It was, yes. I met her soon after she arrived here before the war – 1937 it must have been. She came to study the piano, of course.'

'Of course? She told me she trained in London.' It was

hard to hear a different story from a stranger. But was it the truth? She couldn't be sure of Mme Ramond. She considered telling her about her experiences in Paris. To anyone normal they'd merely sound silly, or worse, mad. *Was* she going mad? She didn't think so. Adam hadn't seemed to think so either, or at least had given her no indication that he did.

'And me – was I here, too?'

And Mme Ramond smiled. 'Of course. You were born here, *chérie.*'

'Oh,' Fay said, not exactly astonished, but feeling a certain shift, as though something had fallen into place. 'Then, please, madame, will you tell me everything?'

Mme Ramond pondered this and sighed. 'I don't think I should. It's not my story to tell, it's your mother's.'

'But she wouldn't tell me. Or couldn't. Why, madame? *Why?*' Fay implored in desperation.

Mme Ramond frowned and Fay watched her anxiously, worried that she'd offended her in some way. Finally, the woman pushed herself up slowly from her seat and reached for her stick. 'Come,' she said. 'I want to show you something that might help explain.'

Fay followed her down the hall into the next room, a handsome dining room painted dark red, and with more of the carved mahogany furniture. Against the far wall stood an ugly cabinet on bowed legs like a bulldog's, and it was to this that Mme Ramond took her. The top half was a cupboard with glass doors and crowded with china ornaments. The lower part consisted of three wide drawers.

'Please,' Mme Ramond said. 'Pull out the bottom one for me, will you? I don't have the strength.'

The drawer was stiff and Fay needed to work it open with both hands. Inside lay neat piles of photographs and a large album with a leather cover. At the woman's instruction she brought this out, and laid it on the thick cloth that protected the heavy dining table.

Nathalie Ramond turned the album towards her and opened it at the first page. Fay found herself looking at a faded photograph of a family group, a mother and father with three boys of varying ages and a girl of about two in her father's arms. All were dressed in their best clothes and stared solemnly at the camera with the same dark-eyed gaze, except for the girl, who was reaching down, trying to steal the cap from the littlest boy's head. There was something about their faces, the eldest boy in particular, that reminded her of the photographs in the drawing room.

'My husband's family,' Mme Ramond confirmed.

'Is that your husband?' Fay pointed.

'Yes. He was fifteen when this picture was taken.' She turned the pages of the album and Fay was surprised to see that the rest of them were filled, not with other photographs but with letters, official forms and newspaper cuttings. She glimpsed headlines in French and English, and grim, grainy photographs of the sort she'd seen in an old magazine she'd found once in a wardrobe when she'd lodged in London. Pictures of ragged, emaciated people with empty eyes, of ugly buildings behind wire fences. Hitler's concentration camps.

'When the war ended, Serge tried to trace them,' Mme Ramond was saying. 'He wrote to all the organizations he could think of, but so many people were doing the same thing and everything was in chaos. Eventually he learned the truth. They were all dead. His parents, his sister, his two brothers. He alone survived.' She closed the album very deliberately. 'And there are some here who still blame him for his survival. They say he was a collaborator. It's nonsense, and so hurtful.'

The fierce resentment in her voice shocked Fay, who could think of nothing to say except a soft, 'I'm sorry.'

'You must wonder why I am showing this to you. It's because you should understand that the story you ask for isn't so easily told. There was so much suffering in those years. Our generation does not like to speak about it. And for some there is much guilt. We would rather bury it, forget about it.'

'Guilt ...?' Fay faltered, realizing for the first time that she was becoming caught up in something she might not be strong enough to bear.

Seeing her stricken face, Mme Ramond said more gently, 'Do not alarm yourself unduly. The guilt – that is something the parents have to carry, not the children.'

'But I was there,' Fay whispered. 'And those other children you spoke of just now. It was not their fault, but they suffered.'

'Yes, they did. But you lived and now you're here. The world is different today and you are ready to take the best from it.'

Still much troubled by this conversation, Fay helped Mme Ramond replace the album and close the drawer, then accompanied her back to the drawing room. But instead of sitting down again, the older woman walked over to the window and looked down the street. For a while she did not speak.

Fay sat down on the sofa and wondered what to do in

the face of this silence. Her thoughts raced. Somehow her own and her mother's stories were caught up in this tangle of tragedy and pain – but how? What had happened? Although she badly needed to know, she also feared it. Perhaps the truth would, after all, be unbearable.

She looked around the room, so gracious with its comfortable antique furniture, the beautiful gilt-framed oval mirror above the fireplace of polished brown stone. There were invitation cards propped on the mantelpiece by the vase of violets, yet something told her that Mme Ramond was lonely. She missed her husband.

'*C'est lamentable,*' the woman muttered, staring at something in the street below. Fay went to stand at her shoulder and see. Walking along the pavement away from them was a family who appeared exotic to her in a Paris street, the men and children dark-skinned, the two women swathed in traditional Arab dress. She noticed a Frenchman on a bicycle passing them in the opposite direction, contempt plain in his expression.

'Algerians,' Mme Renaud said, turning away from the window. 'The cycle of oppression continues.'

'What do you mean?' Fay asked.

'I mean that although France herself was freed, she will not give her colonies freedom. These poor people come here to escape, but they are treated as terrorists.'

'Oh, I see.' Fay thought of the newspaper-seller she'd seen the day before and her conversation with Adam. She opened her mouth to recount the incident, but Mme Ramond was speaking again and studying her, her face a mixture of sadness and amusement.

'Dear Fay,' she said, 'such a funny little girl you were.

And here you are, all grown up. What was it you say you are doing here? Playing in a concert?'

'Three concerts. There was one on Tuesday, our next is a schools programme tomorrow morning, and the last is on Saturday. Then we go home on Sunday.'

'So,' she said, 'a musician like your mother.' They sat down again, Fay on the sofa, Mme Ramond on a high-backed chair near the fireplace.

'Yes, but I play the violin.'

'I must try to come and hear you. And Kitty, she continues to play the piano, I hope?'

'Yes. She teaches.' It struck Fay then how rarely she heard her mother play for her own pleasure, and then she remembered the music for the Moonlight Sonata, on the piano at home. Perhaps she did play to herself sometimes, but when Fay wasn't there. Or had she just never noticed?

'To teach is good,' Mme Ramond continued, 'but she had such talent. It was a shame she could do so little with it.' She paused before saying, 'So, she has hidden away with you all these years and told you nothing.'

'I never knew there was anything to tell. Well, I suppose I sensed that there was, but I didn't actually know. I trusted my mother, madame. I still trust her. Why would she have lied to me?'

'If she did, there would have been a good reason.'

'But now I'm old enough to know the truth.' What was true and what was not? The lovely house in Richmond with the rose bushes, the deer in Richmond Park – had it all been real? Or would that memory be taken away from her? And above all ... She took a deep breath. 'Madame Ramond, what happened to my father?'

'Ah, your father.' The woman relaxed. 'There was a

wonderful man. Never did you see two people so in love as he and your mother. I can at least start with that. I shall tell you how they met. It was, as you English say, a whirl-wind courtship.'

Chapter 12

Kitty and Gene were married in March 1938, five months after their first meeting and several days after Hitler's troops marched into Austria, which naturally cast something of a pall over the celebrations.

They'd discussed at length whether the wedding should take place in Paris or Hampshire, but since their home was to be Paris and Uncle Pepper, to Kitty's great delight, offered to make the journey to give her away, they decided that a small wedding under the ethereal gothic spire of the American Cathedral in Paris, with just a few friends in attendance, would be simplest. Gene's parents in Atlanta had been invited, and his elder sister Sylvia, but his father was ill with a liver complaint, and his mother felt she needed to stay and nurse him. Sylvia was expecting her second child and unable to travel. A vague plan was concocted to visit America later in the year for Kitty to meet them all, but whether this would come to pass depended on Gene being allowed the time away from his work at the hospital. As a junior doctor his hours were long.

Uncle Pepper wired Kitty an extra sum of money, out of which she paid a dressmaker to sew a gown in soft white tulle trimmed with handmade lace. The rest was to be spent on the wedding breakfast: champagne and sand-wiches at the George V Hotel. Gene was taking care of the honeymoon and the expenses incurred in setting up their new home.

Kitty was relieved that it was to be a low-key affair; she would have been nervous at the prospect of anything grander and, anyway, had neither the time nor the resources to arrange it. It was only a shame that Felicity, the one schoolfriend to whom she remained close, would be on board ship for South Africa, where she'd taken on a teaching job, so Kitty would not have a bridesmaid. But the nuns looked after her. On the day of the wedding there was a little ceremony at breakfast when Mère Marie-François presented Kitty with a book of prayers. Kitty had invited them, of course, but the Reverend Mother had explained that as a Catholic order they weren't permitted to attend a Protestant wedding. Miss Dunne was going though, and she had promised to give the nuns a full account.

After breakfast, Thérèse helped Kitty to dress in her wedding clothes, watching with great interest as Kitty applied a little make-up to disguise how tired and pale she looked after a night sleepless from anticipation. The novice brushed Kitty's hair and helped fix her veil, then drew back to study her with a curious expression on her face.

'What is it?' Kitty asked. 'Is something not right?'

The girl shook her head. 'You look so beautiful,' she said. 'But I think now there is not so much difference between us.' She touched her own headdress and finally Kitty understood. Today she was to give herself to Gene. When her novitiate was complete later in the year, Sister Thérèse would become a bride of Christ. On an impulse

Kitty stepped across and took both the girl's hands in hers and they stood together for a moment as though nothing divided them. Then Thérèse's lips curved in one of her serene smiles. 'But we will both be happy, no?'

'Yes,' Kitty replied, smiling back at her. 'We will be happy.'

Like it or not, Hitler's expansionist policies and the alarming fate of Austria were the main topics of conversation at the reception. The latest rumour was that the new French government had addressed a letter of protest to Germany, only to be scorned for interfering in what the Third Reich called their 'internal affairs'.

'Once again everybody will stand aside and let the bullyboy help himself,' Kitty slipping in amongst a group at the bar, was in time to hear blonde Milly Jenkins say. Milly, a journalist, was the type of energetic all-American girl who had the gumption to walk into any difficult situation and ask shrewd questions about it in English, French or German. She had recently visited Berlin incognito and had written up her experiences in the *Herald Tribune*. Kitty liked her immensely, whilst remaining a little in awe of her.

'What else do you really expect?' said Dr Poulon, a gynaecologist colleague of Gene's whom Kitty had met once or twice before. He was a stocky Frenchman in his thirties with prematurely thinning hair and an affable manner. 'Military action would be *une folie* now that Mussolini, Austria's former protector, is allied with Germany. And since France did not lift a finger to defend the Rhineland two years ago, she will not send any forces to save Austria now.'

'Maybe not fight,' Milly conceded, 'but if Britain and America together insisted . . .'

'Gentlemen, ladies, please.' Gene came across to join them, his good-natured face full of happiness. 'No politics today. My wife and I,' here he drew Kitty close, 'have more important things we wish you to attend to.'

'What can be more important than freedom?' Milly protested.

'Lighten up, sweetheart,' Jack, her writer boyfriend, warned – only to be rewarded by one of Milly's famous quelling looks.

'Oh Gene, let them talk about what they will,' said Kitty, who wanted everybody to be as content as she was today. She smiled up at Gene. It was rare to see him trussed up in a formal black suit. He was an open-necked-shirt kind of a man, unconcerned about appearance. That was part of why she loved him. She'd quickly discovered that he was more interested in what people were like inside rather than in what they wore.

'While we still have the liberty,' Milly snapped, unwilling to abandon her soapbox. 'Unlike in Germany or Austria.'

'That could never happen here, could it?' Kitty said doubtfully. 'Not in Paris.' She had read Milly's article about the fearful way people spoke in Berlin, guarded in their opinions, even in private, neighbour suspicious of neighbour.

'Not in Paris,' Jack echoed, and even Bertrand Poulon frowned and shook his head. Not in Paris, the most tolerant and sophisticated city in the world.

'What happens if Czechoslovakia is next?' Milly demanded, as though laying down a trump card.

Czechoslovakia was the last democracy in Eastern and Southern Europe, and its existence depended on French support. 'There would *have* to be war then.' Everyone stared at her, silenced, contemplating the awful thought. What would the French government do if Hitler laid claim to the German-speaking area of Czechoslovakia? France was bound by treaty to go to her aid. No one liked to voice the gloomy answer.

At that moment a waiter came round with more champagne and they turned to him gratefully, holding out their glasses to be filled with golden bubbles. There wouldn't be a war. They were in the most heavenly city on earth and they were young and this was a wedding of two lovely people with a wonderful future before them.

Later, there weren't speeches as such, just Gene, with Kitty at his side, saying a few simple words about how beautiful she was and how happy she'd made him, and thanking everyone for coming, and Kitty blushing with pleasure and embarrassment, then everyone toasting their happiness.

Afterwards, Kitty glimpsed the tall, thin, unmistakably English figure of Uncle Pepper talking to Monsieur Deschamps and her fellow pupil Serge, and went over to join them. She was immensely pleased that her uncle had agreed to come, so rarely willing was he to travel these days. The question of Kitty's studies had already been resolved. She would continue with her present regime. Nothing would change, in the short term anyway.

They spent a few minutes discussing the composer Maurice Ravel, whom Monsieur Deschamps had known well and who had died the previous year, then the teacher made his excuses and took his leave, and Serge found himself taken up by Miss Dunne and an elderly relation of Gene's French grandmother.

Uncle Pepper drew Kitty aside and spoke to her unusually frankly. 'I'm so relieved, my dear, that you're happy and settled. He seems a good man, your Dr Knox. I like him, and I feel he'll look after you. When you get to my time of life, you see, you begin to worry—'

'Don't say that, Uncle,' Kitty cried. 'You've years and years to live yet.' He was only in his late fifties, but to her he had hardly aged. The silvering of his sleek, combed-back hair merely gave him a distinguished look. Always a man of middle-aged appearance, even when young, it was as though he'd finally grown into himself.

Uncle Pepper chuckled. 'That may well be,' he said, 'but I'll certainly sleep easier knowing I don't have to worry about leaving you alone in the world again.'

Her uncle was not demonstrative, but now he reached out a hand to touch her cheek. 'Bless you, Kitty, Elizabeth would have been proud of you. I still miss her, you know.'

And on impulse, Kitty, who could hardly remember her mother at all, leaned forward and kissed him gently on the cheek. While of a solitary disposition, his interests being of the mind, Uncle Pepper had done his best for his orphaned niece. He had encouraged her musical talent and in his quiet, dry way he loved her. She felt tremendous warmth towards him, but also a sadness that it was he who would be alone. Her life was here with her husband now. Paris, not England, would be her home.

'We'll come and see you often,' she assured him. 'And you will always be welcome to stay with us. I know how much you love Paris.'

'I've always been happiest sitting before the fire at home

and reading about it,' Uncle Pepper said. 'But since I'm forced to play the tourist for a few days, I've arranged to take in a little art in the company of your Miss Dunne.'

Kitty and Gene passed a wonderful week's honeymoon in the South of France, in the shabby grandeur of an old hotel whose balconies hung with bougainvillaea. Golden sunshine fell through the trees, dappling the gardens with shadows. Lush bright flowers bloomed in pots on the terrace and their room overlooked a cobalt blue sea that was warm enough for swimming.

When each morning she awoke and found the large, comfortable presence of Gene gently snoring next to her, Kitty marvelled at the joy of being so close to another person. She adored the tender way he made love to her, gentle at first, but quickly stirred to passion as together they explored each other's bodies and found what gave most pleasure. The nights were warm and as dark as velvet, and when their love-making was done they were lulled to sleep by the rhythm of the waves lapping on the beach.

Most days they rose too late for breakfast, but the hotel staff were indulgent and brought them coffee and croissants on the terrace. They talked about their new life together, their commitment to their respective work, their mutual desire for children. Gene had brought a camera along, and they took each other's photograph under the trees. Later, when he showed her the results, Kitty thought she looked stiff and shy, but she loved the picture of Gene. He looked so relaxed and happy. It was the way she always wished to think of him.

When they returned to Paris, they moved into a furnished apartment on the sixth floor of a mansion block of pale ochre stone in St Germain-des-Prés. The street, which rejoiced in the name of Rue des Palmes des Martyrs, was a satisfying mix of neighbourhood shops and residential blocks. The windows in front had pretty wrought-iron juliet balconies. Behind was a paved courtyard with a gnarled old chestnut tree. When the windows were open in summer, they could hear swallows whistle as they swooped and dived in pursuit of insects. Sometimes a woman's voice wafted up from the courtyard, crooning sad songs in a dusky voice.

The flat itself was modest in size, with a light-filled sitting room, a square kitchen and two bedrooms, Kitty's and Gene's looking out to the front. There was some difficulty in getting Gene's wedding present to Kitty, an upright piano, up all the flights of stairs, but it was managed. She'd placed it in a small recess and in order to avoid disturbing the neighbours had laid a folded cloth over the strings inside to mute it when she played. It was made of walnut with beautiful markings, and with its carved legs and music-rest was really very pretty. Kitty bought Gene a gramophone so that they could start a record collection.

Despite having no more domestic skills between them than a pair of babies, as Milly succinctly put it, they found married life to be delightful. Most days, after Gene left for work, Kitty went to purchase the day's supplies from the local shops, then continued to her piano lesson or to practise at the Conservatoire. Initially she tried playing at home, but they'd employed a motherly woman named Jeanette to clean two mornings a week and this made Kitty feel self-conscious. She found she concentrated better altogether if she went out.

Gene worked long hours as ever and was often home late in the evenings. Though she attempted simple meals on the stove for him, the meat was sometimes dried up by the time he got back or she'd burn the vegetables. On these occasions Gene would laugh, which made her cross, but then he'd apologize and they'd go out to a restaurant. Eventually she learned to choose recipes that were quick or wouldn't spoil. At weekends, they'd see friends, visit a jazz club in Montmartre, or go to the cinema. The American trip was discussed again, but put off till Christmas. Gene could not spare the time. And so the summer slipped by.

To Kitty, life was perfect, as long as one didn't read the papers, but soon there was no avoiding the news. It was all that their friends, many of them Americans, talked about, and was the main topic of conversation in the shops. Hitler was deliberately stirring up trouble in the Sudetenland, the German-speaking part of Czechoslovakia, his obvious intention being to snatch it for Germany. If this happened, France was obliged by treaty to go to the Czech government's aid, but as the French Prime Minister expressed it, was it better to sacrifice several million Frenchmen in battle against Germany's horrifyingly great military strength or to break the treaty and thereby give up influence in Central Europe?

Britain's Neville Chamberlain was also keen to avoid war, and when France and Britain gave in to Hitler's demands at the Munich Conference in September 1938, the relief of Parisians was palpable. There would be no repeat of the carnage of the Great War. Lovers would not be parted, families would not be left fatherless, mothers would not lose their sons. Not a few, however, felt uncomfortable, watching from afar as Czechoslovakia was carved up.

Milly, particularly, was outraged. 'Have you read what Saint-Exupéry says in here?' she asked Kitty and Gene one late autumn evening, opening a copy of *Paris-Soir* at the table. Winter was closing in and they'd been forced to retreat inside their favourite restaurant on the Boulevard St-Germain, with its rough wooden furniture and warm country-kitchen atmosphere.

'Are they continuing that ridiculous subscription to thank Mr Chamberlain by buying him a property to fish trout?' Jack said. '"Angel of peace" indeed.'

'Shh. Listen, you'll like this.' Milly read in French from the article by the airman-novelist Saint-Exupéry. '"When peace was threatened, we discovered the shame of war. When war seemed averted, we discovered the shame of peace." There, he's nailed it,' she said, glaring at them over the top of the paper. 'Moral failure all round.'

'But we don't want war, do we?' Kitty said, shooting an anxious glance at Gene, who rarely expressed a political opinion. If France went to war, what would happen to her and Gene? Where would they go?

Gene's hand closed over Kitty's to comfort her. 'No, of course we don't.'

'There's a chance it'll come all the same,' was Milly's warning. 'What will France and Britain do if Hitler turns his attentions to Poland?'

One morning not long afterwards, Kitty awoke early and had to dash for the bathroom to be sick. She put it down to a bad shellfish, but Gene pointed out that she'd been feeling odd before eating the dish in question. When it happened again the following morning, he acted on his suspicions and arranged for her to see his colleague at the hospital.

Dr Poulon examined her carefully and smiled at her nervousness. 'There is nothing to worry about. You are in good health and I cannot think you will have any problems.' Kitty was to have a baby.

She told Gene when he came home that evening, and he whooped with joy, picked her up and swung her round, kissing her still flat stomach repeatedly until, helpless with laughter, she begged him to stop.

'I'll be too heavy for that nonsense soon anyway,' she puffed, smoothing down her skirt. His response was to draw her down onto the sofa and to kiss her thoroughly. She'd never known him so ecstatic and this made her happy, too.

It took her some time to become used to the changes in her body and the idea of the little creature that was growing, imperceptibly, inside her. Because they'd agreed about having children they had never even discussed taking any precautions during love-making. Month after month had passed without consequence, but Kitty hadn't worried. It would happen, Gene assured her, and now it had.

They didn't tell anyone else at first, and passed the days with a quiet joy, complicit in their secret. After his first unruly burst of excitement, Gene began to treat her carefully, giving constant advice about what she should eat and not eat, and curbing late nights. Kitty was at first touched by this, not least because she felt very tired anyway, but as time passed and she recovered some of her old energy, his solicitude was sometimes annoying. They even had what for them constituted an argument – they who had never argued – when one night they went to a club and Kitty insisted on getting up and dancing with Jack to a particularly lively number. After a minute or two she couldn't bear the miserable look on her husband's face and sat down again. Later they made up, clinging to one another on the dance floor for a dreamy slow number.

After three months they judged the pregnancy to be established and began to tell people. When she broke the news to Monsieur Deschamps, he was effusive in his congratulations, but after that she had the feeling that something had changed. He no longer drove her as hard as he once had, and kept asking anxiously whether he was tiring her. Being pregnant, she learned, meant the world wrapped a woman in a cocoon. There seemed to be a general assumption that her brain had softened along with the lines of her body, and even the bustling French midwife at the American Hospital called her *'petite maman'*, as though she had a label, not a name.

Still, everybody's looking after me marvellously, she was able to write to Uncle Pepper in February 1939. *And I'm able to continue my lessons much as usual.* What she didn't put into the letter was any mention of the increasingly dangerous international situation. Although Parisians talked about it endlessly, somehow they carried on under the cosy assumption that France wouldn't be affected. Kitty and Gene and their friends couldn't see how this would be so, though Kitty tried not to dwell on it.

Then at the end of March came the news that Milly had predicted. Hitler issued a demand that Poland return the city of Danzig to Germany, together with the 'corridor' of land that since 1919 had divided East Prussia from the rest of Germany. In so doing, he was swinging the final axe strokes to the Versailles Treaty, which had imposed so much humiliation on Germany after her defeat in the Great War. Now, with Chamberlain finally promising war if the Führer invaded Poland, France had no choice but to stand beside her British ally.

Kitty faced the birth of her baby with an increasing sense of anxiety. Should she return to England, to an English lying-in hospital and the relative safety of life with Uncle Pepper? Or should she stay with her husband? Gene's work was in Paris and she knew he didn't want to leave. And she felt she'd be only half a person without him.

'Even if there is a war,' she heard a man in the queue at the grocer's say, 'we have the Maginot Line. Hitler can't touch us.' This huge system of bunkers with all their complex fortifications ran for nearly 200 kilometres along France's eastern frontier with Germany. What the man didn't mention was its Achilles heel – that it stopped short at Belgium. Still, Gene reasoned when they had dinner with Milly and Jack the same evening, if war broke out, Belgium would stay neutral, so Hitler's troops wouldn't come by that way. Surely France was safe?

And so on 1 September 1939, when Hitler ignored the Allies and marched into Poland, Kitty was still in Paris, waiting for the imminent arrival of her baby.

Chapter 13

1961

'I'm sure you have often been told, *chérie*,' Mme Ramond said to Fay, 'that you were born on the exact day that France and Britain declared war on Germany?'

'The third of September 1939. I'm tired of hearing it,' Fay sighed. 'What I didn't know was that it was here in Paris.' Surely it would say on her birth certificate, though she didn't remember ever noticing. It was her mother who had applied for her first five-year passport when Fay had come to Paris as a schoolgirl. She brought its replacement out of her bag now and studied it, then regarded her hostess with a doubtful look.

'Something is wrong?' the woman asked in a soft voice. 'Let me see.'

'It says London – that I was born in London. Look.' Fay's voice cracked with distress. She passed Mme Ramond the document.

The woman read the entry and exclaimed. 'That is strange, I agree,' she said. She was thoughtful as she handed the passport back to Fay. 'I assure you though, that you were born in Paris. It was in the American

Hospital. Your father insisted that it should be there. One of his colleagues was called out of bed specially.'

'But how could there be a mistake on my passport about something like that?' Fay stared down at the document.

'The war caused many confusions, large and little. It is possible that your mother believed . . .' She broke off. 'Fay, do you trust me?' Mme Ramond's eyes meeting hers were calm and strong.

'I . . . don't know. I suppose so.' There was something about Mme Ramond's account that convinced her. How her parents met and fell in love sounded so wonderful that she wanted to believe it. She recalled the mention of the photograph of her father, now in her mother's bedroom at home, so happy on his honeymoon in the South of France. Everything rang true. But if Mme Ramond was telling the truth, that made her mother dishonest and she didn't like to think about that. And yet . . . if her mother was hiding secrets maybe it was for a good reason.

'I do trust you, yes,' she said simply.

Mme Ramond nodded, satisfied. 'Wait here a moment,' she said. 'I have something for you.' And she left the room with her stick and her slow, painful walk. She was gone some time, and as she waited Fay glanced around the room. Her eyes fell on one of the photographs. Serge – hadn't Mme Ramond said that her husband was called Serge . . . ?

'Do you remember this?' Mme Ramond had reappeared, cradling something in her free arm. She held it out and Fay saw with a stir of interest that it was a carved wooden animal.

'Oh,' she said, taking it from her. The animal was a zebra, about six inches long from nose to tail, fashioned out of plain brown wood painted with narrow black stripes. She knew it from somewhere, but she couldn't place where. As she nursed it in both hands, she found herself stroking the cool smoothness of its polished surfaces, examining its dear black nose, noting the empty indents for eyes. *The eyes.* Suddenly she remembered something. The zebra hadn't always been blind – there had been something in those holes once, tiny black beads. And then a picture rose in her mind. A child's chubby hand – her hand – walking the zebra along a white-painted sill, the ghost of a child's face – her face – reflected in the glass of the window.

'You do remember it, don't you?' Mme Ramond sat down beside Fay on the sofa, her eyes shining in her tired face.

'I think I remember something.' Fay looked down at the zebra and it was as though somewhere inside herself the child she had once been came to life and gave a small sigh of relief. 'It was mine, wasn't it,' she said.

Mme Ramond gave a chuckle. 'It certainly was, yes. A neighbour of your parents, an old man, gave it to you when you were two and you would not be parted from it. The fuss when, in the rush, it got left behind.'

'The rush?'

'When you finally left Paris. But I get ahead of myself. It's important that I tell events in order or you will not understand.'

'You must tell me everything. Everything,' Fay begged. She felt somehow stronger, more convinced of the truth of Mme Ramond's story now she held the zebra. As she studied the small worn animal again, it came to her how when she'd found the child's rucksack in her mother's trunk and had looked inside, it was the zebra that she'd hoped to find. How did Mme Ramond come to have it? There were so many questions she wanted to ask, but it seemed she must be patient.

Mme Ramond glanced at the clock on the mantelpiece. It was half-past three. 'Some refreshment perhaps?' she asked. 'Why don't we have tea.' Fay offered to help, and accompanied her into a narrow galley kitchen to carry a tray for her. After they'd sat down again, Mme Ramond poured glasses of honey-coloured tea which she served with slices of lemon and offered Fay delicate biscuits with an aroma of almond. She bit into one and the buttery crumb melted in her mouth. Again, she glanced at the photograph of Serge Ramond and wondered whether to say anything, but Mme Ramond's expression put her off. She obviously intended to tell her story in her own way.

'When war was declared,' Nathalie Ramond went on, as though she'd never left off, 'Parisians were in a state of shock. Danzig, some asked. Why should millions of Frenchmen die for somewhere as irrelevant to them as Danzig? I remember going out to buy bread and seeing a group of people crowded round a big notice pasted next to the *boulangerie*. Parents must take their children out of Paris, it said. People grumbled and obeyed, but weeks passed and nothing happened, no bombs, no fighting. The army was kicking its heels, and after a while the families all came home again. The weeks turned to months, still nothing. You English called these months the Phoney War. Our phrase for it was *la drôle de guerre*. So, Hitler dared not

attack us, that was just as we'd thought. We relaxed a bit.
Maybe the whole thing would blow over.'

September 1939

Kitty watched her husband, who was sitting on her
hospital bed cradling their newborn daughter, an
expression of wonder on his face. She was exhausted from
the long birth, which Dr Poulon had refused to allow
Gene to attend as he'd 'get in the way', forcing him
instead to pace in agitation outside the closed door of the
labour room. Now, the hours of pain and fear were over,
and despite bits of her feeling not at all right she was
drowsy and happy.

'I cannot believe how tiny she is,' Gene said, measuring
his meaty forefinger against the child's starfish hand, and
laughing when she gripped it. 'I feel like King Kong holding Fay Wray in the movie. Fay – there's a pretty name.
Fay Knox, how about that, Kitty?'

'Fay,' Kitty repeated, liking the sound. 'It's a delicate
name, isn't it? Makes me think of the French for fairy – *fée*.'
Her husband was right. It did suit this waif of a child with
her huge navy eyes, as yet unfocused. They had been
going to call her Elizabeth after the mother Kitty could not
remember, and Kitty didn't want to go back on that. 'Fay
Elizabeth,' she said, wanting to please Eugene.

Fay Elizabeth she was christened. The nuns hadn't
heard of King Kong and were doubtful about fairies.
When Kitty took the baby to see them, they told her that
Fay was close to *foi*, meaning 'faith' in French. 'Elizabeth
is a Godly name, too. Saint Elizabeth was the mother of

Saint John the Baptist,' Mère Marie-François informed Kitty, cradling the child, clearly delighted by her. She made the sign of the cross on the baby's forehead. '*Dieu te bénisse, Fay Elizabeth,*' she murmured before passing the child to Sister Thérèse, who seemed so enchanted by her that the Reverend Mother was quite curt when she directed the girl to return her to Kitty.

A new way of life was gradually established. For the first two weeks Gene hired a maternity nurse to help his wife, a French girl with the face of a Madonna, who imparted an air of calm and order to proceedings that Kitty herself did not feel. The baby was fretful and did not feed easily, and Kitty worried that she was doing every-thing wrong. Never did she feel the lack of her own mother as now, when she most needed advice and reas-surance. The French nurse seemed to manage everything so beautifully when she was there, but in a way that made Kitty feel inferior next to her. Also, she tried to pull rank with Jeanette and upset her, so in the end everybody was glad when her contract came to an end.

After that they managed with Jeanette coming in more often, and by constant use of the local laundry, but Kitty still had to deal with buckets of stinking nappies around the flat, and the tough old bird of a concierge complained if she left the pram in the lobby downstairs. Kitty enjoyed the attention when she took the infant out in it though. Even the baby clothes in Paris were chic, and she loved to dress Fay in stylish matinée jackets and frilly bonnets. If she left the pram outside the butcher's while she nipped in for a bit of steak, ten to one she'd come out to find some black-clad widow had stopped, her worn face softening, to cluck over the baby. And Fay was, though Kitty said it herself, an exceptionally engaging-looking child with her shock of dark hair, wide, long-fringed eyes, button mouth and clear skin.

But even in this cotton-wool babyland, Kitty could not but be aware of the charged atmosphere, as sandbags were piled outside shops and at the bottom of monuments, and people's faces turned anxiously to the sky any time a plane flew overhead. At night the city was blacked out completely, which put an end to the nightclubs. As Gene's friend Jack complained, it was almost worse waiting for something to happen than for it to happen, and it was a while before some sort of normality established itself, though the peace was disturbed occasionally by an air-raid drill. The theatres and cinemas were open, people still gossiped about who was having an affair with whom, and magazines still featured the latest *haute couture*.

Some things were different. There were faces missing from their circle of friends. Few English people remained, Miss Dunne notably being one. Though the US was not at war with Germany, many Americans had been worried enough by the prospect of invasion or bombardment to flee to the South of France or to neutral Switzerland, or had been summoned home altogether by their families. After several anxious letters from Uncle Pepper, Kitty wrote finally to tell him that since nothing untoward was happening she and Gene had decided she should stay where she was. After all, with talk of German U-boats lurking in the Channel, it might be more dangerous to attempt to sail home.

Late in November, when Fay was nearly two months old and had started to smile, Kitty returned to Monsieur Deschamps for her first piano lesson for four months. She was nervous, having left Fay with Jeanette, though the French cleaner had successfully raised four of her own children, so Kitty really had no need to worry. She'd done little practice and had consequently fallen behind, and she was nervous of her teacher's reduced expectations of her now that she was a young mother.

In the event, though she arrived late, he was very kindly and indulgent, but she left afterwards feeling the lesson had been a disaster. Her fingers had been clumsy, her mind skittering away from the black dots of music dancing on the page before her. When she emerged from his room she was close to tears, angry tears that she hadn't done better. She berated herself all the way home and after that day forced herself to practise every time she had a few minutes to herself. Baby Fay quickly learned to sleep through her playing, but she couldn't sleep all the time and Kitty knew it was wrong to wish she did.

'It's very soon,' Gene said, trying to soothe his wife. 'Don't expect so much of yourself.'

'But I'll lose everything I worked for,' she wailed. 'Don't you see?'

For the next lesson she arrived at Monsieur Deschamps' apartment block in time to meet Serge coming out of the lift. She hadn't seen him for months. He'd changed, she saw that straight away. Part of the change was physical – he'd filled out a little, stood taller – but it was also that his air was more confident, and despite the wartime privations he'd managed to acquire a better-fitting suit. They exchanged greetings and she suggested they meet properly at some point. She hesitated to invite him to the apartment because it had become taken over by baby things, and so they agreed to meet the next day at the café by the Conservatoire that they'd frequented before. It was under new ownership, Serge told her, the previous people having left Paris in a hurry when war was declared.

'I hope you don't mind if I bring Fay,' she volunteered, as she entered the lift.

'*Pas du tout*,' he replied through the diamond-shaped bars, and she smiled down at his uplifted face as the lift jerked on its way. The lesson went better that day, thank heavens, and she returned home feeling more hopeful.

The new owners were serving a reduced menu, but otherwise all seemed as usual when Fay entered the café the following day, though it struck her that there were fewer students eating at the tables or chatting and laughing at the bar.

She was surprised at how tender Serge was towards Fay. As she sat with the child on her lap, he exchanged smiles and chuckles with her. 'I remember my little sister when she was a baby,' he told her. 'She used to love sitting on my knee to bash at the piano. I think maybe this one will be a musician.' He carried a recent photograph of his little sister with him, a laughing fourteen-year-old with Serge's dark colouring. She was, he said, six years younger than he was, but they were very close and she wrote to him every week. 'So, Fay, are you a musical baby?' he asked.

'I'm training her to fall asleep when I play Brahms's lullaby,' Kitty said. 'Does that count?'

They talked about the music each was playing for Monsieur Deschamps, and Serge explained how the Conservatoire was continuing most of its classes, though many of the pupils and some of the teachers had left when war was declared. An air of uncertainty blew through its corridors these days, he said.

Serge himself, she discovered with not a little envy, had been doing very well in the four months since she'd seen him. She already knew he'd won a First Prize in Piano at the Conservatoire in July. Now he was actually due to play in a concert for young musicians in two Sundays' time and was practising hard for it, and for a national competition Monsieur Deschamps had entered him for, to take place after Christmas. He'd been earning some money in the meantime playing two evenings a week at a grand hotel near Place de la Concorde. 'If I win the competition,' he said, passion in his eyes, 'I might not have to do that for long. The job is easy, but demeaning. Play this, play that, do I know some foolish American song or other. Pah! *Je me prostitue*,' he said with a look of ferocious disdain. 'But we all have to eat. And at least I am still in Paris.' The implication was clear. He had so far escaped being called up for the army.

It would be hard to imagine his long-fingered musician's hands around the body of a rifle, Kitty thought. She couldn't picture Serge, who poured his soul into his music, marching to orders or running for his life through a shower of bullets. But despite his sensitivity he was tough; he had stamina and the determination to succeed. Perhaps she was wrong to worry about him. She breathed a guilty little prayer of thanks that America wasn't in the war and that Gene was safely in the hospital. Although she was English, she and Fay were on his passport and therefore in the eyes of the authorities they were Americans, so they were all right, too. Gene had told her though, that at the least sign of trouble he would send her home to Uncle

Pepper with their daughter, if he could. They didn't talk of the U-boats.

Christmas came and went. Serge did win the competition, although the prize bursary was not enough to save him from having to 'prostitute' his talents, as he called it. It did, however, bring other opportunities. One freezing February morning, Serge's eyes lit up when he emerged from his lesson to find Kitty sitting on a chair in Monsieur Deschamps' cramped hallway.

'Look, I must show you,' he said, with one of his ironic smiles. He withdrew an envelope from his inside jacket pocket and extracted from it a formal notecard, which he gave her to examine. *Mrs Donald van Haren* was embossed at the top in elaborate silver italics. 'She wishes me to play at one of her salons,' he said. 'What do you think of that?' Despite his studied nonchalance, she sensed his excitement.

'It sounds a marvellous opportunity,' Kitty said, wondering who exactly Mrs van Haren might be.

The lanky figure of Monsieur Deschamps appeared in the doorway to the drawing room. 'Our young friend here has made something of a conquest, it seems,' he said, stroking his moustache.

'She heard me play the Rachmaninoff at the Conservatoire, Kitty. She loves Rachmaninoff, she says here.'

'Will you go?'

'Will he go? Of course he will go,' Monsieur Deschamps said with conviction. 'Serge has to begin to make his name.'

Serge described it all to her later, the mansion in the

eighth arrondissement with the elegant cars parked in the forecourt, the high-ceilinged drawing room hung with blue velvet curtains and furnished in gilt and white. Mrs van Haren herself turned out to be a tall, attractive Frenchwoman married to an American businessman. She was in her thirties with glorious chestnut-coloured hair and large round green eyes that made her appear constantly surprised. 'The American Ambassador himself congratulated me on my playing,' Serge told Kitty, 'and there were writers and politicians present.' Rich old ladies had purred over him, and an old military gentleman with a moustache like Marshal Pétain and a row of medals on his chest had wrung his hand.

But what pleased Serge more than being lionized was that in the post the following day he received a generous cheque from Mrs van Haren 'in honour of his performance', together with an invitation to play at one of her cocktail parties the following week.

Serge Ramond, it seemed, was on his way in society. But so much would depend on the international situation. As the air grew milder and the trees came into blossom, the mood in Paris was hopeful. All right, they might technically be at war, but there was little evidence of hostilities and life continued much as usual. Kitty read a review Jack had written of Josephine Baker and Maurice Chevalier's new show on the Champs-Élysées. Gene talked of their little family going to Avignon for a holiday at Easter. The important thing, Kitty decided, was to focus on the here and now, to let the future look after itself.

In March, a few short weeks later, the future arrived with alarming seriousness. Gene and Kitty first heard the BBC news on the wireless. Hitler's forces had invaded Norway. *La drôle de guerre* was over. Outside the post office down the street more posters appeared, mobilizing troops. The war had finally begun.

On 10 April came the news that the Germans had taken Norway. Nazi troops marched into Denmark. Not long after, it was Holland's turn, then Luxembourg, all falling to the enemy like a row of dominoes. Meanwhile, Parisians reacted in horror to the revelation that Nazi Panzer divisions were forging their way through the Ardennes Forest in France near the Belgian border. The rumours were that the French defending forces were shambolic. It was horrifying! The famous Maginot Line that had cost so much and was supposedly unbreachable had proved no use to France at all. The enemy had simply gone round it.

Belgium was the next to fall. And soon the French and British armies were in swift retreat under the huge might of the German onslaught, falling back through the oft-contested landmarks with their ghosts of the dead of battles past. Ypres, Mons, Waterloo. Steps in an old nightmare.

Sharing a park bench, whilst Fay slept in the pram, Kitty overheard one woman speaking to another of her anxiety for her two sons at the front. Wherever she went – the shops, the Métro, the cafés – there drifted over the city the unimaginable spectre of defeat.

By the end of May the smouldering fear was fuelled by the arrival in Paris of thousands of refugees. From Poland, they came, from the Low Countries, from north-eastern France. They arrived by train, by car, by horse-drawn cart or on foot, laden down with luggage, furniture and blankets. Kitty, visiting the convent one afternoon, discovered that the nuns had taken some of them in. They included a Belgian woman named Marthe and her three children, two boys and a girl. Marthe's face was tear-stained and pinched with worry. She'd become separated from her husband as they'd fled their home town, she told Kitty, and feared the worst had happened to him.

The youngest child, a cheerful girl of five or six called Sofie, took to eight-month-old Fay immediately. Fay was going through a plump stage and her mass of dark curls emphasized her large solemn eyes and gave her a comical look. She chuckled as she tried to crawl after a ball that Sofie rolled for her, while Marthe, Sofie's traumatized mother, explained to Kitty how they'd fled on foot from the advancing German troops, only to be strafed by bullets from their planes. Their handcart ended up broken in a ditch, the family scattered, and in the confusion that followed, her husband could not be found. She'd managed to hitch a lift on a wagon with the children into France, then to get onto a train and had come to Paris that way.

Kitty returned home in a sombre mood. After she'd put Fay to bed that evening she could settle to nothing, and sat alone, brooding on the Belgian woman's story. She often spent evenings on her own these days. Gene, more often than not, arrived home grim-faced and exhausted. He chose not to talk about his work at home, for his own sense of peace as well as to spare Kitty, but tonight when he finally came back she questioned him about the progress of the fighting. She was shocked when he explained about the large numbers of wounded soldiers, French and English, being brought to the hospital by American ambulances. The war, it seemed, had reached Paris.

*

Two nights later they listened to the BBC news with a sense of disbelief. The British Expeditionary Force had retreated to the north coast of France, hemmed in by the enemy on all sides. The only escape route was by sea. Anyone with a boat and in reach of the French coastal town of Dunkirk was ordered to go and help with the rescue. It sounded desperate.

Afterwards, Gene got up and switched off the wireless, then stood staring at it, ruffling his hair but saying nothing. Restless, Kitty rose from her seat and went to the open window. It was still light outside, one of those warm evenings of early summer, when she loved Paris most. Down the street, the drinkers had gathered as usual at the café on the corner and she could hear snatches of accordion music.

Finally, Gene spoke. 'I think you and Fay need to leave for England while you can.' His voice was heavy and firm.

She turned in surprise. 'No,' she said, her voice wild. 'No. We've discussed this before.'

'Kitty.' He came to put his arm round her. 'I've been speaking to someone at the Embassy. If you make your way south-west to Bordeaux there'll be a ship to England.'

'I won't go without you, Gene, I won't.'

'Please, Kitty. If you won't do it for yourself, think of Fay.' He looked down at her earnestly. Dear Gene. She remembered the refugee family, the woman's distress for her lost husband, and wanted more than ever to stay close to Gene. The war was approaching, but surely they were all right in Paris?

'Shouldn't we wait and see what happens? The news isn't all bad. And you said yourself, we'd be safe here. We're on your passport as Americans, after all.'

'There's always a risk though,' he said with a sigh. 'The Nazis may not follow the rules.'

'I don't want to be separated from you,' she whispered, her eyes full of love for him, and he held her tight.

'God knows, I don't want it either.' He sighed. 'All right, we'll wait a while and see what happens.'

A week later, 7 June, Kitty and her daughter were still in Paris, but the Knoxes' sense of hope was being challenged daily. The Germans had established themselves in north-east France, it was said. The French army was falling back. What would happen if the Germans reached Paris? That was the talk in the shops. Would they bomb it, destroy it? Were its citizens in danger? Many were deciding that it was time to leave.

Walking to her piano lesson, Kitty passed through a city in upheaval. On the main roads the traffic was in gridlock, cars piled high with possessions, everyone trying to make their way out of Paris. People on laden bicycles wove their way through the jams, bells ringing impatiently. She'd never seen so many bicycles.

Over the river in the direction of the government offices, ominous columns of smoke drifted to the sky. 'They're burning secret documents, I heard,' Jack had remarked at dinner the previous night. 'All the evidence, no doubt, that threatens Blum's cowardly hide,' he added, referring to the current Prime Minister, blamed for France's shocking failure to defend herself against the advancing enemy.

Kitty passed a shop window being boarded up by a stout old man with a hammer while his wife fussed over their luggage strewn about the pavement. At the Gare d'Orsay she saw a huge pile of battered saucepans, old pipes, a mangled bicycle or two, collected for scrap. It was too late for the war effort now. Crossing the road near an art gallery she was fascinated to see four men loading a huge wrapped picture onto a lorry. The brown paper didn't quite cover it, and at the bottom she could see the painted hooves of a goat-like beast. No one in Paris was dancing now. She got a glimpse inside the truck as she passed. It was already chock-full of paintings. 'Where are you taking them?' she asked one of the men, but he only shrugged and said, 'Wherever Fritz can't get his filthy hands on them,' and she shivered as though the summer wind had turned chill.

She arrived at Monsieur Deschamps' apartment block, to find a scene of disarray. People were hurrying in and out of the building, fetching luggage, calling out instructions or arguing about things forgotten. Boxes and bits of furniture were scattered about, or were being tied onto vehicles. Inside the lobby there was no sign of the concierge, and the door to her rooms was shut and bolted.

To avoid the chaos around the lift, Kitty took the stairs, but when she had edged up past the crowds and emerged at the right floor it was to find a note pinned to Monsieur Deschamps' door. It informed the generality that he had left Paris and apologized for the lack of notice. No forwarding address was given. Although she'd feared this, it was still a shock. She stood there for a minute or two, clutching her music case to her chest, as though it was the only thing she had left. In that moment she saw with clarity that her musical ambitions were over.

She turned away, feeling numb. It didn't matter, she

told herself. She'd think about it later. There were other, more important things now. Fay. She made her way slowly back down the stairs and out of the building, but no sooner had she set off in the direction of home than she heard someone shout, 'Kitty!' and when she looked back, she saw Serge running after her, out of breath. 'You saw the notice?' he said, between gasps. 'I went to find out what was happening at the Conservatoire, then I thought I'd come back to meet you. The Métro was bad, so many people. I thought I'd missed you.'

'What is happening at the Conservatoire?'

'Much the same. Everybody's leaving Paris.'

'What will you do?' she asked.

He shrugged, looking at the ground and shuffling a stone with his foot. Then he said, 'There's been another call-up,' and glanced up to see her reaction. 'It's me this time.'

'Oh, Serge, I'm sorry.'

He straightened and a wary look came into his eyes. 'I might not have to go.'

'How ...?'

'Because of my studies – I'm waiting to hear. Everything's so chaotic anyway. Think about it – if I delay long enough, perhaps I won't be needed.' His voice trailed off. It was horrible to even think of the possibility of France's defeat. 'Never mind that. What about you?'

'Gene wants to send Fay and me home to England.'

'And will you go?'

'I don't know.'

They'd begun to walk back alongside the river. All the stalls were shut up today. No one wanted to buy or sell anything except a fare to safety. When they came to a bridge, Serge stopped, drawing her out of the path of an impatient cyclist. He said, 'I'm going this way. I suppose we must say goodbye.'

'We will see each other again?' She felt a sudden rush of fondness for him.

'I hope so,' he said, regarding her with a grave, unhappy expression. 'But perhaps not for a while. You can always try leaving a message at the Conservatoire.'

'Of course. And whatever happens, I'm sure Gene will still be here at the hospital.'

'Goodbye,' he said, and placing his hands awkwardly on her shoulders he kissed her gently on each cheek, something he'd never done before. She stood for a long while watching his wan figure stride across the bridge until it was dwarfed by the long expanse of the Louvre gleaming silver in the sun. He had been one of her first friends in Paris, bonded to her by music and loneliness.

When Kitty arrived home, Jeanette thrust little Fay into her arms, her eyes refusing to meet her employer's.

'I have to go now,' she mumbled, taking up her bag. She patted Fay. '*Au revoir, mignonne.*' Her eyes teared up. 'I am going to Limoges,' she said with a catch in her voice. 'To rest with my cousin. A little precaution. Until the danger is over.'

'I wish you could stay.'

'I will be back.' She looked up at Kitty, her eyes fierce, her square chin jutted, determined. Kitty knew that her eldest son was on the front line somewhere and that she was worried stiff about him. 'We will win, Madame Kitty. There is no question of it. La France cannot be defeated.'

'Of course France will win,' Kitty said quietly, moved by

the woman's dignity. Fay, who was tired, twisted in her mother's arms and whimpered.

Two days later, Gene came home very late, completely exhausted but with news gleaned from the injured soldiers who were arriving at the hospital in increasing numbers. There had been a major retreat and the French army was disintegrating under poor leadership. 'They say it's chaos at the front,' he said. 'No one in charge knows what they're doing. There's a young lieutenant with a shoulder wound. Says they were given orders to do one thing one moment, exactly the opposite the next. Kitty, we're running out of time now. We have to face reality. Paris may fall. You must take Fay and go.'

'No,' Kitty pleaded. 'I don't want to leave you. Gene, please.' But this time, he wouldn't accept her answer.

Why did Paris have to look so lovely on the day Kitty had to say goodbye? It was 12 June and the air was warm and the window-boxes of an apartment across the street were a mass of flowers, red and blue and white, someone's small gesture for France.

Gene had taken the morning off work to see his wife and daughter safely onto the train, having spent much of the previous day at the American Embassy getting their papers in order. Boats were leaving all the time from Bordeaux, yes, they were assured by the harassed clerk. No, he couldn't book a passage for them, though he proceeded to make several phone calls on their behalf. They should travel down there straight away. 'Or it will be too late,' he said meaningfully, as he turned his attention to the next people in the queue.

The Gare d'Orléans was a scene of chaos as shouting, frightened people fought to get onto trains. Gene went first, using Kitty's case as a battering ram to forge a way across the platform. Their train was packed, people crammed in the corridors, but Gene miraculously managed to squeeze his wife and child through and into a compartment. He stowed Kitty's luggage on the rack and negotiated a space for her between a voluptuous young woman with thick make-up and a frail dowager in a fur coat who had a tiny yapping terrier in a basket on her lap. It was a most unceremonious goodbye. 'Take care, my love,' Gene murmured in her ear as he kissed her and ruffled Fay's soft dark curls. Then he plunged back into the corridor and was gone. All along the train, doors were slamming and people crying out to loved ones and waving or weeping. Kitty strained to see Gene in the crush on the platform, but couldn't see past those still surging to get on, desperation in their eyes. Then a whistle blew and the throng fell back as the train began to move.

At the last moment she caught a glimpse of his tall figure in the crowd, his arm raised in a gesture of farewell. 'Goodbye, goodbye,' she cried, making Fay wave at her daddy until he was out of sight, and desolation engulfed her.

The train gained speed and soon they were on their way out of Paris. Fay buried her head in Kitty's neck and moaned with fear in the darkness of a tunnel, but cheered up when they emerged into daylight, pointing at things they passed or watching the little dog turn in its basket.

Between the confusion of cases and people, a whole family could be glimpsed sitting opposite, placid brown-eyed parents with four children ranging from about twelve down to three. Kitty watched the youngsters hold out their hands as the mother shared out parcels of salami, bread and hard-boiled eggs from a string bag, and the stink of garlic joined the smells of sweat and cheap perfume that already filled the compartment.

From time to time, the train would trundle beside a road, and everybody stared out in disbelief at the long lines of cars jammed bumper to bumper in a great exodus from Paris. Alongside the cars people stumbled, pushing trolleys, prams or carts piled high with furniture, suitcases or children. One man steered a handcart containing an elderly man slumped in a heap. To Kitty all this was shocking, like a medieval painting of hell. People's expressions were anguished or despairing or at best dogged. Parisians had become refugees. It occurred to her that, in a way, she and Fay were, too, and she shivered at the thought. She was relieved when the track curved away, leaving the awful scene behind.

Gradually the houses, the smoking factories and the grimy delivery yards thinned out, giving way to patches of green, then at last they were out in open countryside, with occasional views of churches and villages, orchards, a château, and everywhere fields were lush with ripening crops. As Fay gurgled in delight at the faces made by one of the children opposite, Kitty, lulled by the rhythm of the wheels, gazed out of the window in a reverie, thinking about Gene and the life she was leaving behind.

They were only a dozen miles further on, when the train's whistle sounded, long, low and mournful. The train slowed, then braked violently, jolting to a halt that threw people onto one another. Outside the window, black smoke billowed, casting the carriage into darkness.

'*Qu'est-ce qui se passe?*' everyone asked everyone else.

'*Écoutez!*' Kitty heard a deep-voiced man bellow above the clamour. In the silence that followed the distant crackle of gunfire could be distinguished. Then, from further down the train, they heard shouting, and doors started opening.

A guard passed outside crying, '*Descendez, descendez!*' and the passengers in Kitty's compartment rose as one and scrambled about for their luggage. Outside, people began piling onto the tracks. Kitty helped the old lady with her suitcase before rescuing her own from the rack, then they followed in the wake of the crowd pushing and shoving their way out of the train. A young man caught Fay, enabling Kitty to jump down on the tracks. Behind her, someone handed down the old dowager, whilst her dog yapped furiously in its basket.

Kitty glanced about. Ahead, a field of scrubby green corn rolled away. At the far side was a church tower, a few scattered houses. Passengers milled beside the track, uncertain what to do next, waiting for instructions that didn't come. Some stood motionless, staring towards the front of the train. When Kitty looked for the object of their gaze she drew in a breath of alarm. Far ahead, the sky hung heavy with a swirling dark fog. As she watched, rockets of flame burst through it, orange and purple, like an evil sunset.

'*Les Boches,*' people were murmuring to one another fearfully. Children began to cry and their mothers shushed them. Beside Kitty, the old lady muttered, '*Mon Dieu,*' and crossed herself. In the confusion, it took time to register another noise in the distance. It was the heavy moan of engines above. They were coming nearer and nearer.

Suddenly, overhead there appeared great grey shapes, half a dozen of them, trailing plumes of acrid smoke, filling the sky like malevolent insects.

People screamed in horror and suddenly everyone was seizing children, abandoning cases and plunging into the soft soil of the cornfield. Kitty ran too, with Fay clamped, struggling, to her shoulder. The yellowing stalks knifed her legs as she passed and the sharp scent of sap rose all around.

The planes dropped low and followed them in a rush of hot choking wind. Then came the deafening hammer of gunfire. Shouts turned to screams, high-pitched, animal. Some stumbled but staggered on. Others simply dropped in their tracks. Kitty saw the old lady stop to fuss with her dog, but when she went to help, the woman sent her away. Kitty left her crouched in the cornfield, soothing the animal, her fur coat spread about her like a mantle as the bullets darted down.

Kitty ran on as her breath rasped in her chest. Fay clutched on for dear life, her eyes creased tight shut, her mouth open in an anguished screaming O. Then, mercifully, the planes seemed to tire of their sport for suddenly, as one, they swerved up and away, continuing their journey towards the hellish distant smoke. The train and the helpless refugees must have been a momentary dalliance on their way to more serious business. Now, up ahead, at the far edge of the field, Kitty could see a line of villagers hurrying to meet them. And the church bell began to toll, in furious, urgent tones. She set off once more, the full horror of their situation only now breaking on her, her knees beginning to buckle from exhaustion and the shock.

They were led with many other survivors to shelter in

the church, with the bell still clanging in their ears. Fay hated the sound – she screamed and screamed as Kitty paced, trying to calm her. Finally it stopped as suddenly as it had begun and when the last echo died away, Fay sobbed for a while before falling into a deep slumber, from which she did not stir for some hours. Still Kitty paced with her, but this time it was to calm herself.

All around the church the wounded were being brought in on makeshift stretchers and laid on the floor, near the altar or in the aisles – anywhere there was a space. There was only one doctor, it appeared, a grizzled man with a pointed beard, who bent stiffly to tend to the worst injured. She saw the brown-eyed family thronged round a small figure on the ground, glimpsed a chubby arm thrown out as in sleep and turned away, not wanting to know any more. The doctor called out for ambulances to be summoned, but it became clear that no ambulances would be found. Kitty scanned the crowd for the old lady, but couldn't see her.

Time passed agonizingly slowly. If somebody died, the body was covered up and carried outside. Beyond the door she glimpsed the horrifying rows of the dead. She could not bring herself to go and see if the dowager was amongst them. Village women came with soup and thin mattresses. As night fell she settled herself and Fay as best she could. When she awoke at dawn, Fay was sleeping, but the old lady's dog was nuzzling her face with its cold nose. It pressed itself against her, shivering, its huge eyes full of fear.

Chapter 14

1961

'Your mother told me,' Mme Ramond went on, her voice sombre, 'how the next day, most of those who were able to walk were reunited with their luggage, and shepherded on foot to the nearest station. From there, another train took them back to Paris. The train they'd been on,' she added quickly, seeing Fay's expression of surprise, 'had been damaged in the air raid, and anyway would not have been able to continue because of the fighting ahead. The German forces were tightening their noose around Paris. Your mother had left it too late to leave.'

'So we were trapped here,' Fay whispered. The realization that she'd been present through these terrifying events was still dawning on her. She'd remembered nothing, of course, she had been too young. Yet, perhaps there was something. That bell in Notre Dame on the school trip. The panic it had awoken in her. Maybe she had been remembering a different bell. She explained this to Mme Ramond now.

'I thought it was something about Notre Dame itself that frightened me,' she ended up. 'But perhaps I had been mixing up the two experiences. Do you think that could happen?'

Mme Ramond frowned. 'Possibly, though I'm sure you were correct to think you had visited Notre Dame before. Its atmosphere makes an impression, does it not, even on the very young. The beautiful colours of the windows, the incense, the whispering darkness. The priests know well the power of these things.'

'What happened next?' Fay asked. 'After we returned to Paris?'

Mme Ramond leaned back in her seat and resumed her story.

June 1940

The Paris to which Kitty and Fay returned felt empty and abandoned. It was, however, far from silent. From time to time, dull explosions could be heard in the distance and pillars of black smoke rose into the limitless blue sky. A shower of fine soot like black snow was falling, dusting their heads and shoulders. Hungry, dirty and exhausted, they took refuge in a café before attempting the next part of the journey. The big sad-eyed proprietor explained as he brought Fay warm milk that the French army were blowing up fuel-storage depots.

'It's to stop the Germans getting their hands on the fuel. They'll be here soon, I expect.'

'I hope not,' Kitty said, sounding heartier than she felt.

'Hope is all we have left,' he said, pulling at his moustache. 'The government has abandoned us, the rich people have run like rats. We ordinary people are left to our fate.'

He raised his great hands in a lugubrious gesture of defeat.

'What made you stay?'

He looked around proudly at his neat café with its shining zinc counter, the pastries arranged on doilies in a gleaming glass case. 'I worked hard for this place. It is all I have. I cannot leave it that easily.'

'Well, I'm certainly glad you haven't gone,' she said with feeling.

After lunch Kitty tried to telephone the hospital, but the operator said the line was dead. There being no sign of a cab, she followed the café-owner's advice and took the Métro home. There was a long wait for a train, and when it came it was empty. A ghost train stopping at empty stations in a ghost city. At a kiosk, when they came out onto the street at the Gare d'Orsay, was a newspaper billboard. Kitty stared at it for a few seconds, not quite understanding the headline on it, then hurried on her way, desperate to get home.

When she reached the apartment she cursed herself. She'd left her key with Gene. There was no sign of the concierge, who kept a spare, and upstairs, as she feared, there was no answer to her knock. Fay started to cry with weariness, and the old man who lived next door came out to see what was going on. He was a shy but kindly sort. He couldn't help her gain access to her flat, but he agreed to look after Kitty's case whilst she went to find Gene. If the phone lines were down there was nothing for it but to go by Métro to the hospital in the west of the city.

At Neuilly, Kitty had to walk a long way in the heat, carrying a complaining Fay past fine houses all shuttered and deserted. And yet not everyone had gone. Kitty smiled at a small boy sitting by himself on the steps of one house, playing with tin cars. An old drunk passed them wearing an ancient military jacket arrayed with medals and singing a marching song in a thin cracked voice. He paused briefly to greet them with a fumbled salute.

When Kitty turned into the elegant drive to the hospital, it was to discover a large, jostling crowd of people surging around the entrance to the building. As she approached, she began to wonder how on earth she would get through. Fortunately she spotted a young American doctor she knew slightly loitering at the top of the steps, smoking and looking down on proceedings. She waved and managed to catch his eye. His eyebrows shot up in surprise. He tossed away the cigarette, then pushed through the crowd to meet her.

'Mrs Knox, what the hell are you doing? We thought you'd left Paris.'

'We did, or rather we tried to,' she said wearily. 'Alex, I must find Gene. Who are all these people?'

'It's crazy, isn't it?' He gripped her arm and began to steer her towards the entrance, talking all the while. 'It's been like this for the past couple days. Brits, Canadians, anyone with no money and nowhere to run. I don't know what they're going to do. We can't give 'em all jobs.'

As they gained the coolness of the reception area, Fay began to whimper, twisting and turning impatiently in her mother's arms. Kitty tried to soothe her.

'Thank you for rescuing us,' she told the young doctor.

'My pleasure. Gene should be down here.' He led them along a corridor, eventually stopping at a turning that led to one of the wards. 'This is it. Will you be all right? I must get back to my post. Ask that pretty Sister if you can't find him, she'll sort you out.' Kitty thanked him. He ruffled Fay's hair and was gone.

In the ward the nurses were all busy, but suddenly Kitty saw Gene and relief flooded through her. Something stopped her, however, from hurrying towards him. He was sitting by a bed in which lay a man, quite a young man, it struck her, though it was difficult to be certain as the upper part of his face was hidden by bandages. Gene was leaning forward, a hand clasping one of the boy's as he concentrated on what the lad was saying, and then he spoke quietly to him in reply. He didn't see Kitty, who stood touched by his compassion, the time and care he took with this distressed young man, though he must have had many other patients to see. Then Fay, catching sight of her daddy, gave an impatient cry and he looked up and saw them and his face changed.

'Kitty.' It was hard for her to see his shock and dismay. He murmured something to the young man and hurried over. She almost fell into his arms.

'I'm sorry, we left it too late, after all. It's been so frightening, I can't tell you,' she gasped, just managing to stifle a sob. But already she felt better in the knowledge that she no longer needed to cope all on her own. It felt safe just being here with him.

Gene took Fay from her and put his arm round his wife, holding her close until she was calmer, then he led her out of the ward and into a little side room that was used as an office. Here they sat talking whilst an orderly brought Kitty tea and Fay milk in a bottle. Despite interruptions from the Ward Sister, Kitty unburdened herself of her story, telling him how they'd only been able to reach the outskirts of the city before German planes attacked the train, the awfulness of the aftermath, how they'd passed the body of the old lady, wrapped in her fur coat outside the church. Fay reached for her father, then snuggled into his shoulder and with one small sigh fell deeply asleep.

'My poor darling,' Gene murmured, bending to place a light kiss on Kitty's cheek, but despite the reassurance of his words she sensed he was worried. 'Whatever happens, we'll face it together. Though I wish to God you were both safe home in Britain with your uncle.'

'Safe,' Kitty repeated. 'Maybe we wouldn't have been safe. Anything could have happened.' She shuddered. 'We might not have made it to Bordeaux, or found a place on the boat or ... oh, a hundred things. I'd rather be here with you.' Then she remembered something. 'Gene, earlier I read a newspaper headline. Something about Paris being declared an open city. What does that mean?'

He frowned and moved Fay into an easier position in his arms before answering. 'It's hard to believe, but that is what has been agreed. The Germans will walk in unopposed. In return there will be no violence, no destruction. We've got our Ambassador Bullitt to thank for that. What it means for Brits like that poor guy out there, I'm sure I don't know.'

'He's English?'

'He's from Cardiff. That's Wales, right? Our guys picked him up outside Rouen. His plane had been shot down. If he pulls through then we have to figure a way to get him home.'

'The Germans wouldn't come into the hospital, surely?'

Gene pushed his fingers through his hair. 'We've been assured by the Embassy that they won't, but nothing is guaranteed. Now Kitty, don't worry about him. It's you we've got to think about. If you'll take Fay, I'll find a car for you.' He rose and gently handed over the sleeping child, then spoke quietly into a phone to make the arrangement.

A few minutes later, he led Kitty down by a back staircase to the waiting car, to avoid the crowds. 'Now please don't be anxious. I'll be home as soon as I can, but you've seen what it's like here.'

She nodded and they embraced quickly before he opened the car door and helped her and Fay inside. Then he waited to wave them off. How different it was from the time before. Now she knew she'd see him that evening.

The car had started to move before she remembered. 'Stop!' she cried, and wound down the window. 'Gene,' she shouted back to him. 'I need a door key!'

In the still heat of the apartment, Fay slept on. Kitty unpacked then tried to doze on the sofa while she waited for the baby to wake so that they could go out to buy some food, but she was too wound up to sleep. Everything was too quiet, and every few minutes she would get up and go to the open window to stare down at the empty street. The sun beat down and the air was thick and oppressive.

Across the road, the clock above the jeweller's had stopped at a quarter to nine. It was as though time itself had ceased. The only thing that moved was a little grey dog that trotted up and down the pavement, up and down, up and down, its leash trailing all the while. Kitty wondered whether it had been abandoned or had escaped. It was obviously lost. She went downstairs with a stale crust for it, but it ran from her, so she left the bread in a doorway. When she went out to the shops later, the crust was still there. The dog itself had vanished.

At eight o'clock Gene came home, and she'd never seen him so worn down. 'Tomorrow,' he said in a dismal tone when she asked him what was happening. 'It'll be tomorrow.' Kitty had no need to ask what he meant. As the lugubrious café-owner had said, the French government had retreated – gone, too, were most of Paris's wealthiest and powerful families. Paris lay open to the enemy, but at least the hope remained that it would be left untouched. If the leaders of the occupying forces had any sense of honour there would be no bombardment here, no fires, no looting, no bloodshed. And yet from tomorrow Paris wouldn't be ruled by the French any more. The knowledge was heart-breaking. Neither of them talked much that evening. They were each lost in their private thoughts, sad ones.

Only Fay slept through the night, exhausted by her ordeal. Kitty slipped in and out of confused dreams and awoke at dawn sticky with heat to find Gene's side of the bed empty. She rose, went out and found him standing by the window in the living room as she'd done yesterday. He was smoking and studying the street through half-drawn curtains.

'I just saw one,' he said quietly, drawing her to him and pointing. After a moment she saw him too, a German soldier strolling casually down the middle of the street, a rifle slung over his shoulder. They watched in silence until he disappeared from sight.

'What's he doing, do you think?' she whispered.

'Scouting about, I reckon.'

They watched some more, but nothing else happened.

'I'll put the kettle on,' she said finally. Gene went to get dressed.

'Do you have to go to work today of all days?' she asked. She watched him pace the room as he ate a roll and honey, and knew the answer already. 'Do take care.'

'I always do.' He held her for a long moment before he left.

Ten minutes later he was back, out of breath. 'No trains,' he said, 'and the shops are all shut – I came to warn you. I'm going to drop by Jack and Milly's, see if I can borrow Milly's precious bicycle, unless I see a cab on the way. Otherwise I guess I'll be walking to the hospital.'

She sighed and nodded, foreseeing that it would be a long day.

After lunch, Kitty became aware of a rumbling sound like distant thunder, which continued ceaselessly, growing gradually louder. She wondered what it was, but hadn't the courage to go and find out. Then, without warning, Milly showed up at the door. She said she hadn't seen Gene that morning, so perhaps he'd found a cab, after all. 'I'm going off to watch the parade,' Milly told her. 'I thought you'd come if I fetched you.'

'The parade? You mean the Germans coming in?' she gasped. 'Milly, how could you? Won't it be awful?'

'Yes, it will be, but I wouldn't miss it for anything.' Millie didn't smile, but her eyes shone with a dangerous excitement. 'Nor should you. It's history. We have to be there. Get Fay ready and come on.'

Kitty's curiosity won out. 'You'll have to help me take the pram downstairs,' she told Milly.

They walked out mournfully into the sunlight and immediately the ominous rumbling became much louder. As they made their way across the river they met straggling groups of other Parisians, all with sombre faces, drawn as if mesmerized towards the Champs-Élysées and the source of the racket.

The first blow for Kitty was the sight in the distance of a flag bearing a swastika flying above the Eiffel Tower. At the Place de la Concorde she glimpsed another above the Arc de Triomphe. Meanwhile, the German war machine was already making its progress down the Champs-Élysées. There were gun carriages drawn by gleaming horses, patrols of motorcycles, row upon row of tanks, and then the soldiers, tens of thousands of them, helmeted Wehrmacht, their uniforms immaculate, buttons polished, marching with heavy tread to the menacing brightness of a military band.

Such displays were familiar to her from Pathé films at the cinema, but these had been mere shadows of the reality close up. The sheer strength of the enemy forces was overwhelming. And here they were, marching through her beloved Paris, weapons glinting under a sky of merciless blue. It was as though every wheel ground the breath out of her, every boot stamped its imprint on her spirit. This was the might of Nazi Germany. At that moment it felt unconquerable.

During the course of the afternoon, large crowds of Parisians amassed. For the most part people stood silent and aghast, some with hands over their mouths in shock and horror, others openly weeping, but here and there were people cheering, which Kitty found bewildering. 'How can they? Oh, how can they?' she spoke in Milly's ear.

'They're Germans from Alsace, I think,' Milly replied. 'The enemy within.' She was busy scribbling notes on a pad, doubtless for some article, although where she would be able to place it, Kitty couldn't guess. Milly had already told her that the presses of the *Paris Herald Tribune* had been stilled. I expect she'll find somewhere, she thought. And that meant she would put herself in danger. Milly was smart, but in some ways not smart enough. For her, truth was a shining sword that should never be dulled, no matter the risks. Despite the summer heat, Kitty shivered.

Walking back home, after saying goodbye to Milly, she noticed that many of the shops were opening. The atmosphere in the city, if she had to describe it, was now one of relief. It was as though people were saying to each other that the enemy had arrived in Paris, there had been no destruction, nobody much had been hurt. Perhaps life would continue as normal. It was bizarre and yet at the same time reassuring. Paris might be defeated, but her spirit was not crushed. Kitty had to remind herself that today was only the beginning.

When she reached their building, she lifted Fay from the pram and, since the concierge was not there to complain, parked it in the lobby. But when she reached their apartment she was alarmed to discover that, in her absence, a red seal had been affixed to the door. After puzzling at it for a moment she realized that it had been left by some Embassy official to explain to the occupying force that American citizens lived there. She supposed it should feel comforting, but somehow it wasn't. They were to be marked and observed. Like the Jews, she thought, remembering the yellow stars in the Pathé films. Would it be long before they would see those in the streets of Paris? Her nickname was the City of Light, but would she now become the City of Darkness?

Chapter 15

1961

It took a moment for Fay to realize that Mme Ramond had fallen silent, so caught up was she in the woman's story. When she glanced up, it was to see her sunk in her chair, her eyes closed. Fay was alarmed at how exhausted she appeared.

'Madame,' she whispered, and the woman's eyes opened and she smiled. 'I'm sorry,' Fay said. 'I've tired you.'

'No, you have not, my dear.' Mme Ramond sighed, shifting a cushion to make herself more comfortable. 'It's talking about the past. It's . . . as if one is living it all again.'

'You've told me a lot about my parents. I'm grateful, but there's so much to take in. And I've no idea why my mother has never told me all this herself.'

'You must hear the rest of the story,' Mme Ramond said quietly, 'and perhaps then you may judge for yourself.'

Fay nodded, sensing foreboding in the woman's tone.

'But not today. You are right, after all. I think I am tired.' She stirred from her chair and, crossing the room, she picked up one of the photographs of her husband from the shelves. As Mme Ramond stared at it, Fay was touched to see an expression of pride on her face. 'You know,' the woman said, replacing the photograph, 'he is playing in the Golden Hall tonight. I wish I could be there to hear him.'

'The Musikverein?' Fay said with interest. 'How marvellous.'

'You know Vienna then?'

Fay shook her head. 'One day I hope to go. And to visit the Golden Hall. I've seen pictures. It looks so beautiful.'

'In my opinion it is the best of all the concert halls. Maybe one day you will play there. The war cut off so much opportunity for your mother – but you? The world is open to you. You must be dedicated though. If you marry, you should find a husband who supports you in your work. And it will be harder if you have children.'

'I'm sure you're right,' Fay said a little stiffly. The shrewd way in which Mme Ramond was now regarding her made her feel uncomfortable. She didn't want to have to think about this sort of thing. Not for years and years, anyway. A rush of annoyance surprised her. Who was this woman to advise her like this? A friend of her mother's, she'd said, but who!

Mme Ramond must have sensed all this for she said, 'I'm sorry. All this is still before you. And I forget you are no longer a child who needs protection.'

Fay's irritation subsided. Mme Ramond was an ordinary woman again, not a sinister threat. A woman who deserved Fay's sympathy, too, with her swollen joints, her pain-filled face. And missing her absent husband.

'Fay, I must ask you to excuse me. I'm afraid I need to rest before I go out this evening.'

'Of course. I have to rush myself.' The clock on the

mantelpiece was inching towards half past five. She rose to go. 'Mme Ramond, thank you so very much.'

'It is delightful to see you,' the woman said, pushing herself up from her chair. 'When can you come again?'

'Would you mind if I do? I'm free at the same time tomorrow afternoon.'

'That would suit me very well.'

Fay collected her handbag from the floor and her eye fell on the wooden zebra on the table.

'Take him,' Mme Ramond said, seeing her hesitation.

'Really, may I?'

'Of course, *chérie*. He is yours. I always hoped to give him back to you.' This was said with such warmth and yearning that Fay felt strangely touched. She stowed the zebra in her bag.

She hardly noticed how she made her way downstairs, only that suddenly she was on the street and following Mme Ramond's directions to a Métro station that would take her back to the hotel. It had been an extraordinary afternoon. Over the course of several hours her perception of who she was had been severely shaken. Everything her mother had led her to believe about her infancy – and admittedly that had not been very much at all – she now had to assume was untrue, or at least incomplete. A whole different narrative was taking its place.

But why should she believe Mme Ramond rather than her own loving mother? Kitty had never spoken of any friend named Nathalie or Ramond, but then she hadn't mentioned her Parisian past at all, so perhaps that wasn't in itself significant. She thought of all the women Mme Ramond had mentioned and realized that she'd never once made reference to her own role in the narrative. Who *was* Mme Ramond? Fay wished she'd asked. And yet when she'd been in her flat, such was her trust in the woman's telling of the story, she had sensed it would be revealed when the time was right.

And yes, she did believe Mme Ramond's story. She recognized it instinctively in a way that she'd never recognized what her mother had told her. When Mme Ramond had described the apartment that had been Fay's first home, Fay had seen pictures in her mind of fine net curtains with a flowery pattern blowing in a breeze, of a ball rolling across a paved yard with high white walls around it. Somewhere deep inside she remembered these things, even though she was probably very young when she left. There was her reaction to the tolling bell in Notre Dame, too. Perhaps these disturbing experiences she'd been having in Paris were all actually memories of some sort. If it was true, at least it meant she wasn't going mad, which was the other explanation.

The train was packed with rush-hour crowds. A bashful young man with pock-marked skin gave up his seat to her, but then stood right by her, giving her little glances, so to avoid his attention she brought the zebra out of her bag and examined it, running her fingers over its dear blunt nose and smooth, rounded belly. Once again she saw herself as a child, walking the zebra on a window-ledge. The animal had a name, but for the life of her she couldn't recall what it was. Something beginning with S? Or was it an M? When she looked up next they'd reached the Louvre and the young man had gone.

Fay changed trains at the next station, then alighted at Madeleine. Coming up onto the street, she glanced across to where the great church lay bathed in the early-evening light and remembered the little priest who had been so helpful. How tactless she'd been, she burned with embarrassment to remember, asking him about the war. He'd answered her so mildly, deflecting the question. Who knew what depths of suffering he might be hiding. She was beginning to understand this now. For Paris was part of her own past.

What had happened to her mother here? In some ways Fay could hardly wait to return to Mme Ramond's the next afternoon, but she also dreaded it. She guessed now that she was being led down into some dark area of her mother's life that she, Fay, needed to know about, but which Kitty not only refused to speak of but had also blanked out entirely, it seemed, cutting it out of her life like some vile canker, perhaps in order to survive. She remembered what Dr Russell had said, that her mother was brooding on something, some secret. Was it guilt? What could her mother, from whom she'd only ever received love and kindness, possibly have done?

Fay felt only sympathy for her, and now, walking past the church on her way to the hotel, she experienced a deep longing to speak to her. It would be half past five in England – perhaps somebody would answer, she reasoned, so she retraced her steps to the square and went into the post office where – was it only the day before yesterday? – she'd tried to find the address of the convent. Picking up the receiver at one of several telephone booths that lined the far wall, to her surprise she found herself speaking to Dr Russell.

'Doctor, it's Fay Knox, calling from Paris.'

'Fay.' The man was equally surprised. 'I was on my way out. You were lucky to catch me.'

'I'm sorry if you're in a hurry, but I wondered if you could tell me how my mother is.' She pressed the receiver closer to her ear, winding the flex around her fingers.

'Of course. I spent some time with her today. She's doing well. Brighter, if anything, I'd say.'

'Is she?' Fay said, releasing the flex and smiling. 'That is wonderful. Would you mind giving her a message from me? Tell her that I'm fine, the concerts are going well, and that I've found Nathalie Ramond. That's an old friend of my mother's. Please be sure to tell her that.'

Fay spelled the surname for him, and the doctor promised to tell Kitty. He said goodbye and she replaced the receiver with a sense of lightness. Her mother was getting better!

Chapter 16

Half an hour later, Fay was resting on her bed, waiting for Sandra to be ready and wondering why there had been no message from Adam, when one of the hotel staff knocked on the door. There was someone on the telephone for her – a Monsieur Warner. She hurried downstairs, breathless with anticipation. In reception, she leaned her elbows on the desk listening to Adam's voice ask her about her day. He had an attractive voice on the telephone, warm and low, almost confiding, though because of the background noise at his end she guessed this was because he didn't want to be overheard by the rest of the office.

'I've had a really interesting afternoon,' she said in answer to his question.

'I look forward to hearing all about it. Are you still able to meet me tonight?'

'Yes, of course, but Adam, I simply must have a drink with the others first or they'll think I'm rude. Would you mind picking me up from Harry's Bar at about eight?'

'Not at all,' he said. 'Oh, and you won't need your diamonds tonight. We're going to be new Bohemians.'

'What diamonds are those?' She was amused.

'I only meant we'll be going to the Left Bank.' He chuckled. 'See you later.' And he rang off.

Bohemians, honestly, she thought, grinning as she skipped back upstairs. What should she wear? She had a mental picture of loose flowing dresses and trailing head-scarves, but that was the 1920s, wasn't it, and she owned nothing like that. Maybe he was referring to Simone de Beauvoir, or today's young intellectuals – the Nouvelle Vague, Jean-Luc Godard? She'd glimpsed a picture of the film-maker's pretty new wife on the cover of *Paris Match*, all pale lipstick and a rose in her hair. She preferred the singer Juliette Gréco. Mysterious in black with great kohled eyes ...

Back in her room she washed quickly, dabbed on some cold cream, frowning at herself in the washstand mirror, then contemplated her meagre wardrobe. She selected finally a flared skirt in a stiff, shiny material, matching it with a silky black top, and dressing up the outfit with a pendant on a gold chain. Gold clip earrings, lashings of eye-liner, some pale lipstick, then a quick brush of her hair, which fell nicely into Jean-Paul's layered waves, and she would have to do. She turned as the door opened and Sandra came into the room like a queen in a golden robe and a towel turban, and with her face glowing pink from her bath.

'Oh là là, we *are* chic!' Sandra exclaimed on seeing Fay.

'Are we?' Fay sat on her bed to roll on her stockings, smiling up at her.

'*Très parisienne. Très jolie.*'

Fay laughed. She told her friend about the telephone call and finished, 'I've no idea where Adam's taking me.' Despite the story she'd heard this afternoon she felt very happy suddenly. Her mother was improving and she was looking forward to the evening ahead. Sandra knew nothing of this afternoon's quest, and when Fay changed handbags, something made her hide the wooden zebra in the lining of her suitcase. The past could stay safely in the past for a little while longer.

But the past did not do that at all. As soon as she and Sandra walked into Harry's Bar, she remembered that it was here, according to Mme Ramond, that her father had brought her mother on their first evening together. From the neon sign outside to the dark wooden panelling and plush red seating within, it felt clubbish in that East Coast American kind of way she'd seen in films, and she wondered if it had always been like this or whether it had changed much since 1937. Certainly many of the clientele were still well-heeled Americans and from somewhere further inside cascaded the bright notes of a pianist playing 'The Entertainer'.

Fay was surprised to see only five members of the orchestra at the bar, and they were Frank Sowden and his acolytes: the eldest of the first violinists, the bassoonist and two brass players, in evening suits. 'So where's everyone else then?' Sandra whispered in her ear. 'Frank said—'

'Ah, the fair sex, at last,' Frank interrupted. 'Cocktails, ladies? What'll you have?' His satyr-like face was flushed, as though he'd been making his way down the cocktail menu for some time already.

'A White Lady for me, thank you, Frank,' Sandra said in a prim voice and Fay said she'd have the same.

'Harry's Bar invented the White Lady, don't you know,' Frank said as they watched the barman measure gin and Cointreau into a shaker. 'And the Bloody Mary, if you'll pardon my French.'

'How fascinating,' Sandra said. 'Where are the others? I thought you said everyone was coming.'

'It seems they have no sense of adventure.' Frank pressed his lips together. 'Some of 'em went off to a chamber concert. I don't know about the rest. Tucked into bed early with their teddies, I expect, ready for the schools concert tomorrow.' He sighed. 'It appears we're the only ones to make a proper evening of it. And we shall. Carpe diem, seize the day. Or the night rather. Chin-chin, ladies. '

A glazed look of politeness crossed Sandra's face as she took a large sip of her cocktail.

'Actually, neither of us can stay long, I'm afraid,' Fay said, trying to look regretful. Frank gave a harrumph of disappointment, but she didn't care. If they'd known it was just his small coterie who'd be here, she would never have come. They were the more raffish element of the orchestra, the ones who turned up to the morning rehearsals late and bleary-eyed. It didn't seem to affect the high standard of their playing, goodness knows how, but it displeased the conductor all the same.

'That is a pity,' Frank said, waggling his eyebrows. 'We'd better make the most of you ladies whilst you're here. Where shall we disport ourselves?'

Fay found herself squeezed between Sandra and Frank at a table, the drink relaxing her despite everything. Sandra finished hers quickly and kept glancing at her dainty wristwatch. Whilst the other men argued about where they should go to eat, Frank jiggled his leg against Fay's and rambled on.

'So you're enjoying Gay Paree, are you, girls? Marvellous city, isn't it? Always love coming here. So invigorating after stuffy old London. I was here during the war, you know.'

'Were you?' Fay said, edging her knee away.

'Twenty-sixth of August 1944, we followed de Gaulle and the Frenchies in. The fighting was mostly over by that time though. The Resistance fellows had done the messy business. They didn't muck about, by all accounts. Not that *le Général* was very happy about that. He wanted the glory for himself, you see.' Frank had a solemn air, and despite his reductive interpretation Fay caught a glimpse of a more serious person beneath the habitual banter.

'I don't really know much about it,' she said humbly. 'Only that General de Gaulle spent most of the war in London trying to help his country from there. And after France was liberated he became President.' Beside her, Sandra was laughing at some anecdote the bassoonist was recounting, her head lifted, revealing her long white throat.

'That's right. Well, some of the Parisians weren't at all pleased to be liberated. They'd got their feet under the enemy's table, you see. Collaboration – and worse. I saw some nasty incidents, I can tell you. Rough justice, acts of revenge, that sort of thing.' He looked about him furtively, like a conspirator, then leaned across and said hoarsely, 'I'll tell you what, you don't want to scratch beneath the skins of some of the people in this city. They know things they want to forget about. The war was only yesterday.'

'It feels like ancient history to me.' His words gave her a shiver of dread though.

'So it should,' he continued, his eyes twinkling. 'We need to press on with life, don't we? Now, how are you doing with that tipple? Have another, will we?'

On the dot of seven forty-five, Sandra stood up. 'I hope you'll excuse me, gentlemen, but I promised to be at Maxim's about now.'

'Maxim's, eh? Very nice,' Frank sneered. As she left, Sandra telegraphed Fay a glance of sympathy.

'Hope you meet Monsieur Delon,' Fay told her.

'What's that?' Frank growled.

'Oh, nothing. I'll have to go when my friend comes,' Fay told him. Glancing surreptitiously at her watch for the hundredth time, she wondered where Adam could be. Quarter past eight came, half past, and here she was still stuck with Frank and his chums, who were now gossiping unpleasantly about other members of the orchestra. She hardly heard. She was worried that something was wrong, that Adam wasn't coming after all. Had he gone to a different bar? She went over their conversation in her mind, but still thought she'd got the time and meeting place right. There was a lump in her throat. He'd let her down.

At a quarter past nine there was still no sign of Adam, and Frank was glancing at her pityingly, so she made a decision to cut her losses and return to the hotel. She hadn't eaten, but didn't feel like anything now, and if she did later, perhaps she could order a snack at one of the cafés near the Madeleine. She thanked Frank for the drinks, but then, as she was going out of the door, she almost bumped into Adam coming in. He was agitated and quite out of breath.

'Fay, thank heavens I caught you.' He ushered her outside and stood facing her. 'Something came up I had to deal with. Look, I can't say how sorry I am – are you very angry with me?' His hair was ruffled and the look of dismay on his face melted her heart.

'A little. Not really,' she said, trying to be cool, though in truth she only felt terribly relieved. She waited for him to tell her what it was that had kept him, but he didn't, merely saying, 'Shall we go by Métro? It's only a couple of stops.' They began to walk to the station. It had started to rain, but not enough to matter.

'Where are we going?'

'A restaurant where interesting people go. The décor's a bit on the plain side, but the food's excellent. Are you hungry?'

'Yes,' she said with enthusiasm. For suddenly she was very hungry indeed.

The restaurant on the Left Bank was in a small street off the river, in the shadow of the great gothic edifice of St-Germain-des-Prés. As they approached, the golden light of its window was a patch of warmth in the gloom of the square, and when they entered, she saw that the light came from candles, mounted in old wine bottles around the room.

'I was in too much of a hurry to go home and change,' Adam confessed, when they took off their coats and she saw he was wearing his workday suit. 'But you, you really look the part!'

'Thank you. I wasn't sure what to wear.'

She looked about with pleasure at where he'd brought her, at the Audrey Hepburn film posters on the walls, the communal wooden tables with their paper tablecloths, the rough and ready stylishness of it all. It was busy, but not full. Everyone was dressed in ordinary clothes – there was a young woman mannish in slacks and a polo-neck sweater, her *petit ami* in white shirt and a cravat tied with typical Parisian elegance. The atmosphere was cheerfully noisy and the other diners did look interesting. There were a couple of pale studenty types in jackets with frayed cuffs devouring enormous bowls of stew. A plump woman with short iron-grey hair sat against the far wall, smoking a hand-rolled cigarette, an open Penguin paperback held up in front of her. Two older men and an intense girl of Fay's age argued in loud, urgent French about politics, gesticulating furiously.

Adam seemed to know the patron, a bluff fellow with a white apron tied round his portly belly, who pointed them to spaces at a table in the window, then came across to take their order, inclining his head as he memorized their choices.

They sat quietly over the glasses of glowing red wine he poured them, enjoying the ambience. Adam had still not explained the reason for his lateness, and Fay remained puzzled, though she assumed it had something to do with his work.

The patron brought plates of coarse pâté and wished them *bon appétit*. Adam offered Fay curls of thin toast from a basket. 'When I telephoned,' he said, 'you mentioned you'd had an interesting afternoon. Was it to do with this woman you went to see?'

'Yes, it was.' Here, in the cosiness of the restaurant, Fay felt relaxed enough to confide in him. 'She's the wife of a concert pianist and it turns out that she knew my mother. Adam,' she said, meeting his eyes with growing excitement, 'she says I lived in Paris once. That I was born here. This must be why I keep having those odd episodes. They're memories. Or as much as they can be, given how young I was.'

'Memories? You mean what happened in the Champs-Élysées yesterday?' Adam looked puzzled, so she explained what Mme Ramond had told her. How her mother had met

Fay's American father here, their experiences in the early days of the war.

'And you say this woman was a friend of your mother? How is it you've never heard of her before?'

'I think they must have lost contact.' Fay thought for a bit. 'Or I wonder if something came between them. Well, I expect I'll find out more tomorrow.' She crunched a mouthful of toast and pâté, appreciating the savoury taste as she thought about what the woman had said. 'It's so strange,' she went on. 'All sorts of things are being dredged up. Things I never knew about my mother.' She shook her head. It was difficult to explain her feelings; she didn't understand them herself yet.

'It's as though you have to revisit your whole life, I suppose. Reassess it.'

'It is exactly that,' she said, staring at him in gratitude. He had a faraway look in his eyes, and again, Fay received a sense of unplumbed depths. She was getting the impression that Adam was a much more complicated person than he appeared. Older than his years, she thought.

'Adam,' she said slowly. 'When we first met, do you remember, I borrowed your handkerchief?'

'Yes, I think I do.'

'Well, I tried to give it back to you. And you said something about your father, that you'd inherited his handkerchiefs.'

'Did I?' He rested his knife and fork on the side of the plate in deliberate slow movements. 'It's simply that my father has a lot and I was given some of them.'

'Oh, I see.' She noticed that, after all, he spoke of his father in the present tense.

Their main course arrived, braised veal with beans and

sautéd potatoes. They ate in silence for a while, then Fay said, 'I haven't asked you anything about your family. You seem to know a lot about mine.'

'There's not much to tell,' he said in an offhand manner. 'There's myself and my little sister Tina. Not so little, as she got married last year. We were brought up mostly in London because of my father's job, but when I was twelve we moved to the Welsh borders. That's where my mother's family is from.'

'Are you close, you and your sister? You said you nearly drowned her once.'

Adam swallowed a mouthful and chuckled. 'Yes, despite that despicable episode we are close.' He glanced up at Fay. 'Don't take this the wrong way, but you remind me a little of her. Not in colouring, she's very different. Here ...' He laid down his fork and, feeling inside his jacket for his wallet, brought out a tiny photograph. Fay angled it towards the candlelight until it came into focus. It was a picture of a young woman, dressed for tennis, by the look of it. She was fair like her brother, with a delicate pointed face and large eyes.

'She's very pretty,' Fay said, handing it back to him. 'But I'm afraid I can't see any likeness to me.'

'Well, the prettiness, of course, but it's that look you have sometimes,' he said, smiling at the photograph. 'A bit fragile, but stubborn at the same time, as though you can look after yourself. Tina's as tough as old boots.'

'I'll take that as a compliment,' Fay said hotly. 'I am quite capable, you know.'

'Of course you are,' he said, putting up the palms of his hands as though to fend her off. 'Except for yesterday in the Champs-Élysées. Sorry, that was below the belt.'

A vision of breaking glass, voices filled with hate, the violence. Fay closed her eyes, then opened them again. 'I was grateful to you then,' she said humbly. 'I still haven't learned what that was about.'

'Well, I had an idea and did a little research.' Adam put away the photograph and instead brought out a piece of paper which he unfolded. 'Or rather I asked our librarian to do it.'

'Research? What is there to research?' she said, through a mouthful of food.

'There's a book – a memoir – by a magazine editor who was on the balcony of his office in the Champs-Élysées at the time.'

'What time do you mean?' She stared at him uncomprehending.

'September 1940, it was. Here.' He read from his paper: '"A bunch of thugs shouting 'Down with the Jews' smashed shop windows in the Champs-Élysées." Many of the shops at the time were owned by Jewish families. It must have been terrifying for them.' He looked up, triumphant at his cleverness.

Fay tried to remember her experience of two days before. Ugly shouts and smashing of glass. Had she really been there when she was tiny, and witnessed the destruction?

'It doesn't seem believable, that I'd remember. I'd only have been a baby at the time, just one.'

'It does seem unlikely, I suppose,' he admitted, 'but in the light of what you say about memories ...' He shrugged, then folded up the paper and tucked it back into his wallet.

'And there is another example.' She explained what

Mme Ramond had recounted about the tolling bell of the little village church. 'Perhaps some imprint is made on the mind even at that age,' she pondered. 'Or at least the emotion around it.'

Adam thought of something. 'That was it. Someone dropped a bottle of wine when you and I were in the Champs-Élysées. Do you remember? It must have been that which set off the memory.'

She stared at him. 'Of course!' She noticed the look of warm concern on his face and smiled at him. 'Anyway, I was glad that you were there to help. Thank you.'

'*I'm* glad I was there.' They finished their meal and left, thanking the patron, who held the door open for them.

At the corner across the street, the soft lights of Les Deux Magots café gleamed invitingly. 'I thought we might have a nightcap here,' Adam was saying, but Fay's attention was caught by the name of the street alongside.

She was sure Mme Ramond had mentioned it. It gave her a strange feeling to think she was so near. 'Adam,' she asked him, 'can we go this way? It was round here that my parents had their apartment – on a street leading off this one, I think. Please?'

'Of course,' he said, a little hesitant. 'Do you know the exact address?'

'It was the Rue des Palmes des Martyrs, something like that. I don't know the number of the building, but I remember Madame Ramond saying there was a big clock on the wall opposite, above a jeweller's.'

They walked until they found the road in question and turned down it. It was a narrow street, not very long, which contained a mixture of shops and gloomy old apartment blocks. Unremarkable, really. Fay longed to feel some frisson of recognition, some sense of belonging, but was disappointed to feel nothing of the sort. The shops were all shut up, of course, and the street was silent, there being little traffic at this time of night. It was softly lit by streetlamps with round globes, making it easy to read the signs above the shops. And there was the clock Mme Ramond had mentioned, showing the correct hour, ten thirty, hanging above a sign upon which a ring and a watch were painted.

'This must be it.' Fay stared up at the apartment block opposite, wondering which had been her parents' flat. The sixth floor, she thought Mme Ramond had said. She counted up and her gaze fixed upon a line of windows, from some of which light shone. Perhaps someone was in . . .

Just then, the main door of the building opened wide and a young man in an evening suit emerged and set off down the street the way they'd just come, whistling loudly.

'Come on,' Fay hissed to Adam, grabbing his arm. It was the matter of a moment to catch the door before it closed.

'What are we doing?' Adam said in alarm as they slipped into the building.

'I want to see,' she said.

'You can't just— I was right, you are stubborn,' he said, his eyes glinting in the low lighting of the lobby. The concierge had obviously retired for the night and there was no one to stop them entering the tiny lift. Fay pressed the button for the sixth floor and closed her eyes as she breathed in a musty smell of oil and metal that was in some way familiar. She recognized, too, the peculiar sounds of the lift as it sighed and protested its way up.

When it jolted to a halt at the sixth floor she opened her eyes but did not move. Adam was watching her in the dim light. She gave a gesture of despair. 'I don't think I can, after all,' she said and leaned back against the lift wall, holding her breath and looking back at him.

'You might as well now,' he said – and she let out her breath and nodded.

Adam slid back the doors and they stepped out into a corridor. Fay knew it at once, the scuffed lino with its grainy pattern, the colour of old cabbage. The half-moon shades on the wall casting their faint, eerie light. She turned right automatically, past first one closed door, then, more hesitantly, another. When she reached the third, she stopped, certain now. 'This is it,' she whispered, turning to Adam.

Apart from its number, 605, the door looked like all the others, made of solid wood, its dark varnish chipped and blistering in places. Fay knocked, and when no answer came, she grasped the worn brass door knob, set low on the door. Her hand knew the awkward oval shape of it, the bevelled edge that dug into her hand as she turned it and pushed.

'Fay, no,' Adam hissed, his hand on her arm, staying her. 'You can't simply walk in.'

'It's locked anyway. They must be out,' she said, disappointed, and let go of the handle. For a moment she'd been a child again, a very small girl arriving home, but now the eerie light and the silence unsettled her. Twenty years separated her from that child. She stepped back from the door.

'Let's go,' he said. 'It's late. You should come back in daylight.'

At that moment they heard muffled footsteps and the door to the next apartment opened. A middle-aged man appeared in the doorway. He was a short, stocky individual in a dressing gown, with a fine pair of moustaches and his hair oiled back. He blinked at them with suspicious, red-rimmed eyes.

'*C'est inutile*,' he said in a brisk tone. '*Ils ne sont pas là.*'

'Do you know when they'll be back?' Adam replied smoothly in French.

'Maybe tomorrow,' said the man. 'How did you get in? You should not be here.'

'Someone let us in downstairs,' Adam said. 'I'm so sorry, we'll go now.'

The man looked them over once more and nodded. 'All right, you do that,' he said, and after giving them a final glare, went back inside.

Adam said something to Fay, but she didn't hear what it was. She was staring at the man's closed door. She was thinking that it was the wrong man. Someone else used to live there, the thought of whom aroused in her a maelstrom of emotions. Sorrow, fear, happiness – all these filled her mind.

'Fay?' The mood evaporated and reality reasserted itself. Whatever it was that had happened twenty years ago was gone, lost to the past.

She lifted her eyes to Adam's with a feeling of terrible desolation. 'Yes, we should go,' she said, and allowed him to lead her back to the lift.

Outside, she was glad to return to the life of the main street. They walked back to her hotel through an enchanted City of Light. On the bridge they paused to watch the silent river surge beneath, sparkling with points of silver. The trees in the Tuileries Gardens were garlanded with light, fountains gushed like Roman candles and the Louvre was bathed a soft yellow, as proud as though it were still a royal palace.

They walked side by side, mostly in silence, but it was an easy silence. On the bridge Adam removed his hat and leaned over the parapet to watch the water with the eagerness of a boy, his hair flopping across his face, his hands clutching the stone balustrade. They were strong hands with long fingers and bitten nails, the knuckles prominent. He'd loosened his tie, and standing beside him she was acutely aware of the pulse throbbing in the delicate niche between the tendons of his neck. He'd missed a little patch on his upper lip when he'd shaved, and the hairs there gleamed golden. She yearned to reach out and touch his hair, to find out if it was as soft as it looked.

Sometimes, as they walked, he glanced at her with such attention that she felt he was there for her alone, but sometimes his eyes flickered away, restless, and she sensed that he wasn't thinking of her at all, but was somewhere else, somewhere troubling. Once he stopped to light a cigarette and frowned as though he were alone and deep in his own thoughts, and this was disconcerting.

They passed the cafés of Place de la Madeleine, packing up for the night now, and turned down the quiet street to the hotel. Adam slowed and gently touched her arm, causing her to turn towards him.

'I've enjoyed this evening,' he murmured, fully present for her now, his eyes scanning her face as though taking in every detail.

'Me, too,' Fay said, a little unsure, though she didn't know why. 'Thank you for dinner and everything, for putting up with my reckless ideas.'

'Making me sneak about perfectly respectable people's apartment blocks like a thief,' he said, with a light laugh. 'Perhaps that makes up for me being late in the first place.'

'Oh, don't worry about that,' she replied. 'All forgotten.' But it wasn't quite. He'd never given a reason for his lateness.

'You're sweet.' He stood somewhat hesitantly.

'Well,' she said, 'I ought to go in now. It won't do to yawn all the way through the concert tomorrow.'

'No, of course not.'

'Well, goodbye then,' she said.

'Good luck with the performance. I may be busy tomorrow evening, but perhaps the following day?'

'Perhaps.' It felt like a rejection.

He must have seen her disappointment for when she put out her hand to shake his, he held on to it. 'I really am sorry about tomorrow night. There's a political meeting and I promised I would go to report on it. I really want to see you again, please be sure of that. '

'Of course,' she said, a little mollified. 'I expect I ought to go out with the others tomorrow anyway.'

'Good night,' he said and watched her go inside.

Upstairs, she discovered that Sandra hadn't returned, although it was getting on for midnight. The room looked bare and depressing under the faint brassy hue of the ceiling light, but when Fay switched it off in favour of the bedside light, and climbed into her narrow lumpy bed it felt cosier, the darkness around a welcome cocoon. She couldn't settle though, her mind full of all that had happened that day. She was puzzled by Adam. She still felt about him as she had at their first time of meeting, that somehow they knew one another deep down, that some shared experience tied them together. She'd always believed this to stem from the fact that they'd both lost their fathers, but now it appeared that this wasn't the case. His father was not dead. What she felt very certain about was that there were still things he was keeping from her. It occurred to her that perhaps she was only imagining this closeness, that he was merely being polite by seeing her, for old times' sake maybe, or because she was a young English girl and he felt a responsibility to help her enjoy her visit.

I don't need looking after, she told herself. And yet it appeared that she did. This evening, outside her family's old apartment, she'd been prepared to simply walk inside. What if she had, and someone had been there? Perhaps the past was driving her on, thrusting itself remorselessly into the present.

She thought again of the man with the grand moustaches who'd emerged from the flat next door. She'd never seen him before. She'd expected a man to live there, but not that one.

As she drowsed, a picture formed in her mind of a man reading. Whenever she saw him, which was quite often, because he didn't go off to work in the morning like her father, his nose was in the pages of a book. Whether waiting for the lift, or outside in the street, her mother would have to repeat her greeting before he'd look up from the page and stammer a reply. At first Fay was shy of him, for his skin was lined like a winter apple and he wore thick-lensed spectacles that made his eyes appear unnaturally large, but she liked the way his greying hair stood on end like a halo when he pushed his spectacles up on to his head and how he smiled down at her, not stern or falsely cheerful like some grown-ups, but with complicity, as though he remembered exactly what it was like to be nearly three.

Another picture took the place of the first. They met him coming out of the boulangerie, carrying his book under one arm and a baguette under the other and he nodded to them as he passed. Fay stared bewitched at his departing figure, then pointed, laughing, and said a word she still couldn't manage yet, but which her mother understood: 'Zipper'. Her mother gave a delighted 'Oh!' and squeezed her daughter's hand. The man was wearing a pair of bedroom slippers. After this, Fay always spoke of him as 'M'sieur Zipper'.

Chapter 17

Friday

When Fay woke it was to a faint dawn light filtering through the curtains and the soft purr of Sandra snoring in the other bed. She remembered her dream. It had been the man next door who'd given her the zebra, she knew that now. 'Zipper,' she whispered to herself. Maybe she'd called her zebra Zipper because he'd given it to her, or simply because it was striped, like his slippers.

When she went downstairs to breakfast at eight she left Sandra sleeping. She had tried to wake her, but Sandra had muttered, 'Too early, go 'way,' so she let her lie. After all, the morning's concert wasn't until ten. There was no sign of the two or three others from the orchestra who were staying in this hotel, and Fay ate her rolls and jam alone.

She was enjoying a second cup of the milky coffee when the receptionist she'd spoken to about finding the convent entered and came across to her. '*Une lettre pour vous, made-moiselle,*' the woman said with a polite smile as she placed an envelope on the table by her plate.

'*Merci.*' Fay picked the letter up and examined the envelope, wondering who would write to her with a French stamp. Tearing it open, she slid out a single folded sheet. By the letterhead she saw it was from the priest she'd met at the convent. It was short and to the point, but as she read it a sense of excitement stole over her.

> *Dear Mlle Knox,*
>
> *Since we met I have remembered something that will be interesting to you in your search for information of your mother. I ask you to come and see me at the church or my office at a time of convenience to us both. Please telephone me at the number above.*
>
> *Be assured of my good wishes.*

And a scrawled signature underneath: *André Blanc.*

She brushed at some breadcrumbs that had fallen on it and read it again, wondering what he could possibly have found. She must go to see the man as soon as possible – but when? Not until after the concert, that was for sure, and she was supposed to see Mme Ramond in the early afternoon. It was past nine now, she saw, glancing at her watch, and she should wake Sandra. Perhaps she would ring the curé in a moment.

With an auditorium full of excited children the orchestra members were more relaxed this morning. They were to play a light programme: *Peter and the Wolf*, the Nutcracker Suite and a Mozart overture – nothing very demanding, but an air of enjoyment was vital to the success of it. It wasn't only Fay, therefore, who was shocked when Frank appeared in the Green Room beforehand looking deathly pale and with all the signs of a hangover. She noticed the conductor giving him a black look. The rest of his coterie simply looked tired. Sandra, remarkably enough, was as fresh as a flower.

Fay found her spirits lifted by the playfulness of the music, and for an hour or two she was able to forget her tiredness and all the worries that beset her. Music did that for her, took her out of herself, and she sensed the rapt attention of the young audience. Music was a gift she could give them, too. So the concert flew by.

There was no time to visit the priest, Fay told herself in the Green Room afterwards. She'd tried to ring him earlier whilst she had been waiting for Sandra to get dressed, but there had been no answer.

'That was rather fun,' James, the violinist with silver hair, remarked, breaking into her thoughts.

'They were very appreciative,' Fay agreed.

'You sound as though you know what you're doing, I must say,' he said in an encouraging tone.

'Do I?' Fay loosened her bow, pleasure swelling in her at his compliment. 'I feel I'm keeping up, at least.'

'That's the most important thing.'

She was leaving the Green Room to look for Sandra when she bumped into Colin as he came marching in. 'Oh!'

'Steady,' he said, grasping her arm. 'Ah, Fay, a quick word if I may.' She allowed him to steer her out into the corridor, wondering if she'd done something wrong.

'How do you feel you're getting on?' His eyes, thankfully, were kind.

'Oh, it's going well, I think.' Nervousness made her gabble. 'I'm enjoying myself enormously.' It was the truth. When she played, it was as though she became a part of the music as it swelled and ebbed, and this satisfied something profound in her.

'Good. Just thought I'd check. There might be an opportunity for you to continue playing with us – we'll see.' He patted her arm in a paternal fashion, and she saw that his thoughts were already on something else.

'Thank you, that would be wonderful,' she replied as he moved away. What had *that* been about? she wondered. She watched him pick up a sheet of music and return it to the oboeist who'd dropped it, exchanging some quip about notes floating in the air.

'Teacher's pet are we now, eh?' came a familiar voice from behind. She looked round to see Frank who, close up, looked puffy-faced, his thinning hair greasy. The stink of stale alcohol was on his breath.

'I think he was simply being polite.' She was shocked at Frank's change of attitude to her.

Frank made a dismissive gesture, but before he could say anything else Sandra hurried up and hoiked her away to have lunch.

'You looked as though you needed rescuing,' she whispered as Fay followed her to the cloakroom.

'I did. He was being a little unpleasant.'

'I'll say. Taking his bad mood out on you. I suppose you didn't see?' Sandra said, as they found their coats.

'See what?'

'At the end you rushed off, but I was messing about with my music-stand and heard Colin call Frank back. I didn't hear the exact words, but Colin was clearly tearing him off a strip. Frank looked ghastly when he walked past me just now.'

The two girls pushed open the back door and walked out on to the street.

No wonder Frank had seemed so resentful of her just

now, Fay thought. It must have stung, seeing her being complimented by Colin, and yet it was unfair of him to be so changeable. He'd been almost fawning last night. She recalled the drinks he'd bought her and wished now she hadn't let him.

'He's a funny old stick,' she sighed.

'That's a generous way of putting it. Of course, everybody's used to him – he's played with the orchestra forever. I say, shall we find somewhere we can sit outside? It's so warm.'

It was sunny and there was a light breeze. A perfect spring day. Still, Fay could not relax and enjoy it. It was partly Frank, but everything else crowded in, too: thoughts of Adam, and her forthcoming visit to Mme Ramond to hear more about her mother. Then there was the matter of the priest's letter to follow up. She had better try telephoning again later.

'Fay?' Sandra broke into her reverie. 'Are you all right? You're not really bothered by Frank, are you? Don't, he's not worth it.'

'No,' Fay said. 'It's been a long morning, that's all.'

'Come on, let's try here.' They'd come to an elegant café with round tables outside. At one, two young men in sunglasses, drinking lager, eyed them appreciatively. At another, a Parisian matron in an elegant woollen suit was slipping bits of bread to a greedy terrier sitting in her lap, a napkin tied round its fat neck.

The girls settled themselves at an empty table and after a moment a jolly-looking waiter stepped out and took their order.

'Now,' said Sandra, when he'd brought their wine. 'Confession time. I simply must tell you about last night.

We all went back to Georges' place after the meal. So modern. Leather sofas, a glass coffee table – and you should have seen the kitchen.'

'And did you meet Alain Delon?'

'He wasn't there, but it was quite a party. There was a girl who was in that film called *Breathless* – terribly pretty face. Now you must tell me about your evening with Adam, you naughty thing.'

Fay laughed. 'I'm afraid I haven't been naughty at all.' Still, she was careful to ask questions about Georges and his film friends for most of lunchtime, so that she didn't have to talk about Adam.

Sandra was very entertaining company. 'There was an older man who begged me to go for a screen test,' she said, smiling, 'but Georges got annoyed and told me this director was always promising parts to girls he fancied, so I said no. I think Georgie Boy gets a teeny bit jealous.'

Because lunch went on, Fay was late for her appointment with Mme Ramond. The lift in the apartment block didn't come right away so she ran up the stairs instead, the clack of her heels echoing in the stairwell.

The door to the flat opened at once to her knock. Seeing Fay flustered and out of breath, Mme Ramond's eyes widened in alarm and the colour drained from her face.

'What's wrong?' she croaked, clutching at a silver crucifix she wore.

'Nothing,' Fay said in surprise. 'I'm sorry to be so late. I was lunching with a friend and it was difficult to get away without seeming rude.'

'Oh, that's all.' The woman visibly relaxed as she let Fay into the apartment. 'I feared you weren't coming.'

Fay apologized again, finding the woman's concern out

of all proportion to her being a few minutes late. Was it simply the anxiety of a lonely woman, or something more? Perhaps Mme Ramond's unburdening of herself was as important to her as it was to Fay. If so, there was some mystery at the heart of this matter that wasn't just to do with Fay and her mother, but with Mme Ramond too.

She followed the older woman into the drawing room where cups and saucers were laid out on a tray, along with a plate of palm-shaped biscuits. Whilst Mme Ramond made tea, Fay took a seat on the sofa and looked about her. The room was exactly the same as yesterday, the music in its neat pile on the gleaming piano, the clock ticking peacefully on the mantelpiece and yet – was it her imagination? – there was an expectant atmosphere, as though the room itself was waiting.

One thing was different. On a side-table lay an old scrapbook with a creased cover, and now she'd noticed it her eyes kept being drawn to it. Then she heard Mme Ramond's soft footsteps, and the woman appeared carrying a full teapot, which she placed on the tray.

'I spoke to my mother's doctor yesterday evening. I thought you'd like to know that he said she's a little better,' Fay told Mme Ramond, who sat down in the chair next to the table with the scrapbook.

'I am relieved to hear that,' Mme Ramond whispered. She leaned forward, checked under the lid of the teapot, gave a nod of satisfaction and poured the tea. After Fay refused a biscuit the older woman settled back in her chair.

'I am surprised that you say your mother never married again,' she began. 'She was still very young and I always thought her so lovely and graceful, so full of life. There never was anybody?'

A picture came briefly to mind that Fay hadn't thought of for years. One afternoon when she was thirteen she had arrived back early from tea with a friend and gone round the side of the cottage to the back door. There she saw her mother by her beloved rosebed with Mr Stewart, another teacher from the school. Mr Stewart was kissing her in a very thorough sort of way, but as she watched – horrified, but fascinated, too – Kitty pulled away from him and said something in a voice too gentle for her to hear the words. Shocked, Fay ran back the way she'd come. For weeks afterwards she'd stalked her mother and worried, but when no word of the incident was mentioned and life continued as normal, she let all memory of it fall away.

'I think that maybe she had the opportunity,' she told Mme Ramond now, 'but nothing came of it.'

'That is understandable. She loved Eugene so much. She told me once, she never regretted staying on in Paris during the war, not for a moment. She had nobody else, you see. Her uncle, she loved very much, but I think he was used to being alone. She didn't worry about him, whereas of course she'd have been frantic about Eugene if she'd returned to England, leaving him in Paris. And since the Occupation itself was initially peaceful, she did not feel you were in danger. Though in the end, of course, the danger was extreme.' She shook her head. 'But no, that comes later in the story. First things first, as you say in English.' And she smiled. Then she took a sip of her tea, a tiny bite from a biscuit and wiped her fingers on a serviette.

'After the relief at the quietness of the Occupation we were fearful, that summer of 1940,' she continued. 'Above all, we felt a great sense of sorrow and shame. How could it be, we asked ourselves, that France had been so swiftly and completely defeated? This was the talk, everywhere you went. It was a strange and awful time.'

Chapter 18

Under the terms of the official French surrender signed at Compiègne on 22 June 1940, France was carved into four zones. The northern coast around Calais was to be administered by the Nazi authorities from Belgium, Alsace-Lorraine in the east was absorbed into Germany, the greater part of France including Paris and down to Bordeaux in the west was to be Occupied territory, and the southern rump designated 'Free' France, able to manage its own affairs from the spa town of Vichy, but under the close scrutiny of the Nazis. The long border that divided Free and Occupied France was vigorously policed by Germany, expensive passes being required to travel between the two jurisdictions.

In Occupied Paris, the power of the victor was felt immediately. Hitler himself paid a short but symbolic visit to the city the day after the Armistice. Citizens suffered a curfew – from dark till dawn they were not permitted outside. Since cars were banned for ordinary citizens there was little traffic; instead, armed soldiers patrolled the streets. British nationals were required to register their presence and found themselves required daily to report their whereabouts at a nearby Kommandantur office, a nuisance Kitty was spared by virtue of being married to an American.

Nothing, though, could save her from terrible fears for her homeland. The newspapers, now in German hands, were filled with demoralizing stories indicating that Britain was about to be crushed beneath the jackboot. As Kitty pushed Fay's pram through streets hung with Nazi flags, she found it impossible to ignore the propaganda posters everywhere. There was one she particularly loathed, of Churchill depicted as a murderous octopus devouring a screaming victim.

Outside Paris was a German airbase, and at nights she lay sleepless with anxiety, listening to the roar of planes on their way to bomb England. Never had she felt such an attachment to her home country as now, when she was an exile and Britain was in danger.

Eugene did his best to comfort her. Together they'd sit close to the wireless to listen to the BBC of an evening, the sound turned down low in case someone heard and reported them to the authorities.

Sometimes Kitty reflected how life in Paris had narrowed right down to herself, baby Fay, and Eugene – when he was home, for the nightly curfew meant that if he was on a late or an early shift he slept at the hospital, leaving her to spend a lonely evening. In September, a harsh rationing system was announced, and each morning she'd have to set out with Fay on a challenging search for food, joining the eternal queues at the shops, alert to rumours of where fresh milk might be bought for Fay, or eggs or green vegetables or fresh meat – simple fare that she'd always taken for granted. Attempts to beg for extras were sometimes met with kindness, but some Parisians were afraid of being seen to consort with foreigners.

Over the summer, those who had fled Paris before the

Occupation, including the Knoxes' concierge, started to return, and the pressure on already short supplies began to get serious. At the same time, other people would simply vanish. One morning Kitty stood in the queue at the fruit stall eyeing the runtish apples on display and wondering if their allowance would stretch to a couple in addition to a few plums, when it occurred to her that she hadn't seen the Austrian couple recently. This pair of middle-aged women were memorable because they were always together, and because of their distinctive appearance. The elegant taller one wore a mannish hat on her short greying hair, a boiled wool skirt and jacket, whereas her companion was petite and darkly mercurial. Kitty had been used to seeing them most mornings. Occasionally they would stop to admire Fay. It was the man next door, Monsieur Klein, who told her they were Austrian, for he knew them from the library. For a week or two after they had disappeared she looked for them and worried, but even Monsieur Klein didn't know where they lived and she had no idea how to find out what had happened to them.

She saw quite a bit of Milly and Jack, and of a young Frenchwoman who looked after a little girl named Joséphine, the same age as Fay, whom she first met one afternoon at the park near the apartment. This young woman's name was Lili Lambert, and Kitty liked her the instant she set eyes on her, sitting on a bench feeding crumbs to the sparrows, the round-eyed child on her lap pointing at the birds and squealing with delight. Lili was a couple of years older than Kitty and rather like a sparrow herself – being small-boned, with a pert, pointed face and quick black eyes. She was alone in Paris, her husband Jean-Pierre having been called up to the front, as she told

Kitty early in their friendship. He had been taken prisoner by the Germans during the last days of May and despatched to Germany. She'd heard from the Red Cross that he had been sent to work in an arms factory on the Ruhr. Recently she had received a letter from him. She took it out of her bag now. It had been folded and refolded many times. Lili did not offer to read it to Kitty, nor did Kitty ask. But Lili held it tightly as though it were a talisman that connected her to Jean-Pierre.

'All I can do is wait,' she told Kitty. 'Wait and hope that the war will end soon and that Jean-Pierre will come home safely. Meantime at least I have work and somewhere pleasant to live.' The child, Joséphine, belonged to a French business couple, and Lili had moved in with them to save paying rent on the rooms she'd shared with Jean-Pierre. Kitty took to coming to the park when she could if the afternoon was fine, and quite often she'd meet Lili. They mostly spoke about the children and their own upbringings – Lili's family lived near Nice – but they had another interest in common, which was music. Lili had first come to Paris to try her luck as a singer and had scraped a living by it. Most of the nightclubs were closed now, and anyway, Jean-Pierre, a bank clerk, wouldn't have liked his wife to return to that kind of life, so the job she had now was better, she told Kitty. Still, Kitty enjoyed hearing her stories about the rackety life of the clubs and Lili even taught her a song or two. She had a light, expressive voice and rolled her Rs as she sang. Despite her troubles Lili was by nature a cheerful girl and their times together were full of laughter whilst the babies crawled on the grass if it was dry or slept in their prams in the autumn sunshine.

One afternoon, two Wehrmacht soldiers came into the park, taking the air maybe, or keeping an eye out for signs of trouble, and the women fell silent as the men passed, averting their eyes until they'd gone. Her fear of them accompanied Kitty all the way home, and when she carried a sleeping Fay out of the lift she felt that terror still. She jumped therefore when a door opened and Monsieur Klein came out, several books under his arm. He caught her alarm.

'Oh, it's only you, madame, I'm sorry,' he said, picking up a book he'd dropped. 'One can't be sure these days ...' He trailed off.

'Are you all right, monsieur?' she asked him and when he said he was, she asked politely whether he was going to the library.

'Not exactly,' he said, and paused. 'When I visited last week they told me they had no record of my name and that I wasn't to come any more.'

Kitty studied him with surprise. 'But you go there every day! How can they say that?'

'I don't know. It was the usual woman on the desk, but she wouldn't even look at me. However ...' His expression brightened. 'I have a good friend who will borrow books on my behalf. I am returning these to him now. Good day.' He touched the black hat he always wore as he passed by and entered the lift.

'That's how it is for Jews all the time now, Kitty,' Eugene explained to her that evening when she recounted the conversation.

'I didn't know Monsieur Klein was Jewish,' she said, surprised. 'He doesn't look it. How do they find out?'

'It could be in the records somewhere or maybe it's just his name.' He sighed. 'Or more likely, somebody dropped a word in an official ear. It's happening all around us now.'

'But he's a harmless old man, Gene, anyone can see that.'

'Perhaps the lady at the library took a dislike to him. These days there doesn't have to be a reason.'

'It's so unfair. I know, nothing's fair any more. But it's not enough now to keep one's head down and try not to cause any trouble.'

'It's still the safest way,' he pointed out, coming to put his arm round her. He looked down at her with concern. 'It's important that you behave very carefully. Think about Fay.'

'Fay and I will be all right,' she said. Nothing would happen to them, she told herself. The soldiers strolling through the park today had touched their caps politely to Lili and Kitty and smiled at the children. They were far from the raping, pillaging vandals that everyone had feared. Not that this stopped Kitty from hating them.

Eugene was having a rare night off. He looked scruffy and exhausted, she thought, noticing the furrows that had appeared on his brow.

'They expect too much of you,' she told him.

'It's hard doing our work properly when our every step is observed.'

She knew that the pressures at the hospital were considerable. Although the Germans had to respect the work of the institution, they monitored its activities carefully, especially in respect of any Allied servicemen who were treated there. These patients were supposed to be transferred into German hands once they were better, but she knew that this wasn't always the case. Back in July she'd asked after the injured Welshman she'd seen Eugene with on the day she and Fay had returned to Paris and gone to find him at the hospital.

'According to official records, he died,' was all that Gene would tell her, and when she asked him if that was really what had happened, he replied, 'Don't ask me any more. It's better that you don't know. Too many people's safety depends on it.'

'I'm worried about you, Gene,' she said now. 'You need looking after.'

He hadn't visited a barber for some time, so after supper she made him sit on a kitchen chair while she cut his hair. She worked carefully, feeling the warmth of his head beneath her hands and loving the familiar oily fragrance of his hair as she snipped until the floor around was covered in small bright curls. 'There you are, my shorn lamb,' she said finally, handing him a mirror.

'Wonderful,' he said, beaming at his reflection. 'I would have had to pay the barber.'

'A tip would be acceptable,' Kitty said, trimming one last stray lock. She put down comb and scissors, and as she lifted the towel from his shoulders, he caught her hands and swung her round so that she landed in his lap, laughing. He rubbed his nose against hers and kissed it.

'How much are you asking?'

'Only everything,' was her reply.

'Already yours,' he said simply and with such heart she felt the truth of it. She had his love, had borne his child and they would endure this together. So many were worse off than they were, she thought as he kissed her again, this time long and deeply. But she still worried about him.

'Oh, Gene,' she whispered when they broke apart. 'I don't know what you're involved in at the hospital, but take care, my love, won't you? Take care.'

Kitty came to sense more strongly the fear that pervaded the city when she visited Jack and Milly. The couple lived in rooms in a shambolic building above shops in a street leading off the Boulevard St-Germain. They'd decorated the place themselves and furnished it with interesting odds and ends that they'd collected over the five years or so they'd been together in Paris. No one could call the result fashionable, but it suited the sort of people they were. Since they both worked from home, two desks took up one wall of the living room where they'd sit together, the room hazy with smoke, Jack quietly writing in a foolscap notebook and Milly bashing away on a typewriter, stopping occasionally to curse and vigorously rub at some error or snatch up the ringing phone and speak loudly into it. How Jack put up with this disturbance, Kitty never knew, for he was always complaining about the lack of peace and quiet, then they'd argue and Milly would fly off the handle and tell him to go someplace else if he didn't like it. Recently it had become common for Kitty to catch sight of him in the café on the corner of the street, his hat pushed back on his head, his notebook and a cup of coffee on the table in front of him as he smoked and watched the world from the window.

One afternoon at the end of September when Kitty called by it was to find Milly and Jack in a gloomy mood, having received the news that the office of an underground newspaper Milly had started writing for had been raided and the publisher, a close friend of theirs, taken into custody.

'Do they know about you?' she asked Milly anxiously.

Milly made an impatient noise. She was like a caged animal today, pacing the room, smoking and brooding, whilst Kitty watched and Fay stood by Jack's chair, pulling at his jacket, puzzled that he didn't want to play swinging games with her today.

'She published under a pen name, thank God,' Jack put in. 'Unless they get her real name out of La Tour,' he added glumly.

'He won't tell 'em anything he doesn't have to,' Milly said, squashing her cigarette into an already overloaded ashtray. She paused for a second, as the implication of what she'd said struck home with all of them. Suppose he had no choice about talking. 'Oh, the poor, poor man,' she burst out. 'Do you think—'

'He's gotten the best legal help, Milly,' Jack broke in. 'La Tour's attorney is married to a German girl. It's proved useful recently.'

'It might not work this time,' Milly muttered, picking at a nail. 'Not after he printed that cartoon of von Stülpnagel. I can't bear it. There must be something we can do to help.'

'Well, there isn't, Milly.' Jack handed Fay back to her mother and went to put his arms round his girlfriend. She looked up him and smiled sadly. 'It's no good, sweetheart,' Jack said. 'You'll put yourself in danger and I can't live without you.' He stood with his arms tight around her, swaying to soothe her.

'Oh, Jack,' Milly mumbled in a strange, hiccuping voice.

Kitty was shocked. She'd never seen Milly cry before, but now Milly was weeping freely, with great hoarse sobs that wrenched at Kitty's heart.

She could think of nothing to say. It was a glimpse into a world she knew little about and didn't want to know. She almost wished she hadn't come today, but they were her friends; she cared about them. 'Stay safe,' her husband had told her, but it wasn't that easy.

The publisher La Tour remained in prison for two weeks, then was suddenly and miraculously released. When Kitty next visited, Milly was jubilant, but explained that there was no point in him even trying to resume his underground activities. All his printing equipment had been seized and he was aware of being watched. None of this would stop Milly from writing, but how would anyone read what she wrote?

There was so much to write about as the forces of Occupation tightened their grip. In September, Jews, Africans and Algerians who had originally fled the city were barred from returning to their homes, and their property was confiscated. The Knoxes awoke one day to find that the shutters of the Jewish jeweller opposite had been daubed with obscenities during the night. Eugene would come home from the hospital with stories of German interference in the operations of the American Volunteer Ambulance Corps who tended to the wounded of any nationality. By the end of September, the Corps had been forced out of service.

Chapter 19

The winter of 1940–41 was the cruellest Kitty had ever known. The new year brought heavy snow that turned to ice, making it treacherous to go out. Every day was a remorseless struggle to find food, for the weather brought the fragile supply chains to a standstill and even vegetables were scarce for they could not be dug out of the frozen ground. The sign *Nothing left to sell* was a not unusual sight to see in shop windows by midday.

A rare bright spot was a parcel sent for Christmas by Gene's mother in America, but which didn't reach them until January. An excited Kitty unwrapped chocolate, tins of meat and packets of dried fruit with wonder, her stomach growling with hunger at the thought of eating these treats. There were baby clothes for Fay, too, which were beautiful, but sadly too small, so she gave them to a woman with a baby girl downstairs, who received them with amazed delight. Kitty and Gene gave some chocolate to Monsieur Zipper, and invited Jack and Milly round for a feast, so all too quickly everything was gone.

One freezing morning when she braved the weather to shop, it was to find the bread at the baker's stale and a tired grey colour, and the only vegetables on the market stall were rotting turnips, presumably scavenged leftovers from a previous season. Worse, there was no milk to be found anywhere, and Kitty was panic-stricken about what to give Fay. She was overwhelmed with gratitude therefore, when later that morning she answered a tap at the door to find waiting outside the tall square figure of Adele Dunne, the Englishwoman she'd met at the convent. Miss Dunne was enveloped in a coat that looked as if it had been made out of an army blanket and a floppy felt hat with snow dripping off it.

'Surprise!' She held out two tins of condensed milk in her gloved hands, smiling like a naughty schoolgirl.

'Adele, you lifesaver. We're desperate!' Kitty cried, taking them from her and ushering her inside.

'I do hope I'm not intruding. The tins were a personal gift to me from a friend, and I immediately thought them a good excuse to see how you were in this dreadful weather.' Miss Dunne's comforting English tones brought to mind school pinafores and cycling on winding country lanes. Never had Kitty been so glad to see her.

'We're down to our last tin,' she told Miss Dunne. 'It's simply impossible to find any in the shops. Look, Fay – milk.'

Fay toddled across and clutched at her mother's skirt. The child was swathed in jumpers and her face was tired and pinched. She withdrew her thumb from her mouth and stared up at this strangely dressed figure with curiosity.

'Hello, Fay, dear, I don't expect you'll remember me. My, you are growing up fast.' Adele Dunne smiled down at the child as she unpinned her hat, then extricated herself from her coat and soaked brogues. Fay stared with solemn eyes at the woman's much-darned stockings. Miss

Dunne sank onto the sofa with a sigh of relief. She looked reassuringly the same as ever, Kitty thought. Perhaps her broad face was a little worn, but her cheeks were rosy from the cold air and her eyes were bright and interested.

Kitty fetched a towel for Miss Dunne's wet feet and made what passed for tea, using a little precious milk. The apartment was freezing, but there was nothing to be done about that. Fuel had to be saved for the evenings when the temperature plummeted.

'What's your news? I expect you're kept very busy,' Kitty said, settling Fay in her lap with a cup of the watered-down milk. The little girl drank it down, her wide eyes fixed dreamily on the visitor.

'Oh yes, we're certainly that. There are so many who need help.' Miss Dunne talked of the church where she worked, which tried to aid any who came within its doors regardless of religion or race. The tide of refugees flowing into the city had dribbled to a halt with the Occupation, but there were plenty already here who needed help: families from Belgium, French-speakers expelled from their homes in Alsace-Lorraine, children who'd lost parents, parents who'd lost children, widows too old or ill or poor to join the daily scavenge for food.

'The Red Cross do their best,' she explained, 'but the rules are so pettifogging. Why can't the Germans make up their minds?' She complained about having to trek every day to report to the authorities. 'Such a waste of everyone's time. They know full well where I am and what I'm doing.'

More serious were the games the Nazis played with rations. 'One moment we're allowed extra for our nursing mothers, the next we're not.' Then there was the constant harassment. 'Last week they threatened to close us down completely. Harbouring enemy aliens, they said. Enemy aliens my foot, I told them! They're frightened, half-starved wretches.' Now Miss Dunne had started to talk, she couldn't stop. It was as though she needed to unburden herself. 'Last week, half a dozen Gestapo arrived out of the ether. They turned everything upside down, searching for goodness knows what. The place was in uproar. Anyone without the right papers they simply bundled into a van, including a mother with a young baby, Kitty – and there was nothing we could do to stop them.' Miss Dunne's face was a picture of distress. 'And it's so difficult to find out what happens to people.' It wasn't just this woman who had vanished, either. 'Someone might turn up every day for a while then simply disappear. We do our best to make enquiries. Sometimes I can't bear to find out. Such stories, such awful stories ...' She drifted to a halt and sipped gratefully at her tea. 'Oh, it is nice to see you, dear.'

'Are you still living at the convent?' Kitty asked, cradling the now sleeping child. She knew from visiting the nuns in August that Miss Dunne had moved back there. The French family she'd been lodging with before had needed to make room for some elderly relatives and regretfully turned her out.

'Such good people, the nuns. They didn't want payment except for food, you know,' she told Kitty, 'but I insisted. That poor Belgian girl Marthe can't pay a thing.' The refugee family was still in residence, the mother doing her bit by helping Sister Thérèse with the cooking and cleaning. The children attended the church school. 'There's quite a ragbag of other people, too,' she said, 'but we all muddle along. Mère Marie-François has been in bed with bronchitis. All those hours spent kneeling in that cold church, if you ask me.' Miss Dunne's attitude to religion was brisk and practical. 'She's past the worst now though.'

Kitty was concerned. 'I must visit again soon. I never seem to have time, though if you asked me, I couldn't say what I've been busy doing. This morning I queued at the butcher, then again at the baker's and came back with almost nothing. If something needs fixing I end up asking a neighbour or doing it myself as Eugene's often not here, though it's been easier since they've relaxed the curfew, and when he is at home the poor man's too tired to deal with broken saucepan handles.'

'Everybody's exhausted,' Miss Dunne sighed, rubbing her feet with the towel. 'Simply finding the strength to stay alive is tiring.'

'Gene's worried that the Germans intend to close the hospital, which would be dreadful. Not that he tells me much. I think he wants to protect me, but I don't need protecting. I'd rather know things. Then I can prepare.'

Miss Dunne regarded Kitty with a sympathetic expression. 'It must be hard for you, dear.' She nodded towards the piano. 'Do you ever play now? I suppose you don't have time.'

'Not often, no.' All that belonged to another life, a life that was closed to her now. She thought longingly sometimes of her lessons with Monsieur Deschamps. She'd visited his apartment before Christmas, wondering if he'd returned, thinking perhaps foolishly that she could at least have the occasional lesson with him, but there had been no answer when she knocked. No one was at home next door either, so she'd been unable to find out if he was back.

Serge might know, but she hadn't seen him for some while. She must write to him at the Conservatoire. Something else she hadn't had time to do.

'I saw that dark-haired young man from your wedding,' Miss Dunne said suddenly, as though she could read Kitty's thoughts. 'The boy pianist. Just by accident, in the street.'

'Serge, you mean? Did you speak to him?' Kitty asked, immediately interested. 'How was he?'

'I tried to speak to him, but he behaved very oddly. At first I thought that he hadn't recognized me. After all, we had only met on that one occasion, but then I realized he did know me but didn't want to be seen with me. He kept glancing about anxiously so I took pity on him and walked on.'

'I hope he's not in any kind of trouble,' Kitty said, frowning.

'That's what I wondered,' Miss Dunne said. 'He had just come out of a rather grand-looking apartment block in the Faubourg St-Honoré. Near that big hotel the Germans have turned into offices – perhaps you know it? I expect it was being near that which made him nervous.'

Speaking to an Englishwoman with the Gestapo about would be seen as dangerous. Kitty thought Miss Dunne was right, that must be the reason.

That evening she wrote a note to Serge, asking if he'd heard from Monsieur Deschamps, and suggesting that they meet. She sent it to the Conservatoire but received no answer, which was worrying. Perhaps Serge was in difficulties of some sort.

One darkening February afternoon, Kitty and Fay returned home from meeting Lili and Joséphine, but when she eased her key into the lock she was surprised when the door opened a few inches and through the gap she saw Eugene place a finger to his lips.

'Papa'!' Fay cried and stretched her arms towards her father. 'Papa!'

'Come in quickly.' He took hold of Fay and pulled Kitty inside. She was surprised to find the apartment unlit. By a glimmer of light from the window she saw someone rising, with some difficulty, from the chair by the piano. It was the tall, spare figure of a man.

'I must apologize for interrupting—' the stranger started to say. It was an educated English voice with a soft burr. Then Eugene cut in.

'Kitty, may I introduce Flight Lieutenant John Stone. John, my wife Kitty and our daughter Fay.' A British RAF officer! There was something in Eugene's voice that warned Kitty not to react. The air had a dangerous taste of metal, like on an icy day.

'Flight Lieutenant.' Kitty could hardly see the man's face, but she shook the outstretched hand and found it reassuring in its warmth and firmness.

'Please call me John,' he said. 'I'm very sorry to intrude on you like this.'

'No more apologizing, please, John,' Eugene said. 'It is I who should be sorry. Kitty, John may have to rest up here a couple days. I know I should have asked you first, but there wasn't the chance.'

'I see,' she said, slowly unbuttoning her coat. To avoid thinking about her fear, she started to worry what she could give John Stone for supper. There were two gristly chops waiting in the kitchen, the only meat she'd been able to buy for some days. Perhaps she could eke them out with the last of the bacon fat. At least there was a tin of beans left, and ...

'Where will he sleep?' she asked.

'On the couch, do you reckon?' Eugene said. He was cuddling Fay close, but he laid his free hand on Kitty's shoulder to comfort her. 'It'll be fine. Our plan went wrong, that's all. The place he was supposed to go to didn't work out.'

'I'm sure I won't be here long,' Stone added.

Kitty nodded. What plan? What place? She was hardly able to think straight. To hide her troubled feelings she went to draw the blackout curtains across the windows. When she switched on the table lamp and saw their visitor in its weak light she gave a sharp intake of breath. The man must once have been handsome in a fair-haired, sturdy English fashion, but now the left side of his face and neck was livid, the skin puckered and the eyelid drooping. He returned her searching gaze though, without flinching.

'Apologies for my appearance, but I assure you it looks worse than it is.' His voice was gentle. 'I didn't bale out quickly enough – thought I could save the plane. Stupid, really.'

'When?' she managed to ask.

'Six weeks ago. We were on a bombing raid over Normandy. An old farmer who'd seen our plane catch fire came out searching for us. He and his wife picked me out of a hedge, carried me home somehow and sent for a local doctor, who patched me up the best he could before handing me over to these chaps.' He indicated Eugene.

'How did he get to you?' Kitty asked her husband. It was so bewildering.

'It's best you don't know,' Eugene said. 'He reached us, that's the important thing. But now he's better we were trying to get him home.'

Kitty sat down on the sofa, her mind finally beginning to work. Had Mme Legrand on the desk downstairs seen Stone? There was no thinking what might happen to them all if he were discovered. How could Gene do this to them? Did he not think of little Fay? Fay, in danger. The thought was too much

'Well,' she said, getting up. To her horror she was trembling. 'I'd better see what there is for supper.' And she fled to the kitchen.

It was there Eugene found her a moment later staring down unseeing at the plate of bloody chops. He put his arms round her and held her close. She looked up at him blankly, unsure whether to berate him or weep.

'I'm real sorry,' he murmured. 'I think you know how I'm involved. There's a few of us at the hospital, I won't tell you their names, but we don't like to hand these guys over to the Germans, so when they're well enough we try to get them out. It was my task today to take John to a safe house in Montparnasse, but when we arrived we found someone had gotten there ahead of us. The lock was bust and we daren't risk going in. I couldn't think what else to do with him except come here. No one saw us, Kitty, I'd swear on it. Even Madame Legrand wasn't at her desk.'

'You can't be certain you weren't seen,' she said. 'Gene, it's not me I'm worried about, it's Fay.' In all honesty she was frightened for all of them.

Now she was getting used to what had happened, part of her was proud of her husband. She felt a kind of relief, too, that Gene had explained things better. So much made sense now. Gene's preoccupied manner, the continual feeling he was hiding something from her. She had known about the young Welshman but hadn't realized that he was helping other Allied servicemen, too.

'For God's sake keep all this quiet, Kitty.'

'You don't need to say that. I'm not stupid.'

'I didn't mean that.' He gave a weak smile. 'I don't know why I said it. Now I'd better go rescue Stone from Fay. She seems to have taken a shine to his shoelaces. He's a great guy, you know. He won't be any trouble.'

Just then came a pattering of small feet and a cry of 'Mama!' and Fay ran into the kitchen, her arms held out. Kitty swung her up, held her close and kissed her, taking comfort in her sweet-sour infant smell. She closed her eyes and for a moment knew an intense joy. Here were the people she loved most in the world, her husband and her child. *Let no one try to take them from me*, she sent out a silent pleading.

Flight Lieutenant Stone hid in their apartment for two nights. Once, Kitty awoke, hearing him shout out something in English, and for a minute or two lay rigid with anxiety, thinking someone had broken in. Then she realized that he was simply dreaming. She hoped no one else in the building had heard him.

In the daytime Gene went to work as usual, so Kitty was left with Stone, and the unenviable task of stretching the rations to feed the extra mouth. When she went outside she was more wary than usual. Once, in the newsagent where she was buying some envelopes, a German officer came in for cigarettes. Fay, trotting off across the shop, bumped into him, bounced back and sat

down squarely on her bottom, looking up at him in astonishment. Full of apologies, Kitty rushed across, but the
man only laughed. 'Careful, *Liebchen*,' he said. He bent and
took Fay up into his arms, his expression tender.

The little girl turned rigid with fear, and sensing this,
the man hastily handed her back to Kitty.

He touched his cap. 'I have a daughter like her,' he said
in heavily accented English and Kitty realized that she'd
somehow given her nationality away. She tensed, waiting
for him to ask for her papers, but he merely nodded cour-
teously, paid for his cigarettes and left.

'Madame!' the woman behind the counter called to her
as she went out, and she remembered she'd not paid for
the envelopes. She fumbled with her purse and dropped
coins that clinked and danced across the counter.

She came to like John Stone very much in the short time
he was with them. He was thirty-one, an experienced
pilot who'd flown many missions without mishap before
this one. His co-pilot, she learned, had not survived the
parachute drop and Stone could not speak of him without
distress, so Kitty avoided the subject. It was easier not to
talk of the war at all, she found, so they spoke of more
cheerful things, of places they both knew in Hampshire.
Stone was a director of the family's shipping line, running
cruise ships out of Southampton. He loved ships and the
sea, but the war had cut business dead and the vessels
had been commandeered for troop transport. He'd
always wanted to fly, so he'd chosen the RAF above the
Navy, and Kitty sensed that he fed off the danger of the
bombing raids. He'd been frustrated by the long weeks in
hospital, and now he was restless, keen to start the

perilous journey home to England and to get back in the
air.

In private Kitty wondered whether he'd be allowed to
fly again. His eye, miraculously, was undamaged, but he
didn't hear her sometimes when she spoke and his left
arm would twitch involuntarily.

Despite her affection for him, she was glad when he
was gone. It happened one midnight. Eugene went ahead
down the stairs to see if the way was clear. Kitty thrust a
packet of food into Stone's hand, as he whispered farewell.

'Has he far to go tonight?' she asked Gene when he
returned.

'No,' was all Gene told her. 'And it's no good asking me
what next. I haven't been told.' *The less we know, the less we
can tell*. That was the unspoken message. But she could
hear the relief in his voice. She was glad that they'd helped
Stone. She asked Gene to find out whether he'd made it
home, but time passed and there was no news. All she
could do was to carry him in her thoughts. She remembered how Mère Marie-François always said that this was
a kind of prayer.

There were plenty of other people to worry about. One
rainy February lunchtime, when Kitty returned home
from shopping, she found Sister Thérèse waiting for her in
the foyer. The concierge must have felt honoured to have
a nun visiting, for she had found her a chair, and by the
clattering sounds from her room had gone to fetch her
refreshment. All this was quite unlike her usual peremp-
tory behaviour.

'Oh, Kitty, *Dieu merci*,' Sister Thérèse said, rising to her
feet with an air of distress. 'I came at once. It's
Mademoiselle Dunne. She's been taken.'

'Taken, where?'

It seemed that two French policemen had arrived at the convent at breakfast-time that morning, asking to see Miss Dunne. They were respectful and ill-at-ease, apologizing profusely to Mère Marie-François for disturbing the community. When Miss Dunne came to the door, the policemen told her to pack a few things and to accompany them to the local police station. She protested and assured them that her papers were in order, but they quietly insisted. Thérèse had gone up to help her pack.

'We didn't know what was happening,' the nun said. '"Don't worry," Miss Dunne told me, "I'm sure it's a misunderstanding," but she hasn't come back, Kitty, and we do not know what to do. Père Paul went down to the police station to find out, but so many other people were waiting there with the same questions and the police would tell him nothing useful, so he came home. The Reverend Mother thought you should hear of it at once and that maybe Monsieur Knox could discover what is going on.'

'I will telephone him right away,' Kitty said, as the concierge came out of her room bearing a glass of water and a small round bun on a plate for Thérèse. 'Perhaps someone at the Embassy can find out.' The concierge put through the call to the hospital and to her surprise Kitty was able to speak to Gene almost immediately. He promised to do his best. By this time Fay was becoming fretful, hungry for her lunch, so Kitty invited Thérèse upstairs, but she declined.

'My thanks to both of you,' she said, returning her plate and glass to the concierge, 'but I must hurry to Mademoiselle Dunne's place of work. They'll be wondering why she hasn't arrived this morning.'

'You don't want me to go?' Kitty asked, seeing how upset Thérèse was, but the girl insisted that she would be all right.

Gene arrived back that evening with bad news. His contact at the US Embassy hadn't needed to make enquiries as the networks were abuzz with the news. It appeared that dozens of foreign nationals, predominantly British women, had been rounded up that day. No one knew as yet what was being done with them.

'You don't think they'll come for me, Gene?' Kitty thought to ask. Gene didn't think they would because as his wife she was protected by his American citizenship.

Two weeks of worrying passed, during which Gene and Kitty heard conflicting rumours. Finally a postcard arrived from Adele. It gave little information, but Kitty rejoiced in the mere fact of it: *Perfectly safe and in good health*, it said. *Don't worry about me, but please write*. Across the message in heavy black type was stamped the name: *Frontstalag 142*. As Kitty remarked, Adele's bland message amounted to no information at all, but it was reassuring all the same. Frontstalag 142 was an internment camp not, to Kitty and Gene's relief, in Germany but near a French town called Besançon, which Kitty later found on a map to be near the Jura Mountains, close to the border with Switzerland.

Gene passed her back the card, thoughtfully. 'At least we know where she is and that she's alive,' he said.

'But it's not fair that she should be locked up, Gene. She's a harmless middle-aged lady, who was merely being useful.'

'To Germany she's an enemy alien and there is no doubt where her loyalties lie, Kitty. Try not to worry too much, there's no reason for them to ill-treat her.' But he did not smile and there was something uncertain in his tone.

Kitty visited the convent with the news and the nuns were glad to hear that their dear Mademoiselle Dunne was safe. She helped Thérèse pack up a few more of Adele's clothes to send to the camp. Under her bed Kitty found several of the woman's sketchbooks. She turned the pages to examine the array of arresting portraits of the refugees whom Miss Dunne had helped, faces etched with pain or sorrow or bewilderment, moving and powerful. One of the pads was new, and Kitty slipped it in amongst the clothes for posting, along with some pencils she discovered in a drawer. The rest of Adele's things the nuns promised to look after for her. It was all anybody could do.

It was several weeks before a note of thanks for the clothes arrived, though the sketchbook and pencils were not mentioned. Some time after that, a cheerful postcard came to say that the internees had been moved to better premises at Vittel, some miles further north, and that conditions were very good there. But after that, for a long while, there was no news at all.

Nathalie Ramond had been speaking for some time but now her soft voice fell silent, and she leaned back in her chair, her eyes closed. From the way she massaged her gnarled hands, Fay sensed the woman was in some pain.

'I'm sorry,' she said then, her eyes fluttering open. 'I have somehow lost my thread.'

'You were telling me about Miss Dunne,' Fay prompted. 'I knew her when I was a child. I had no idea that she'd been through so much.' Fay recalled her as a benevolent aunt-like figure in old-fashioned tweeds and had never given a thought to what lay behind the appearance. The story was astonishing.

'You know Miss Dunne?' Mme Ramond's face lit up.

'She lived near us in Norfolk. I'm afraid she died when I was nine or ten.'

Mme Ramond looked sad. 'Ah, but I should have liked to have met her again. You know, the war would not have been won without the Miss Dunnes. I don't mean the fighting with tanks and bombs, but the war of hearts and minds. She had a natural instinct for what was right and good, and always lived by it. For most of us life is more confusing and sometimes we mistake the way.'

The bitterness in Mme Ramond's tone both puzzled and alarmed Fay. Not for the first time, she perceived that some unimaginable darkness swirled beneath the woman's narrative. Was it the same darkness that lay behind her mother's distress? The worst was yet to come in this story, she knew, but she had to find out what it was.

'Shall I continue?' Now Mme Ramond was studying her with an expression of great tenderness, and the tenderness gave Fay hope.

'Yes, of course,' she said.

'It's difficult to decide where to start next ... but ah, I think I see.'

Chapter 20

1941

The winter snows melted in the pale spring sunshine, but life in Paris grew even harder. Rations remained strict and it wasn't always possible to buy fresh vegetables, meat or milk. Kitty worried each night over what to feed the family the following day. Once or twice they were blessed by donations from Gene's wealthy American patients or ate meagre meals in cafés or restaurants. They were luckier than most. But it wasn't just the food, it was the growing sense of threat. From what they heard on the BBC, and news circulated by their Embassy, Paris's American community grew more certain that their country would be brought into the war. America was helping Britain in all the ways a non-combatant could, sending supplies and even surplus American destroyers. In response, a German U-boat sank an American merchant ship off Brazil, and the US Embassy in Paris was pressurized by the Nazi authorities into closing, though for a long time it resisted, determined to serve those American citizens who remained in Paris in the face of all advice to leave.

Now, if challenged for her papers by a German soldier,

Kitty heard the words 'Your husband is American,' pronounced with an icy politeness. The message was clear. Americans were no longer welcome in Paris.

'I've been trying to talk Milly into going home,' Jack said gloomily one evening, when they all met in a restaurant in a back street near Kitty and Gene's apartment. Kitty's friend Lili, nanny of little Joséphine, had come to babysit Fay whilst Joséphine's family were away for a few days. 'There's nothing for us here. We should have gone months ago.'

'So many of our friends have left,' Milly sighed. 'There's you two, of course, and Miss Beach at the bookshop – she'll never go, insists Paris is home. And it's more and more difficult getting anything I write published.' Since the La Tour affair, Milly had become a person of interest to the authorities. Once or twice she'd been summoned to a police station to have her papers checked, and recently, she'd been interviewed by a Gestapo officer concerning her purpose in Paris. He'd asked her repeatedly whether she knew the identity of 'Odette', the pen name under which she'd published several articles for La Tour. In these circumstances it would have been foolish to do anything further to draw attention to herself. 'I feel like a prisoner here,' she had confessed to Kitty a few days after that incident. She had sounded bitterly unhappy.

'I think Jack's right, you should leave,' Kitty said. 'But oh, we shall miss you both so much.'

There was one small element of happiness. 'We've decided to get married. Jack says it'll be easier for us when we travel. That doesn't sound very romantic, does it, but I couldn't bear to be separated from him so I guess that means it's the right thing to do.'

This was the closest Milly would ever get to telling Kitty how much she loved Jack, though it was blindingly apparent to any that knew them. Their recent troubles seemed to have brought them closer. Milly was no longer the outspoken young woman who'd arrived in Paris six years ago and won Jack's heart. She hardly took risks now. She'd become more careful and, Kitty thought, more caring. Life here was no longer full of colour and laughter. Instead it was monotone and full of shadow, but this made the underlying bones of people's characters stand out, and she saw that Milly's was strong and true.

It was different for Kitty, having a child. Although she felt desperately worried about her future, Fay also helped her take pleasure in the world. With the spring came the swallows darting in the air beyond their window, the blossom hung as thick and heavy as always on the trees, and a gentle sun warmed their faces as they walked in the park with Lili and Joséphine. Kitty shared her little daughter's delight and wonder at these things. Fay helped her live for the moment.

It was a fine Wednesday morning in early April that Eugene and Kitty witnessed Jack and Milly's quiet wedding ceremony in the American Cathedral. The Knoxes were practically the only guests, for by now nearly all their other friends had decamped. A week later, Kitty and Fay went to wave them off at the Gare d'Orléans on the first leg of a long and arduous train journey that would take them across the Spanish border and on to Lisbon, where they'd managed to book berths on a ship for New York. For Kitty their departure was one of the saddest moments of the war so far. She'd never imagined that Milly would leave Paris. For Milly it was accepting defeat – and she had never done this in her life before.

During April, Gene came home with anxious reports about the future of the hospital. The question was whether it should remain under American management, given that the United States was likely to be brought into the war. Eventually, it was decided to deliver it into the control of the French Red Cross, and this happy arrangement left Gene and his colleagues much relieved, for its work could continue as before. Everywhere in Paris, Americans were in retreat. At the beginning of May, the US Embassy finally closed. Americans still had the hospital, their own library, churches and charities to assist them. But apart from that, they were on their own in Occupied Paris. If their country went to war with Germany, there would be no one to protect them.

'Madame Knox!'

She heard the man's voice as she was wheeling Fay past the Métro station near the Quai d'Orsay one June afternoon. She'd been walking by the river simply to get out of the flat. There was something about the river that comforted her, the way it continued to flow, the same as ever, as the city changed around it. The man was climbing the steps from the station and at first she didn't recognize him. Then she saw it was her former piano teacher.

'Monsieur Deschamps!' She waited for his approach, thinking him less spry than when she saw him last. He kissed her soundly on both cheeks and smiled at Fay, who was sitting in her pram, staring back at him with her serious expression. 'I'm so glad to see you, m'sieur. I had no idea you were back in Paris.'

'I suppose I should have written to advise you,' he sighed. 'I returned some months ago, but I'm afraid I have been doing very little teaching. I have been ill, you see.'

He wore a greyish look, she thought. He had always been on the thin side, but now his clothes hung off him and something of his old vigour was gone. She saw him glance away to where a pair of German soldiers loitered on duty outside the railway station, chatting to one another as they kept a casual eye on the crowds that passed in and out. The fellows were too far away to hear their conversation, but still, their presence put her on her guard.

Monsieur Deschamps must have felt the same because he said, 'I'm on my way home now. Perhaps you'd like to come back with me? I can at least give you some music to practise – if you still have time to play, that is.'

'Thank you. I try to make time, but it isn't easy with this little one.' Kitty smiled at Fay, who gave her a gap-toothed grin and began to suck at the wooden zebra the man next door had given her, for she was teething. Kitty gently eased the animal from her, and when she creased her face to protest, pushed a rattle into her hands to distract her.

Monsieur Deschamps' flat was the same as it had always been, except messier, and it was a bony, sallow-faced woman with a dead expression in her eyes who brought Kitty a glass of water instead of the lively little maid of before, of whom there was no sign. The mess was caused by dusty cardboard boxes that lay piled against the bookcases, some split open with the contents spilling out. Kitty had to grab the toddler, who had made a beeline for them and started pulling out sheet music, creased and yellowed with age. A violin case that hadn't been there before lay under the piano.

'All this belongs to a colleague who's been interned,' Monsieur Deschamps explained. 'A fine player, very fine, but the brutes who took him left his apartment in a terrible state. Since Germany invaded Russia they'll imprison anyone they suspect to be a Communist. Communist, pah. It's a crime now to have a Russian name. His neighbour contacted me after it happened. I'll keep everything safe for when he returns.' The last words were spoken with a false heartiness.

Kitty nodded, compassion rising in her. She was becoming used to these sad stories. They haunted her dreams, though she tried not to dwell on them, tried to distance herself. It was the only way. She'd seen something similar happen to the watchmaker and his wife who lived opposite. One late afternoon, a fortnight before, a van had drawn up outside. She'd looked down from the window to see two soldiers jump out and shoulder open the shop door, then after a moment the old couple were brought out, the man complaining and the woman wailing. She'd watched with pity as they were pushed into the back of the van, which drove off at speed. Soon afterwards, another vehicle arrived with two men in overalls who arrived to clear the shop of its contents, hammering bars across the door before they left. Now it stood empty, and passers-by threw litter in the porch. Who had denounced the couple and for what imagined crime, nobody had any idea. Nor did anyone wish to speak about it, in case they were next.

Monsieur Deschamps was sifting through the contents of a drawer in the music cabinet that stood behind the drawing-room door and muttering as he selected the scores. 'Beethoven. We have to remember there are good Germans, you know. Ah, and here is my old friend Ravel –

how I miss him.' He pushed shut the drawers and took the music over to the piano, where he sat and spread open the Beethoven score – a Sonata Kitty didn't recognize – on the music-rest and began to play.

Kitty sat on a chair beside him, Fay in her arms, and once more allowed the surge of the music to fill her. Her teacher played with his old strength, and the heights and dips of the harmonies released something in her that had been stopped up by the fear and stress of the last months. Sometimes his playing stumbled or slowed as he turned a page, and sometimes she saw his eyes were closed, the emotion naked on his face as he played from memory. How was it that the composer knew such a language of feeling that through Monsieur Deschamps' playing communicated to her what being human was all about? When the movement came to an end, they were quiet for a moment.

'That was beautiful,' Kitty whispered. 'Beautiful. Thank you.'

'Beethoven says the things we cannot put into words, no?' Monsieur Deschamps said, exactly echoing her thoughts as he closed the score and gave it to her. 'Perhaps you would play it at home, and when you feel you know it well enough, come and see me and I'll listen to you.'

She tucked the music under her arm and said, 'The Ravel – I'd love to hear you play that. Serge used to play that for you, didn't he? I heard him once. Have you had any contact with him?'

To her dismay Monsieur Deschamps rose from his stool, snatched the Ravel from the music-stand and cast it down on the piano. 'I had forgotten,' he said in a voice trembling with anger. 'We shall not play this piece, after all.'

'What's wrong?' she stammered, feeling Fay stiffen in her arms.

'When I think of all I've done to help that young man. Gone. Thrown away. It turns out he has no courage at all. He shall not come here. Ever again.'

'Why, what has he done?' she cried. 'I've truly no idea.'

'If you do not know, you do not need to,' Monsieur Deschamps snapped, pacing the room, a mixture of rage and sorrow on his lined face. 'There is nothing you can say in his defence. We shall not speak of him any more. No. He has betrayed music, betrayed his friends, and worst of all, he has betrayed France.'

'Monsieur!'

'No, not one more word.'

He was breathing audibly now, as though fighting for breath, and the greyness of his face was tinged with blue. He made his way across to a small side table from which he took up a bottle of pills, fumbled two out in his hand, and swallowed them down with water from a carafe. Kitty watched, bewildered. Whatever medication it was he'd taken worked quickly, however, for quite soon he was breathing more steadily, and his face returned to a more normal colour.

'Is there anything I can do? Shall I fetch your maid?' she asked, starting from the chair, but he shook his head.

'No, I am soon recovered,' he said, 'but tired. The doctor says I must be calm, but that's all very well. It's impossible to be calm in these terrible times.'

Kitty sat down again. Fay wriggled off her lap and tottered over to the door, where she stopped and looked back enquiringly at her mother.

'Go home,' she said.

'Yes, we ought to. Monsieur,' she said, rising, 'thank you so much for the music. I'll come and see you again soon, though please don't feel you must give me a lesson. It seems that you should look after yourself.'

'All I have is my music, Kitty,' he said, giving a weak smile. 'To teach you has always been a pleasure. I'm so glad to have met your daughter, too,' he said, winking at Fay. 'She has something of your determination, I believe.'

'She keeps me strong,' Kitty said fondly. 'I don't know where I'd be without her.'

It was the simple truth. Fay was nearly two now, and developing well, despite the erratic nature of her diet. She had grown into a quiet child, shy with others but with a strong sense of who she was. She loved to sing to herself and to play with a favourite toy, a set of wooden animals that she marched into an ark. One of the zebras had unfortunately been lost, and there had been much excitement when M'sieur Zipper, as she called him, had given her the one she clutched now. She had often looked at it longingly on his bookshelf.

Was she an over-protective mother? Kitty sometimes feared she might be, but Fay and Gene were her little all. She would do anything for them. Anything. Even give her life.

The following week, Kitty could not stop thinking about Serge. Was he in trouble? What had he done to offend his old teacher so deeply? She recalled that Miss Dunne had seen him in the Rue du Faubourg St-Honoré, and he had pretended not to know her. This might be genuine – he'd only met her once, at Kitty and Gene's wedding, but perhaps it was part of the mystery. She discussed the matter with Gene, who thought it puzzling, but showed no surprise. The normal rules of social behaviour had been suspended. Now, survival was all. For some reason she couldn't explain, she was determined to find out if Serge was all right. She wrote another note for him at the Conservatoire, urging him to be in touch, and this time she left Fay with the downstairs neighbour and delivered it herself.

She felt odd walking into the building now. It was a part of her life that was gone, but she had never meant to let it go. She'd had to leave it behind because of Fay, she told herself. There was no point being nostalgic about it. This fierce reasoning didn't prevent envy rising in her, envy for the trickle of students coming past with instruments and music cases as she waited at the desk to present the letter she'd brought. It was just at that moment that she heard her name called and turned to see Serge himself, as thin and nervy-looking as ever.

'What are you doing here?' he said in a low voice, but his face lit up with pleasure all the same.

'I wanted to see you,' she said, stuffing the letter, no longer needed, back into her bag. 'I met Monsieur Deschamps, you see.'

'Ah.' He glanced quickly about, then took her arm and steered her out across the courtyard, where their feet rang on the flagstones, then in through a far door and down a corridor until they came to an empty practice room.

'No one uses this much, it's too dark. We can speak more freely here,' he said, drawing her inside and shutting the door with the quietest of clicks. He went over to the oblong window and glanced through it as if nervous that someone could see them. She watched him, feeling troubled. It was as though he was haunted by something.

Apparently satisfied that they were alone he sat down at the elderly upright piano that gleamed in the pale patch of grey light coming from the window. 'Do you know this waltz?' he asked, and began to play a rich lilting tune from memory.

'It's Brahms, isn't it?' she guessed, coming to stand by the piano, facing him, and he nodded as he continued to play, but now in a fast and furious style that would have sent the dancers madly whirling. Halfway through the concluding phrase he stopped suddenly and lifted his hands from the keyboard.

'The German Romantics – that's all they want,' he said in a savage tone. 'No Scriabin, never Debussy or Bartok.'

She stared down at him in puzzlement. 'Who are the "they" you're talking about?'

'Don't you know?' he said in a fierce, low voice. 'I assumed you'd come to condemn me like the rest. Deschamps won't speak to me, you know. He'll cross the street if he sees me coming – the man to whom I owe so much. The man who encouraged me to go in the first place. It cuts me to the bone, Kitty.'

A glimmer of understanding. 'Are you talking about that American woman you used to play for?'

'Mrs van Haren. She's not American, though – her husband is. She's French. He has returned to the States, but she would not go. She and her husband Donald have lived separate lives for years. Everybody knows this. She likes me to play for her friends. The trouble is that some of her friends now happen to be Germans.'

And not just any Germans, either. Serge drew up a chair

for her, and as he lit a cigarette and smoked it, he spoke of his visits to the opulent apartment of Chantelle van Haren. Kitty sensed his relief that he'd found someone to confide in and she listened quietly, only interjecting occasionally to ask for some small clarification.

'You remember how grateful I was when she first invited me to play Rachmaninoff? She loves Rachmaninoff, but she never asks me to play his music for her now. He's Russian, you know, and lives in New York, and she says her new friends call him a degenerate.'

Kitty recalled Serge's wonder and excitement when he'd first described to her the spacious and elegant apartment, the grand reception room hung with blue velvet and lit by glittering chandeliers. Here he'd played on a grand piano of polished ebony for Mrs van Haren and her guests. Milly, who knew who all sorts of people were, had pointed her out in the Champs-Élysées once, a tall, slim and fashionably dressed woman with thick auburn hair, stepping out of an open-topped car.

'She was very good to me,' Serge went on. 'I think the truth is, she was sometimes lonely – though you wouldn't have thought it. But her husband was often away or busy, and anyway he did not share her interests. She married him at seventeen, she told me, before she knew anything about the world and men, and when the heat of their passion burned out they grew apart. She likes to surround herself with talented people, writers and artists and musicians. Some have been her lovers, I think, but not me. She treats me more like a pet, a lapdog,' he snorted, 'happy to take any small scrap of attention she'll throw my way.

'I used to confide in her, but not any more. I told her too

much, you see. About my family and how concerned I was that their sacrifices for me should not be in vain. I was terrified, that with the war I would be prevented from continuing my studies. Like the other men here, I feared we'd be called to fight. Some were and few have returned, it is terrible. But one day Mrs van Haren took me aside and spoke to me. She said I'd be all right, that I would not have to go, that she'd spoken to somebody she knew. I was relieved, I can tell you. Though I felt guilt, too – guilt that I was to be spared and my fellows were not.'

'That's what you were talking about when I saw you that last time,' Kitty remembered. 'When we said goodbye, near the bridge.'

'Yes, yes. It seems a lifetime ago, does it not? Before the Germans came.' At this he stopped, rose from the stool, stubbed out his cigarette in an ashtray on the windowsill and stepped silently to the door. There he listened a moment, then opened it with a sudden movement and peered up and down the corridor. Apparently satisfied, he closed it again, and returned to his seat.

'It is necessary to be careful,' he said, before taking up his story once more.

'After the Occupation, it did not take long for things to change at Mrs van Haren's salons. She did not invite me quite so often, but when she did, I went eagerly. I was so grateful to her, you see. Each time I went, some of the faces I used to see had gone and new ones took their place. Gradually I felt less comfortable. The old soldier with the medals I never saw again. One or two of the writers stopped coming and Miss Markwell who worked at the American Library ... I believe she soon left Paris. Instead there are others, a distinguished German writer, Ernst

Jünger, is one. And a French novelist, Louis Claude, an obsequious little man. I remember the first time, a year ago, Kitty, when I found myself shaking hands with a German officer. Think how I'd have gone out of my way not to sit near one in the Métro! Chantelle van Haren introduced us in her drawing room, and what could I do but shake his hand and force myself to smile. It would have been rude not to.

'After that, I promised myself that I would go no longer, that I would turn down the next invitation if it came. But it didn't prove that easy. The next time, Mrs van Haren wrote me the most charming letter, saying how much my playing had impressed her guests, so I sighed and went once more. And then found myself going again and again. The Germans were on the whole cultured men, and always most civil to me. They asked always for Brahms and Schumann. Never anything modern. However, then the most worrying thing happened.'

At this he broke off and looked up at Kitty, his face a picture of misery. 'Do I shock you, Kitty?' he asked. 'Perhaps you despise me now, for playing for the enemy. I feel ashamed. Sometimes I think Louis Claude feels the same, for when I meet his eye at these parties he looks away. We laugh at these people's jokes, we eat the food – good food such as is impossible for ordinary people to buy these days – and drink the best wines. I assume that like me, Louis Claude has his reasons. It's not something we can speak about. So, do you despise me?'

'Not despise you, no,' Kitty said slowly, 'but I find it difficult to understand. Why should you feel loyalty to that wretched woman? I've heard about her from my friend Milly, who said she's amoral, that she uses people.'

'I see that increasingly. I suppose she *is* using me. She likes to have power over people, to twist things to her advantage. I think underneath her glamour, her sophistication, she is still a child. But a child who plays dangerous adult games.'

'Games?' Kitty echoed, wondering what he meant.

Serge was silent for a moment before beginning to explain. 'Several weeks ago, when I went there I arrived a little early to lay out my music and was surprised to find Mrs van Haren alone with a German officer I'd never seen before. He must have been in his fifties, a veritable Prussian type – you know, sitting with that very taut, upright bearing and with eyes that seemed to look straight through me. She introduced me to him – his name was Propaganda-Staffel Emil von Ullmann – and the way he nodded and drummed his fingers on the arm of the chair . . . well, this was the first man I'd ever met of whom I can honestly say I was terrified.'

Serge lit another cigarette before going on. 'He was polite enough to me, asked me sharp questions about my studies and my ambitions, and I stammered out answers as truthfully as I could. Madame, however, was in what I could only call a skittish mood. I think she was nervous of him, too, because she was flirting with him and he wasn't responding. Her desperation was making her tongue run away with her. I was horrified when she started to tell this man about my family – how my mother was Polish, from a long line of musicians, and how well I'd done considering my parents had so little money. I don't think she meant anything unkind by it, only to draw his interest, but he could see I was agitated and he scrutinized me more closely than ever. Nothing was said, and yet I felt he had seen something in me I'd rather he hadn't. I held my breath in case she mentioned what I'd stupidly told her about my mother's claim to be related to Leopold Godowsky, but fortunately she did not. Perhaps she realized she'd already gone too far.'

He looked at Kitty and she looked back at him, feeling very much at sea. When she didn't twig he gave a little shrug and said, 'No matter.'

'I'm sorry,' Kitty said, 'but why is Godowksy significant?' She thought desperately of what she knew about this world-famous Polish pianist, who'd died in New York just before the war. And then she saw it. He was a Jew.

'I think I see,' she said quietly. 'I know you lodge with a Jewish family, but I didn't know you were Jewish.'

'We're not,' he said swiftly. 'That is, my father isn't, and I've never thought of myself as Jewish. My mother's proud of her heritage, but she's never wanted anything to do with religion. She's never come with us to Mass, but nor did she ever attend synagogue.'

'I expect it will be all right. This man von Ullmann – did he say anything, or act differently towards you afterwards?'

'No,' Serge admitted, 'but now I don't know what to do. If I stop attending Mrs van Haren's parties she might be offended and I'll lose the commissions her influence attracts for me and maybe her protection. And if I continue to go . . .' He spread his hands in an expressive gesture. 'Well, I might attract unwelcome interest.'

Kitty was quiet for a moment. She understood now why their teacher had been so angry and disappointed in his star pupil. Part of her thought, how could Serge have let himself get into this situation? And she gave silent thanks for Gene. Gene would never have fallen into a trap like that. He was straight as a die, knew right from wrong. His calling as a doctor meant he placed a high value on human life. She thought how he was risking his own life by saving Allied soldiers and airmen from capture by the Germans. A man of conscience. But what of Serge? How had he lost his way? He'd been taken under Mrs van Haren's patronage before the Occupation and told himself he was being loyal to her. And in doing so had slipped into a kind of collaboration and possibly put his whole family in danger. She saw his dilemma very clearly, but could not advise him.

'Perhaps the danger is not as bad as you fear,' she tried to soothe him. After all, Jews apart from German Jews had not been significantly targeted. Things could be a great deal worse. She remembered fleetingly how some of the black jazz players Gene had loved to hear had been interned. At least they were believed to be alive. Perhaps survival was all that could be hoped for.

She stood and reached for her bag. 'I have to go, Serge,' she said. She'd already left Fay longer than arranged and there were chores to do.

'Will I see you again?' Serge had been sitting despondent, smoking, but now he leaped to his feet. 'I can't blame you if you say no, but it would help me to know I have one true friend.'

'Of course we are still friends,' she said gently, 'but I'm not sure how I can help you.'

'No,' he said with a hollow glance, 'but to know you do not reject me will be something.'

'Be careful, Serge,' she said, kissing his cheek. 'Please, be careful.'

The way he twisted his mouth into a worried smile did nothing to reassure her as she opened the door and closed it quietly behind her.

This time, as she made her way back to the entrance, she could not wait to leave the Conservatoire building behind. To get home safely to her husband and child, where she would do her best to conserve the illusion that their little family home was a haven from the storms of the dark and dangerous world outside.

Over the summer of 1941, Paris became increasingly cut off from the world. Kitty and her husband were experiencing financial difficulties. Gene's salary was far from generous and he had spent the money that he'd inherited from his grandmother on his studies and setting up house. It worried Kitty dreadfully.

Communications between Britain and France had become virtually impossible, and Kitty had no knowledge of how her Uncle Pepper was faring. Although England was safe for the moment from invasion – Hitler's ill-advised Russian campaign had taken up his attention and resources and put paid to that – she missed her home in Hampshire badly, and wished she could find out what was happening there.

It was difficult, too, communicating with Gene's parents, but sometimes a letter would reach them, weeks or months after it had been written and with phrases blacked out by the censor. From one of these letters Gene learned that his father was ill. He had been given an operation on his stomach and was expected to recover, so Gene did not become over-concerned. It was an awful shock therefore when a telegram announced that he had died suddenly.

Gene was devastated. His relationship with his father had been distant in adult life, not least because of the man's liking for bourbon, but Gene had warm memories of him from his childhood and he wept for the loss of those halcyon days as much as for the bitter and cantankerous character his father had become.

He and Kitty spoke earnestly of whether they should try to leave, but the journey was so long and difficult that they would be far too late for the funeral, and then it would be impossible to come back. Gene knew what he had to do – his lot lay with the sick and injured of this war. It was decided that they should stay.

By July their personal finances became so bad that he wrote to his parents' attorney in New York. He didn't wish to bother his grieving mother, he told him, but the fact was that he was very short of money. Fortunately, the man was able to make arrangements to wire some over. Kitty didn't find this out until much later.

There was something else she didn't know. After the visit of Flight Lieutenant Stone there were no more such incidents. Gene told her nothing about his activities, but she guessed that they continued. In particular she wondered if the blowing of the safe house where Gene was to have taken Stone had had repercussions.

They had a terrible fright one airless night when they were awakened in the small hours by the scream of brakes outside. A car's doors slammed. Torchbeams strafed the air. Gene leaped out of bed and listened, but no one appeared to enter their building. Instead there came shouts outside and the thump of running feet. A throaty German voice cried, '*Halt!*' before a crack of gunfire sounded. Shortly after this the car sped off and the street fell silent once more. Eugene went to peep past the black-out curtain, but could see nothing.

'I'm going down,' he said, switching on a lamp. He started pulling his trousers on over his pyjamas.

Kitty sat up. 'Gene, no!'

'I must, sweetheart, in case someone's hurt.' She fell back on the bed with a sigh. 'Don't worry, I'll be careful,' he whispered and went out, shutting the door behind him. She lay tense with her eyes closed, listening, waiting. It felt like forever before he returned, but it was actually only a couple of minutes

'Couldn't see anyone, dark as the devil outside,' he remarked cheerfully, undressing. He turned off the light and clambered into bed. When he rolled over and put his arms around her she felt his heart thudding against her back.

She turned and hugged him close. 'I know you have to do these things,' she said in his ear, 'but I hate it. What if something happened to you? What would Fay and I do?' They'd be alone, poor, defenceless. Her mind ran ahead. They'd be sent to one of the camps, probably. Did they intern young children? She thought they must do if there was no one else to look after them. She ran over the names of people she knew. Who would have Fay? One of the French doctors' families, perhaps – Dr Poulon, possibly, who'd delivered Fay. Or Lili, but she didn't know Lili's employers so that wouldn't work.

'If anything happens to me, Kitty – not that I'm saying it will – you'll have the insurance. It's not much, but it would be something.'

'That's not what I mean.'

'No, but seriously.' He kissed her bare shoulder, then

she felt the warmth of his breath on her neck. She thought of something else, the thing that haunted her, that she usually pushed away.

'You're not doing anything ... dangerous, are you?'

'Of course not,' he said quickly – too quickly, she thought.

'Gene?'

'Don't ask me anything,' he said. 'Nothing at all. I cannot tell you.'

She had heard all she needed to know in the tone of his answer. He'd never spoken to her in that curt way before. She wriggled out of his grasp and shuffled over to the chilly extremes of the mattress.

'Kitty,' he whispered. 'Kitty, darling,' but she would not reply, and when he sought to comfort her, she pushed his arm away. She'd never felt so angry. Or frightened. Were she and Fay worth so little to him that he'd risk his life and maybe theirs helping strangers? And what would happen when America came into the war? They would all be enemy aliens then.

It took a long time that night for her anger to subside. *I'm being selfish. Whatever he's doing I should be proud of him*, she told herself, but part of her refused to be unselfish and proud. She wanted to be safe.

Summer turned to autumn, and America moved closer to the edge. Snippets of news were greeted by the little expat community in Paris with a mixture of excitement and foreboding. The US government introduced a peacetime draft to call up soldiers for training. In November it repealed the Neutrality Act it had passed in 1939. Eugene and Kitty once more discussed leaving and this time, finally, decided they should do so, for Fay's sake. They began to put together plans. But then something happened to make them delay.

It was a miserable rainy day in late November and the pavements were slippery with the last of the autumn's dead leaves. Kitty held Fay's hand as they waited to cross the Boulevard St-Michel. They stepped down into the road, but then a cavalcade of motorcycles roared into view and they retreated hastily to the kerb. Little Fay slipped and as Kitty jerked her upwards to stop her falling, she missed her own footing, her left ankle twisting under her. Because of the noise of the traffic she felt rather than heard the bone break. Quick hands seized her just in time, or woman and child would have fallen under the wheels of the sleek limousine that swept past, its swastika pennants snapping in the wind.

The accident required an operation to pin the ankle. As Kitty lay in bed in the American Hospital, sick and woozy from the anaesthetic, she knew that their travel plans would have to be put off. For a fortnight at least, Gene said, until the wound had healed and she was confident on crutches.

On 7 December they woke to the news that the Japanese had bombed American ships in the Pacific port of Pearl Harbor. Four days later, Germany saw fit to declare war on America.

Once again, Gene and Kitty had left it too late to leave.

'It's becoming chilly, *non*?' Mme Ramond said, getting up to switch on the electric fire that stood before the grate.

'A little,' Fay conceded, privately thinking it perfectly

warm in the room. It must be mid-afternoon, for sunshine still poured in through the window. 'But what happened, Madame Ramond? Were my parents all right?' She thought of her mother, injured, trapped in Paris. She herself must have been about two. If only she could remember clearly. There were things she recognized in Paris, the corridor of the apartment block where she'd lived, the sound of glass shattering, other fragments, but she could bring nothing back by will. It wasn't surprising really. She had been too young to store proper memories.

Nathalie Ramond put her hand to her face in a brief, protective gesture, then glanced around the room, as though looking for inspiration. Her eyes alighted on the scrapbook lying on the table. It was old, the cardboard cover peeling apart at the corners, the spine worn down to expose the threads that bound it. She lifted it onto her lap and, holding it part-closed to stop loose pages from escaping, she searched until she found the page she wanted. Carefully, she passed the book to Fay, who examined it. And caught her breath.

She knew the man in the photograph at once. He was a little older than he'd been in that honeymoon picture at her mother's bedside. His hair was shorter, though curly, but the smile was the same – a broad, open smile, that you couldn't help liking. He was sitting on a low brick wall and his attention was fully on the little girl whose arms he held as she balanced on the wall before him, looking out of the picture with a shy, uncertain wonder. The child had a mop of shoulder-length wavy hair with a ribbon tied into it. It was as dark as the man's was fair, but Fay could still see the likeness between them. It was something about the child's eyes, she thought, the fullness of the lips.

'I've never before seen a picture of myself when I was little. My mother told me they'd all been lost when our house was bombed. It is me, isn't it?' she whispered, looking up at the older woman with an expression of rapture.

'Of course it is. It was taken near the time of your mother's accident. You were two years old, a sweet child.' She gestured with her finger and thumb. 'A tiny edition of your mother. Ah, you liked to sing to yourself. Such a pretty voice. That was before they took your father away. You were never quite the same after that.'

'Took him away?' Fay echoed, and felt a responding emptiness. She studied the photograph one more time before closing the album.

'Early one morning in the middle of December, your father was arrested at your flat and sent with other American men to an internment camp in the North of France. Your mother was beside herself, and of course she was left in charge of you, alone and with a broken ankle. You were too young to know what was happening and the arrival of the police that morning must have been very frightening to a young child.'

'I don't remember it,' Fay said, closing her eyes. Her mind refused to try.

'It wasn't for long he was gone, a matter of weeks. Your father's employers made an official complaint. He was vital to the work of the hospital, a good doctor, no threat to anyone, what was the use of imprisoning him? He was freed soon after Christmas. The whole thing had been – how do you say? – sabre-rattling by the authorities. At the time they guessed nothing of your father's activities.'

'My mother must have been terrified out of her wits.'

'She was. You must have sensed that also. The Gestapo,

however, kept an eye on them after that. They both had to report each week to their local police station, and sometimes they'd receive a visit from a Gestapo officer. His name was Obersturmführer Hoff. I remember your mother hated him even then. He was very correct in his manner, with eyes of such pale blue they were almost colourless. He would ask about their movements in great detail and examine their papers. She told me she was terrified of saying the wrong thing. She felt like a hunted animal that is tempted to give itself up. When he'd gone, your poor mother would be left literally shaking.

'What with all this and the viciously cold winter that followed, when there was hardly any electricity or fuel and it was increasingly difficult to get food, how could you not be affected?'

Chapter 21

'By the early summer of 1942,' Mme Ramond said, 'instead of feeling relief after the terrible deprivations of the winter, life for Parisians became even more challenging.'

The war was not going Germany's way. Their forces were engaged on too many fronts and their winter campaign in Russia had sucked up men, supplies and, crucially, morale.

In Paris, the Nazis were enraged by the activities of the Resistance, who were becoming increasingly sophisticated in their mission to make the enemy's job more difficult. Hitler's response was to clamp down hard. He gave the policing of the Occupied Zone into the hands of a man with a reputation for complete ruthlessness. His name was Major-General Carl Oberg, and he was a member of the Nazi Party's security agency, the SD – the *Sicherheitsdienst*. In appearance he was like a cartoon evil Nazi, with a shaved head, rimless glasses and a fanatical expression. He was obsessed with two aims: to pack as many Jews as possible into trains to Poland, where they would be put to death, and to crush the French Resistance. His horrifying brutality was to earn him the nickname 'The Butcher of Paris'.

Kitty and Gene sensed the change of mood immediately. New regulations were issued thick and fast. One morning at the beginning of June, when Kitty ventured outside she saw that new posters had been pasted on the hoardings at the end of the street. Instead of crowding round them as was the usual habit, however, people averted their eyes and hurried past. Kitty saw the word *Juif* and stopped to look, reading with a sense of increasing revulsion. All Jews, the posters said, were to wear the *étoile jaune*, the yellow Star of David, sewn onto their outer garments. They were forbidden to enter a variety of public places: libraries, swimming pools, restaurants, parks – the list went on. As she stood there, trying to come to terms with the reality of it, she heard an all-too-familiar sound, the regular tramp of hobnail boots, a voice barking '*Eins, zwei, drei!*' She turned away as the patrol marched by.

That same day, she began to notice people in the street wearing yellow stars, shamed, cowed figures, branded for all to see. Her spirits lifted slightly at the sight of one angry-eyed man walking tall, wearing a row of military medals next to his star. A French youth spat on the ground as the Jew went by, but his older companion cuffed the boy's arm, saying, 'What are you doing? He fought for France, you fool. He is one of us.'

It happened late one morning a few days afterwards. Kitty returned from shopping with Fay to find an unmarked, matte-grey van parked outside their apartment block. Its back doors were open and the driver, a uniformed policeman, was pacing about smoking. He nodded to Kitty and closed one of the doors so she could get the pram past on the narrow pavement, but as she manoeuvred it into the lobby and unclipped Fay's harness, she was filled with unease. The concierge was nowhere to be seen and in any case had stopped complaining about the pram, so she left it where it was and summoned the lift. She waited, but it didn't come. It must be stuck somewhere. Her sense of unease grew.

'We must take the stairs, sweetie, I'm afraid,' she said to Fay. 'See if you can count them.' Fay's little voice sang out, 'One, two, one, two,' as she climbed, clutching the iron railing.

At the second floor they paused to catch their breath. Up above, men's voices could be heard, and odd thudding noises, echoing down the stairwell. These grew louder as mother and daughter resumed their climb. Halfway up the last flight, Kitty stopped. Whatever was happening, it was on their floor. Angry shadows leaped on the wall ahead. There came a muffled cry of pain and a roar of what sounded like '*Venez – vite!*' then a door slammed and a tableau formed at the top of the stairs. Two policemen were dragging a man in a shabby black suit. It was Monsieur Klein. She caught a glimpse of his face. His spectacles were gone. He was deathly white and blood streaked his chin. Kitty gasped and drew Fay back into the shadows. After a moment she heard the lift grille clatter into place and then the whines and creaks of the machinery as the lift began to descend.

Fay had seen it all. '*Maman,*' she whispered and buried her head in Kitty's skirt. Kitty lowered her straw bag, hefted the child onto her hip and held her close. The bag toppled over and her shopping tumbled out.

Above, all was quiet now, so she abandoned the shopping, walked up the last few steps and peered into the corridor. Monsieur Klein's door was closed. Something had been scribbled on it in white chalk, but before she could read what it said, she heard a sound and looked round. At the other end of the corridor a woman stood in an open doorway, her arms folded. When Kitty caught her eye, she retreated inside and closed her door without a word.

'*M'sieur Zipper, maman?*' Fay asked, twisting in her mother's arms to face her.

Kitty did not answer. She was staring at Monsieur Klein's door. The scrawled writing read *Sale Juif*. Dirty Jew.

'I should have helped him,' Kitty cried, throwing herself into her husband's arms. She'd had difficulty getting Fay to sleep, the little girl was so agitated and afraid, but finally she'd fallen back exhausted in her cot, her long-lashed eyes closed, the hot tears drying on her flushed cheeks.

'What could you have done, honey?' Gene said, hugging her close. 'You did all you could, keeping yourself and Fay out of sight.'

'I don't mean then,' she wept. 'I meant before. We should have seen what was coming.'

'There was no indication of danger. Someone must have denounced him.'

'But why? He was harmless. And kind, Gene, so kind.'

'Life doesn't work like that now. It must have been to someone's advantage to get rid of him. We'll probably never know.'

Kitty's suspicions focused on the woman she had seen further down their corridor. A childless widow, she was the only inhabitant to have a mat outside her door for visitors to wipe their feet on. She also had a German lover who came by night. A dapper man, his soft footsteps could sometimes be heard padding down the corridor. Sometimes she'd smell his scented hair-oil in the lift in the mornings and know he'd been there.

Kitty rubbed the chalk message off M. Klein's door, still feeling guilty. The fact remained that M. Klein had lived next door and had been their friend, and yet they had been able to do nothing to stop him being taken away. For some days afterwards, Fay would ask her if he'd returned and eventually Kitty told her that he'd gone to live somewhere else. The little girl looked at her for a long time after this then said, 'Poor M'sieur Zipper. Gone,' whenever they passed his door.

In the weeks following, his flat remained silent and empty. No friends called to enquire of him, and as far as she knew, no one came for his possessions. Each time she passed the empty flat, she felt his absence like the warning twinge of a hidden disease.

Kitty had become used to days when some special operation was underway, the presence of extra soldiers in the streets, the horns of the outriders' bikes clearing a route for an official cavalcade to pass. Often she never learned what it was about. But there was something different about 16 July.

The raids began at dawn. She was woken by vehicles roaring down the street. Soon, shots could be heard in the distance. Sleep was impossible after that; she lay anxious as Eugene breathed gently beside her. He was exhausted, poor man. Long hours at the hospital, insufficient food and the need to be constantly on his guard had taken their toll. When had she last heard him laugh? She couldn't remember, yet from the passion with which he spoke about his work she knew that beneath his weariness his spirit still burned bright.

When Fay came in at six and snuggled into the bed between them, Kitty rose to visit the bathroom and became aware of a low, distant rumbling, like a storm gathering on the horizon. She went to the window and raised the sash and the rumbling grew louder, yet the sky was a cloudless blue. A hot day was in prospect, she thought. There was a strong smell of traffic fumes and though the usual sounds echoed up from the street below, a tension hung in the air. She turned back to the room and went to lift the child into her highchair, taking comfort in the usual routines, the whistle of the kettle, Eugene running water in the bathroom.

All morning, the noise of heavy traffic continued, and down in the shops, people pursued their business with a subdued air. Everyone was aware that something was going on, but there were conflicting rumours as to what. It was while she was queuing at the butcher's, in the hope of a few strands of stewing meat, that the butcher's wife, a beady-eyed woman with a dumpy figure and an ear for gossip, came in and remarked to her husband that 'they', whoever they were, said it was all going on at the Vélodrome. Others joined in with questions, and by the time Kitty had stowed her tiny parcel of offal in her shopping bag she'd learned that a huge Gestapo operation was in place. Jews were being taken from their homes and assembled in the vast sports stadium near the Champs de Mars.

An awful silence fell over the shop and Kitty was pleased to take Fay's hand and leave, trying to absorb the shock of this news. All those poor people, some the Knoxes' neighbours perhaps, herded together – and what was it for? What were the Gestapo going to do with them? And then a thought that turned her blood cold: was Serge amongst them?

She wasn't sure what to do, but as she put the shopping away and warmed some thin soup for lunch a resolve strengthened in her mind. She had to find him and make sure he was safe. After they'd eaten she hastened downstairs with Fay and knocked on the door of the lady with the baby, begging her to look after Fay for an hour or two. It was only as she left the building that she remembered that she didn't know Serge's precise address. It was somewhere in the maze of streets in the Marais district, she knew, in a street of jewellers' shops, but which number she had no idea. This meant she had to go to the Conservatoire first to enquire. It took the porter some time to find out the information she needed, then she checked to make certain that he wasn't in the college, before taking the Métro to Place de la République. By this time she felt so anxious she was jittery and hurried along with lowered eyes in case anyone noticed.

Rue du Temple was a long, narrow street running straight down towards the river at Notre Dame. Despite the mid-afternoon sunshine it was cast in shadow. The grilles were down on many of the shops, and sentiments similar to the one on Monsieur Klein's flat had been daubed on some of the doors.

She found the number she wanted without much trouble. The shop itself was *closed until further notice*, a handwritten sign told her, and when she rang the bell to the dwelling above there was no answer. After a moment, she crossed the street and looked up at the windows. Though the shutters were open the curtains were drawn across and the glass reflected darkly back at her. She was turning to go when her eye caught a tremble of a curtain as though someone had lifted it to peep out, but when she looked again, all was as before. She glanced about in case anyone else was watching.

A man was standing at a street corner a dozen yards away. He wore his hat down low so she could only see the lower part of his face. It was a narrow face, close-shaven, with a mean twist to his lips, but it was his hands she noticed as he smoked his cigarette. Who would wear leather gloves in July? He saw her interest and touched the brim of his hat in acknowledgement. She ignored this, and instead set off down the street towards the river. She hardly noticed where she was going – she simply wanted to get away from him. But when she checked behind her a moment later, there was no sign of anyone following her. Perhaps he was of no significance. She walked on more slowly now, deep in thought. If anyone had been in the flat, they hadn't been prepared to reveal themselves. Had it been Serge? Who else could she ask about him? The lovely face of Mrs van Haren hovered in her mind, but she'd need to find out where the woman lived, and anyway, she might be putting Serge in more danger by stirring that particular wasps' nest. She would ask Gene.

Her pace quickened. She was glad to leave the shadows of the Rue du Temple and to emerge into the open, cross-ing the dusty expanse of ground by the Hôtel de Ville with its forbidding German sentries before reaching the pearl-grey bridge over the river.

It was as she undressed alone that night in the weak light of the bedroom lamp that she became aware of a gentle tapping sound. Someone was at the door of the flat. Kitty pulled a dressing gown on over her underwear and went to see. Outside, the figure of a man separated himself from the shadows and for a moment she thought she saw those leather gloves and drew in a sharp breath. But then a shaft of light fell across his face.

'Oh, thank goodness,' she breathed. It was Serge.

Grasping his arm, she pulled him inside and shut the door, saying in a low voice, 'Serge, I was so worried.'

'I'm sorry,' he whispered, setting down a small suitcase. Fear rose from him, she sensed it in his shallow breath, the quick pulse of his blood. 'I saw you this afternoon, but I daren't come down. Not till *he'd* gone.' She had no need to ask who 'he' was.

'Gene's not here,' she said, directing him to sit with her on the sofa. They conversed quietly for a while. Serge had received an anonymous letter the night before warning him to stay away from his apartment and to tell no one. He had slept the night in a cupboard at the Conservatoire 'with the ghosts of all those musicians', he managed to joke, then, torn with guilt at having left the family he lodged with, couldn't help himself returning to Rue du Temple to find out what had happened to them. There was no sign of them, but no sign of any struggle either. He'd just been packing a few things when he'd peeped out of the window and noticed the man in the leather gloves. Each time he'd looked he'd seen the man. Then Kitty had arrived, and after that the man had left. Whether he'd been right to be wary of him, he couldn't say, but he'd been fearful enough to wait till darkness fell before setting out once more.

'It's she – she who betrayed me,' he kept saying over and over again. 'Mrs van Haren, of course,' he snapped when Kitty asked. 'I thought I'd be safe with her, but she couldn't keep her mouth shut, could she?'

'But think – perhaps it was she who sent the note warning you?' Kitty saw no yellow star on his coat and wondered if he'd ever worn one. If he'd been stopped and his identity checked, he could have been arrested simply for that omission, but perhaps it was the only safe way for him to travel during curfew. And now he was here, what was she to do with him? She didn't need to glimpse the not-quite-closed door to the second bedroom to remember Fay, within, sleeping innocently on her front, her knees curled to her chest as was her habit. Kitty swallowed. If only Gene were here, he'd know what to do, but he was on call at the hospital tonight and wouldn't be back until tomorrow evening. All she knew was that if Serge was found here, she'd be deemed guilty of hiding him – and who knew what would happen? She'd heard stories – everybody knew one – of prison and torture.

Serge's eyes were dark pools of fear in his white face. His hands with their strong, sensitive fingers worked at the brim of the hat in his lap. He was her friend and he was in trouble. There was only one thing Kitty could do now and that was to find him something to eat and make up a bed on the sofa.

Sometime in the early morning they awoke to the sound

of distant gunfire. It was from the prison in the Avenue Foch, she'd heard the butcher's wife say. She had to clamp her hands over her ears whenever where she heard it now, knowing it must be an execution.

She did not sleep well, then in the morning had to drag herself out of bed with heavy-lidded eyes. She found Fay playing on the floor by the sofa, showing Serge the animals from her ark. Kitty remembered how good he'd been with her when he'd met her as a baby.

The day inched by and it was as though she walked on broken glass. Everything she did had to be thought through first, to make sure Serge's presence was not suspected. The shutters and the curtains must be opened as usual – everything must be as usual – but this meant Serge had to keep away from the windows in case he was seen by someone from a window opposite. If she went out he must not answer the door or flush the lavatory or run the tap. He should not smoke or make a sound of any sort. The inability to smoke and his constant fear made him tetchy by the end of the first day.

Gene's expression when he walked in through his front door at six o'clock and saw Serge could only be described as horrified. 'He had nowhere else to go,' Kitty said, when Gene drew her out to the kitchen to speak to her privately.

'So I imagine, damn the man,' Gene said, pushing a cigarette between his lips and lighting it, but the pity in his voice belied his words. 'He can't stay here, of course.'

'Of course not,' Kitty echoed, twisting a tea towel round her hand and imagining a visit from Obersturmführer Hoff.

'No, Fay,' Gene commanded.

Fay had climbed on a chair to get to the bread bin. 'Tea for man,' the girl said, trying to hide the stolen heel of a loaf behind her back.

'We have nothing to feed him on, Gene,' Kitty said, trying to keep her voice level. 'What do we do?'

'I'm trying to think,' was her husband's answer.

'I'm sorry to cause you this trouble,' Serge kept repeating, his eyes desperate. He was worried about his family in Orléans. 'I need to get a message to them,' he said unhappily. 'To find out if they're safe.'

'We'll work out a way,' Gene soothed, 'but we must be careful.'

'Of course,' Serge said, slumping in his chair.

After supper – a particularly sparse meal given the extra mouth – Gene went out. He didn't say where he was going, but he didn't return until after midnight. Kitty heard him as he let himself in and came into the bedroom where she was lying awake in the dark.

'Where did you go?' she whispered.

'To see a pal who might be able to help. They're going to sort out something quickly, but in the meantime Ramond will have to stay here.'

Kitty screwed up her eyes and sighed, then said, 'How long?'

'I don't know, Kitty, it's no good asking. There are so many similar cases just now. Tomorrow maybe, or the day after. It depends what can be fixed up for him.'

A day or two. Not that long. Surely they could bear that.

'I don't like it either, sweetheart, but we must help him, of course.'

'Of course we must.'

*

Everything must be as usual. Kitty had arranged to meet Lili in the park the following afternoon. She was actually glad to get away from the flat and from Serge, whose moods veered between misery and extreme nervousness, and it would be good for her and Fay to be out in the sunshine. She picked out some books for him to read, buckled Fay's shoes on for her, and went out. As she pulled back the grille of the lift, the door of the apartment with the mat opened and the same woman looked out. When she saw it was Kitty, she closed the door again. They met the man who visited her as they stepped out into the vestibule. He called a greeting to the concierge and winked at Fay as he passed.

Today, Lili was not her usual cheerful self. Her small, heart-shaped face was creased into a frown, and when Joséphine fell over and got a grass stain on her white pinafore, Lili brushed at it and scolded her. She and Kitty sat together on a bench while the children played with a ball. Kitty studied Lili gravely and put her hand on hers, asking what had brought her so low. Wordlessly, Lili dug into her handbag and brought out a postcard. From Jean-Pierre, her husband, Kitty imagined – but when she turned it over, she saw Lili's own handwriting on it. It had been stamped by some German official, but the ink was smudged and impossible to read.

'It was returned to me a few days ago. What does the stamp say?'

'I don't know, Lili. Have you asked anyone else?'

'Who? My employers are away and I don't like to take Joséphine to the Kommandatur.'

'I expect everything's all right. You'd have heard if it wasn't, I'm sure. It must be a mistake.'

'Yes,' she echoed. 'It must be a mistake.' She gave Kitty a whey-faced smile.

Kitty's thoughts flicked back to Serge. The weight of the knowledge of him was with her all the time. Waiting, she thought. This war is all about waiting, and the news, when it came, was so often bad. Poor Serge didn't know what had happened to his family, but she had an awful feeling. *Don't*, she told herself. It was too easy to be pessimistic, always to fear the worst.

'Why don't you take it to the Red Cross?' she told Lili, wondering why she hadn't thought of this immediately.

Lili gave a nod, took the postcard and thrust it back in her bag, then tried to cheer up. They spoke about plans for Joséphine's third birthday, which was coming up shortly. The girl's mother had acquired some sugar for a cake and they were saving up butter. 'There won't be chocolate icing, but she's got some old vanilla.'

The sound of slow footsteps made Kitty look round, but the path was hidden by bushes. It left her with an odd tingling feeling, as though they were being spied upon.

Eugene arrived home in time for dinner carrying a paper package which contained half a small chicken, a gift from the grateful family of a wealthy French patient. Quite how they'd acquired it was better not to ask. Normally Gene would pass on such presents to the hospital cook, so everyone might benefit, but this time he'd asked to take some home. 'I felt we needed it,' he said with one of his old carefree smiles. Kitty seized the meat immediately and it wasn't long before the air was redolent with the delicious smell of fried poultry.

'Such bliss,' Kitty said, licking her fingers after the feast and laughing at Fay sucking at a drumstick. 'I'll make soup tomorrow from the bones.'

The taste of proper food cheered them up for the evening, but once Fay had gone to bed, the mood turned sombre, for Gene had found out more about what had happened the day before at the Vélodrome, the bicycle stadium.

'It was a planned operation, of course,' he told Serge and Kitty. 'They took everyone they rounded up there – thousands of them. Many were children, Kitty.'

'No,' Kitty breathed, pity welling up. 'What will happen to them, Gene?'

Gene sighed. 'They're putting 'em on trains. Sending 'em off goodness knows where. Listen, Ramond, my contact said they're mostly Jews who are not French citizens, so it may be your family is all right.'

'My mother is Polish,' Serge told them, 'and my father's from Belgium, so I'm not sure.' He covered his face with his hands for a moment. 'I wish there was some way we could get news. Perhaps I should go there.' His hair was rumpled and his expression dazed.

'Don't be ridiculous.' Gene's voice was stony. 'You'd be picked up in an instant.' He went to the mantelpiece for the matches, then lit a cigarette and gave one to Serge. 'No. We must get you out of here as soon as possible. It won't be long now, I'm sure of it.'

'Where will I go?'

'Somewhere safer than here, that's all I know.'

'Don't worry, Serge. We'll take care of you,' Kitty told him. Serge looked so lost, she thought, so strained and hollow-eyed she knew they couldn't do otherwise. But oh, she wished he could be gone, because if they were caught with him, she dared not think what might happen to them all.

The next day was no less tense. Serge looked as though he'd slept badly. He sat on the edge of the sofa, passing Fay building blocks in a desultory fashion for the house she was making. Kitty folded up his bedding and took it into Fay's bedroom, out of the way. It was while she was thrusting it into a cupboard there, that she heard the piano being played.

'Serge – ow!' she cried, bumping her head on the roof of the cupboard in her haste. 'Serge, don't.' He had launched into a complex piece she recognized immediately as Chopin – one of his Ballades, which Serge played fluently and with a passion that came from his very heart.

'Stop it, stop it!' she cried, but only when she grabbed at his hands to tear them from the keyboard did he come to himself. 'Someone will hear you, or see you or something. Come.' She closed the lid of the instrument and led him back to the sofa where he sat morose.

'Anyone hearing that would know it wasn't me,' she told him gently. 'I hardly play now, and anyway, you're miles better.' He looked at her then and she was so pleased to see his smile that she burst out laughing.

Suddenly she was serious again. 'Serge,' she said, 'listen. You must not play the piano.'

Everything as usual. Although he offered, she could not leave Fay with Serge when she went out shopping, because a neighbour might wonder what was going on. She did not acknowledge another, deeper reason, which was fear for Fay should the Germans come when she was out. She would never forgive herself if something happened to her daughter when she wasn't there. Never ever. She told herself this as she and the little girl waited for the lift, and after Fay declared that she didn't want to go in the pram today, Kitty held her hand tightly as they stepped out into the street.

Chapter 22

The queues for food were particularly bad that morning. There had been some news the day before about an explosion on a main railway line and the authorities often reacted to such acts of resistance by disrupting the distribution of food. Inevitably there was grumbling. Milly would have berated the grumblers, but Kitty felt some sympathy for those struggling to keep their families alive.

In the butcher's, where the queue wound out of the shop, they waited nearly half an hour, watching the small piles of meat in the window diminish. Inside, the butcher's wife was still talking about the events of the day before yesterday. 'Pushed them into railway wagons, they did, like animals, but at least they give animals water.' Kitty couldn't bear to hear about it, and it took a supreme act of will for her not to walk out again. Her reward was some beef dripping and a quarter pound of stinking tripe. The butcher smiled down at Fay and coiled on an extra piece when he weighed it. She paid quickly, feeling sick as she picked up the packages and made a hasty exit.

Out in the fresh air she looked up at a sky of radiant blue. She took a deep breath and urged a reluctant Fay down to the main street. There was a stall at the covered market selling wild strawberries, someone had said in the meat queue. She'd not eaten a strawberry for years and Fay had never had one. She was too late, of course. The strawberries had gone, if indeed they'd ever existed, but she bought a lettuce, not a very green one, then walked home, stopping in the grocer's for a tin of condensed milk on the way. It was as she pushed open the door to their building that she happened to glance up the street. Outside the tobacconist, a man was leaning against the wall reading a paper. She couldn't see his face, but for a moment she watched him before Fay gave an impatient cry and pulled at her mother's hand.

In the lobby her mind worked as she nodded to the concierge and crossed the floor to the lift. What was it about the man that piqued her interest? It was something she recognized about the way he stood – but it wasn't only that. It was his fingers, gripping the edges of the paper. Even at this distance she had seen that he was wearing gloves.

It was early afternoon and Kitty was sewing, trying to let out a dress of Fay's that was too tight about the chest and shoulders. Serge sat at the modest dining table in his waistcoat, his jacket hooked over the back of his chair. He was writing a letter to his parents, a task that was causing much sighing and rasping of his jaw, and once Kitty caught him wiping his eyes with the back of his hand.

She was thinking it was about time to wake Fay when there was a knock on the door, a timid knock, but still enough to make them stare at one another in frozen horror. It woke Fay, too, who cried out, so there was no pretending no one was in. Kitty gestured and Serge rose instantly, gathering his jacket and his notepaper, and tiptoed into the main bedroom where he pushed the door until it shut with a gentle click. They'd rehearsed this. He would hide in the wall cupboard, though if anyone looked inside . . . she banished the thought from her mind.

Instead she flew to the door and opened it, and felt a tremendous relief and surprise to see her friend. 'Oh, Lili!'

It was indeed Lili, but Lili without Joséphine. She wore a troubled look and said in an uncertain voice, 'Kitty, I am sorry to come without warning.'

'That's all right,' Kitty said, widening the door. 'Come on in.'

As Lili entered, Fay peeped round the door of her bedroom, two fingers in her mouth, her other hand clutching her zebra. Lili greeted her, and Fay briefly removed her fingers to smile, then popped them back again.

'Do sit down, Lili,' Kitty encouraged.

Lili took the sofa and Fay came and sat next to her. Kitty, sitting in Gene's chair, glanced swiftly about the room, but was relieved to see no evidence of Serge's presence. The door of the main bedroom remained closed. What if Fay asked after Serge? How would Kitty answer? Although Lili was Kitty's friend, she couldn't let her know. She had to get her out of here as soon as possible without arousing her suspicions.

'We were just going out,' she said, thinking of an idea. 'To get some air, see if you were in the park, in fact. Would you like to come?'

'No, thank you,' Lili said. 'I'll only stay a moment. I ought to go back to Joséphine. I left her with a neighbour, you see.'

'Has something happened?' Kitty wondered, sensing the girl's unhappiness.

Lili's head drooped. 'I visited the Red Cross this morning, as you said,' she sighed. 'There was a long wait, but then I spoke to a woman and showed her my postcard. She couldn't read the stamp either but she said to leave it with her. They'd make enquiries. That's all. I just thought I'd let you know.' She finally met Kitty's gaze and Kitty was struck by the desperate expression in her eyes.

Kitty said, 'I suppose that is the best thing to do, to ask them to find out. At least you're doing something.'

'Something,' Lili echoed. 'I can't bear the waiting.'

'Oh, poor you,' Kitty whispered, going to sit beside her on the sofa to take her hand. 'I do feel for you. But there's plenty of room for hope. I'm sure it's only that a mistake has been made.'

'Yes, I expect you are right. Thank you.' She gently pulled away her hand. 'Kitty, may I have a glass of water, please? I have walked a long way in the heat and—'

'Of course,' Kitty cried, standing up, 'How remiss of me. I should have thought.' She went out to the kitchen, Fay at her heels.

As she was at the sink, Fay asked where Serge was. 'He'll be back soon,' she assured her, 'don't worry.'

When they returned to the sitting room Lili was standing near the front door, repinning her hair in a mirror hanging there. She turned and took the glass, thanking Kitty, and drank, then placed it half-empty on the table next to the dress Kitty had been altering.

'This is a pretty blue,' she said, picking up and spreading it in her hands.

'It is, isn't it?' Kitty said, stepping over. 'Like cornflowers. I'm trying to move this seam.' She pointed at the garment, showing her. 'I'm not much good at this sort of thing. Do you think this will hold?' She stopped as she realized Lili wasn't looking at the dress at all. Instead she was staring at something on the table that had been hidden by the dress. It was a sheet of paper written over in bold black ink, the French words clear to read. It was a page of Serge's letter that he'd started and discarded for some reason. *My dear parents, I am so worried for you. How are you all? The news here is ghastly but for the moment anyway I am safe . . .*

For a moment her mind went blank and then it cleared. 'Oh, the neighbour must have dropped that here when she brought the newspaper,' she said in as normal a voice as she could muster. 'I'll take it back later.' She forced herself to pick up the letter slowly, to fold it and slip it into her handbag.

When she turned round, it was to see Lili looking at her calmly, the dress still in her hands.

'You have made a good job here, your stitches are so neat,' she said brusquely, handing it back. 'Now I shall go. As I say, I have left Joséphine too long. Goodbye, my little Fay.'

Kitty opened the front door for her. 'Goodbye,' Lili said in a cold voice.

'Goodbye, Lili,' Kitty replied, dismayed. It was as though all trace of their former friendship had vanished.

When she went inside and closed the door, Kitty leaned against it for a moment, going over everything that had happened. Lili had come out specially – to tell her what? No news at all. She'd drunk a glass of water and gone. If she hadn't seen the letter, all would have been well. That Lili didn't believe her about the neighbour's newspaper remained a possibility, but Lili had no other reason for suspecting her of anything. She was her friend, for goodness sake. She was upset about her husband, that was the reason for her strange manner.

Kitty opened the door of her and Gene's bedroom and went to the cupboard. 'Serge?' she whispered, knocking on it, and was almost struck by the cupboard door as it shot open and Serge stepped out, unfolding himself.

'There's a nail sticking out at the back,' he complained, rubbing his hip, then he stopped and said, 'Did you come in here, or was it Fay?'

'I didn't,' she said. 'I don't think Fay did either, did you, darling?' Fay, who stood in the bedroom doorway, shook her head.

'Someone opened the bedroom door a few minutes ago and came in. I would swear it.'

He and Kitty stared at each other. It was as though a giant hand reached out and crushed her heart in her chest. It wasn't possible: Lili was her friend. Yet she was certain now that Lili knew something. The question was what? And what might she do with the information? She remembered the man with the leather gloves. It could be no coincidence that she'd seen him twice. Who was he? Some accomplice of Obersturmführer Hoff? He didn't look like Gestapo.

'Serge,' she began. His back was to her and the slump of his shoulders spoke of defeat. He no longer looked spruce, but dejected and a little wild. There were so many people looking like that whom she passed in the street. So many lived lives in the shadows, hoping only to survive, to escape the notice of officialdom. How many more were hidden away, never going out?

It came to her in a flash what she should do.

'Serge,' she said urgently. He turned round and she saw the desperation in his eyes. 'You have to leave.' She could see the situation clearly now. 'We'll go with you. There's a back entrance where we put the rubbish – we'll take that.'

Whilst Serge fetched his case, she snatched up her handbag, a few things for Fay, then scribbled a note for Gene that gave nothing away. She had an idea. All the while she was thinking, working it out.

Reaching the back stairs meant passing the nosy woman's apartment. Kitty signalled silence to Fay and scooped the child up into her arms. They passed the door with the mat and Serge held open the door to the staircase and shut it behind them with a small sound that echoed its way down the narrow stair. This they descended and unlocked the heavy door at the bottom. Outside, they found themselves in a back yard shadowed by a high brick wall and lined with a row of dustbins. Kitty checked, but there was no one else about. They turned left and walked quickly down the path that skirted the back of the building, dodging right along another, eventually emerging onto a quiet back street. She knew at once where they were when she noticed the little piano shop that she used to visit.

'Where are we going?' Serge whispered to her, looking bewildered. Fay was whimpering and wanting to get down, but Kitty wouldn't let her.

'The convent,' she said, and registered his surprise. 'It's the only place I can think of and it will only be for a short time. We must travel separately though. I can't risk it with Fay.'

Serge looked so tragic that a pair of passing French policemen looked at them curiously, so Kitty leaned

forward and kissed Serge on the mouth, saying loudly to
Fay in French, 'Say goodbye to Papa, he's going to work,'
and waved Fay's hand for her while the child was astonished into silence. 'Rue St-Jacques, the bookshop by the
Métro,' she hissed to Serge when the policemen showed
their backs. She gave him a little push and watched him
set off down the pavement in a stiff wooden gait that in
her anxiety she convinced herself would attract suspicion.

'He's not my papa,' Fay said.

'Shh, Fay, we're playing a little game,' Kitty said as they
walked in the other direction to catch the Métro further
along the line.

Fay liked games, though she didn't know the rules of
this one. She clutched her wooden zebra and snuggled
into her mother's shoulder.

The Métro was crowded. There were empty seats next to
a pair of German soldiers who were talking and laughing
together, but people chose to stand rather than take them.
An elderly Frenchman in a pristine old-fashioned suit
insisted on Kitty having his seat and she spent the journey
with Fay held tightly on her lap, expecting at any moment
that the soldiers would turn and see her and arrest her.
However, when the doors slid open at St-Michel-Notre-
Dame they got off unnoticed.

Fay insisted on walking up the steps herself, so by the
time they reached the barrier, Kitty's nerves were in
shreds. She looked about for the bookshop, thinking at
first it had gone, then realizing it was in fact several shops
down from the Métro, not right next to it as she'd
thought. To her consternation, some of the books in
the window were in German, but she entered anyway,

leading Fay by the hand and nodding at the middle-aged woman behind the counter who was thumbing through a sheaf of invoices. A quick glance about confirmed Serge's absence.

'Are there children's books upstairs?' she asked the woman, who nodded, but before she could move to the staircase the door opened and the bulky silhouette of a Gestapo officer filled the entrance.

Kitty gave a little gasp and gaped at him, but he merely inclined his head politely and turned to ask the shop-keeper in heavily accented French about a book he had ordered, so she recovered herself and carried Fay up the stairs. At the top she almost bumped into an agitated Serge. Wordlessly, she steered him round the corner of a bookshelf where they conversed in urgent whispers as Fay sat on the floor exploring a picture book and the officer's deep voice rumbled up from downstairs.

After a minute or two, they heard the man leave the shop. Kitty managed to separate Fay from the picture book and carried her complaining downstairs, leaving Serge behind. 'They are nice, but expensive,' she said to the woman, who shrugged and did not return her goodbye.

Outside, as she waited to cross the road, Fay in her arms, she looked all about but could see nothing to worry her, no sign of the Gestapo man, nor anyone watching. A soldier seemingly on duty outside the Métro was flirting with a plump nurse.

She waited for a grey van to pass before crossing the road, looked around once more and set off down the street that led to Sainte Cécile's Church and the convent. Just before the bookshop became hidden from view, she glimpsed the door open and Serge step out. She watched him saunter to the kerb in her wake. Good. But now, as they came to the tiny alley that led to the convent, different worries took over. What was she to say to the nuns? They'd looked after refugees, but could she persuade them to risk their lives by hiding a Jew, a man whose very religion they might abhor?

Some instinct told her they would. Anyway, there was nothing else she could do now. She hurried down the alley with Fay, her chin set with determination.

The convent was as it ever was, the small square empty and baking in the afternoon sun, the cherry tree in full leaf, the row of pots tended by the Sisters blooming with tiger lilies and jasmine. It immediately made Kitty feel safe and cared for, this refuge from the world, as it had on her first day in Paris. Fay was struggling so Kitty put her down and with a cry of joy she ran to push open the gate. Kitty waited until, a moment later, the nervous figure of Serge emerged from the shadows of the alley.

'No one saw me, I'm sure,' he told her, glancing behind him. 'Is this the place?' He looked up at the building, a doubtful expression on his face.

'Yes. Don't worry,' Kitty replied, understanding his anxiety. 'The nuns are friends.'

It was one of the older nuns, Sister Clare, who opened the door, peering over her wire spectacles in surprise at the three figures on the doorstep, but she ushered them in, closed the door and bolted it. 'They're all in the sitting room,' Sister Clare said, smiling down at Fay.

She went and knocked on the closed door to Mère Marie-François's small sitting room, listened, then pushed it open. Kitty walked in then stopped, struck with amazement.

There were three people in the room: the Reverend Mother and the curé, Père Paul, both seated. Coming forward to meet them, looking as astonished as his wife, was Gene.

Fay ran to him and her father swept her up into his arms. 'What happened?' he asked Serge and Kitty in urgent tones.

'Oh, Gene, it was Lili.' Serge was introduced and in a few brief sentences Kitty told Gene of her belief that their apartment was being watched, about Serge's letter and Lili's suspicious behaviour. 'I couldn't think where else we could go,' she said, appealing to Mère Marie-François, who inclined her head, as serene as always. 'And here you are, Gene, and . . .'

'Come and sit down. You are very welcome,' Mère Marie-François said to Serge, and, addressing the older nun, 'Sister, perhaps you would take the little girl for Thérèse to amuse, then bring us all some of that disgusting stuff they call coffee these days.'

'Yes, Mother.'

Sister Clare held out her hand, but Fay shook her head until Kitty said, cajoling, 'Go with Sister Clare, sweetheart – maybe Sofie will be there,' and the mention of the little Belgian girl was enough to make Fay change her mind. As she reached the door she looked back, clutching her zebra, and sent her mother the brightest of smiles.

'*Un petit ange*,' the curé murmured, rising to his feet. 'Bless the child.' Then with a kindly gesture, he said to Serge, 'Come with me now, monsieur, and we'll get you settled,' and he unlocked a door at the back of the room which Kitty had never been through before.

'Stay here, honey,' Gene told her. 'He'll be all right.'

'I should like to go with him.'

Seeing the stubborn expression on her face, Gene shrugged. He picked up Serge's worn case and they followed the curé into a lobby which led to a utility room with a sink and a boiler that stood idle and silent. The curé pushed aside an old coat hanging on a nail and hooked his finger into a crevice in the wall behind. The wall hinged open – it was made of some light material – and behind was revealed a dimly lit room furnished with a pair of bunks and a table and chair. On the bottom bunk a figure sat up and a dark-stubbled face peered up at them in bleary confusion.

'Serge Ramond, this is Squadron Leader George Craven,' Gene said. 'George,' he added in English, 'you have a pal for a few days. Don't worry, we'll get you both out of here soon.'

Serge and the pilot nodded to one another, then Serge shook hands with Gene and Kitty and thanked them, his brown eyes filled with anxiety, before the curé closed the gap in the wall once more.

Kitty's mind was struggling to keep up. She'd hoped that in leaving Serge she'd feel the lifting of a burden, that someone else would be responsible for him now and keep him safe. Instead, with the appearance of the British pilot a whole new area of anxiety had opened up. They trooped back into the sitting room where the Mother Superior still waited.

'We will look after them,' Mère Marie-François assured them as the curé relocked the door, 'with God's help. Now, what can Sister Clare be doing? ' She went out to see.

'How long have you been bringing people here, Gene?' Kitty asked, her voice low and trembling. She felt betrayed. The convent was her special place, but all the time the curé and the Reverend Mother had been colluding with Gene and it didn't feel like her safe place any more.

'I dared not tell you,' he said. His voice sounded calm, but there was a catch in it.

It was difficult to think straight. Her feet seemed to give way under her and she sank onto the hard settee. Despite Gene's prevarications she had tried to kid herself that the rescue of the Welsh boy and Flight Lieutenant Stone had been isolated incidents. Now she was thoroughly disabused. It was clear that by treating and rescuing Allied servicemen, Gene was putting himself in constant danger. Gene had been trying to protect her by telling her nothing and she'd been happy not to know. Now, though, she glimpsed how lonely Gene must have been and felt guilty for her deliberate blindness – for she'd not been able to support him.

'Are you all right, honey?' he asked, coming to sit by her and taking her hand. She shook her head.

'I'm sorry,' she whispered. 'You've been doing so much to save people and I've been no help at all to you.'

'Of course you have,' he said, his voice low, but full of passion. 'Coming home to you and Fay is what I love best. You are my haven, Kitty. You know that.' He smoothed back her hair and kissed her and she clung to him.

'What do we do now?' she said. 'Maybe our flat has been searched. Surely we can't return home?'

'I think we have to. It would look wrong if we didn't, do you understand?'

'What happens if they're waiting for us?'

*

But no one was. The flat was as she'd left it. There was no sign of forced entry, and nothing had been disturbed. And yet ... As she walked through the rooms she caught the very faint scent of a strange tobacco, and some of the items in her chest of drawers appeared to have been rearranged.

'I haven't noticed anything,' Gene told her.

'Gene, I'm not a child. Don't talk to me as though I were.'

'I'm only trying to reassure you.'

They were both of them on edge though, over the following few weeks. Kitty, who'd expected to feel relief that Serge had gone and they were safe, felt quite the opposite.

Chapter 23

The end of July and the beginning of August were days of oppressive heat. It made no difference if the windows were open or closed, people wilted. A silence descended over the streets. Kitty shopped early in the morning and she and Fay sweltered in the flat until late afternoon when the sun grew less merciless and they'd venture out. She avoided the park where they used to go in case they saw Lili. Sometimes she wondered whether she'd imagined Lili's odd behaviour, but in the middle of the night she took the opposite view. Lili had come to the flat, something she'd never done before, and alone. Serge said she'd trespassed into the bedroom where he was hiding. She must have done this while Kitty was in the kitchen fetching the glass of water for her. Kitty was curious to discover whether Lili had found out any more about Jean-Pierre, her husband. Perhaps someone was using the situation to put pressure on Lili? She didn't confide in Gene about this. He'd have said Kitty's imagination was running away with her.

Still, she avoided the possibility of seeing Lili just in case. And when she entered or left the flat with Fay she always hurried, in case her neighbour down the corridor was watching. A French couple moved into Monsieur

Zipper's flat next door. They looked ordinary enough and nodded to Kitty in a friendly manner if they met each other going out or coming in, but Kitty was as unwilling to chat as they seemed to be. It was safer that way.

And so the weeks passed and she grew used to the tension so that it supported her, propelled her through the days. Her job was to watch over Fay and Gene, to keep them close. Fear made her do this job well. She could never be off her guard.

She tried not to think about Serge, shut in that cell-like room at the back of the convent, with little daylight, cut off from his beloved music. She quizzed Gene about the British man with him until he told her that he had been moved on in his dangerous journey home, but there might be others to take his place. Maybe, she imagined, Serge was allowed out sometimes, to sit in the quiet back courtyard or to play the piano in the church. She hoped so, or his place of safety would be to him a cruel prison. Awareness of his suffering made her realize how much she cared about him. He could be prickly with her, but there was something vulnerable about him that roused her sympathy, and she felt a deep connection to him because of that time when they'd both been lonely newcomers to Paris, and in their shared passion for music.

Towards the end of August the weather became cooler, and one afternoon Kitty set out with Fay to visit her old piano teacher Monsieur Deschamps. She hadn't practised the Beethoven he'd given her as much as she'd hoped, but she remembered his complaint of being ill and felt guilty for not going before. To tell the truth, his bitterness over what he saw as Serge's treachery had kept her away. She felt a certain loyalty to Serge and could not of course tell the old man about what had happened to him. She could not tell anyone. She sent a note to her teacher, but received no answer. This worried her and she became determined to visit him. He might after all be unwell again.

It was the concierge at his apartment block who broke the news. 'Oh no, madame, you have not heard? Monsieur Deschamps passed away, oh a few weeks ago. I am so sorry.'

Kitty stumbled out her thanks and turned away. The poor man, she hadn't realized he'd been quite so ill. And now she wished from the bottom of her heart that she'd been to see him before. How easy it was in life to look the wrong way and miss something like this. When she tried to explain to Fay why they weren't seeing the old man with the piano, after all, she felt a terrible despair. He'd been a kind and encouraging teacher, and now that he'd gone, the whole reason she'd come to Paris had vanished, too. At a time when there was so much loss and grief, she still felt his death keenly.

Serge would be upset, too, she knew he would. He'd always held the old man in high esteem, and though he'd been terribly hurt by his rejection, he understood it. For Monsieur Deschamps in his old-fashioned suits represented the old French sense of honour. His were ideals that demanded complete loyalty and Serge would have respected that, even if he couldn't live by it himself.

Serge. She had to tell him.

It wasn't much further to the convent and Fay's face lit up when Kitty suggested they go. Kitty looked about carefully before crossing the Rue St-Jacques and taking Fay to the Place des Moineaux. The convent appeared as peaceful as ever in the sunshine, but when one of the Sisters opened the door, the greeting she gave was less enthusiastic than usual.

'May I speak with the Reverend Mother?' Kitty asked, wondering what was wrong. The Sister reluctantly widened the door to admit them.

'Please wait here while I fetch her,' the Sister mumbled, and Kitty and Fay idled in the hallway while she disappeared. Fay ambled over to stare at the figure of the young Virgin at prayer in the niche by the door, just at her eye-level. She was often told not to touch, but she liked to look at the girl's sweet face.

'Kitty, I'm so pleased to see you!' Thérèse came out of a room at the front of the house that the nuns used as a sitting room, her round face so vivid with pleasure today that she looked pretty, despite the severity of the plain coif that hid her hair. 'Hello, Fay!' Fay ran to her and Thérèse sank down to speak to her, and caressed the child's hair. She took Fay's hand.

'Sofie's in here, I'm teaching her to sew,' and Fay went first into the room, Thérèse and Kitty following. The girl Sofie was by herself today, laboriously tacking a row of stitches across a strip of old sheeting. Fay sat down close beside her to watch her work.

'Here, you want to do the same?' Thérèse said to her, reaching into a cloth bag on the low table before them and withdrawing a patch of canvas. 'I've a tapestry needle here, Kitty, not sharp at all. You can try this, Fay.' Poking the needle into the canvas she showed the child what to do.

They were watching her prodding at the cloth, her tongue poking between her teeth as she concentrated, when Mère Marie-François appeared at the door. There was something in her face that made Kitty rise at once and go to join her in the hall.

'Kitty, how can we help you, my dear?' Her voice was as calm and sweet as ever.

'I . . . hoped to see Serge. There's some news. No, not of his family, but our old teacher. I'm afraid he's died and – well, I thought Serge would like to know.'

'I can give him the message later. You can't see him now, I'm afraid. The moment's not convenient.' She glanced towards the closed door of her private sitting room. Someone else was in there, more than one person. She could hear the murmur of voices, men's voices. One, she thought, must be the curé. Was the other Serge? She felt her breath catch in her throat.

'No,' she heard the curé say, his voice suddenly nearer and louder. 'No, no, it is not possible. There is danger enough.'

The other man said something she couldn't quite hear, but she knew its rhythms. At once she was alert. 'Is that Eugene?' she whispered in surprise, and when the nun did not deny this, 'What is Gene doing here? Please, tell me.'

'Perhaps you should go in,' the Reverend Mother said wearily, and knocked at the door of her own room. The voices fell silent as they entered.

Kitty could hardly believe her eyes. There was Gene, standing by the fireplace smoking a cigarette with an air of nervous strain. The curé was starting from his chair, his face suffused with emotion. The third member of the party she also knew: Dr Poulon from the hospital, the man who'd delivered Fay. 'Mrs Knox,' he said in his formal way, coming forward to shake her hand.

'What are you doing here?' She sensed a terrible tension in the room. She looked from Gene to Dr Poulon, alarmed by their sober expressions. Finally, Eugene spoke – gently, but in an urgent voice.

'You shouldn't be here, Kitty. Go home. Please, go home. I hope you haven't brought Fay?'

'What is this about?' she asked, feeling a tingle of panic.

'I simply can't tell you, only that we've nearly finished.' He sighed. 'Perhaps you'd wait for us a moment outside, then I'll take you home.'

'Gene, please . . .' The panic grew.

'Kitty,' he said, exasperated, but then relented. 'All right. A cell we worked with has been betrayed. We are discussing new arrangements.' The other men watched her, their faces impassive.

It was Dr Poulon who spoke. 'This is very discourteous of us, Mrs Knox, but I'm afraid we need you to wait outside.' It was a voice that brooked no argument.

Wordless, Kitty turned and left the room. Mère Marie-François followed, shutting the door behind them.

'Come into the church, child,' she said. Her light touch on Kitty's shoulder was calming, but it was also a command. 'Perhaps you'll play for me while we wait.'

She led the way through the passage into the pale light of the church. The protective cover of the piano had been folded back and the elegant lines of the instrument gleamed in the shadows. How lovely it appeared in the lazy sunshine, though Kitty hardly noticed.

She sat at the keyboard and lifted its lid. 'I have no music,' she said dully, brushing her fingers across the keys.

'Play whatever you can remember,' the Reverend Mother said, sitting down on a chair in the front row.

At first her mind was frozen, then she glanced at the row of chairs where Eugene had sat that first time, when he'd come into the church uninvited. And now it came to her what she needed to hear. And very softly she began to play the long, ethereal opening chords of the Moonlight Sonata.

As she played, it was as though the music took hold, possessed her, and her anxiety ebbed away. '*Listen*,' she heard Monsieur Deschamps' voice say in her mind. '*Listen to the music, make it sing to you.*' And she let it sing, and its powerful, brave beauty spoke of all her love for Gene, all her fear, feelings too deep to put into words. Music was her voice, and through it she would speak.

When she came to the end of the movement and the last lingering chord faded away, a light rustle and a sigh reminded her of the presence of Mère Marie-François. Kitty looked up to see the old woman sitting straight-backed, her hands folded in her lap. Her eyes were closed and her cheeks glistened with tears.

What happened next shattered the moment.

Engines roared outside. The building trembled. Kitty covered her ears and flew to the window. She stood on a chair in time to see half a dozen motorcycles and a grey van surge into the square. There came the squeal of brakes, doors slamming, then all was a confusion of armed men and harsh voices.

'The Gestapo!'

Mère Marie-François gasped, then hastened to lock the main door to the street. Kitty leaped down and ran to the one which led back to the convent. Eugene, Fay – her only thought was to reach them. She gained the passage only to see the door ahead of her burst open. Fear possessed her but the man who rushed through, barging into her, was thankfully familiar. It was Eugene and he was carrying Fay.

'Take her!' He passed Fay over, then shut the door he'd come through and bolted it. Then, seizing Kitty's arm, he ushered her back into the church. There they found that Mère Marie-François had pulled back a carpet from the floor by the piano and was wrestling with a brass ring set in a flagstone on the floor.

'Help me!' she cried. 'It's the crypt, you can hide,' and Eugene went and seized the ring. The stone gave suddenly, lifting on its hinge to reveal stone steps down into darkness. Out of this a chill stole up, a chill of damp stone underground, and a stink of earth and death and decay. Kitty shivered and Fay cried out in fear.

'I can't take her down there,' she whispered. 'I simply can't.'

'It's me they've come for,' Gene said, his breathing heavy. 'Me and Poulon. I'm sure of this, Kitty. It's nothing to do with Serge, it's the other thing. With luck they'll let you go.'

'Oh, Gene,' she said, trying to digest this new and horrifying news. 'What can we do? And Dr Poulon . . .?'

'He's safe, I promise. I had to find you, to let you know – not to tell them anything.'

'Of course I won't, but—'

'There's no time,' the nun commanded in a tone Kitty had never heard before. 'Go, monsieur. The Lord will look after Kitty and the child.'

Eugene took one last loving look at his wife and went down into the hole. Kitty, desolate, set Fay on the ground and helped force the trap door shut. When it was done, they spread the carpet back over the spot. All the time Fay watched, clutching her zebra, her face a mask of distress. 'Papa,' she said. 'Papa.'

The piano. Kitty ran to its far side and gave it a shove, intending to shift it further onto the carpet, but it didn't move. She pushed the heavy instrument again, harder, and this time she felt the castors give. She tried again and it moved a couple of inches further. It was half on, half off the carpet when there came the sudden sound of gun-shots.

Chapter 24

'She stepped away from the piano,' Mme Ramond's voice was tense, 'as a commotion came from the passage to the convent. The brutes had broken through the door. They rushed into the church and—'

'Why didn't she hide?' Fay cried, unable to stop herself.

'What?' Mme Ramond was still lost in her story.

'My mother wasted time when she and the Reverend Mother could have escaped with me by the front of the church. After all, the Gestapo wouldn't have known my father was in there. Would they?' She faltered.

'I don't know – I suppose they did not. But Eugene would not have had time to explain that to Kitty. Anyway, who knows how any of us will act in a crisis? Perhaps they realized there were soldiers outside in the street. There probably were.'

'If the door between the church and the convent had been locked from the church side, the Gestapo would have guessed they were hiding something.'

'You may well be right.' The woman sounded impatient. 'Perhaps Kitty didn't hide because she believed your father when he said that it was only him the Gestapo wanted. The raid was not about them hiding

Serge at all. It was to do with one of the British patients at the hospital whom Eugene and Dr Poulon had helped. I'm certain of this.' Her voice had risen in frustration. She had to compose herself before going on.

'Four officers had arrived in the church, all armed. Kitty and the Reverend Mother were standing on the carpet, Kitty holding you, and they were surrounded straight away and questioned. "Where is Dr Knox?" their leader demanded of Kitty. There was no mistaking those almost colourless eyes. He was Obersturmführer Hoff, the officer who'd visited them at the flat and questioned Gene so coldly. Of course, she would not tell him anything. At his order the other three began to search the church, whilst he paced up and down, snapping out questions at Kitty. What was she doing here? Where was her husband?

'It was then that Père Paul came hurrying in and remonstrated with them for disturbing the House of God, but the commanding offer told him to get out of the way. What else could the poor man do but stand aside and watch helplessly as they pulled up the skirts of the altar cloth, tore curtains aside and ransacked the vestry in their search.

'And the irony was that all the time, they were standing by the piano, on the carpet that covered the place where Eugene was hiding. Fay, you began to cry, and Hoff lost his temper and directed the Reverend Mother to take you away. Even your mother seemed to think this was best. It must have been terrifying for you.'

'When I visited the convent earlier this week,' Fay said slowly, 'I remembered the thud of boots on the stairs and people shouting ... and the statuette smashing on the floor.'

'When the Reverend Mother took you back into the convent, the men were still searching.'

1942

Fay had been sitting with Thérèse and the Belgian children having a drink in the kitchen, when she heard the roar of the vehicles and saw her father run past the open door. She cried out 'Papa!', left the table and followed him.

Moments later, the Gestapo burst into the convent. Hoff ignored the curé's protestations and set his men charging through the building. Shouts could be heard from overhead as they entered all the rooms, rounding up everyone they could find, including the Belgian family, and bringing them downstairs. Others began a detailed search of the ground floor. It was Hoff himself who shot out the locks of the doors to the church.

Later, everybody was herded through to the church, to find Hoff and his oppos tearing the place apart.

'Concern leaped into Kitty's eyes when she saw you back again,' Mme Ramond continued. 'There you were in Sister Thérèse's arms, wailing and holding out your arms to your mother, your cheeks streaked with tears, but she could do nothing. Hoff paced up and down studying everybody. His eyes were cold with anger, everyone could see that.

Sister Gabriel and Sister Clare, who were the oldest, were allowed to sit, but the rest of us were made to stand whilst his men continued to ransack the church. Sister Gabriel started muttering prayers over her rosary as he paced, and he shouted at her to stop. There was a silence. Then you started to cry again.

'It was after that when it happened. He crossed the floor to where Kitty was standing by the piano, as if to speak to her, and suddenly he stopped and looked down. He tested a patch of the carpet with his heel, before crouching to feel the spot with his fingers. Then Kitty was hauled aside whilst two men pushed back the piano. Her face, it looked so desperate, as he peeled back the carpet to reveal the brass ring in the trap door.

'He took hold of the ring himself and he pulled. Everybody was so quiet, you could hear them breathing. The door opened on its hinge with a grinding sound and there came a rush of cold air from underground, a horrible icy cold like death itself. Sofie, the little Belgian girl, gave a gasp.

'"Silence!" Hoff snapped.

'He produced a torch and, going down on one knee, shone it into the hole. I don't think he could see anything. He shouted, "Come out!" and we waited like Jesus's friends who witnessed Lazarus emerge from his tomb. But nothing happened.

'Hoff drew his pistol and fired it into the hole. The crack rang round the building. Kitty's eyes were wild, her face bleached white. Again there was nothing. Hoff climbed down the steps with torch and gun. One could imagine his torchlight flicking over the stone coffins of the long-dead until it met Eugene's eyes blinking out of the darkness.

'What happened next I cannot exactly say. A shout echoed up from the hole, then came sounds of a scuffle. Kitty tried to run to the hole, but one of the officers

dragged her back. Two of the others peered down, directing their torchbeams and arguing, then one climbed down
after his leader. Kitty cried, "Gene!" and struggled in her
captor's grip, but he pinned her arms more tightly behind
her back and pressed his hand over her mouth.

'From down below came an explosion of shots. The
nuns cried out in terror. Kitty struggled, but the man had
her pinioned.

'A moment later, a dishevelled Hoff emerged from the
crypt, still holding his smoking weapon. His face was
inscrutable.

'"He resisted arrest," he announced to the generality.
Then, "Clear the church," he ordered his men. "They can
all go. Frau Knox, however, comes with us in the van."

'Kitty gave a terrible cry: "*Gene ...*"

'Hoff would not look at her.

'It was over.'

'He murdered my father,' Fay whispered.

'Yes.' Mme Ramond spoke the word like a sigh. 'In
France, you know, we have the *crime passionel* – violence
committed in the heat of passion. This killing was in cold
blood: like an execution. I have often thought about why.
Perhaps your father did or said something unwise down
there underground. Perhaps the German could not bear to
be humiliated in front of all those women. We will never
know. I did not see them bring the body out. None of us
did. They sent us all back into the refectory, whilst they
combed the convent quickly once more. Perhaps they
were looking for Dr Poulon or one of the Allied servicemen, I do not know. They left without finding the room
where Poulon and Serge were hiding.

'Your mother, they took away with them. She fought as

they led her out to the van, her face ravaged with shock. She was searching for a last glimpse of you – her lips shaped your name. I stood by the window in the kitchen with you so that Kitty could see you. She gave you one final lingering look before they lifted her up into the back of the van and slammed the doors.

'A moment later, she had gone.'

The sun had moved off the window of the Ramonds' flat and the room was falling into gloom. Hardly able to bear what she'd just heard, Fay rose and crossed to look through the glass down to the street below. Her gaze focused on a young man on a motor scooter who had stopped to speak to a demure girl clutching a music case and she heard their laughter. Further down, a portly man with a balding head and a white apron swept soapy water from the pavement outside his shop. A little girl skipped along beside her elegant mother. A withered old man in a jellabah loitered at the street corner smoking and looking up at the sky where Fay saw the silver glint of an aeroplane. Peaceful scenes, but only twenty years ago, any of these people might have been shot in cold blood, like her father had been. Or have witnessed it happen to someone else. It was difficult to believe, but it was true.

Was this the heart of her mother's secret then, the story of how Fay's father, Kitty's beloved Gene, had been executed? Why hadn't he been taken prisoner instead? How was it that Serge and the other man, Dr Poulon, had not been found? There was so much that might never be answered.

There was something else that was troubling her, something worrying at the corner of her mind that Mme

Ramond had said – but she couldn't think what it was for the moment, couldn't quite catch hold of it.

But now her mind was moving on. She turned and asked Mme Ramond, 'What happened to my mother? Where did they take her?' She came and sat down on the sofa once more.

'Initially she was taken to the Gestapo headquarters in the Avenue Foch. Père Paul was able to discover that much, but after that, for a long time, nothing more.'

Fay suddenly remembered what she thought was odd. It was a mistake Nathalie Ramond had made. How had it not registered at the time? The woman had said it so naturally that Fay hadn't noticed. Or maybe it was something that unconsciously she'd known for a long time. She knew who Mme Ramond was now.

'You said "we".'

'Excuse me?'

'Just now, when you described the scene in the church. You said "we". You were there, Mme Ramond, weren't you? You saw it all.' And now she felt anger, anger and frustration, that this woman hadn't told her the truth. All this time she'd shielded her identity from Fay.

But now, instead of being defensive, Mme Ramond's expression grew tender. She smiled and in the soft light it was as though all the years fell away and the marks of pain dissolved and she was familiar. Fay remembered her. A gentle young woman with a serene face and an infectious laugh. Fay's eyebrows knitted as she strained to recall her more clearly.

'Do you remember, Fay?' this new tender version of Mme Ramond whispered. 'There was a song I used to sing you, a silly nonsense song about planting cabbages.

It always made you laugh.' She began to hum. '"*Savez vous planter les choux, à la mode, à la mode . . .*" That's how it went. You used to love to sing. Such a sweet voice you had.'

'I know you,' Fay whispered in gathering wonder. 'I do remember. You're Thérèse, aren't you? Sister Thérèse. But . . .' She studied the woman before her in her neat wool suit, the crucifix at her breast, the gold ring on her finger. 'You're married.'

Mme Ramond glanced down at her hand. 'If you're a nun,' she murmured, 'you wear a ring to show you're a bride of Christ. But I was released from my vows. My name is Nathalie now. It always was my name, of course – I was born with it. I only became Thérèse when I entered the convent. I had always had an attachment to the Little Flower of Lisieux.'

She raised her eyes to meet Fay's. Fay was so full of questions but she didn't know where to start. This new knowledge made everything different in ways she couldn't begin to comprehend. The whole story about her mother. Everything.

'Why did I leave the convent?' Mme Ramond said. 'Is that what you wish to ask?'

'Yes. And about Serge.'

Mme Ramond folded her hands in her lap and sighed. 'Tomorrow I will tell you,' she said. 'The next bit is difficult for me to relate and I don't have the strength for it now.'

As Fay rose to go, Nathalie Ramond asked her to pass the old album that lay on the sofa next to her. The older woman opened it on her lap and turned the pages until she came to the photograph of Fay and her father.

'Here we are, my dear,' she said. She separated the

photograph from the page with care and passed it to Fay, who looked up at her enquiringly.

'I can't remember at all how I came to have it. Take it, it's yours.'

'Oh, thank you,' Fay said, thrilled, examining it again with feelings of tenderness. Then with care she hid it in her handbag.

Chapter 25

'*Mademoiselle,* wait – you have a letter.'

Fay thanked the hotel receptionist, seeing with surprise and pleasure that the letter was from her mother. She went into the breakfast room, which was empty, settled herself at a table and slit open the letter with the handle of a teaspoon someone had forgotten to put away.

The note inside was written on cheap paper in Biro, probably all the hospital had. Her mother had written quickly, agitation evident in the handwriting, which was less even and elegant than usual. In it, Kitty went straight to the point.

My darling Fay

Dr Russell has given me your message and I knew I had to contact you straight away. I'd simply no idea you'd meet Nathalie Ramond or that the wretched woman was even in Paris. I urge you not to talk to her, Fay, or if I'm too late, don't believe everything she tells you. I repeat: do not believe her. It was because of her I nearly lost you.

I realize now that I should have spoken to you myself and told you everything, and when you return, if you can bring yourself to even speak to me, I shall try to explain properly. I never did when you were a child because I

*wanted to protect you, and later – I'm ashamed to say
this – I did not have the courage. Now my failure torments
me in every waking moment. I know I've let you down
badly all over again.*

*I hoped you'd see your old rucksack with the label and
remember something of what happened, and, if you did,
you'd find Mère Marie-François, or the old curé, I think his
name was Paul Lavisse.*

I'm so sorry, darling, sorry for everything.

*I hope the concerts are a big success and that you're
having a lovely time, Fay. I can't wait to see you again to
have a proper talk.*

*Dr Russell is looking after me very well. I think we are
almost friends.*

*From your loving mother,
Katherine Knox*

Fay read it through a second time, her hand over her mouth, her face strained with despair. It not only upset her that her mother sounded so distressed, but because what she said threw Fay into confusion once more. What part of Nathalie Ramond's story should she believe? All of it or bits? Which bits? What should she do and whom should she trust? Over the last few days her world had shifted on its axis, and now, just as she'd been getting used to the new perspective, it was shifting once more.

She laid the letter on the table and stared sightlessly ahead, her chin resting on her hand, her lips quivering. She felt like crying.

She was suddenly angry with her mother. What right had Kitty to tell her what to believe, whom to listen to? Her mother herself had lied, it now seemed. It was up to her, Fay, to decide, and she knew what she wanted to do. She would hear out Mme Ramond's story, and then she'd weigh everything up and judge which was the correct version. The deer park and the whitewashed house in Richmond, or the convent and the apartment on the Left Bank? Or both? Her mind whirled. Did the stories fit together, or was one – or both – a lie?

Fay was still reflecting on the letter when a gruff voice interrupted her thoughts. She looked up to see a middle-aged man, somewhat broad in the beam, and with a fringe of hair around his otherwise bald head. He wore a short apron and carried a set of keys.

'I'm sorry?' she said, blinking.

'It is I who must apologize for disturbing you.' He went to the corner of the room where there was a small bar and proceeded to unlock the padlock on the grille that stood round it.

'Oh no, no. I was only sitting here thinking.'

'Not bad news, I hope?' he said, lifting a section of the counter and squeezing through behind it. 'Your letter – it has upset you, no?' He took a cloth and started polishing glasses.

Fay smiled briefly and shook her head. 'It's from my mother,' she said. 'I've done something to annoy her, that's all.'

'Ah,' he said, his face lighting up. 'That is part of growing up. We must learn to make our own decisions and this cannot always please our mothers.'

'No, I suppose it can't,' she said thoughtfully. She watched him pour an amber liquor into two glasses.

He passed one to her, taking the other himself. 'Let us drink to our mothers. Where would we be without them, eh?'

She swallowed a mouthful of the brandy and coughed as it burned its way down. Somehow it made her feel better, more brave. She took another sip, which this time was more soothing.

'We all love our mothers,' the barman said, and drained his glass. 'But remember, mademoiselle, you must follow your heart.'

Whether it was the brandy or the man's words of advice, she couldn't say, but when she climbed the stairs to her room to change for dinner, she knew the right thing to do. She would go back to Mme Ramond to hear the last part of her story, she simply had to. Despite the rambling nature of the letter, her mother sounded better, stronger and more eager to talk. Fay had the right now to demand the truth from her. She was no longer a young girl to be comforted by untruths.

Sandra was in the room, lounging on her bed in a petticoat, smoking and listening to the French news on a tinny transistor radio. 'Not much happening in the world. President de Gaulle's presenting some medals in Paris tomorrow,' she remarked to Fay, yawning. She reached over and switched it off. 'I hope the city won't be too crowded. It's our last chance for some shopping.'

'Didn't you do some this afternoon?'

'No. Georges took me to a poky little theatre to see the most ridiculous melodrama. Oh, did you take that phone call? Someone came up asking for you a moment ago.'

'No, I didn't.' That must have been while she was in the breakfast room.

Fay hurried back downstairs to find that it was Adam who had called and left a message. He could meet her after all this evening, if she was free. She rang him back quickly and managed to catch him before he left the office.

When she replaced the receiver her mind was so full of him that she almost forgot to ring the curé. She tried his number straight away, but again, nobody answered. He was probably out taking the evening service.

After Fay had left that afternoon, Nathalie Ramond returned to her drawing room and for a long time sat thinking of the past. Today had been difficult and she hoped that she'd been right to say the things she had and to leave out the others. It was hard to remember clearly the exact order of events that had taken place at Sainte Cécile's that dreadful day nearly twenty years ago, but the manner of Eugene Knox's death she recalled as though it were on a piece of film playing on a loop before her. She closed her eyes to shut it out.

Chapter 26

Twilight – *l'heure bleue* – wasn't that what they called it in Paris? Fay could see why. It was like a change of scene when the light of day dimmed and the colours of the sky segued into night. As she walked out of the hotel on her way to meet Adam, a woman was pulling down the shutter of the gift shop opposite with a long pole. Next door, a café-owner was stacking tables and chairs to be carried inside. Outside the fruit shop, a girl in navy overalls swept the pavement with long, weary strokes.

If daytime Paris was furling her wings like the starlings roosting in the trees of Place de la Madeleine, her nightlife was about to spread its gaudy plumage. A necklace of coloured lights now fringed the awning of the tourist café on the square, where a waiter was chalking names of the specials on a slate. The Art Nouveau lanterns by the Métro glowed with tender mistiness as Fay hurried down the steps.

When she emerged from the station in Montmarte, Adam was waiting, a solitary figure dressed in a dark suit, leaning on a railing and staring up in contemplation at the dome of the church of Sacré-Coeur, which dominated the indigo sky like a giant vanilla ice cream.

'Hello, Adam,' she called, and saw his expression of wistfulness change to a delighted grin. He returned her greeting and kissed her cheek.

'You look nice.' His quick eye appraised her – and she was glad she'd worn her mother's gold stole to go with the black cocktail dress. The look, completed by court shoes and long gloves (borrowed from Sandra), not only complemented his, but felt right for the mood of the evening. The indigo velvet sky, the strings of tiny lights in the trees, the bright chatter of the crowds ... tonight the air was charged with excitement.

It seemed natural, the way she slipped her arm in his and he squeezed it gently. 'I've booked a table at a little place I know not far away. The scallops there have to be tasted to be believed.'

'Lead me to them,' said Fay, who'd never eaten a scallop. They crossed a square where a few artists were still offering to draw portraits of tourists and set off down a winding street lined with ancient, misshapen buildings – shops and restaurants mostly – with intriguing dark alleys branching off on either side.

'I'm sorry about the short notice,' he said. 'I wasn't needed tonight, after all. You aren't in trouble, are you, for letting the others down?'

'No, it didn't seem to matter,' she replied. Dinner tonight had been at one of the other hotels, and was expected to be a quiet affair. Sandra had promised to convey her apologies, though she herself was planning to leave immediately after the meal to meet her amour at a nightclub. 'What were you expecting to have to do?'

'Oh, there was a meeting I thought I'd have to go to, but in the end it was all right.' She sensed by his tone that he didn't wish to speak about it, so while thinking it strange she didn't pursue the matter.

Anyway, now they'd come to a cheerful-looking restaurant, its frontage lit by a trail of coloured electric bulbs. There were tables on the street and much decorative greenery. Inside, a bosomy woman in a close-fitting lace dress showed them to a pretty corner near the window where there was a round table set with white linen, sparkling silver and glass and a spray of pink blossom in a vase.

The scallops were indeed delicious, served with a buttery sauce, and the pale wine, which was drier than Fay was used to, slipped down delightfully. She wondered how something so cold could make you feel warm. When they'd finished, the waiter bore away their plates and brought lamb fragrant with garlic and so tender it fell from the bone.

Fay found herself opening up to Adam, and he listened with serious concentration, nodding occasionally, or taking a sip of wine as she related all that Mme Ramond had told her about her mother, and how she'd protected Fay. She spoke with a catch in her voice as she described her father's death. The shock and sympathy showed naked in Adam's face, and when she faltered he reached out and caught her hand.

After she'd finished speaking they were silent for a moment, then, 'That's awful,' he managed to whisper.

'But I know who she is now – Madame Ramond, I mean. Adam, she's been hiding it from me all this time, deliberately, and I'm so confused. I think she must have done something she's ashamed of. I – I don't know what the truth is.'

'Hey, slow down,' he said. 'What do you mean, you know who she is? I thought she was a friend of your mother's.'

'Yes, but I didn't know exactly who.' And she explained about Sister Thérèse, who'd known her mother from the moment she arrived in Paris, who had seen her dedication to her music, and watched as she'd fallen in love and married and had Fay. All the things that Thérèse would never do, shielded as she was from such matters in the confines of the convent.

'And then this letter arrived from my mother.' She unclipped her handbag and drew out the envelope. As she did so, she glimpsed the hurried script and remembered the rawness of the words. Should she show this letter to a stranger? Her mother might not like it. But Adam wasn't a stranger to Fay. Not any more. She felt close to him, as though they'd known each other for years. Yes, she wanted him to see it. She unfolded the single page and passed it over.

'Are you sure?' he asked, seeing her hesitation, and she nodded, so he took it.

Was it really possible to feel like this about someone you'd met so few times? Fay asked herself. Then she remembered the story of her parents – and knew that it was. Kitty and Eugene had known almost instantly that they were meant for one another. The question was, did Adam feel the same about her?

All this she thought as she watched him read the letter, his forehead creasing. She ate and felt better simply for having shared her burden.

'How very puzzling,' Adam said, returning the letter to her. 'You seem to be caught in the middle of all this. What do you think you'll do?'

She thought about her argument with herself earlier. 'What I want to do is to hear Madame Ramond out. I've begun to remember more things, Adam.' And as she said this, she knew it was true. She remembered Sister Thérèse now, her pleasant dimpled face, the sigh of her habit as she moved. When Fay had visited the convent she'd recalled the tramping of boots on the stairs, her fear as the Gestapo had searched the building.

But there were things she did not recall. Of her father's death, nothing. Her mind simply refused to engage with it, though when she thought about it now it conjured a faint feeling of terror, like the fleeing coat-tails of an evil dream.

'It's as though I've been handed pieces of a jigsaw,' she told Adam. 'But there are still some missing. And there's a great area of sky where I can't see where to put the pieces I've already got. Madame Ramond must have some of the missing pieces and my mother may have others, but I'm the one who has to fit them together and make sense of them.' She glanced at her mother's letter, lying on the table. 'Or decide whether they belong to the puzzle at all. It's my picture, you see. The picture of my life. I *have* to understand it.'

'How will you know what is true,' Adam asked, 'if there are conflicting accounts? Who is telling the truth? You see, it's not just you. We all have to face this. People have different versions of what happens. Everyone is sure that theirs is the right one. Take the episode I told you about when I rescued my sister from drowning. My mother insists that she was nearby, and that she rushed over to help pull Tina out, but I don't recall her being there at all. Did my five-year-old self remember more clearly than she did, or did I distort such an event to put myself at the centre of it?'

'That's strange, but you're right, of course,' Fay said quietly. 'I don't know how I shall determine what is the truth, but I'll try to get as close to it as I can.'

Adam nodded. 'I understand.'

'Madame Ramond gave me something.' Again, Fay reached for her handbag. This time she withdrew the photograph of herself with her father. Once again she gazed at it, appreciating how safe and comforted she must have felt with him, how fondly he held her. She passed it across to Adam, who examined it, his face softening.

'You look very like him in some ways,' he said, glancing up at her. 'It's your expression. You both have the same smile.'

'Thank you,' she whispered. He couldn't have said anything that she'd wanted to hear more.

They finished their lamb in companionable silence and ordered sorbet, which arrived in tall scalloped glasses and which they ate with long spoons.

The restaurant was filling up now, the air swirling with the smell of food, with smoke and conversation. From somewhere near the back wafted the sounds of jazz piano. Adam lit a cigarette. Each was lost in their own thoughts, but in a way that seemed natural, not because they couldn't think of anything to say to one another.

The waiter came with coffee. 'I'm looking forward to your concert,' Adam said, stirring sugar into his. 'It's a programme of Russian music, isn't it?'

'Yes, you'll enjoy it, I think. Colin seems most worried about the Tchaikovsky. He's unkind enough to say we sound hysterical rather than ecstatic in one of the movements.'

'Relief at reaching it, perhaps?'

'Not at all, it's a lovely piece. '

'It's helpful to know for my review. I shall watch you all for signs of hysteria.'

'Adam, don't! I shouldn't have pointed it out. I'm glad you're coming though.'

'It's my job. And anyway, there's a much more important reason.' And now when she met his eyes it was hard to look away.

'I wish I could see you tomorrow,' he said, 'but I think I'll be tied up most of the day.'

'Working?' she asked, trying to mask her disappointment. They didn't have much time left together.

'Not really.' He took a final draw on his cigarette, then took a while stubbing it out in the ashtray. 'There's to be a military parade tomorrow down the Champs-Élysées.'

'Sandra heard about that on the radio. It's to do with the President awarding medals, isn't it?'

'Yes, to mark some wartime anniversary.'

'And you'll be reporting on it.'

'I want to go down and see what's happening. I have a feeling there might be some sort of trouble.'

'Trouble?'

'Nothing major, I assure you. It's just these things can become a focus for . . . well, discontent.'

'What do you mean? Will it be dangerous?'

'Not for me.' He was looking round now, as though he thought someone might be eavesdropping. 'I'm worried about some friends of mine, that's all.'

'Oh.' Things were starting to become clear in her mind.

'Is this something to do with the meetings you've been going to?' but now the woman in the lace dress had arrived with their bill and he didn't hear her.

After he'd paid, Adam leaned back, smiling at her. 'There's a nightclub nearby where they have rather good bands. I don't suppose you fancy going on there?' He appeared to have forgotten their previous conversation.

She shouldn't be back too late, but she didn't want the evening to end. 'Why not?' she said.

They walked out together into the night, holding hands, down a street busy with milling, laughing people. Cars and scooters were forced to edge past cautiously. After a few hundred yards Adam showed her down a steep flight of stone steps and they entered a cellar with black-painted walls and a small stage drenched in gold light. Here a piano and a saxophone and a voluptuous singer wove together melancholy love songs that melted the heart. Adam bought drinks and they stood together listening. Several couples were slow-dancing and after a while Adam leaned across and spoke in her ear: 'I haven't had much practice since that school trip, but will you have a go?'

'I'll risk it,' Fay replied, smiling. He held her close to dance, and she felt the warmth of his breath in her ear as they swayed to and fro in time to the music. She shut her eyes and gave herself up to the moment, the music flowing through her and Adam's cheek brushing hers.

It was getting on for midnight when they emerged into the cool air. Adam tucked her arm in his and they ambled together somewhat aimlessly back the way they'd originally come. The streets were quieter now and some of the restaurants and cafés were starting to close for the night. Others, clearly prepared for the long haul, were still busy with customers.

'I suppose I shouldn't be too late,' Fay said, in an unconvincing tone.

'I'll find you a taxi, shall I?'

'Mmm, or you could walk me to the Métro. Will there still be trains?'

'For another hour at least.'

'What about you? You live nearby, don't you?'

'Yes,' he said. 'We'll be passing the end of my street.'

She turned to him. 'I'd love to see it,' she said, on impulse. 'If you wouldn't mind, that is.' She stopped, worried that she'd crossed some line. It was just she hated the thought that she would leave Paris soon and wouldn't have seen where he lived.

'Would you really?' he asked, his eyes searching hers. 'I don't mind at all, but you really mustn't expect anything glamorous.'

'I won't if you'd rather not,' she said gently, biting her lower lip. 'It's only so ... I can imagine you being there. When I think of you.'

'When you think of me. I like that.' And when he smiled she felt elated.

'Here we are.' They turned down a dimly lit street where the sounds of nightlife receded, and buildings of several storeys rose on either side. Here and there a light showed at an upstairs window, which helped to illuminate the uneven pavement. Beyond a row of shuttered shops, Adam stopped and unlocked an unassuming-looking door. Inside was a tiny lobby where he pushed a button and a linoleum-covered staircase was revealed in the sepia glow from a naked pendant light.

'I'm afraid it's at the top,' he said, and started to climb.

'How many floors?' she gasped after the sixth flight brought them to a third landing.

'I'm on the next. Not far now.'

Outside a door on the top floor, as he twisted the key in the lock, the landing light snapped off. 'Damn,' he said, out of the darkness, and she giggled, but he got the door open.

'Wait a second while I tidy up a little,' he said, going in ahead. A light glowed suddenly and she heard the sound of him moving around like some animal, and drawers and cupboards being opened and closed, then his slight figure darkened the doorway and he found her hand and drew her inside, saying, 'Mind the shoe rack here.'

They were in a large attic room with wooden floors and a sloping ceiling. There was a casement window set high in the gable end. Because the light was on, the glass reflected back at them blackly. The room was chilly and he switched on an electric fire. Immediately it looked more cosy.

'Oh, Adam, it's lovely.' She found herself looking about for clues to his life. Against the highest wall stood a wardrobe and a bookcase full of books. There was a single bed in a corner, untidily made. Much of the rest of the room was taken up by an ancient desk. On it was a type-writer with a leaf of paper scrolled up, haphazard piles of documents and photographs, and a large glass ashtray.

'What do you do about cooking?'

'There's a kitchen on the floor below. The bathroom's down there, too. I eat out a lot. I'm not much of a cook, to be honest, and I find eating on my own a bit lonely. It's not easy to invite people here for meals either.'

Although he said this in a perfectly ordinary way, not sounding sorry for himself at all, Fay did pity him. He must have friends here in this city but it could be a solitary life.

'I like it,' he said. 'It's quieter than you'd think, and I can just shut myself away from the world and get on with my writing. Yet it's quite central. It doesn't take long to walk to the office. The other people in the building are pleasant, though they keep themselves to themselves. And there's one thing about this place that I love above all . . .' As he said this he went and took a short pair of steps that rested in a corner, positioned them beneath the window and climbed up. Here he unfastened a bar and pulled the window open, then pushed back the shutters.

'Come on,' he said, turning to her. 'It's perfectly safe. Put on that jacket if you like, it can be chilly.' When she was ready, he stepped out first then reached down a hand to help her up. 'Mind your feet there. Now you're all right.'

They had climbed out onto a flat roof crowded with fragrant plants in pots and edged with a low wrought-iron rail that shone white against the darkness. Instinctively she clutched Adam's hand, not daring to move, knowing it was so high up, then gradually her eyes adjusted to the light and she saw he was right. There was no dizzying drop to fear. Instead, a jumble of rooftops spread in all directions in a man-made landscape of valleys and hills. She could see other terraces like this one. Ridged roofs and gabled windows jutted up, and all around were the lights of night-time Paris. Further up the hill loomed the dome of Sacré-Coeur, only half-obscured by other buildings. Adam pointed out the flashing light at the top of the Eiffel Tower, in the opposite direction, far in the distance. Overhead was spread the canopy of the sky, with a bone-coloured moon veiled with snatches of cloud, and all around, bright winking stars. A light wind ruffled her hair, and she was glad of the sports coat and the warmth of his hand in hers.

'It's completely marvellous,' she whispered.

'Isn't it? I love it up here,' Adam said. 'It's surprisingly peaceful, even in the daytime.' He was right, the night-time noises of the street sounded muffled, like the sea. 'I often bring a chair out here and sit and look at the view and think great thoughts.'

Fay was very aware of him close to her, squeezing her hand, but sensed, too, that he was a little preoccupied.

'Yes,' he sighed, 'it's a good place to think. It makes you look at the world from a new angle.'

'It certainly does that,' she breathed, and noticed far-off spiky towers bathed in a pinkish glow. 'Look, is that Notre Dame?'

'Yes, very distinctive, isn't it?'

She wanted badly to lean into him, to lay her head against his shoulder, but something stilled her – an alone-ness about him. And after a while he said, 'Shall we go down now? I've got a bottle of Calvados somewhere.'

Back in the room, the window firmly closed, he pot-tered about finding glasses and her eye fell on some items on the chest of drawers. A photograph and a wooden carv-ing. There was something about the carving that interested her. She took a step nearer. It was the willowy figure of a woman, about eight inches high, very graceful, and carrying what looked like a bundle or a basket on her head.

'She's lovely, isn't she?' Adam said, pouring amber liquid into two tumblers. 'African, I expect you know. A friend here gave her to me.'

'She's beautiful,' Fay agreed. 'May I?' And when he nodded, she picked up the object and turned it in her hands, feeling the smoothness of the wood. Although it was simply done, whoever had made it had a natural talent, an affinity with the way the grain ran, and she loved the vitality of the figurine. It reminded her a little of her zebra – there was the same care in its making. It made her feel a connection with Adam to think that he had a carving like she did. That it was something he loved, she was in no doubt. It showed in the way he took it back from her as he handed over her glass, and stood it in its place.

He noticed her curious eyes move to the photograph. '*La famille* Warner,' he said, passing the frame to her. She was standing in shadow and had to move over to the standard lamp to see it clearly under the reflections on the glass. A mother, a father and two children all in best coats and hats outside a church. The boy was about ten, his wide smile immediately recognizable. 'This is really you?' she teased and he gave that same smile. 'And I remember Tina from that picture you showed me in the restaurant. Oh, your mother's so pretty.' Mrs Warner was neat and merry-looking with soft blonde hair like her son's. His father was dark-haired, with round glasses and a felt hat with a brim. It was difficult to read his expression. Surprised? Perhaps he simply didn't like being photographed.

'Nice,' she said, holding it out to him. 'You look a happy family.'

She knew immediately that she had touched the scar of some old wound, for Adam took the photograph from her and weighed it in his hand before pushing it into the shadows on the chest of drawers.

'We were happy then,' he said in a measured tone. Did she imagine the slightest of stresses on 'were'? He must have sensed her unease, because he laid his fingers on her arm for a brief moment in a gesture of reassurance. She waited, uncertain of what to say.

He dropped his arm, turned away and picked up his glass, took a large mouthful and swallowed. 'There's something I ought to have told you before,' he said.

Raising her eyebrows in reply, she sat down with her drink on the pair of steps, feeling the fiery apple brandy sear her throat as she watched him pace the room. What could be wrong? She wanted to hear it and she didn't want to. What if it meant he couldn't love her or that she shouldn't love him?

Finally he dragged out the chair from under his desk and straddled it, then sat looking into his glass, agitating it so that the Calvados swirled in a miniature whirlpool. 'It's wrong not to say. I haven't before, because I'm ashamed.' His eyes fastened on hers. 'I don't know what you'll think.'

He still seemed undecided, but now it was like a loose thread in a favourite garment she couldn't leave alone, even though pulling at it might unravel the material altogether. There could be no lies between them. 'Adam?' She looked up at him gravely. 'You've got to tell me. It's not fair otherwise.'

'I know.' He reached into his jacket for his cigarettes and took them out, then seemed to change his mind, for he pocketed them again.

'All right then,' he said, with a bitter sigh. 'Fay, you've been spending the last few days with the son of a jailbird.'

Fay blinked. Whatever she had expected him to say, it wasn't that. For a moment she couldn't feel anything and her brain refused to function, then she was aware of the life flowing through her. Suddenly everything fell into place. The way he had rarely mentioned his father, a certain vulnerability about him. The fear she'd felt left her and now she was quite calm. Her world had not been turned upside down. They were still here, together, in this room. Nothing had changed between them, or not that she could see. She met his eye with a steady gaze.

'Go on, tell me about it,' she said evenly, and watched him breathe deeply and his shoulders relax.

'You're not shocked?'

'Not shocked exactly, but certainly surprised,' she said carefully. 'You haven't told me what your father did yet.'

'It was fraud,' Adam said. 'But even worse than that, he lied, Fay – he lied under oath and betrayed a friend.'

Fraud was bad, but at least it wasn't murder and still she felt calm. She listened as he told her the whole story. He spoke fluently, as though he'd had to tell it before, or had at least long brooded over it.

Adam's father, Geoffrey Warner, had been a director of a property company based in the City of London. One of his fellow directors was an old schoolfriend named Rupert Fielding, the other a former colleague of Fielding's. The three of them had set up the firm together after the war, and because of the national building programme that followed the cessation of hostilities they did rather well. But then Geoffrey had made a mistake, a bad mistake. He'd bought a large family house in Chelsea where he moved with Adam and Tina and their mother, and to pay for the deposit asked Fielding for a personal loan. The man had turned him down. This led him to do something, the reason for which he later said was inexplicable. Unknown to the others, ahead of an expected windfall from a deal that was going through, he'd covertly borrowed some money from the company account, imagining that he'd pay it back quickly and no one would know any the better. The problem was that the deal collapsed because of the unexpected death of the other party, and Adam's father suddenly had no way of replacing the money he'd taken.

'What he should have done then, of course, was to sell our house, even though we'd just moved in, but he couldn't bring himself to disappoint my mother, who has always thought the world of him and was so proud of this concrete sign of his success. He, meanwhile, thought – not unreasonably – that money would soon come in from somewhere, since business was going so well, but before that could happen their bookkeeper spotted the discrepancy in the accounts and it all came out. My father begged his fellow directors not to make anything of it, and offered finally to sell the house and pay back the money. Rupert Fielding was reluctantly in favour of this in order to avoid the scandal, *and* because my father was an old friend of his, but the third director refused to countenance this course of action and called in the police.

'I was only twelve at the time,' Adam said, 'and my parents told me nothing to begin with, but I was old enough to be aware that something was very wrong. Police turned up at the house once or twice and there were long conversations behind closed doors. My mother went around all the time looking as though she was about to burst into tears. They had rows, terrible rows, and I would lie awake listening to them shouting at each other. She had to tell us something in the end. The trial when it happened was a very public affair because the third director was married to the daughter of a government minister, and there were newspapermen camped outside our house. After several days of this, my mother sent my sister and me to stay with our grandparents in the country. The grandparents told us nothing because they wanted to protect us, but this was worse because we worried all the same.'

What happened, Adam went on to explain, was that under all this pressure Geoffrey Warner lost touch with reality. He got it into his head that Fielding had let him down. If Fielding had lent him that money, he thought, the whole situation would never have happened, and, what was more, he latched on to something he claimed Fielding had said and twisted it against him. He said Fielding had told him he could take the money from company funds and that he'd 'square it' with the other director, and, against all legal advice, insisted on making this the main plank of his defence. Fielding hotly denied he'd ever said this and in the end the jury believed him rather than Warner. The damage was irrevocable. The business collapsed in disarray. Adam's father went to prison for six years.

'You can guess the effect of all this on a twelve-year-old boy and a ten-year-old girl,' Adam said. 'It was intolerable, utterly, miserably intolerable. We lost the house anyway, of course. There was a huge legal bill to pay. We moved to live with my grandparents. It was partly a matter of money, but my mother also, somewhat foolishly, thought we'd have a better time of it there, but of course people read the papers, don't they? Everybody knew. And Tina and I were treated badly at school until the other kids got bored. Some of the children were forbidden by their parents to be friends with us. But worst of all, I think, was ... oh, Fay, he was my *father* – he'd fought in the war and won a medal, and yet he'd done this awful thing.' She saw his throat contract as he swallowed and the tic of his pulse.

'It must have been horrible,' she whispered. It didn't take much to imagine how it might have been for him. Like most boys, Adam would have seen his father as a hero, doubly so if he'd been decorated in the war. To have seen him convicted as a thief and a liar – it didn't bear thinking about. And Adam would have carried all this like a stone in his heart.

'Oh, Adam,' she said again. And in a moment of impulse she went to kneel at his feet, laying her cheek against his knee.

'Hey,' he said softly, stroking her hair. 'It's all right. *I'm* all right. It's just ... you had to know.'

'I did,' she said, lifting her head. 'Thank you for telling me.' Then, 'If it was six years, I suppose he's out now, is he?'

'Yes. It was the year after we met on that school trip they let him out. I was off to university then, and glad to go. For me it was a chance to start again. No one much knew who I was there or thought to connect me with him. The case was old news by then. But he suffered, he suffers still. And it's been hard for my mother and my sister. Tina getting married has perked everyone up no end. It means a clean sheet for her, you see. People can stop feeling sorry for her at any rate. But for me? Every now and then I meet someone who recognizes the name. "You're Geoffrey Warner's son, aren't you?" *Fingers in the till, eh?* That's what they think, even if they don't say it.'

'Adam, I'm sure that's not always true. I certainly wouldn't think that.'

'No, but you're different from everyone else, Fay. You understand.'

'I hope I do,' she said soberly. 'Ow.' While he'd been talking she'd sat very still on her stool.

'Are you all right?'

'I've got cramp,' she laughed. She kicked off her shoes and hobbled over to the bed, where she sat down flexing and curling her feet.

'I can rub them if you like?' This, hesitantly.

'No,' she said, embarrassed. 'It's better now. Go on.'

'I was wondering if it mattered,' he said, his eyes not leaving her face. 'About my father.'

'It sounds awful, the whole thing. Terrible for you all.'

'But does it – I don't know – affect what you think about me?' He waited, still gazing at her, poised as if on a knife's edge for her answer.

'No,' she said finally. 'How could what your father did be your fault?'

There was relief in his face, but still anxiety. 'You don't think it's in the blood then? Or in my upbringing or something? Sometimes ... well, this might sound stupid, but I feel I need to prove it to myself. That I'm not like him.'

How dreadful and grown-up it sounded, to have to demonstrate that one was not like one's parents.

Everything Fay had discovered about her mother and father over the previous few days had made her feel just the opposite – that she *wanted* to be like them, especially her father, brave and true as he was. She remembered then that she was angry with her mother for lying to her, but still, she hadn't sorted out the reason for her mother's behaviour yet, nor what the exact nature of the lies was. No, she felt much sorrier for Adam.

'I think you're a good person,' she said quietly, 'a very wonderful person,' and she saw the light come into his face.

He swung himself off the chair and stepped over to her and she rose from the bed to meet him. Now his arms were round her and she leaned into him and tipped her face up to his and they kissed with small tender kisses that became deeper, more searching. And he pressed her close, and she felt his lips on her hair and her eyelids and he whispered in her ear, 'Darling Fay, oh, my darling,' and bent to nuzzle her neck. A rush of warmth flowed through her, causing a poignant stab of tenderness.

After a while he said, 'How d'you undo this thing?' his voice rough with longing as he tugged at the brooch of her stole. She unpinned it for him and the shawl fell about their feet. He kissed her some more and ran his hands over her body, pressing her close. Then he set her at arm's length to look at her and there was a new confidence in his eyes that made her body turn electric under his gaze.

He rested his hands on her arms. 'May I?' he murmured, turning her round. His fingers on her zip were clumsy with impatience, but he got it undone, and helped her pull down the sleeves so that a moment later it joined the stole on the floor. And he lifted her up and went and laid her on the narrow bed. When he lowered himself beside her they kissed again. She felt for the buttons on his shirt.

And now each kiss, each caress woke deeper surges of desire within her as they twined together, exploring each other's bodies blindly with hands and lips, the touch of skin on skin ... and she was lost in his warmth.

There came a time, however, when he drew away, brushed back her hair and studied her face in the circle of light thrown by the lamp and she shivered, though whether from cold or his sudden absence she couldn't say. 'What is it?' she said.

'Don't you think we ought to stop?' he asked. 'I mean ...'

'No,' she said, loving him for his thoughtfulness. It was her first time, but she was surprised that she was so sure. She couldn't bear to let him go. Here, in this little attic, away from the busy world, they were not bound by ordinary ties. Here, she could give him the love and the certainty he needed, and take the same for herself. She felt she knew him, knew him deep down, and something vulnerable in him called to the same in her. They were two halves of a whole. All this she knew, but hadn't known long enough to put into words.

He smiled a smile full of tenderness and adoration, pulled the blankets over them both and bent to kiss her once more.

She drifted into languid wakefulness to find herself alone in the bed, the room bathed in bright sunlight. Rolling onto her elbow, she saw no sign of Adam. Come to think of it, she had briefly surfaced to hear him moving about earlier, but had sunk back into deep sleep. What time had that been? And what time was it now? Casting about for her wristwatch, her hand came upon it eventually under the bed. She squinted at the face. Half past eight. She groaned and fell back on the pillow, wondering where Adam could have gone and whether he'd be back soon, then slipped into a doze wherein her mind roamed happily over the pleasures of the night before. She remembered how they'd lain together afterwards face to face, and the softness of Adam's breath on her in the darkness. She came to. The room was beginning to feel hot. Probably she ought to get up. Sandra might worry about where she'd gone.

Adam had penned her a note. She found it propped up on his typewriter. *Darling girl, I didn't like to wake you. See you this evening after the concert. All my love, A.* She hadn't seen his handwriting before. It was like learning another side to him, the tiny, stylish italics contrasting with the generous downstrokes of the A. She stowed the note in her bag, glad to have something at least of him. Last night she'd felt so sure of him, but this morning that certainty was beginning to leak. Why had he taken off without an explanation? Had he gone to the office? He hadn't mentioned needing to leave quite so early. She dressed quickly, pulling the stole round her shoulders and slipping her shoes on, then let herself out. Before she closed the door she took a wistful look round the room. Mean and shabby some might think it, but to her it was perfect. It would be a part of her for ever.

Chapter 27

Saturday

It felt faintly racy to be going out in a cocktail dress and evening shoes at ten o'clock in the morning. The cheeky young man who served Fay at the café near Sacré-Coeur gave her a complicit wink across the counter. She smiled back as she sipped her café au lait. The Fay she'd been in London would have minded about being treated this way, but here in Paris she felt different, a new person almost. Was it simply to do with how she felt about Adam, or was it the city itself, or maybe something about her that had changed? She couldn't decide.

She ate the almond croissant the boy set before her and planned out her day. She'd take the Métro back to the hotel, freshen up and change her clothes. There was to be a short rehearsal ahead of the concert that evening, and before that she was to visit Mme Ramond, but the rest of the morning was hers. There was not that much time, but she knew what she needed to do. She'd visit the curé at the convent, and then she'd go back to her parents' old apartment in Rue des Palmes des Martyrs. The current occupants might be home. She badly wanted to see where she'd once lived. Maybe it would help her remember more.

Arriving back at the hotel, she found there was no one on reception. The key to the room was on its hook – Sandra must be out – so she leaned over the desk and took it. Upstairs she found the chambermaid's trolley in the corridor and when she entered the room saw it had already been made up. Either Sandra hadn't slept there or she'd risen early for her and gone. Fay washed and dressed quickly, found a more comfortable pair of shoes and went downstairs. In the lobby she hung the key back in its place and headed for the front door, then hesitated. It would be sensible, she supposed, to try the curé's number again first.

She was glad she did. The telephone at his house rang for a long time, but at last a faint-voiced woman answered in French and it took some effort for each to make the other understand. Eventually she discerned that the curé wasn't at home and, no, he wasn't at the convent either. He had gone to visit his brother in hospital. Fay was advised to telephone again after lunch. She thanked the woman and replaced the receiver and left the hotel intending to take the Métro to St-Germain-des-Prés, feeling somewhat frustrated in her plans and wondering what on earth it could be that the priest had to tell her.

The Rue des Palmes des Martyrs was full of life this morning, the shops open and market stalls set out on the pavement. A cyclist rang his bell furiously at Fay when she stepped into his path without looking and, to gain entrance to the apartment block, she had to squeeze past a badly parked car and a pair of women with prams, chatting.

The concierge was at his desk today, a middle-aged man

with a cherubic face reading a newspaper while a radio emanated jangly French rock and roll. He gave her only a cursory nod when she volunteered her business and pointed to the lift. As she waited, the radio announcer interrupted Johnny Hallyday with the news. She caught the words *'le Président'* and *'l'Arc de Triomphe'* as she rehearsed what she should say to the occupants of the flat. The only thing she needed to do, she decided when the lift arrived, was to keep her account simple.

When she emerged at the sixth floor she felt again that sense of threat. Was it merely the semi-darkness of the narrow corridor – or had the events of twenty years ago left their mark? Still, she told herself, there was no need to be fearful. Nothing here could hurt her now. This didn't stop her pausing outside number 612, listening as she laid her palm on the familiar bevelled handle of the door. She could hear the rise and fall of a woman's voice within, and lifted her hand and knocked.

'Bertrand!' A moment later the door was opened by a boy who, judging by his short slight stature, was twelve or thirteen, but when he smiled at her and said, *'Bonjour?'* in a growl that cracked at the second syllable, Fay realized he must be a year or two older than that.

She returned the greeting and asked in French, 'Your mother or father, are they at home? May I speak with one of them?'

'Ah, oui, ma mère est ici.'

'Qui est là, Bertrand?' The boy moved away as a small wiry woman came to the door. She had a patient, gentle face, with deep shadows under her eyes.

'I am sorry to trouble you, madame,' Fay said. 'My name is Fay Knox. I'm from England and I'm visiting

Paris.' Fay then managed to say that she used to live in this flat as a child and she wondered if she would be allowed to see inside.

The woman's face registered astonishment, then reluctance. 'It is not very convenient now. We have been away, you see, and only returned last night.'

'Please, I'm going back to London tomorrow.'

The woman sighed. 'I suppose you can come in, just for a moment.' She cast a glance down the corridor as though checking whether anyone was there, then widened the door for Fay to enter.

Fay found herself in a bright but untidy living room with windows that looked out at the building opposite. In an alcove near the window, a vase of drooping tulips stood on a gate-legged table. Something else used to be there, she sensed, but what? Her gaze swept the rest of the room eagerly. It did feel familiar, somehow, but much smaller than when she'd been a child, which was to be expected. A mahogany dresser filled the wall opposite the windows. She had sudden knowledge of how satisfyingly the brass handles of the drawers would rattle if she touched them. The sofa and chairs were surely different, and she had no memory of the geometric pattern of the carpet. She wasn't certain what she'd hoped to find here – some sort of connection with the place, she supposed, a sense of belonging – but she didn't, she really didn't. Other people lived here now and in a hundred ways they'd made it their own.

She turned to them, the woman and her son. They were watching her silently as if to see what she'd do.

'I remember it a little,' she said slowly. 'How long have you lived here?'

The woman thought for a moment. 'It was soon after the Libération we came,' she said. 'Some years before Bertrand was born. We were lucky. My husband knew someone living in this block who told us one of the flats was empty.'

'My family lived here during the war,' Fay said softly and the woman nodded.

'Someone said there had been a married couple with a little girl and then they had gone away. The girl, that was you?'

'Yes.'

The woman frowned. 'What did you say your name was?'

'Fay. Fay Knox.' She spelled it out for her and the woman looked more engaged than she had up to now.

'Knox,' she said to herself. 'Well, Mademoiselle Knox, perhaps you'd like to see the kitchen? Come, it's this way – though of course,' she said with a little laugh, 'perhaps you remember.'

Fay did remember. She followed the woman into the small square kitchen where the dirty breakfast crockery lay stacked by the sink. Three plates and three bowls. Maybe the third ones belonged to Bertrand's father. Apart from the number of inhabitants, everything was different to how it must have been when Fay lived here. The stove was of a more recent origin, and there was a modern Formica worktop, and cupboards where she didn't expect them to be.

Remarking on this, she added, 'It's very nice though, isn't it?' She peeped out of a window to see a paved court-yard below with an old gnarled tree just coming into leaf.

'Thank you,' said the woman, looking pleased. 'This

cabinet is the old one, though.' She pulled open a deep drawer under the worktop and started to rummage through the contents: light bulbs, bits of folded brown paper, coils of string. Fay wondered what she was looking for. 'Everything is so untidy,' she sighed, eventually giving up and shutting the drawer.

It occurred to Fay to wonder what had happened to the Knox family's possessions. 'Was anything left here from our time?' she asked. 'When you moved in?'

'All the furniture, of course – the flat is rented furnished – but there were no clothes or anything personal, if that is what you mean.'

'Yes.' Perhaps her mother had come back for their possessions. She thought again of that strange feeling in the living room that something was missing and suddenly knew. It was where the gate-legged table was now – the table must have been moved there to fill the empty space. 'Was there a piano?' She remembered the bulk of it, the grain of the wood, her small hands bashing the keys. She had a vision, too, of her mother playing, the swiftness and sureness of her fingers dancing up and down the notes.

'No,' the woman said, frowning. 'There was no piano.'

They walked back into the living room. Bertrand was nowhere to be seen, but after a moment the door of what must be a bedroom opened beside the mahogany dresser and he appeared in the doorway, looking furtive. 'Was this your room once?' he said, standing aside. 'You can see it if you want?'

'Thank you,' she said, curious, but before she could move there came the sound of a key in the lock, then the front door opened smartly and a surly-looking man strode in. When he saw Fay he did an exaggerated double-take, and shut the door behind him in the showy, deliberate manner of someone who liked to control.

'Who is this, Monique?' he said. He extracted from his jacket pocket a parcel wrapped in butcher's paper and handed it to his wife. He was a bull of a man with a strong physical presence. He also exuded the sour smell of last night's wine. In the doorway to the bedroom Fay saw the boy twitch nervously.

'It's all right,' Monique told her husband in a calming voice. 'She's not come to make trouble. She lived here once, before we came – is that not interesting?'

The man did not seem to think so. He glared at Fay with narrowed eyes.

Fay stood her ground, meeting his resentful gaze with her steady one, annoyed rather than frightened by this unpleasant man.

'I am sorry to disturb you,' she said quietly. 'But your wife is right, I have not come to make trouble.' She moved towards the door. 'Thank you for showing me the flat,' she said to Monique and Bertrand. And smiling at Bertrand, who smiled nervously back, she let herself out, pulling the door closed behind her. She walked down the stairs, not wanting to wait by the lift in case the boy's father came out to see if she'd gone. She was not sure what the visit had achieved. It was important to her that she'd seen the place, but it had not settled anything. There had been nothing there that meant anything to her, not really, and she felt sorry for Bertrand, overshadowed by a man like that.

The cherub-faced concierge hardly looked up from his paper as she passed him on her way out into the street. For

a moment Fay stood dazzled by the sunlight, then crossed
the road and dawdled past the pavement stalls looking at
the displays, enjoying being outside in the fresh air.

'Mademoiselle!' She glanced up to see the boy,
Bertrand, hurry across the street towards her, breathing
hard. He reached her and held out something whiteish
and creased in his hand. She took it. It was a small envelope, the flap sealed with tape that was brittle with age.
She smoothed it out to read the name on the front and
looked at him in surprise.

'Where did you get this?'

'My mother found it a moment ago,' he muttered in his
hoarse voice. 'She said to tell you it had been waiting in
our flat when she and Papa moved in. She didn't know
what to do with it so she put it in a drawer and forgot
about it. It's taken her a few minutes to remember which
drawer.'

'She kept it all those years?' Fay whispered in amazement.

He nodded. 'Was she your mother or something?' he
said, his eye on the envelope.

Fay stared down at it. On it was written *Mme K. Knox*
and at the top, in the corner, *Privé*. Private.

'Is,' Fay corrected him. 'She *is* my mother.' And as she
said this she received a tender picture in her mind of her
mother waiting for her in the hospital garden, and felt
tears prickle behind her eyes.

'You will give it to her?' His voice squeaked. His boyish
enthusiasm for this mystery moved her and she smiled at
him, noticing the dark down on his upper lip.

'Of course I will. I'm going back to England tomorrow
night. Please, would you thank your mother for me?'

'Yes. Wait, there's something else.' He lifted the flap of his jacket pocket and took out a small object, which he held out in the flat of his palm. 'Is this yours? I think it must be. I found it a long while ago under a floorboard in my room. There was a gap by the skirting board and perhaps it fell down there once.'

'Yes, it is mine,' she said, taking it from him in surprise. She held it up, examining it. It was a wooden zebra, much smaller than Zipper, its stripes faded to grey. 'It must be the one I lost from my Noah's Ark,' she told him. The one she had mourned, whom Zipper was to replace, though Zipper would surely have been too big for the ark. 'I don't know what happened to the rest of the animals, but it doesn't matter really. It's nice to know that this little fellow wasn't completely lost.'

'Would you like him back? He belongs to you,' Bertrand said, using the 'tu' form, as for a friend. He sounded hesitant though, and she sensed his attachment to the toy. She imagined his secret delight in finding it, maybe when he'd been a quite small child himself.

'No,' she said, giving it back. 'You've looked after him better than I did. You keep him.'

And waving away his thanks, she bade him goodbye and watched him walk back inside. She still felt sorry for him, but he was a nice boy and perhaps he'd be all right.

Chapter 28

In a café by the river, Fay stirred sugar into her *citron pressé* and examined the envelope more closely. It told her little more than she knew already. It was of thick paper, and there was no show-through when she held it up to the light. The script of the address was distinctively French. She considered briefly the possibility of opening it – the tape would be easy to peel away – but rejected the thought immediately. The very idea was abhorrent. She had learned how her mother had lived through a time when ordinary people were spied on, when letters were opened by censors and black lines struck through private messages. If she opened a confidential letter addressed clearly to her mother, she'd be as bad as the censor. She unclipped her handbag and thrust the letter inside. It had waited many years to be read. It could stand a few days more.

She sipped the bitter-sweet drink and watched tourists browsing the stalls on the quais for books and prints, or crossing the bridge to where the ornate façade of the Louvre gleamed downriver on the other side. Tomorrow evening she would have to leave this beautiful city behind and return to England. It saddened her. She had discovered so much about the past that tied her to Paris, but mysteries still remained. And most of all it would mean leaving Adam. She would see him tonight, after the concert, and as she finished her drink she enjoyed a little day-dream about their meeting. It was best not to think about tomorrow at all.

A church clock struck nearby. Half past eleven already. Two hours to kill before going to Mme Ramond's. Fay considered what best to do with her time. Visit the convent, perhaps, or spend an hour looking at paintings before a bite of lunch. She wanted to try the convent. Using a phone box inside the café she got through to the curé's housekeeper with the tinny voice. No, the curé wasn't in yet, but he was expected back for lunch at one.

She left some coins on the table to pay for her drink and set off across the Pont Royal, which eventually brought her to the Tuileries Gardens with the Louvre to her right. And it came to her, looking across the barren expanse of ground in front of the museum, that she didn't want to see pictures today. It was too lovely outside in the sunshine. So instead she turned left and walked briskly along the fine, tree-lined paths of the gardens. She could hear ahead, faintly, coming and going on the breeze, the brisk sounds of a brass band. Curious, she followed in their direction, and this took her all the way to Place de la Concorde.

There, at the edge of the huge piazza, steel barriers had been erected to contain the crowds, for quite a number of onlookers had gathered, some using cardboard periscopes to get a view. As she approached, she could glimpse the nearer of the two great fountains that flanked the lofty Egyptian obelisk at the centre of the square. The road itself had been blocked to traffic. Tricolor flags flapped in the wind above a handsome mansion on the far side, lending the scene a bright, ceremonial air.

The music grew louder, and she edged her way to the front to get a clearer view, wondering whether she might see Adam. Along the road towards her rolled two tanks. Behind them a military band was marching. She watched them pass, then came squadrons of soldiers in khaki and red berets, and a cavalry unit, the horses' hooves ringing on the road. Soon after that, a fleet of cars followed. Their destination was the far side of the square where, in the distance, the parade halted and the squadrons turned at a shouted order to face the obelisk. Dignitaries stepped out from cars. The band started to play 'La Marseillaise' as in the distance, a long black saloon car with graceful lines swung slowly into the square from the Champs-Élysées.

'*Général de Gaulle, le Président,*' she heard people mutter. There was jostling as the crowd pressed forward. A few of them, she'd been noticing, were Algerians, brown-skinned men like the one she'd seen arrested at the Métro station, but women, too, in traditional dress with gold-threaded headscarves. They were being joined by others, and as their numbers grew Fay sensed tension build in the air. She glanced round nervously, wondering if she ought to leave, but the crowd was too dense now, pressing her against the barrier, and she couldn't move. There was no sign of anyone who might be Adam.

Across the square the black car slowed to a halt near the lines of soldiers. A young officer stepped forward to open a rear door and Fay craned her neck trying to see the figure who was climbing out, but now the reception party gathering around the car blocked her view.

At that moment, as if at a signal, the crowd started pushing forward. Next to her, an Algerian man was pulling a board from under his coat. Others were doing likewise. Two men lifted the railing aside and people surged into the square, raising their placards and calling out slogans. The womenfolk followed, making strange whooping cries. All around the square it was happening. There were dozens, a hundred – no, hundreds – of Algerians, pouring into the road, moving as one body across the square towards the President. Two women stopped near Fay to unfurl a banner. On it were printed the words *L'Algérie pour les Algériens*.

A whistle shrieked, then dozens of gendarmes appeared from the other side of the square and bore down on the demonstrators. Fay watched in horror as they thrust their way amongst the Algerians, threshing about with truncheons or with the butts of pistols, or simply wrestling them to the ground. The air was filled with screams, angry shouts and grunts of pain. A falling placard spun into the crowd, hitting Fay on the arm, then someone barged into her from behind; she stumbled and would have fallen, had not another bystander caught her arm and steadied her. He was middle-aged and French, in a working man's jacket and a beret. He rescued her handbag and helped her towards some steps in the gardens, saying, 'Are you all right, mademoiselle? *Les terroristes*, that's what these people are. They're not in Algiers now. They should go home.' She thanked him and politely refused his offer to find her a taxi. Eventually he went away still muttering about, *'ces terroristes.'*

She was all right, she discovered, shrugging off her jacket and examining her arm. The placard hadn't drawn blood, it had merely grazed her. There would be a bruise. Otherwise she was just shaken. She pulled on the jacket again and stood up, wondering which way to go. There were still gendarmes everywhere, but the altercation seemed mostly to be over. Dark blue vans were drawing up, and she watched with concern as some of the demonstrators were rough-handled into them and driven away. Then, in the distance, with a stab of joy, she caught a glimpse of a blond head. *Adam!* she thought, but then he was hidden again by the dispersing crowd, and though she strained to see, he was gone.

She had begun to cross the gardens towards the Métro when she passed an embroidered slipper lying in the dust. On a nearby step two young Algerian women sat with their arms round each other. One was crying and the other was comforting her. All the while, the triumphant strains of the military band could be heard in the distance. The crying woman was missing a shoe and Fay went back and picked up the slipper and took it to her, a small gesture of how she felt. The other received it, giving a brisk nod of thanks, then her face changed to alarm as she saw a gendarme approaching, and she hustled her companion to her feet. They hurried away in the direction of the river. Fay, too, moved on, but more slowly and in the opposite direction.

Back at the Madeleine, she sat alone in the café across from the hotel, picking at a sandwich and unable to get the disturbing events that she'd witnessed out of her head. She tried to tell herself, as she had with Adam only the other day, that the Algerians were trouble-makers. They couldn't expect to spoil a solemn state ceremony without repercussions. After all, a small handful of Arab activists were violent, had killed innocent people, even Adam had admitted that. The demonstrators just now had been unarmed though, and the brutal response of the police, especially towards the women, had shocked her to the core. The irony struck her that twenty years ago, it was Parisians themselves who had suffered like this at the hands of the Nazis. How was it they appeared to have forgotten this recent past? Suffering did not seem to make people kinder.

She was still wrestling with these weighty matters as she made her way to Place des Vosges for her appointment with Mme Ramond. She was almost there when she realized she'd been so caught up in her thoughts she'd forgotten to try the curé's number again.

Chapter 29

July 1942

The hidden room at the back of the convent had once been a storeroom lined with shelves of bottles and jars. It had been the curé's idea to build a false wall to disguise the door, and an ingenious one. The room being long and narrow, with only one of a row of several skylights for a window, it would be difficult for the casual observer to notice its existence. Only if they looked down on the building from a bedroom window and counted, or compared the inside width of the scullery with that of the outside of the building, would they ever begin to suspect. The disadvantages were that the room was dark and cold in winter, and visitors had to pass through the Reverend Mother's sitting room to get to it, but neither of these difficulties was insurmountable. The scullery was rarely used and there were long periods when the hidden room was empty.

Only a few of the nuns knew about the men who came and went from it, and those who did were cautioned never to speak of the matter, even amongst themselves. Thérèse had to know because she prepared the food, and it usually fell to her to take it to them and fetch any small essentials that were required. She would wait for a quiet moment when there was no one around to ask questions, then tap on the door of the sitting room. If anyone did see her they might suppose that the tray she carried was for Mère Marie-François, although since the Reverend Mother normally ate in the dining room with the rest of the community, they might wonder.

A deep-seated, childlike part of Thérèse thrilled to the business of knocking on the false wall and opening the secret door. She was ashamed of these feelings, for the poor wretches the room concealed went in fear of their lives and she dared not think what retribution might be visited on the whole community if they were discovered. The men would usually come out to sit at the table in the scullery, and while they ate she would clean their room. Afterwards, they might go out into the courtyard to walk and feel the sun on their faces and to smoke. They could not smoke in their hiding place – it was one of so many ways in which they might have given themselves away if ever the convent were searched. The courtyard was not overlooked by other buildings and the curé could not bring himself to forbid them the respite. It seemed safe enough.

The British airman who was there when Serge arrived did not remain at the convent long, another three days maybe, and after that Serge was on his own in the room for several weeks before the Gestapo raid. He found solitary confinement testing and the loneliness got to him so dreadfully that Thérèse used to sit with him as he ate. Having had no company, he would talk too much, but she liked to listen and answered his eager questions about the world outside as best she could. She told him very little, in fact – that the bread today was greyish and gritty because that was all there was in the shop, that she'd visited Notre Dame that morning to pray because an errand had taken her past the West Door, that the stray cat she fed in the square had slipped into the convent and given birth to three kittens in the laundry cupboard. She didn't tell him about the posters that had been pasted up in the Rue St-Jacques threatening death to *résistants* and their families, nor how she thought of him each time she saw a young man in the street wearing a yellow star.

Serge liked to hear about her life in the convent. Although his mother was Jewish he'd been brought up a Catholic, if he'd been brought up as anything, and could not imagine how the nuns endured so many church services. She tried hard to make him understand. The women were at peace here, she said. They felt secure while pursuing their duties. Sainte Cécile's was not a closed order and their life was not without its pleasures. And this was true, or at least, she'd been happy with it before Serge came.

She told him about her upbringing. Nathalie Boulanger, as she had once been named, had been a tranquil child, always dutiful. Her elder sister, Louise, had been the tempestuous one who had upset their mother in particular, and it was in Nathalie's nature to compensate for that. Shy, studious and musical – she had a lovely voice – Nathalie had not made friends easily in the raucous streets of the industrial suburb where they lived and where her father worked as a supervisor at the Renault factory, and this wasn't helped by the priest at the school she attended marking her out as 'spiritual'. When she was fourteen, he asked her parents whether she might have a calling to become a bride of Christ, and when they spoke to her about it the idea came to have a certain appeal. Being a nun would give her a position in life and a job to do, Nathalie thought, and it stopped her worrying about her lack of friends and her shyness with boys. Thereafter her mother and father spoke of her calling with pride, and so her future was sealed. It seemed that she wasn't meant to marry and have children, she was to dedicate her life to God.

Louise married at eighteen, having been seduced by a young mechanic, and their parents breathed a sigh of relief. Their daughters were settled. Louise and her husband Gustave had gone on to have two little boys, and Nathalie had become Sister Thérèse. It was terrible that war had come and Gustave had been forced to go to Germany where his skills with vehicles were being put to use making tanks.

She explained all this to Serge hesitantly and over several mealtimes – the nuns were not encouraged to dwell on their past lives. He listened with interest and in return told her about his own childhood, and of the intense expectations his family had of him. Music was his passion and his parents had made real sacrifices to pay for his lessons and he'd felt he mustn't disappoint them. And he worried about them now, for he'd had no news of them. Serge and Thérèse saw that though their upbringings had been quite different, in their strong sense of duty towards family they had something important in common.

Still, there were some things Thérèse kept to herself, even at confession. Some of the nuns taught young children at a school nearby, and Thérèse longed to do this too, but the Reverend Mother said that because she was the

youngest and fittest her work should be the shopping and
cooking and heavy housework. She'd always been obedient to this, and by and large enjoyed it. Shopping, for
instance, took her out of the convent and meant she could
listen to people talk and learn what was going on.

Recently, however, she'd lost her sense of contentment.
She'd seen the cherry tree in the front courtyard blossom
in the spring, then the dark green leaves come and the
fruit form and swell, and knew that when the leaves red-
dened and died she would be here still, serving the other
nuns and growing older. On the rare, precious occasions
that she was allowed to visit her sister and the little boys,
she was always left with a sense of wistfulness that there
was something she'd missed.

She did not speak to Serge about any of this, but it stole
up on her bit by bit that she was dissatisfied with her life
and that these shared few minutes with him were what
she looked forward to most in her days. She admired his
passion for his music, and understood his unhappiness at
being cut off from it. He spoke bitterly of the situation he
was in, how unfair he felt it was that he'd been labelled a
collaborator by the teacher he revered, how he suspected
that his supposed friend Mrs van Haren had betrayed
him, although conceded that perhaps she hadn't meant
to.

What an odd pair they were, the young musician and
the nun. Each felt trapped in a different way by their situation. As they sat together at the worn table in the
scullery, or on a bench outside in the sunshine, she found
herself noticing things about him as she'd never done with
any boy at school – the sharp planes of his face, the gloss
of his black hair and his fine dark eyes. There was an

unhappiness in him, a deep unhappiness born of frustrated ambition and loneliness, but she saw sweetness, too, and vulnerability, and longed to be able to comfort him. She brought him paper, so he could write music, and gave him an old book of Psalms from the church, with which he amused himself, inventing harmonies that they sang together softly, their voices intertwining.

'All this went on for several weeks, but everything changed completely the day your father died,' Mme Ramond said. 'The whole community was in shock. Such brutality happening in our midst, in our very church – it was inconceivable. Many of us had known Eugene and liked him and, of course, we worried about your poor mother. And you, Fay – we had to look after you. It was a simply dreadful time.'

She passed her hand briefly across her eyes as though trying to shield herself from her memories and said, 'I am not certain what to tell you next.'

'My mother, surely. What happened to her?'

'Yes, of course, your mother,' Mme Ramond sighed. 'It's difficult to tell things in the right order. The following day, the curé went to Gestapo headquarters to ask after her, but they sent him away with the usual official language that told him nothing at all. It was some weeks before we heard anything definite. In late September there was another round-up of enemy aliens, this time mostly of American women. Kitty was lucky. They released her from prison, but sent her to an internment camp.'

'Lucky!' Fay broke in. 'In what way was she lucky?'

Mme Ramond examined her with narrowed eyes and a

humourless smile. 'Because think what they *could* have done with her – if they'd decided she was guilty of something. She'd hidden her husband from them. Suppose they had accused her of collusion in his activities?'

'If they'd found Serge, I suppose,' Fay said, still confused.

'Exactly. Or if the Gestapo had known about John Stone hiding in their flat. I suppose we'll never find out what they knew and why they didn't charge her. So yes, she *was* lucky. They only locked her up in a camp with other enemy aliens. I say only, but for her that was suffering enough. Because she was separated from you.'

Mme Ramond's voice was gentle and when Fay studied her face she found in it only compassion.

'What happened to me?' Fay asked, but a part of her already knew. There were pictures that were coming into focus more clearly in her mind. Walking her toy zebra on a windowsill, being carried by a woman in a black dress, feeling the rough material against her cheek. She glanced at her left hand where there was a tiny scar on a knuckle, and she remembered her pain and distress after a white cat scratched her because she'd tried to play with its kittens.

'You stayed with us in the convent, of course. Do you really remember nothing?'

'I recall a little,' Fay admitted, 'but not much. It's … well, it's as if my mind won't go there. There's … a kind of emptiness.' Yes, that word felt right. Or numbness, that was better.

'You missed your parents so much, you poor child,' Mme Ramond said. 'I tried my best with you, so did Sofie's mother, but we could see you withdraw into yourself. It was so sad. For a long time you would ask where they were. It was the Reverend Mother who explained to you that your father was dead. I don't know if you really knew what that meant, except after that you stopped asking about him. We were at a loss as to what to tell you about your mother. We wanted to protect you, to keep you safe.'

And Fay remembered. '"She's had to go away for a while." That's what you said, wasn't it? "She's gone away, but she'll be back."'

Mme Ramond nodded. 'How could we get a child of three to understand about a war and an internment camp, about prison and barbed wire?'

'Gone away,' Fay echoed. 'Those are dreadful words to a child. My mother had never gone away before. But something awful had happened and I didn't know what, only that it was my fault that she'd gone. My fault.'

She looked at Nathalie Ramond and was surprised to see that the colour had drained from her face. 'Your fault? Why should you think that?' the woman whispered.

'I don't know, I just do.'

'I don't understand why you should think it your fault that your mother went away. There was a war on. Many children were separated from their parents, but they didn't blame themselves.'

'I think they did sometimes,' Fay said carefully, still puzzled by Mme Ramond's defensiveness, 'because nobody explained to them.'

'What good would explaining do? Children should be protected from the adult world.'

'Is that why my mother told me nothing of all this?'

Mme Ramond stroked the knotted knuckles of her hands. 'I don't know,' she said. 'You'll have to ask her.'

It was the stern and evasive way she spoke that upset Fay and made her remember her mother's letter. *Don't believe everything she tells you. It was because of her I nearly lost you.* She had to ask, she really did.

'Madame Ramond, what happened between you and my mother?'

The hands grew still. Mme Ramond closed her eyes briefly, then she said in the faintest of voices, 'You must let me continue. The story is not told. Please let me do it my way, then maybe you will understand.'

Fay could see that she'd upset the older woman. 'Of course,' she whispered. 'I'm sorry.'

It was as though Nathalie Ramond had not heard her. Her gaze was far away. Finally, with effort, she spoke.

'Sometimes,' she said, 'we would hear from your mother, but not often. And Mère Marie-François would never allow the letters to be shown to you. She feared they would make you unhappy, you see, and of course you could not read in either English or French.'

'Which did she write in?' Fay couldn't help interrupting.

'Oh, English, but the Reverend Mother could read English and would translate for us. The letters were always short. I think there was a great deal that your mother was not allowed to say. Perhaps writing was difficult for her, too. She would mostly write platitudes, that she was being treated well and that there was a great deal to keep them busy there. Oh, and there was good news. Miss Dunne was there, safe and well. And, of course, she asked after you.'

And apparently no one had told Fay this. She supposed Mère Marie-François had thought she was being kind.

Perhaps it was the way that she'd been brought up herself, with the understanding that the less children knew of sad things, the better. Yet she was sure that she'd have wanted to know what her mother had written to her, to have been told that she missed her daughter, even if it had made Fay distressed. A great sadness broke out in her now to think of all those missed chances.

'You shared a bedroom with Sofie for several months,' Mme Ramond said, 'but then something happened, one of the few good things in that terrible time. Sofie's mother heard from the Red Cross that they'd been contacted by her husband, who was looking for them! He'd survived! After the family had become separated from him he'd been gravely wounded by enemy fire, but had been looked after by a Belgian family and had eventually recovered. He had been trying to find them for some time, but all his attempts had failed. Until now. Sofie's mother took the children and went at once to meet him near Rouen where he was living, and they simply never came back. She wrote to us from time to time and though they were experiencing many difficulties she sounded happy. We did not ever see them again, and we missed them.'

'I don't remember Sofie properly, but I'm glad that she found her father.'

'You were close. She was like an elder sister to you, and when she and her brothers went away you could not be comforted. I did my best, but as I say, it was a time of great unhappiness for all of us.' She paused for a moment. 'I had my own private sorrow that I confessed to no one. After the Gestapo raid, the curé decided it was too much of a risk to hide Serge and Dr Poulon on the premises. We would be under surveillance, you see. Dr Poulon left during the first night. I don't know what happened to him, whether he survived. We were told nothing; it was safer that way for all of us. Then nobody could put anyone else in danger if questioned. And Serge ... I wouldn't have known what had happened to him if he hadn't told me. Neither the curé nor Mère Marie-François said a word. It was All Saints Day when I took him his lunch – I knew at once that something was wrong. He appeared agitated, and when I set down the tray, instead of sitting down to eat, he came and took my hands ...'

Nathalie Ramond closed her eyes and turned up her palms and an expression of great tenderness passed over her face. 'And he said, very gently, "I have something to tell you," and his eyes were fixed on mine. "They're moving me tonight, Nathalie," he said. *Nathalie*. He'd never called me that before, but later I discovered that was how he thought of me, as Nathalie, not Sister Thérèse. I didn't correct him, I was too stunned and upset. "I'm frightened," he whispered.

'"Oh don't be, don't," I told him. One of us had to be strong and he needed my strength, for it was his life that was in danger. "Do you know where you're going?" I asked him, but he didn't and so he couldn't tell me. He was leaving, I knew not for where nor whether I'd ever see him again, but there was nothing else to be done but for me to accept it. Just as I'd accepted all the other things that had happened in my life, which had always been directed by others. "I shall pray for you," I told him, but he said nothing to that, just continued to hold my hands and to look at me, his face tender and expectant.

'Then, "Nathalie," he said again, only that, and I could not tear my eyes from him. He leaned forward suddenly and pressed his lips against my forehead. "When all this is over," he said, "I shall come and see you again."

'"You must not," I tried to say, but my heart was breaking and the words came out as a sob and I snatched my hands away. I don't know what else we might have said or done had not the curé arrived at that moment to speak to Serge about arrangements. We sprang apart, but the old man was so distracted by worry himself, anxious that Serge be gone, that he did not notice anything amiss.

'"I must speak with Monsieur Ramond now, Thérèse," was all he said, dismissing me.

'"Goodbye,"' I said to Serge. "May God go with you." It was hard to keep my voice even, but somehow I managed it. Then I left the two of them together.

'Serge left during the night, so quietly I did not hear him go, though my sleep was full of dreams of doors opening and closing, of voices calling for help. It was the last I saw of him for a very long time.'

Mme Ramond paused and her face was grave. Fay waited, not liking to interrupt. When the older woman spoke again it was as though she was speaking from somewhere deep in the past, unaware of Fay's presence in the room.

'For a long period after he went, I was miserable, utterly miserable. For the first time in my life, you see, I had fallen in love. Though I denied it to myself, of course. Such a thing was terrible for a nun. I simply told myself that I missed a friend and was worried for his safety. But as time passed I still could not sleep or eat much, and all I could think about was him and how happy I'd felt when I was with him. I knew it was wrong, but that happiness had seemed so wonderful I couldn't think why it should be thought wrong. I became very confused. There was no one I felt I could speak to. I stopped taking the sacrament or going to confession, but for a while no one seemed bothered. We were in a state of such shock and confusion that my behaviour seemed no odder than anyone else's.

'As the weeks passed, the pain of separation grew less sharp, though I often thought about Serge. I wondered where he'd gone, but I don't think even the curé knew for sure, or so he said when I asked him. A safe house not far away, was all he said, and so I comforted myself by imagining it: an upstairs room, maybe, an attic with a sunny window, and he'd have books to read, even if he couldn't play his music.

'And then one day, I took you out for a walk, Fay. The Jardin du Luxembourg wasn't very far from the convent, and the shortest route took us down a narrow residential street where we heard the sound of loud piano music coming from an open window high above. I remember stopping in amazement to listen to the river of notes flowing out into the air, the brave passion of the playing. Although it was mid-morning, there was hardly anyone else about and we listened for a couple of minutes before the playing stopped abruptly and someone closed the window. Do you remember any of this?'

Fay shook her head.

'I felt transformed with joy hearing that music. I got it into my head that it must be Serge, and after that I often used to take you that way. But I was always disappointed. I never heard the music again, yet I was sure that it had been him and it helped me to walk under that window and feel close to him.'

'And was it him?'

'No.' For the first time for a long while, Nathalie Ramond smiled. 'It turned out that he'd been taken to a house in the suburbs, nowhere close at all. It had been someone else altogether playing that day. But I always bless whoever it was, because it gave me something to latch onto, some kind of hope.

'The other thing that helped me was you, Fay. You were only three, a lonely child and quiet, very different to how you had been. You rarely smiled and there was a tentativeness about you that I would have worried about if I hadn't been so distracted by my own unhappiness. Still, helping Sofie's mother care for you gave me pleasure, and when the family left, it was June of 1943, you became my responsibility and that was very good for us both.

'But all that time, beneath the daily routines, the endurance, the waiting, I was changing. I was no longer the dutiful young girl who had done what was expected of her all her life. The routines of the convent were no longer enough for me. I still believed in God and tried to serve Him. I still liked the convent. The other nuns were mostly kind. Many of them I loved. But I did not feel as I once had, that I belonged there for ever. Loving Serge had opened my eyes to other possibilities. Those things I had believed did not interest me – a husband, children – I came to realize I wanted desperately. For the moment though, I had no courage to do anything but carry on as I had been. There was you to look after, and I could not leave you. And where would I go, anyway? My parents would be ashamed if I left the order and went home, and anyway, I did not know for certain that it was possible to be released from my vows.

'Winter passed. The cherry tree blossomed again in the

spring, but the daily routine became no easier. The search
for food, the confusion of new regulations, the harshness
of repression. Twice more the Gestapo visited us and the
convent was searched, but after the second time they
mostly left us alone. I could not get enough for us all to eat
and some of what we did have the Reverend Mother
made us give away. There were so many people in Paris
with greater needs than us, you see. You had to be fed, Fay,
and the children in the school, and then there were people
who came to the convent seeking charity, desperate cases,
some of them. We could not help them all.

'During February, Sister Clare developed pneumonia
and died. Sister Philippe passed away not long after – she
was found dead in her bed one morning, poor soul. Both
were elderly, and the extreme cold and lack of nourish-
ment had weakened their systems. It was I who prepared
Sister Philippe's body for burial. I tell you, she was so
light, hardly more than skin and bones.

'Somehow the rest of us kept going, and news about the
progress of the war brightened our spirits. I was like a
magpie, bringing home small scraps of gossip from the
shops, or the curé would tell us things. We began to hope –
yes, hope. It was a long time since we'd had much of that.

'It was in early 1944, before blossom time, that I went to
the Reverend Mother and asked how I could be released
from my vows. To my relief, she did not seem surprised
and dealt with me kindly. She said she'd noticed how in all
sorts of small ways I'd become more distant. I hadn't been
aware of this, but now I recognized what she meant. I had
not often gone to confession, for fear I'd blurt out my
secret about Serge, and I'd been wrapped up in myself,
less open, less easy to read. It wasn't that I did not wish to

serve God any more, I promised her, but that I felt I'd changed somehow and that my future life lay beyond the convent. We agreed that I should think about it further, and if I still felt the same she would speak to the curé and they would see what could be done. After this conversation I felt much better. I did what she said and brooded deeply, but did not change my mind. Even if Serge never came back, I felt that I must leave. When the curé spoke to me in May, it was agreed that when France was free – and we had reason to believe that this would not be long coming – I would seek to leave Sainte Cécile's.

'You can imagine the excitement when, in June, came the news that the Allies had invaded Normandy. For me the joy was mixed with anxiety. What would I do with myself when I left the convent? And another very important question: what would happen to you, Fay?'

Mme Ramond sighed and Fay looked up to see her studying her with a tender look. 'Perhaps we should have some tea,' the woman suggested.

'I'll come and help you,' Fay said, getting up, glad to leave the past for a moment. As she followed Mme Ramond to the kitchen, she saw how heavily she leaned on her stick and it was difficult not to feel sorry for her. Yet she sensed the woman's pride, that she did not want Fay's pity. Indeed, she would not let her make the tea, but insisted on pouring the boiling water herself and fetching the milk from the fridge, only accepting her offer to carry the tray, rather than using the small trolley she kept for the purpose.

When they were settled once more, Mme Ramond sipped her tea and warmed her hands on the cup, but it appeared difficult for her to continue her tale. Finally she said, 'I hope that you will listen to everything I have to say. I must not rush, because every detail is important and I need to make you understand. Your mother does not know all of this. She only knows her side of the story. She never wanted to listen to mine.'

'Of course I'll listen,' Fay said, wary, 'but I wish I could remember more. Then it might seem real to me.'

'I need to tell you about a decision I made,' Mme Ramond said carefully. 'At the time it seemed the right choice to make. But your mother has never forgiven me for it.'

Chapter 30

August 1942

The cell in the prison in the Avenue Foch was long and narrow, and tapered inward at the window end, which made Kitty feel as if the walls were closing in. It contained a straw mattress, a wooden chair and a bucket. If she stood on the chair, it wobbled, but she could see out of the tiny barred window. It looked out onto the end of a brown brick building and a patch of sky, which was the only part of her surroundings that varied. She must have been on a side of the building that lay in shadow, for there was never any sun.

Not that she cared much, in those terrible long weeks, whether the sun shone or not. She just wanted to be assured that the world outside this cell still existed. It helped her to remember that she wasn't alone.

After they brought her to this prison, handing her down roughly from the van, she was taken to an interrogation room where Obersturmführer Hoff questioned her for several hours in his clipped English. What had Gene been doing at the convent? Where was the airman he was hiding? Who else had he helped get away? Who else from the hospital was involved? To most of these questions she could answer truthfully, 'I don't know, I don't know.' Her husband had done well in protecting her. At one point she burst out, 'Why are you asking me these things? My husband told me nothing. Nothing.'

'Why were you hiding your husband then if you believed he'd done nothing wrong,' the man shot back. His colourless eyes betrayed no warmth, no guilt, and she hated him.

'Because he told me to. He's my husband.' *Was.* 'Why did you kill him? He wasn't armed. He'd done nothing to you.'

'He resisted arrest. But it is I who ask the questions.'

He asked them again and she gave him the same answers. We're going round in circles, she thought and her attention roamed. A scene played over and over in her mind. It was of Hoff disappearing down into the crypt, his shout and the volley of gunfire that followed. Gene. She had not been allowed to see his body. They'd denied her even that.

'Where is Dr Poulon hiding?'

'Where have you taken my husband?' she asked.

'Answer my question, please,' he said, but his hand, placing a cigarette between his thin lips, trembled slightly and she saw it. Even a man like this, with a cruel mouth and eyes like chips of grey metal, could be weak sometimes, and despite her misery the thought satisfied.

'I don't know what you're talking about,' she said, folding her arms and staring at him. She was beginning to think that he didn't know much about the whole thing either. He'd suggested no names of Allied airmen, no specific incidents, there was nothing he could connect her with. He was casting about in the dark.

He switched the direction of his questioning to the convent and its inhabitants. Why had she been there? 'It was my home when I first came to Paris. The nuns are my friends.' Who were they hiding? 'Nobody.' But now she was frightened. Fay. Did they care that Fay was still there in the convent and that the child was her daughter? They must do, surely. She remembered Fay's face, pale in the dimness of the church, her cry of anguish that made Kitty give up all hope, the last glimpse of her shadowy form through the window, one childish palm pressed against the glass, before they shoved Kitty into the van. That face and Fay's cry were to haunt her for many nights yet, more nights than she'd known she could ever endure.

'I don't know anything,' she repeated stubbornly and turned her head away. On the wall of the interrogation room was a splash of something brown. She averted her eyes.

The officer picked up his cap from the table and the chair grated as he pushed it back. 'Enough now,' he said. 'We'll speak again tomorrow.'

At the door he hesitated. For a moment he was silent, as if searching for words long unused. Finally he looked at her and said, 'My sympathies for your loss,' then bowed his head and left the room.

He questioned her in the same room the next day and for several days after that, but he learned nothing from her. Sometimes he tried to trick her by mentioning some name or other and claiming information about them. But the names did not mean anything to her and she wondered if he was making them up. Seeing the truth in her puzzled face, he changed tack, moving back to the convent and the same old line of enquiry, but she could see that he was losing heart. After that, days passed without questioning, then it stopped altogether. Kitty lay on the mattress in her cell in a miasma of misery, thinking about Gene and praying that her daughter was safe. She felt she could not ask after Fay without drawing attention to her existence, and hoped that her daughter was still at the convent and being well looked after. Thérèse would care for her, she loved all children. Kitty had seen the way she had been with Sofie and her brothers as well as Fay.

At regular intervals, food arrived – thin grey porridge and a crust of hard bread, or a watery stew made of rotting vegetables and a lump or two of fatty meat. She did not care what it was, she had little appetite. Days passed and nights, their transition marked by the brightening or dimming of light from the window. The nights when there was no moon were of a dense blackness. Most days she was taken to exercise in a back yard with a stubby ash tree in its centre and a high wall topped with barbed wire. Here she and several dozen other women were made to walk in a wide circle round the tree. A guard would call a vicious 'Silence!' if anyone was caught in conversation.

One day she noticed how the leaves of the tree were edged with brown and wondered how long she had been imprisoned.

'*Quelle est la date?*' she breathed to a proud-faced Frenchwoman at her side. '*Quel jour est-il?*'

'*Le dix-huit Septembre,*' the woman muttered and the shout came to be silent.

18 September. It had been on 23 August that Gene had been killed. She'd been here almost four weeks. Her throat tightened. How long would she be kept here? What would they do to her? She glanced around at the other women. Some faces were the same, but there were often new ones and others she no longer saw. This made her wonder about the mornings when she was woken by the sound of gunfire. There was one girl whose eyes were crazed with pain: what had been done to her? Kitty pushed these dark thoughts from her mind. She would think only of Fay and try to keep going, praying that her daughter was safe.

On the morning of 24 September, after she'd eaten the sludgy paste that was breakfast, a female warder thrust her head round the door and told her sharply to collect up her possessions. *'Mach schnell!* Hurry!'

'Where am I going?' she asked, not daring to hope, but the woman merely repeated that Kitty should hurry. She glanced about. She'd been given some prison clothes but didn't have much else. They'd taken away most of the contents of her handbag. She bundled everything up in the jacket she'd arrived in and followed the warder.

'Am I being released? Tell me,' she pleaded as she was led downstairs, to be answered only by a grim glance. Perhaps the woman did not speak English.

In the entrance hall her purse and keys and wedding ring were returned to her by the officer on the desk and her hopes began to rise. 'Are you letting me go?' she asked him, but he did not even meet her eye. He went and unlocked the front door and gestured to her to go through. 'Goodbye,' he said, in English and she found herself outside on the steps blinking in the sunshine. The door closed behind her with a final sound.

She was free! But there was no time to feel relief, for at the bottom of the steps a soldier was waiting. *'Kommen Sie mit mir,'* he said, and ignoring her protests, escorted her across the street to where a large, covered, military truck was waiting, its engine running. As he helped her into the back she saw with astonishment that it was already full of women. He closed the doors and after a moment the truck lurched into movement.

The other women were Americans, she quickly discovered; she was the only Englishwoman, there by virtue of her marriage certificate. Since they'd all been collected from their homes, they'd been able to bring luggage and she'd had to clamber across their suitcases with her modest bundle to find a seat. She recognized one or two. Sitting next to her was the wife of a French doctor at the American Hospital whose name she thought was Sarah; another was a middle-aged woman she'd seen at the library sometimes. Although nobody had any idea where they were going, they were putting on a cheerful face, and despite her profound disappointment that she wasn't free, Kitty felt comforted to be among them. For their part, they regarded her with open curiosity. She knew she'd lost a bit of weight, but now she realized she must look dreadful. She answered their questions as simply as she could and could hardly bear the warmth of their sympathy, which made her want to cry. Beside her, Sarah, who must have already known about Gene, gently squeezed her arm.

The truck wound its way through Paris, stopping at one house after another to collect more American women, and now the word 'interned' was being whispered and there was much speculation about where. Not Germany, it was to be hoped. Kitty was in a panic at being taken further away from Fay. Was there nothing she could do? 'I'm worried about my daughter,' she told Sarah, who nodded. Her two were with her husband. 'I think Fay must be with the nuns,' Kitty said. Sarah didn't know.

'I'm sure she must be safe,' Sarah said. 'Perhaps we won't be gone for long. My husband will get me out soon. They'll see that it's a mistake.'

But there's no one to argue my case, Kitty thought sadly. No one at all. She didn't think anyone at the convent would take up the matter with the authorities. Their bravery was of a different kind, the kind that quietly endures.

And now the truck was speeding along a road where the sound of city traffic was left behind. Through chinks in the tarpaulin she glimpsed trees and expanses of water. When eventually they stopped and the soldier ordered them out, she knew at once where they were. It was the Bois de Boulogne, in peacetime a busy public park which she'd sometimes visited with Gene, but today it was bleak and empty. The truck had deposited them at the door of the Jardin d'Acclimatation, home to the city's zoo. As they were hurried into the glass-enclosed structure and past rows of empty cages, Kitty remembered how it had been before the war. She'd seen giraffes and a bad-tempered elephant, deer and darting fish in the aquarium. Where had the animals been taken, she wondered, or had they been destroyed? She was aghast when one of the soldiers with them stopped and unlocked a large cage then ordered the protesting women inside. There were many already there. It was, she remembered, the monkey house. It had been cleaned, but there was still a whiff of its previous inhabitants. Now they were the animals, to be fed and stared at by their captors.

The women were kept there for several days, sleeping in makeshift dormitories. More arrived each day until there were several hundred of them, far too many for the number of beds. When it rained, water dripped from the roof onto their faces. Some quickly became ill. At night, Kitty heard some crying themselves to sleep. Others walked up and down the aisles, unable to settle. The braver amongst them taunted the German soldiers who circulated with flashlights, desperately trying to count them all. Kitty lay curled up on her cot wearing all the clothes she possessed against the cold, quietly thinking about Gene and Fay.

The wide assortment of women astonished her. There were nuns, artists, French brides of American soldiers from the Great War, prostitutes, a dancer or two, a book-seller, various women wearing expensive clothes and jewellery, the wives of officials and Vichy politicians. There was one in particular, an older woman with silvery white hair and a New York accent, who tested everyone's patience by complaining vociferously about everything being 'not what she was used to' until one of the dancers told her to 'stow it'.

Although more women arrived, a few were also released – on grounds, it seemed, of age or ill health. Eventually this included the silver-haired woman, which was a great relief to everyone. Kitty decided to approach the harassed official charged with organizing these releases, and who she'd heard speak English. 'I have a young child,' she told him.

He stared at her for a moment. 'What is your name?' he asked, and when he found it on the list, read something handwritten by it and shook his head. 'There are many in your position,' he said, dismissing her. She was curious to know what he'd read. Whatever it was, it had informed his answer. She turned away, not knowing what to do. Later she begged some writing materials from Sarah and penned a short letter to the Reverend Mother explaining what had happened to her and asking after Fay.

On the fourth morning, most of the women were taken from the monkey house to buses waiting outside the zoo. By this time, there were crowds gathered, of friends and relatives clamouring to see their loved ones, and more soldiers had been brought in to prevent them surging forwards and impeding operations. 'Where are we going?' the women asked repeatedly, but the soldiers did not appear to know. After each bus was loaded up it departed, to the great distress of the onlookers. Gauging that the driver of hers was French, Kitty took care to sit near the front and on the journey asked if he'd post her letter. 'It's just to let my daughter's carers know that I'm well,' she assured him, and when he agreed, slipped him the envelope and a coin for a stamp.

The bus took them out of Paris to a remote railway station where a train of shabby third-class carriages awaited. The compartments the women were packed into were filthy. They still didn't know their destination. The doors were sealed and the train travelled east. Again, there were rumours that they were being taken to Germany and Kitty's fear grew.

They travelled all day and for most of the following night, with a tiny packed lunch to sustain them and nothing to drink. At Nancy the train was held up by an Allied bombing raid, but only the German soldiers were allowed to leave the train and seek shelter. The women clutched each other in terror as bombs exploded in the darkness around. When the planes had passed, the soldiers returned and the journey continued. In the morning the train arrived at Vittel station and everyone was ordered to disembark. It was blessedly well short of the German border.

After the grim prison in Paris and her wild imaginings of what might await Kitty in Germany, Frontstalag 194, the internment camp near Vittel, came as something of a relief. The complex itself was extraordinary. At some time during the nineteenth century the village had been turned into a luxurious holiday resort, and the Nazis had created the camp by fencing off some of the grand hotels, which were grouped together in a lovely park. Seeing it for the first time, full of Englishwomen, who hung out of the hotel windows and cheered to welcome the American new-comers, it was only the barbed wire on the surrounding fences and the billowing Nazi flags everywhere that indi-cated to Kitty that this was a prison. She learned soon afterwards that the Germans were using Vittel as a show-camp, to convince the international community that they were abiding by international law and treating innocent British and American internees well. First impressions of pampering though, were quickly dispersed: everyone's luggage was thoroughly searched and articles believed to be compromising confiscated. These included paper and envelopes, torches, which might be used to signal to the Allied enemy, and any books deemed to be suspicious.

Their accommodation not yet being ready, they had to crowd into rooms already occupied. Kitty and Sarah man-aged to room together, with two English girls their own age, who were at first a little disgruntled to have to share their grandiose surroundings. Their first-floor suite was spacious with a balcony overlooking the park and with a view of the valley of the Vosges Mountains beyond. There were gloriously high ceilings, proper beds and, joy of joys, a private bathroom. Here Kitty had finally to confront her appearance in a mirror. It was a shock. Her face looked grey and wasted, her eyes sunken in their sockets. This was the legacy of the weeks of her imprisonment by the Gestapo.

Given generous rations of food, which they cooked in their room, and lots of fresh air, she began to look better. She managed to buy a few clothes from other inmates, with the little money she had with her, and necessities such as a toothbrush. Everybody hoped the next consignment of Red Cross parcels wouldn't be long in coming. She was amazed at the range of activities on offer in the camp. Much was organized by other Englishwomen but there were also tennis courts and a bowling green, and in one hotel a hall with a stage and even a grand piano – not, unfortunately, perfectly in tune, as Kitty discovered when she sat in the half-darkness of the hall and played a desultory scale.

She tried to tell herself that in many ways she was lucky, considering the fate she might have suffered at the hands of the Gestapo, but still a heaviness blanketed her heart. In Vittel she was clothed and sheltered and fed, and if not treated exactly with kindness, certainly without cruelty, yet she was mourning her husband, lost in the most brutal of circumstances, and she had been parted from her only child.

The camp felt crowded. There were already over a thousand women here before Kitty and the nearly three hundred Americans arrived, but there were also some men, mainly older, released from the camp at St-Denis near Paris to join their wives. It was a few days after her arrival, while she was speaking to one of them in the food queue, an English schoolmaster who'd not wished to abandon his work when war broke out – that Kitty heard her name spoken. She looked round to see behind her a woman whose face was dear to her.

'Adele!' she cried. 'I wondered if I might see you here.' Adele Dunne had never been demonstrative, but now the two women clung to one another in their joy. Then they collected their rations and ambled back together.

Miss Dunne appeared to be much her usual self, her face more lined perhaps, and her mousy hair streaked with grey. She was wearing a long skirt, a lace blouse and a short jacket, an outfit thirty years out of date, but which oddly suited her. She threw Kitty a look of concern.

'Don't ask, I know I look dreadful,' Kitty mumbled.

'What has happened? Is Dr Knox well? And young Fay?' She asked this tentatively, then read the answers in Kitty's face.

They stopped to sit on the steps of a pavilion to talk. And now Kitty told her everything, hesitantly at first, but then it all came tumbling out in a rush, about Serge and the nuns, Gene's death and her subsequent incarceration.

'Dear God.' Miss Dunne clutched the cooking pot in her lap and closed her eyes as she absorbed the shocking news and for a while after Kitty had finished was quite speechless.

'Please,' Kitty laid her hand on her arm, 'I need you to be strong for me. I have to stay strong or I won't be able to go on. Fay . . .'

'Is Fay all right?' Miss Dunne asked swiftly. 'Where is she?'

'I think she must still be with the nuns. I wrote to Mère Marie-François a few days ago. It was before we came here, so she won't know where I am.'

'There'll be some way you can let them know. The nuns will look after her, I'm sure of it,' Miss Dunne said firmly. 'Perhaps she could be brought to live here.'

'Is that allowed?'

'Sometimes, yes. But would you want her to?'

Kitty considered this. Yes, she wanted Fay with her badly, very badly, and Miss Dunne was right, some women did have children with them. It would be a long journey for Fay though, and what would it do to the child to imprison her here? Kitty must confirm where her daughter was and whether she was happy, then she'd decide what was sensible to do. She mustn't be selfish.

'I've also known of women who've been released because of having young children,' Miss Dunne told her. 'You must apply.'

'Yes, I must,' Kitty echoed with uncertainty, remembering her last attempt to do that. Again, she wondered what had been written next to her name on the list the officer had consulted at the zoo.

Miss Dunne was not a popular figure at the camp and it didn't take Kitty long to find out why. She spoke German fluently, and was amongst several women who worked at the Kommandant's office, helping with the record-keeping. 'It's just clerical work,' she explained to Kitty. 'I do it because I enjoy it.' Some of the other internees thought it amounted to collaboration with the Germans and made a point of not speaking to her. Miss Dunne never tried to justify her work to Kitty, who simply didn't believe that her friend was capable of betraying anyone and accepted her naïve explanation at its face value.

Miss Dunne never spoke about anything she might have discovered during her work – Kitty supposed this was a condition of the job – except for one thing. When, after she'd been at the camp for a fortnight, she asked Miss Dunne about her application to be released, the other woman was quiet. Finally she said, 'I'm afraid that they are unlikely to let you go. You were right. There's a note on your file that says as much. I don't know for sure, but I think it's because you're still under suspicion of some sort. I'm very sorry.'

This news, although Kitty had suspected it, was a blow and she became very cast down. Even a letter arriving from the Reverend Mother lifted her spirits only slightly. It was warmly expressed, but said little beyond the fact that Fay was well and, that although she missed her mother, kept up good spirits. They all sent their best wishes and hoped that Kitty would be released soon. There was no suggestion of bringing Fay down to see her. Perhaps it was for the best, Kitty told herself, putting the letter safely away to reread later. It might upset both of them to see each other and then have to say goodbye again. Anyway, there had been an outbreak of measles at the camp. Some of the children had been very ill indeed and the rumour was that one had died. It wasn't a good place to bring Fay at present.

In the weeks and months that followed, Kitty kept herself as busy as she could. She was much in demand to give music lessons as part of the impressive education programme organized by a committee of English stalwarts in the camp. However, she still found plenty of time to brood.

The shock of Gene's death was gradually ebbing away, but it was succeeded by anger, and, what is more, anger with Gene. How could he have put himself in danger in that way when she needed him so much? This was unreasonable, she knew, and she was ashamed of this feeling, but she felt it all the same. She went over and over in her mind the events that led up to his death, wondering what she could have done differently. If only Fay hadn't been there. She worried that what had happened would affect her daughter for ever. How traumatic, to see her father going down into that frightening dark hole and not come out again. Had Fay understood what had happened to him? Kitty hadn't been given the opportunity to find out.

In time the anger faded and thankfully her best memories of Eugene started to emerge, burnished and shining. Her husband had done only what he'd had to, helping others, and it was one of the things for which she'd always loved him. *Yes, but he should have put us first,* a voice would argue in her mind. He tried to, was her counter-argument. He had managed to keep her ignorant of his dangerous acts of resistance. She would not have known anything at all if he'd not needed a safe place for Flight Lieutenant Stone. And Gene hadn't complained when Serge, who was her friend, had come to them. He had accepted it and done what he regarded as the right thing.

Kitty had always known she'd have to share Gene with his work. She remembered the night they'd become engaged, when she'd been so bitter that he had missed their date because of being needed at the hospital. He'd as good as told her then that she'd be marrying his work.

Men had their duties and women had theirs. Hers had been to support him, she thought resentfully, and to the detriment of their child. And now she must do everything to survive and endure for Fay's sake. One day this war would be over. Germany would be beaten: that was what the rumours were saying and Kitty believed them. She would find Fay and go home to England, home to Uncle Pepper and Hampshire, and never mind if life was dull, they would be safe. But it would be a life without Eugene. How would she bear it? She wondered, not for the first time, what they'd done with Eugene's body. Had the Gestapo taken it? Was there a grave where she would be able to mourn?

In February 1943 came a piece of bad news that she hadn't expected. It was a letter from Uncle Pepper's solicitor, who'd finally heard by a roundabout way official news of Kitty's internment. He was very sorry to have to tell her that her uncle, Anthony Fletcher, was dead. He'd died the previous summer, apparently, following a short illness. Her uncle had left her some money and he, the solicitor, would see if he could send her some via the Red Cross if she was in need. He was duty bound to remind her though, that Mr Fletcher's house had been leased from a local landowner and the lease having lapsed with her uncle's death, it had had to be cleared. His effects had been placed in storage pending Kitty's return.

She refolded the letter and closed her eyes against grief as memories of her uncle flooded her mind. His kindness to her and his dry affection. The way he'd encouraged her music and wanted to do his best for her. It was because of him that she'd come to France in the first place. And met Gene. She remembered how relieved her uncle had been at her wedding, believing her to be happy and settled. How anxious he must have been about her, hearing nothing from her for so long.

'What a shame. He was a very nice man,' Miss Dunne said when Kitty broke the news to her. 'We had such a lovely time visiting the Louvre together while you were on honeymoon. He was so knowledgeable about the paintings. How very sad for you.'

'I don't have anywhere to go home to now,' Kitty said, with a catch in her voice. In losing Uncle Pepper she had become an orphan all over again. She didn't remember her real parents, not properly. He had eventually taken their place and provided not just the material things she needed, her education and stability, but a steady, patient love. A bachelor who'd been middle-aged for most of his adult life, he had been the most unlikely candidate to bring up a lonely small girl, but his guardianship had turned out a success for both parties and she felt the loss of him deeply.

'I felt like that when my father died,' Miss Dunne said, patting Kitty's hand. 'I had no one else, you see. When we return to England, you and Fay must come and stay with me in Norfolk.'

'If we return,' Kitty said, wistful. 'Sometimes I don't believe we ever will.'

'Now, now, it is our Christian duty always to hope, Kitty, dear. Naturally you're sad about your poor uncle, but remember what you told me when you first came to Vittel. You must think of Fay and be strong for her.'

All this made Kitty miss Fay more than ever. Again she applied to be released. Again her application was refused. After this she wrote a letter to Mère Marie-François asking after Fay and suggesting that one of the nuns bring her to visit. She gave it to one of the French doctors in the camp hospital to post, but did not receive a reply. She wondered whether the letter had ever arrived at the convent. Or perhaps the response had gone missing or been intercepted.

In her most desperate moments Kitty entertained the idea of escape, but in the end she didn't have the courage. What would happen if she were caught? She had heard that runaways could be shot. Anyway, the only place she would want to escape to was Paris – and what was the point of going back there? She'd put both herself and Fay in danger then. No, better to stay where she was.

In the spring of 1943 something happened that drew her out of her own predicament. Several hundred unusual visitors arrived in two successive trainloads. Some of the women wore furs and velvet hats, others were dressed more shabbily, having lost all their possessions. The group included men, young and old, in their number, and many children, emaciated and terrified-looking. An air of fear and exhaustion hung over the whole group and the news quickly spread through the camp that they were Polish Jews, traumatized survivors of the Warsaw Ghetto, which had been destroyed by the Nazis. They had come to Vittel, many of them, clutching doubtful paperwork claiming Latin-American citizenship or promises of sanctuary in Palestine that their captors, perhaps in a rare moment of clemency, felt bound to investigate. Or maybe they just hadn't known what else to do with them. At Vittel, the Poles were housed together away from the rest of the inmates in an hotel by itself. This was linked to the main complex by a specially erected wooden bridge which, Kitty heard, was a bitter reminder to them of the one the Nazis had constructed to the Warsaw Ghetto.

It was from these newcomers that many of the internees learned for the first time the phrase 'the Final Solution' and the names 'Auschwitz, Treblinka and Dachau' and were appalled. All sorts of whispered stories circulated, so horrifying that Kitty didn't know whether to believe them. Many of the most traumatized of the Jews had endured the cruelties of the Nazi camps or had family members who were still there or had died in one.

Kitty came to befriend one of the women, Rejcel, who reminded her of a girl she'd seen in the prison exercise yard in Paris, being fair-haired, slender and listless with a hollow-eyed look. She had with her a ten-year-old daughter, Anna, who played the violin, and Kitty approached Rejcel originally after hearing the child practise, wanting to help.

Like Kitty, Rejcel had lost her husband in dreadful circumstances. She had no idea of the whereabouts of her younger daughter, Iza, or of her parents, but feared they must be dead. She and Anna had escaped the round-ups by crawling through Warsaw's sewers.

Vittel must have seemed like paradise to Rejcel after all that they had endured, but if so it was an empty one because she was without the people she loved. Rejcel wept often, but in a strange and unexpected way, talking to her helped loosen the tight band of grief around Kitty's own heart.

Most of this group of Polish Jews lived at Vittel for a year. During the winter of 1944 the news gleaned from outside started to bring hope to the internees. Italy had surrendered to the Allies early in the autumn, and now the war in Africa was slowly being won.

Vittel was directly under the flight path of the British planes on their way to bomb Germany, and Kitty's heart couldn't help lifting as the raiders passed overhead in ever-increasing numbers, for this was further indication that the tide of war was turning in the Allies' favour. Surely it wouldn't be long before France would be free. None of the rumours offered hard information about when or how. Patient, she must be patient. From time to time a letter arrived from the convent to assure her that Fay was well. For now she had to be satisfied with that.

Then in the spring came an awful sign of the increasing defensiveness of Germany's position. A train with boarded windows drew up at the station in Vittel. Most of the internees thought nothing of it, but the Polish Jews understood its significance straight away and panic ensued in their enclave. They were right to panic.

Kitty watched in consternation the horrifying scenes as the first batch of Jews was marshalled together by the Germans. At least one woman killed herself by taking cyanide rather than get on the train. Another jumped from a fifth-floor window. Miraculously, she survived and was taken to the camp hospital. A few, however, were discovered by the authorities to have mysteriously vanished, and searches of most of the buildings ensued.

Kitty looked anxiously for Rejcel, and was relieved to see that she wasn't in this first group to be deported, but there were others she knew who were. She ran to ask one of the SS soldiers where they were being taken. As ever, she was ignored, and when she persisted in her request was pushed roughly aside.

'They are only being transferred,' the more benign camp Kommandant was telling everyone. 'Nothing to worry about.' Some of the other internees were naïve or fearful enough to believe him. A few who protested found themselves branded as tiresome meddlers and confined to their hotels for a month. Kitty narrowly escaped being one of these.

After the train left, witnesses delivered the dreadful news that it was travelling east, in the direction of the German border. Much later, Kitty was to learn that in response to the increasing likelihood of defeat, the Nazis had stepped up their programme of extermination. Most of these poor people were never to be seen again.

Rejcel and Anna were safe this time, but Kitty had never seen Rejcel so terrified. She talked all the time about how they would be next. However, as the days passed, a new look of determination came into her eyes. 'We have to escape,' she told Kitty. 'Another train will come. I know what will happen. This is what they do.'

'How, though? How will you get away?' Kitty knew that some of the inmates had connections with the Resistance outside. Sometimes internees did vanish. Some escaped and never returned, and you never heard what happened to them. Of those who were caught, some were shot. Others were brought back to the camp and deported to heaven knew where. For Kitty it wasn't worth the risk. But for Rejcel the choice was starker. 'I want to help you,' Kitty whispered, her mind working quickly. She was sharing a room just with Sarah now. Perhaps they could hide Rejcel and her daughter there?

'No, that would put you in danger,' Rejcel replied when Kitty explained. 'I've already spoken to a woman who can help. She knows people outside. Don't ask me any more, I beg you. It's better that way for all of us.'

And so it came about that when she looked for Rejcel a few days later, Kitty was told by the matronly woman they'd roomed with that Rejcel and Anna had gone. They'd been helped to escape the night before. *She didn't even say goodbye*, Kitty thought, but if their disappearance was a shock, it was also a relief. She lived on her nerves for weeks though, fearing the news that they'd been caught. But no news of any kind came. A few other Jews vanished, too, but most stayed, dreading the consequences of being apprehended. Maybe there wouldn't be another deportation, some told themselves. Maybe they *would* get to Brazil or Palestine, or wherever it was that they'd pinned their hopes on going.

They were wrong. In May another of the windowless trains arrived at the station and the whole pattern was repeated. The Poles' cries of desperation as they were rounded up were terrible. Kitty could not bear to watch.

After that, very few Jews remained. Some, Kitty knew, were concealed about the camp until means were found to facilitate their escape. It came as some surprise to hear, long afterwards, that Adele Dunne had used her position in the camp office to help.

Chapter 31

Summer 1944

Once again the camp at Vittel was abuzz with rumours. The inmates discussed with breathless excitement the news of the D-Day Landings, of Allied successes in Northern France and the merciless bombardment by the Allies of German cities. Then one hot day in the middle of July, the camp's sound system rang out through the dusty grounds with momentous news. The names of nine hundred people were read out. They were to get themselves ready to leave the camp, to be repatriated. Kitty was one of them.

'I can't just go,' she told Miss Dunne in a panic. 'Not without collecting Fay.' Adele was also on the list and she was in a hurry to pack. Everyone was told they could take up to forty pounds' weight in luggage, but still the rules were ridiculous. No paper, even scraps. Or books or envelopes. Strip searches were threatened.

'Of course you can't,' Miss Dunne replied. 'You'll have to tell them. Not everyone's going at once. Perhaps Fay can be fetched. Why don't we find someone who'll telephone the convent? Or we can write. Oh Kitty, you can't miss this opportunity to go home.'

Home. Kitty wasn't sure what she'd do when she arrived in England, but she longed to be there. Paris wasn't home, not now, without Gene. There was nothing to stay for. So many of the people she'd loved had left or been lost. Milly and Jack, her teacher, Monsieur Deschamps. And Serge, what had happened to Serge?

In the end she found the doctor who had once smuggled out the letter for her and begged him to help her. He was a slow, careful man who considered her request gravely, then nodded. 'I will do my best,' he told her, and she gave him the address of Sainte Cécile's. Father Paul must have a telephone number, though she didn't know what it was.

It was with mixed feelings that she watched the first group of excited internees leave to board the train going west to the coast. It was a proper train with proper carriages, it was said, not those ominous box-cars. Miss Dunne was among them, a spare upright figure in her old-fashioned clothes, her face burnt brown by the baking summer sun, but still looking unmistakably English with her bright, dignified expression and an inelegant pair of sensible shoes. 'Remember, Kitty,' she told her, 'if we don't see each other again en route, it's Little Barton where I live. Primrose Cottage. Ask anyone there, they'll all know it.'

'I'll find you, Adele. Thank you. And good luck.'

Sarah, her roommate, had been allowed to leave a couple of months before, returning home to Paris, so Kitty had the room all to herself now. She lay awake that night, worrying about Fay and hoping against hope that her daughter would arrive in time for them to travel home with the other internees.

The day of departure grew closer, but there was no sign

of Fay. 'I sent your letter,' the doctor assured her. 'It seems the telephone system has been down in that part of Paris, so it's difficult to find out what is happening, but I expect they'll come. The only other thing you can do is to fetch her yourself.'

'Would they let me do that?' she asked.

'I don't know, but if you like I'll help. Come and see me again this afternoon.'

When she sought him out he was in his office, writing up reports. He put down his pen and his face lit up with a broad smile. 'There's a train to Paris in the morning. It's been arranged. Two of the guards are to go with you.'

'Two? What do they expect me to do? But thank you, Doctor.' She was indeed relieved.

'And someone at the camp office is to telephone your Father Paul to know to expect you.'

Again, she thanked him. Once, when she'd consulted him about persistent headaches, she'd told him about Gene, and he'd always remembered that her husband had been a doctor, too, and had been especially kind.

The return to Paris seemed to pass more swiftly than the awful journey down to Vittel. Kitty shared her compartment with the guards, who ignored her, instead talking and laughing with each other as they played cards for small change. When night fell she slept, wrapped in a coat, trying to block out their snores. When she awoke it was morning and they were arriving in Paris. *Today I'll see my daughter!* She was so nervous with excitement she could not eat.

'Gone? Where? When?' Cold shock coursed through Kitty's limbs.

'I'm sorry, my dear,' said Mère Marie-François. 'When we received the letter from the doctor at Vittel we discussed it at length, and decided that Thérèse should take Fay to you. They left two days ago and should be there by now. Your trains must have passed each other.' The Reverend Mother clutched the rosary she wore in an unusual sign of distress. The presence of the guards seemed to fill the entrance hall. One asked something in German. The Reverend Mother answered in the same language. The guard looked puzzled, then shrugged and explained the situation to his comrade.

'I've told them Fay isn't here,' the nun said. 'They'll take you back to Vittel. Surely you'll meet them there.'

'I hope so,' Kitty said.

There was a train from Paris that passed through Vittel later that morning. They boarded it, but it was an hour late in leaving and Kitty could hardly keep still for anxiety. When it finally lurched into movement, her relief was palpable. In late afternoon, however, it came to a halt so suddenly that they were almost thrown across the carriage. Kitty's German guards were on their feet and leaning out of the window, trying to discover what was happening. There were rumours of difficulties further down the line.

'Bomb,' one of the guards explained to her in English and mimed an explosion. It appeared that an air raid had damaged the track during the night. The train sat there for the rest of the day, waiting for it to be repaired.

Chapter 32

Thérèse had never travelled so far before, and certainly not by herself. Not that she was quite alone, she had Fay with her, but that made her doubly nervous because she had such an important task to perform. She was to take Fay on the long train journey from Paris to the spa town of Vittel. She hadn't even seen Vittel on a map, though she knew it was somewhere beyond the industrial city of Nancy, on the edge of Occupied France and near the borders of Germany and Switzerland. She didn't want to leave Paris and she dreaded the moment when she would have to say goodbye to Fay, but the Reverend Mother had said she should be the one to do it and so she had to. She'd packed Fay's little rucksack with her few items of clothing and a book of children's Bible stories to read on the way and prepared a basket of food. She hoped it would be enough to last them for the journey, though it was a far cry from the generous picnics that she'd been given on outings as a child.

Fay was in a strange mood, by turns excited and tearful. 'Aren't you looking forward to seeing your mother?' Thérèse asked her as she helped the child on with her cardigan and fitted the rucksack over her shoulders.

Fay thought a moment and nodded uncertainly, then

leaned against Thérèse. The young woman felt her warm arms through the thick cloth of her habit as Fay hugged her tightly and she hugged her back, surprised and not a little moved by the unusually strong rush of affection. Fay had never been a demonstrative child, and since losing both her parents she didn't always like to be touched. If she wanted reassurance she would clutch her wooden zebra and stroke its smooth striped sides. Zipper was safe in the rucksack, Thérèse had made sure of that.

Before they left the convent, she sent Fay to the refectory to say goodbye to the other nuns eating breakfast there whilst she went to fill a bottle of water for the journey. She knew it was a wrench for all of them to say goodbye to the little girl and couldn't have borne to see their tears.

Father Paul travelled with them on the Métro to the Gare de l'Est, to make sure they boarded the right train, and it was only after they'd waved him goodbye and settled in their compartment that Thérèse noticed Fay's rucksack was undone. Her clothes were all still inside, but a frantic search revealed that the toy zebra was missing.

Had Fay unbuckled the bag herself – and if so, when? Was it she who had taken Zipper out and left him somewhere? When had she last had him? Fay was clear that she'd undone the bag to check that he was in there when Thérèse had sent her for a last-minute visit to the lavatory. Then there had been a hurry to leave and she hadn't rebuckled the bag properly. 'We'll find him and send him to you,' Thérèse said. With luck the toy had been left at the convent rather than falling out on the street.

For a long while after this disaster, Fay sat opposite

Thérèse cast in her own private shadow, her slight figure very upright, a tragic expression on her face as she stared out of the window at a passing view she did not see. She would not speak, and from time to time Thérèse wondered if her eyes were gleaming with tears. If so, the tears did not fall. She ate the bread that Thérèse passed her and sipped the water, and when night fell she consented to lie with her head in Thérèse's warm lap where she quickly fell asleep.

She was fretful in the night, and when she woke her face was flushed and her forehead hot to the touch. Her eyes glittered with fever. Thérèse got her to drink a little of the water and after a while she revived.

When they arrived at Vittel, their train slid past another waiting at the other side of the platform. It was packed full of women, some of the younger ones leaning out of the windows, chattering and calling out to one another. Half a dozen German soldiers were loading a last few items of luggage.

Anxious to find out what was happening, Thérèse helped Fay with her bag and lifted her down from the train. How light she was, her shoulderblades protruding like wing buds under her thin cardigan. She gripped the child's hand and hurried her across to the other train. A station guard moved past them, closing the doors.

'Where is this train going, m'sieur? Who are these people?' Thérèse asked him.

'*Les Anglaises et les Americaines,*' he replied, as though it should be obvious to her. '*Elles rentrent chez elles.* They are going home.'

'Home? You mean to England?'

'Yes, to England, America, wherever, I don't know.'

'Do they go through Paris?'

'Paris? No, they can't get through that way. South-west, they'll go. Portugal, I'd say. Now, if you'll excuse me ...' And off he went, returning a dropped hat to a laughing fair-haired girl in a threadbare jacket who was leaning out of a window.

'*Madame Kitty Knox, est-elle ici*?' Thérèse asked the fair-haired girl, starting to panic. 'This is her daughter.'

'Mrs Knox? I know who you mean. Wait a minute.' The head disappeared from the window and Thérèse heard Kitty's name repeated in the compartment.

Down the train the final suitcase had been loaded and the guard was closing the last door.

The young woman's head reappeared. 'She's not in this carriage,' she told Thérèse, 'but she should be somewhere further down. Someone here heard her name read out.'

Thérèse's grip on Fay's hand tightened as they hurried along the train, asking for Kitty. The guard passed them, checking the doors, a flag in his hand.

'Kitty Knox, she is here?' Thérèse asked a swarthy woman at a window in the next carriage. Again the woman withdrew and another consultation took place before she reappeared. 'Someone says they might have seen her down at the front,' she said.

'*Excusez-moi?*' The woman's accent was difficult for Thérèse to follow.

'That way,' the woman repeated, pointing.

A whistle blew. '*Attendez!*' Thérèse cried, hitching up her habit as she pulled Fay along to the next carriage. 'Kitty,' she cried, searching the rows of faces behind the glass. The women stared back, puzzled.

'Hey,' cried the swarthy woman from the previous

carriage. Thérèse swung round wildly. 'The front. Further that way,' the woman said, pointing again up the train.

The train gave a sudden judder and the engine let out a great hiss of steam. 'Kitty!' Thérèse shouted in great alarm. '*Attendez, attendez,*' but the guard was too far away to hear.

'Please?' She lifted Fay up to the woman at the train window.

'Come on, ups-a-daisy,' the woman sang out and the little girl flew through the air in her arms. For a crazy moment Thérèse wondered if she should get on too, but it was too late, the train was beginning to set off. She ran to a carriage door and managed to open it, but it moved beyond her reach. Further down the platform, a soldier leaped forward to slam it. The train gathered speed, then cleared the end of the platform and was away.

Thérèse was left standing there alone, gazing after it. Had she done the right thing? The soldiers glanced at her without interest as they passed, ambling off in a relaxed group to the exit, talking and laughing, their duty done for the day.

She went and sank down on a rickety bench, her heart full of grief and confusion. She'd not said goodbye to Fay, not properly, and now the girl was gone, caught up, swept away. The women would take her to Kitty, she assured herself. Kitty must be on the train. Hadn't the swarthy woman said so? She, Thérèse, had done the right thing. So why was she visited by this sense of unease like smoke drifting from a smouldering fire? She pondered, and eventually the fire leaped into life as the truth came to her. *Kitty would never have got on the train without her daughter, if she could help it*. The knowledge surged through her veins like molten lead, heavy, hot, deadening. She sat motionless for a long time, unsure what to do. Then, slowly, she forced herself to stand. Step by reluctant step she made her way out of the station and looked for the entrance to the camp.

Chapter 33

'And that,' Nathalie Ramond said, 'was the last time that I saw you.'

'The last ...?' Fay echoed, frowning. She was trying to catch the tail of a memory. A woman's voice saying 'Ups-a-daisy,' then surprise and fear as a strong pair of arms pulled her flying through the air, the ground rushing away beneath her feet. She'd landed in a swaying carriage compartment where there was a crowd of strange faces. Fay closed her eyes, remembering an exotic scent and the sound of female laughter.

'You were on a train going west,' Mme Ramond's voice brought her back. 'All the way back to England, safe with your mother. Or so I believed. Only I was wrong. Your mother wasn't on the train at all. When I asked at the camp, they searched for her and found she wasn't there and for a while I was reassured. Then someone in the camp office remembered that she'd gone to Paris to collect you. No one had seen her return. Hearing this, well, you can imagine, I was horrified. I'd had only a split second to think and I thought I'd done the right thing – but I hadn't, after all. If there had been more time I could have searched the train, but I still should have known that your mother would not have left for England without you. Not unless they'd forced her to.'

'And what if they had – forced her, I mean? You couldn't know.'

'That is true, yes, but at the time I didn't think about that. I simply believed the woman who said your mother was on the train. Anyway, the Kommandant's secretary managed to speak to somebody at the convent, but for a time nobody knew where your mother was.

'I stayed overnight in the town. It wasn't until the following day that your mother returned. Her train had been held up by bombing damage to the tracks. When I told her what had happened to you, well, of course, you can imagine her distress. She begged and pleaded with the Kommandant to put her on another train so she could follow you, but it seemed this wasn't possible at short notice. What we didn't know at the time was that because of the fighting and attacks on railways by the Resistance in Southern and Central France, it was dangerous to travel. If your mother had known that, she'd have been even more worried about you than she was. The Kommandant kept saying there would be a train soon, and trying to reassure her that the other women would look after you, Fay. And after that I didn't know any more. Your mother was furious with me. She questioned me and questioned me about my decision to put you on that train, and told me I was stupid. Stupid or bad, very hurtful things, but I accepted them. They were my due. I had failed her and, more important, I'd failed you. It didn't count for her that I'd looked after you for so long. Still, I understood. If you'd been my child and someone else with responsibility for you had failed in that duty, I'd have been angry, too. I offered to stay with her, to travel to find you, but she wouldn't have it. And after a day or two I was summoned back to the convent. I went to her room to say goodbye, but she would not even open the door. And so, utterly miserable and defeated, I returned to Paris.'

'What did my mother do then?'

'I don't know. We didn't hear anything. For us in Paris the climax to the war was not long in coming, and for a while everything was chaos. In the middle of August 1944,' Mme Ramond went on, 'as the Allied armies surrounded Paris, a great spirit of resistance began to burn in the city and the Germans found it impossible to keep order. On the twenty-fifth, Général de Gaulle marched in, triumphant. You can imagine the strength of our rejoicing. But there was confusion, too, and recriminations; awful things went on.'

The woman sighed, as though remembering these things, but then she smiled.

'For me, a whole new life began. One day in early November, I was relieved and delighted to receive a letter from Serge. He'd been able to leave his hiding place, but life was still very hard for him. He had travelled at once to Orléans to look for his family, but found his childhood home boarded up and empty. When he'd questioned the neighbours he learned that his parents and siblings had simply been picked up by the police one summer's morning in 1942 and taken away. No one had seen them since. He was trying desperately to make enquiries, but the authorities were deluged with such requests and he wasn't able to find anything out. He'd recently taken a room near the Conservatoire and was back at his old job, playing the piano at the hotel. He asked if he might come to visit me at the convent.'

'And of course you said yes.'

'I did – after asking the Reverend Mother's permission. The following spring I secured a release from my vows. The other nuns were surprisingly kind and I was very touched by this. And shortly after, Serge and I were married.'

Mme Ramond's eyes were soft with love. 'We have had some wonderful times together, you know, though there has been tragedy too. Serge was devastated to discover that none of his family had survived the war, and he will never recover from that. It might have helped if we'd been able to have children of our own, but we were not blessed in that way. And then this arthritis has meant I haven't been able to support him in his work as much as I'd like. Still, Serge has had great success with his music, and we have each other. Yes, we have been happy.'

Fay sensed this to be true. Nathalie Ramond had always been loyal, but she'd also followed her heart. This thought reminded her of the letter her mother had sent warning her against believing the woman. She supposed that Kitty was referring to the young Thérèse's mistake in putting Fay on the train alone. But Mme Ramond had admitted her mistake and had always rued it. Was her account true? Fay could hardly ask her. It would sound offensive. Instead, when she rose to go, she kissed Nathalie Ramond on both cheeks.

'Thank you,' Fay said. 'Thank you for looking after me when I was small. Whatever happened to me after you put me on that train, I can see that it wasn't your fault.'

'Thank you, dear,' Mme Ramond said, very moved.

'That means a great deal to me.'

'I'm not sure that I will be able to see you tomorrow, but I will write.'

'Thank you, *chérie*, I should like that. And one day I long to see ... No, I must not even hope ...'

'You would like to see my mother again?'

'Yes, but I fear that she has never forgiven me.'

'Maybe she will,' said Fay, 'when I explain to her how you told me the truth.'

After Fay had gone, Nathalie Ramond went to the window and stood there, staring out, but she did not notice the sunshine, or a pair of laughing young girls hand-in-hand on the pavement below. She was thinking about the nature of truth. She had been brought up by her parents always to tell the truth, and all her life she'd tried to do so. She knew that truth shone light in dark corners, that it enabled reconciliation and forgiveness. 'The truth will set you free,' the Bible had taught her, and she had always believed that. She had seen for herself how, when Serge found out the terrible truth of what had happened to his parents, his brothers and his sister, the knowledge had freed him. He had fallen into bitter despair, yet somehow, with her support and the succour of his music, he had found within himself the courage to go on.

She'd told this child Fay the truth about how she had mistakenly put her on the train in Vittel, and Fay's reaction had been more generous than she'd hoped. The dear girl had forgiven her, and she blessed her for that. But there was something she hadn't told her, something so dark and difficult she couldn't think of it without pain.

Sometimes, as in this case, she disagreed with those

who insisted on the sanctity of the truth. This was why she had chosen to lie about it to Fay.

She pressed her forehead against the cold glass of the window and closed her eyes, remembering again the horror of the day Gene died. The facts as she'd relayed them to Fay were shocking enough, but they weren't the complete truth.

Only when one has been caught up in a chaotic, fast-moving and emotional event oneself can one fully appreciate how difficult it is to make good decisions in such a situation. Only she truly understood how she came to that spur-of-the moment decision made in good faith on Vittel station. And only the people present in the church when Gene was shot could comprehend completely what had happened that day.

Fay's mother had obviously never told her daughter the truth about it, and Nathalie Ramond would not do so either. Never, ever. There are some truths that should never be told because they hurt and destroy more than they can ever heal. Eugene Knox's downfall came as a result of his daughter telling the truth. Fay had been nearly three, too young to know how to lie. What she did was simply not her fault. It was what came naturally to her.

Mme Ramond pressed her fingers to her temples, wondering if one of her headaches was coming on. She closed her eyes, unable to fight the pictures flying into her mind. Of what happened after the Gestapo had rounded up everyone they'd found in the convent and sent them into the church.

Hoff and his men had practically given up their search for Gene, and Hoff's frustration was plain to behold. There he was, standing at a loss before a bunch of terrified women and children and a fussy old priest who were all watching him, waiting for him to fail.

The tension was all too much for Fay in Sister Thérèse's arms. She didn't understand what was happening, only that everything was frightening and wrong. She began to cry. 'I want my papa, I want my papa,' she moaned, and Sister Thérèse had done her best to quiet her.

It was too late, however. Hoff's curiosity was drawn. He consulted with the officer holding Kitty, then went across to the little girl and said to her, surprisingly tenderly, 'Where is your papa, *Liebchen*?'

Kitty gasped, 'No, Fay!' only to feel a hand clap across her mouth.

Hoff asked her again.

Fay knew exactly where her papa was. She was afraid of this man, but she was an obedient child.

She pointed.

Chapter 34

Saturday

'You look as though you need a stiff drink,' Sandra said as she stepped into a full-length black dress and pushed her arms into the sleeves.

'I do, but I daren't,' Fay said, doing up the zip for her. 'I'd really make a mess of the pieces.'

She'd left Mme Ramond's flat to go straight to the rehearsal, where she'd found it impossible to concentrate. Her fingers had played the notes automatically, but her heart hadn't been in the music. All she'd been able to think about was the death of her father, her mother's suffering ... then there was the account of herself as a small girl, sent far away all alone on a train full of strangers. What had happened to her next? If only she could remember! The scenes Mme Ramond had described spooled through her mind with such vividness that at one point she didn't notice the conductor asking them to start a particular passage again and, scrabbling for the right page, she knocked the score off the stand. James's eyebrows had knitted in disapproval.

She must, she told herself as she finished dressing, simply must focus her whole mind on the concert. Not only was it the climax of their tour, to be attended by an alarming array of dignitaries, but it was her final chance to prove to Colin that she was worthy of a place in his orchestra.

It was important to look her best, too. She leaned towards the hinged mirror on the chest of drawers to clip on a pair of sparkling zircon earrings, then sighed at her reflection. Tonight in the weary light of the room her dark eyes looked huge and luminous in her pale face. She patted on more face powder. As she slicked on pink lipstick, she thought of Adam, whom she'd see later. A rush of longing warmed her cheeks, to be succeeded by despair. She was going home tomorrow. This might be their last time together. Only for a while, she assured herself, trying to be reasonable, but couldn't stop a lump forming in her throat. It would be unbearable to say goodbye.

'So, big night tonight,' Sandra remarked as she pushed her narrow feet into elegant black shoes. 'We're sold out, apparently.'

Fay dragged her thoughts back. 'I heard. Do you think the Prime Minister is really coming?'

'So Colin says. I suppose we do have to go on to the reception afterwards.'

'Can't see how we can get out of it.'

'At least Georges is invited. We might bunk off early though.' Sandra dabbed on scent from a bottle and the smell of Nina Ricci filled the air. 'I shouldn't wait up for me if I were you. It's our last night, after all.'

'Won't you try to see each other again?' Fay asked, surprised. 'I thought you were rather fond of him.'

'Oh I am, but that's hardly the point. He's in Paris, I'm in London. It wouldn't work, Fay.'

'Wouldn't it? It seems a shame.'

Sandra gave a light laugh. 'Easy come, easy go,' she said, but Fay was sure she detected a sadness in her voice and wondered whether Sandra was kidding herself. Fay couldn't live the kind of life the other girl did, moving between men, loving and letting go, and she wondered how long it would be before Sandra herself came to tire of it.

'What about you?'

'What about me?'

'You are a dark horse! You know I'm talking about your young man.'

'He's coming to hear us. It's his job to write about the concert, after all. He'll come to the reception, too.' She couldn't bear to compare her relationship with that of Sandra and Georges. Surely she and Adam were of a different order altogether. She didn't mean to be secretive, it was that it seemed too fragile and important to be exposed to Sandra's casual eye. 'Don't you think we ought to go?' she rushed on. 'You look lovely, by the way.'

'Thank you,' Sandra said, pulling on a short black jacket. 'So do you.'

Sitting quietly in her place, her instrument tuned, Fay looked about at the gathering audience, trying to calm her whirling mind. The hall with its fine wooden panelling and inlaid geometrical patterns was packed with elegantly dressed people. There, in the nearest of the boxes, was a stern bearded man, who James, her fellow violinist, whispered was indeed the French Prime Minister, sitting with his dark, striking wife. Somewhere, she thought as she scanned the rows of seats, must be Adam, though she couldn't see clearly against the lights. Adam. The thought of him briefly filled her mind. Now the last few latecomers were settled in their seats and the air of expectation rose. *Concentrate*, she told herself fiercely. She mustn't think of anything except the music.

The leader of the orchestra took his place to enthusiastic applause, and there was more as Colin hurried on stage with his bright, brisk demeanour. He mounted the podium and bowed low to the audience before turning to the orchestra and raising his baton in a sign to begin. There came that moment of stillness when all eyes were focused on him, bows poised and breath held. Fay emptied her mind of everything except her first note. Then it began, the dark, dramatic pulsating beat of the Dance of the Knights from Prokofiev's *Romeo and Juliet*, which always thrilled her. Then it was the violins' turn to soar, and at once she was there at the heart of the music, oblivious to all else but the part she was playing, the beat of Colin's baton and the surge of sound building all around. She didn't need to urge herself to concentrate any more, for the music filled her mind, possessed her, took her to another plane.

This was where she wanted to be, doing what she wanted to do, and she poured all her passion into her playing, seeing in her mind's eye the whirl of the dancers for whom the piece had been written, feeling their yearning, their joy, their despair. And it was as though she shared it too. All the sorrow and confusion and delight of the last week poured out in her playing. And all too soon the piece was over. She raised her head, exhilarated and panting, as a rapturous applause began.

'That went rather well.' Great praise from the austere James, spoken as the clapping finally faded. Fay smiled to herself as she shuffled the music on their stand ready for the second piece of the night. It was one she adored, Rimsky-Korsakov and the beautiful haunting voice of his *Scheherazade*. As they played, Fay could imagine the clever young bride telling her fascinating stories through the sultry Arabian nights to beguile her impatient husband and save her own life. The leader of the orchestra was playing the violin solo. As Fay listened, a thought floated into her head. *One day it will be me playing that.* She wanted it badly, she saw suddenly. Again, she poured all of herself into the music, to the exclusion of all else.

Backstage at the interval, she half-hoped that Adam might appear, but when he didn't, she wasn't worried. He was probably with some journalist friend or other, caught up in the crowds at the bar. She was content to sit by herself, checking her instrument and drinking a glass of water as she prepared her mind for the long final piece of this Russian programme, Tchaikovsky's Sixth Symphony, written for his beloved nephew and first performed only days before his own demise. Her mind was calmer now. She knew she could do it, she could master herself like a soldier preparing for battle. And now it was time to return to the stage. She walked with head held high, set for the task ahead.

At the end of the concert the atmosphere in the Green Room was electric with excited chatter as the musicians manoeuvred instruments into cases, and collected coats. Someone banged on a table to gain everybody's attention and Colin stepped onto a chair to speak.

'Congratulations, everybody, I'm extremely proud of you,' he said, and there was an answering cheer.

'Sad to think it's all over,' James said laconically as he checked his tie in the mirror. 'Coming across the road to the bunfight?'

'I hope so,' Fay said. 'I must look out for someone first.' She was still buoyed up by the music, her nerves taut with the glory of the playing, but now all she could think of was Adam.

She took the violin case and hurried out into the auditorium to look for Adam, scanning the crowds still flowing towards the exit, but seeing no sign of him. Instead her attention was caught by the sight of a middle-aged woman with a stick making her way in the opposite direction towards the stage. With surprise, Fay realized it was Mme Ramond. She hurried to meet her and they exchanged kisses.

'Nathalie, you didn't tell me you were coming.'

'I had bought tickets. I did not tell you as I wasn't sure if I would feel well enough.'

'I'm so glad you did. Thank you!'

'No, thank *you*, Fay. It was a most wonderful concert. I loved to see you play. You looked as though you were enjoying it, my dear. You appeared to be transported!'

'I was, I really was. I must confess, I felt quite shaken after what you told me today and I didn't think I would play my best, but I did.'

'That's the sign of a real musician. It's just a pity that Serge was not here. He would have loved it, too.'

'Is it Monday that he returns?'

'Tomorrow evening now, but you will have left Paris by then, yes?'

'I'm afraid that the train leaves late afternoon.'

'You must come back to Paris very soon and meet Serge. He will be delighted when I tell him I've seen you. I do hope that your mother is well again quickly.' Mme Ramond hesitated, her manner wistful. 'I should so like to see her again.'

'I will speak to her about it,' Fay said quickly. She sensed it would be a difficult task to persuade her mother. She thought of everything that she had to tell her, the questions crowding in her mind. It was clear from her letter that Kitty had not forgiven Sister Thérèse for her mistake. Would she do so now that Thérèse was Nathalie Ramond, older and wiser and struggling with ill health?

Mme Ramond turned to look up the hall towards the central exit. A woman of similar age was standing there and Mme Ramond waved to her.

'I have to go now,' she told Fay. 'My sister is waiting.'

Fay walked with her as she made her slow progress. 'I want to thank you again,' Fay said. 'For telling me everything. Perhaps I'll start to remember more when I speak to my mother. But I wanted to say that I do remember you now. I remember ...' she faltered '... that you loved me. So thank you.'

The former nun looked up at her quickly and smiled, and through the lines of pain Fay could once more glimpse how she must have been before her illness. 'I did and I still do, Fay. It was very wonderful to see you again, all grown up, and with such a talent. I am so proud of you.'

'Thank you. That means so much to me.'

'And now we must say *au revoir*.' She laid a light hand

on Fay's shoulder and kissed her on both cheeks, then Fay watched her walk back up the aisle to meet her sister. At the top Mme Ramond looked back to her one more time and smiled, and then the women were gone.

At once Fay felt a sense of loss. She hadn't really asked Nathalie enough about Serge or their life together. It would have to wait for another time. And for now Mme Ramond faded from her mind. She needed to find Adam.

He wasn't anywhere in the auditorium. It was almost empty. There were several men on the stage clattering about with music-stands, and the percussionist was packing up his drums. Fay went up to the central doors at the back and stood scouring the crowds in the foyer, but couldn't see him, so she turned and made her way back to the Green Room. Perhaps he would come to find her backstage.

'Fay!' It was Sandra in the Green Room, pulling on her coat, her cheeks flushed with warmth and excitement. 'Are you coming to the reception? I'll walk with you, if you like.'

'Yes,' Fay said uncertainly. 'I was looking for Adam.'

'Haven't you found him?'

'No. Have you seen him?'

Sandra shook her head. 'He's probably waiting outside. Hang on, just finding my gloves.'

He wasn't outside and a glumness settled over Fay. Where was he? He'd said he'd be here.

'Georges didn't come to the concert either, the wretch,' Sandra said, trying to cheer her up. 'I'm meeting him later on at the reception. I expect we'll see Adam there. Did you say that he was invited?'

'He said he was.'

'There you are then,' Sandra said, which sounded meaningless, but it somehow cheered Fay.

They walked together until they came to the hotel where they'd been the first night, when Fay had stood on the balcony and listened to the beguiling music before Adam found her. Again there was a drinks reception, with hundreds of the same kind of people who had been present last time, but now there was a large group that included Colin standing around the Prime Minister, waiting to be introduced. Fay stared around, only interested in seeing Adam, but there was no sign of his blond head, his tall, laughing figure, his eager face, raised to look for hers.

She joined a circle of people from the orchestra and sipped champagne, not really listening to them. Frank was blustering about something again and gradually she tuned in. It was about it being his last concert for the orchestra, but by the time she started to engage properly, the announcement for dinner came and they all began to drift towards the restaurant.

Two dozen white-clothed tables lay sparkling with glass and silver under the soft light of chandeliers. Afterwards, Fay didn't remember much of the rest of the evening, so anxious was she about Adam. She drank a little too much and picked at the food and politely listened to the elderly Frenchman next to her talk about his love for the works of a long-dead English artist of whom she'd never heard. Across the table, Sandra and Georges talked to each other. Sandra looked very happy and animated, hanging onto his every word, Fay thought. Georges was certainly sitting close to her, whispering in her ear, but Fay noted that he was always glancing at people passing, exchanging greetings with some of the men, and admiring the women a little too openly, and she felt sorry for her friend.

Fay left with her violin as soon as she politely could after the dinner and took a taxi back to the hotel, wanting to be alone. When she collected the key from an old man on reception she hadn't seen before, she asked if there were any messages. He took his time finding the right pigeonhole, then inspected a slip of paper he found before passing it to her with a gravelly *'Voilà.'*

She took it, and seeing that it was a telephone message from Adam, read it quickly. He had rung just after she and Sandra had left for the concert.

Je suis désolé, the receptionist had written down. Desolate. It sounded more sincere than the casual English 'sorry'. Adam was desolate that he would not be able to come tonight because of – here the receptionist had crossed out the word for 'emergency' and replaced it by the one for 'difficulty'. It seemed he would telephone again in the morning.

Fay walked slowly upstairs, rereading the message, glad to have heard from him but wondering what was wrong. The thought of an emergency was worrying, and clearly he'd thought so too, which had made him soften the word to 'difficulty'. What could be wrong? Had he been hurt during the demonstration? She hoped it was nothing bad to do with his family. Still, she was comforted. He hadn't simply declined to turn up this evening. There had been a good reason, and he was *désolé*.

In her room, feeling suddenly fed up and exhausted, she changed for bed as quickly as she could, taking the trouble only to fit her black dress over its hanger in the wardrobe and to wipe off her make-up with a few strokes of cold cream. But when she turned out the bedside light and lay at last between the cool sheets, she couldn't settle. Her mind was full of everything that had happened that day. Adam, the demonstration that morning, the concert music that still played in her head, but above all there was the story that Nathalie Ramond had told her that had swept away her foundations. It seemed that there had been a long period when she was young when she'd been separated from her mother who was in the Vittel internment camp and the nuns had looked after her. That explained the familiarity of the convent when she'd visited, her memories of playing there with her toy animal. There had also been the feeling of terror that had engulfed her when she'd imagined shouts and the thud of boots on the stairs. Perhaps that had been the day that her father had been killed.

There was so much though, that she didn't remember. She must have wiped out altogether the scene of what had happened in the church that day. Had she even understood what was going on? And Mme Ramond hadn't said what happened to him afterwards, whether the Gestapo had taken his body away. That was something else she'd failed to ask her.

And that dreadful time – all those months – when she must have missed her mother, but nobody had properly explained where she was or when she would see her again. And then they told her, the nuns, that she would travel on a long train journey with Sister Thérèse to find Kitty, except she hadn't found her. Instead she had been thrust onto another train full of strangers. The woman who took her had said something Fay didn't fully understand, because she hadn't spoken English for so long. She recognized the word 'safe' though, and 'mother' and heard the clatter of the wheels as the train gathered speed ...

July 1944

The woman was kind, blowsy-looking with untidy greying hair and a face that sagged under her make-up. She smelled strongly of perfume. Fay knew this wasn't her mother, so who was she? She had a sense of her mother deep down inside, but no memory of her face. The blowsy woman made a space for Fay to sit. Somebody gave her some bread and a piece of sausage and called her a 'poor thing'. Another gave her something sweet and strong to drink from a bottle. After that the blowsy woman tucked a coat round her and she fell asleep.

When she woke, she was bathed in perspiration and the sight and sounds of the compartment moved in and out of focus. The blowsy woman stroked her hair, felt her forehead and exclaimed. Fay was given water from a different bottle then taken to a smelly lavatory to relieve herself. Back in her seat she fell asleep again.

The next thing she knew, she was falling into pitch dark, the women were crying out. There was an awful mechanical screeching as the train ground to a halt. The blowsy woman gathered her off the floor and cuddled her and she cried, but despite the noisy confusion she fell asleep again, the tears drying on her cheeks. When she woke once more the train was still at a halt, but her fever had gone and she felt much better. Her stomach growled with hunger.

Outside, it was sunny. The view from the window was beautiful, with meadows and trees stretching as far as the eye could see. They were told the train track was damaged, but that they could get out and the women jostled each other in their eagerness. They all sat together in the grass amongst the flowers. Men could be seen working on the track in front of the train. An eager fair-haired girl from Fay's compartment was dispatched to look for Kitty. When she returned her eagerness was gone. The women all stared at Fay and talked to each other in whispers of dismay.

Fay plucked wild strawberries and popped them into her mouth as she watched a ladybird climb to the top of a plant with delicate white petals. Above, a blazing sun moved imperceptibly across a sky of opaque blue. The women grumbled or slept or delved in their suitcases for bits of smuggled food, which they shared, always making sure Fay had some. The younger ones played cards, or laughed or sang or squabbled. The men appeared to finish their work on the track and went away, but for a long time nothing happened.

The air cooled and the blue sky darkened to ultramarine, to navy, then indigo, and points of starlight began to gleam. Finally a whistle blew and everyone rushed to climb back on board. The sky was black velvet when the train started on its way again.

Two mornings later, the train trundled through a battle-torn landscape and entered a city of smoking ruins. It edged slowly into the remains of a station where Fay pointed at the ridiculous sight of engines upended in craters. Gangs of ragged men were tearing at the rubble, urged on by German soldiers with whips. The women were made to change trains and after another long wait were relieved to leave the scene behind. They sped out into open countryside again. The train carved its way through green fields, then a gorgeous plain of golden sunflowers, and entered a long, dark tunnel. It emerged to pass along the side of a steep gorge above a rushing river.

Night followed day, followed night, and Fay felt as if she'd been travelling for ever. The air grew hotter, the colours of the houses changed from white and grey to ochre, with roofs of baked terracotta. They were in a region of terraced hills patterned by rows of small trees. The train stopped at a small station where police milled about the platform, and the women were made to disembark. Fay followed the blowsy woman, whom she had learned to call Cynthia, as she lugged her suitcase along a road to a hotel. It was a shabby place with overcrowded rooms. Fay spent several nights there on a straw pallet on the floor and woke each morning covered in red spots that itched all day. There was strange food, too, fatty spicy sausage, olives, which she detested, and a cold salty soup that caught the back of her throat. She made friends with a mongrel dog that slept on the veranda and wondered what would happen next.

It was here, on the border with Spain, that the trouble began. At the hotel Cynthia searched Fay's bag for her papers, but there was nothing, nothing to state legally who she was or where she belonged. '*Anglaise,*' Fay said, when a woman who spoke French asked her. '*Ma mère est anglaise,*' but this was all she could remember of what Thérèse had told her.

'You will have to pretend you're my daughter, sweetpea. *Ma fille,*' Cynthia said, pointing first to Fay. Fay was beginning to remember her English. Cynthia was from England, too. She didn't understand Cynthia's argument with the border guards, but knew she must pretend to be her daughter. She obediently held the woman's hand until everybody stopped arguing and they were allowed to pass and climb onto another train with the other women. This train set off up into the mountains, the women watching the majestic landscape with whispered awe.

After they'd descended the other side, the train raced across Northern Spain towards Portugal. This time at the border, Cynthia hid Fay in the lavatory until the guards had passed along the train. And now the hot, exhausted women, who'd been travelling for a fortnight, began to be cautiously excited. Freedom was within reach. Portugal had remained neutral during the war, and it was from Lisbon that they would board ships to England or Canada or America, wherever was home.

Fay, who could not follow all their talk, grew quieter and quieter. She wondered what would happen to her, where her mother was, whom Thérèse had promised she'd see. When at last the train drew into Lisbon and the passengers began to gather their luggage, she slipped her arms through the straps of the canvas rucksack and followed Cynthia down onto the platform.

Cynthia walked across with her suitcase to a tall man in a cream suit and a Panama hat, one of the Embassy party sent to meet them. He was pale-haired with a grave face and mild hazel eyes. Fay waited as he and Cynthia conversed. She heard her mother's name mentioned – Kitty Knox. The man studied Fay with concern. She looked back at him, shy and silent. He smiled down at her kindly, then crouched in front of her and took off his hat to speak.

'My name's Lawrence York. How old are you, Fay?'

In answer she held up her hand with fingers splayed, and slowly folded down her thumb.

'Four? Goodness me,' he said in surprise, for he had thought her younger. He straightened up, and taking a pipe from his pocket, blew sharply into the bowl then inserted it into the side of his mouth; all the time, his eyes remained fixed on her. 'Well, Fay,' he said, taking out a tin of tobacco, and the pipe trembled between his teeth as he spoke, 'we'll have to sort out how to get you home.'

Home, she thought, not understanding. Paris was home. Here she was, alone in a strange place where the heat poured down and this kind man was going to send her back to Paris. Maybe her mother was in Paris.

'Home to England,' he said, and her heart sank. England wasn't home.

And even Cynthia was leaving her.

'Goodbye, sweetpea,' Cynthia said, and ruffled Fay's hair. 'And the best of luck.' She acted sad, but Fay detected an air of relief. She watched Cynthia pick up her case and walk away without looking back. She was alone with this man who was sending her to England.

'Come along,' he said, and took her hand.

For a long time after that the days all melded into one. She lodged with a wealthy Portuguese family in a pretty villa overlooking the sparkling Atlantic Ocean. She'd never seen the sea before! The mother was a gentle person who bathed her, brought her fresh clothes and sent her old ones to be washed. There were two boys, a few years older than Fay, who played boys' games, but she was shy. When they asked her to join them to kick a ball about, she shook her head, and sat on her hands on a bench in the garden to watch them, hardly moving, her shoulders hunched, her expression grave.

The family didn't speak much English and no French. She couldn't understand their Portuguese, so she fell into the habit of not speaking at all. The elder boy was learning the violin and, seeing her interest, he showed her how to position it under her chin and to move the bow across the strings. The first time that she made it sing, she smiled up at him with pleasure.

Early one morning Major York returned and told her it was time to go. The woman packed up some clothes in her canvas bag. She fitted it on to Fay's back and buckled up her shoes for her, tutting because they had become so tight. Fay climbed into the back of York's black car, clutching the leather seat as they wound through Lisbon's narrow streets to the sea. She was amazed to see the harbour spread out before them, busy with ships and little boats, and was overwhelmed when the car drew up in the shadow of a vast grey battleship. They got out. Queues filled the gangways. The decks of the ship were packed with bright, excited passengers, calling and waving to the people below.

York took Fay's hand and led her up another, quieter gangplank near the bow of the ship. At the top a petite young woman in neat naval uniform was waiting.

'Fay, this is Third Officer Briggs. She'll be looking after you on the voyage. Take good care of yourself now and send my best wishes to England.' York patted Fay's shoulder, nodded at the little Wren, and was gone.

'Third Officer Briggs is an awful mouthful. Call me Sally,' the young woman said. Her eyes shone with happiness.

Her fiancé was a senior officer on board and they were on their way back to Southampton. They were getting married next month and she would see her family in Gloucestershire.

During the nightmare week of the voyage, Fay hardly saw Sally at all because the ship was overcrowded and the crew so busy. Instead Sally gave her into the care of a recently widowed woman with a little girl of seven, whose bed Fay had to share. Then the girl became ill and the mother hardly quitted the cabin. Fay was left to roam the boat alone. She recognized some of the women from the train from Vittel, though there was no sign of Cynthia, and they'd give her food or take her on deck to watch the flying fish. But much of the time she was alone, a ghostly figure one might easily miss, sitting quietly in a corridor.

Southampton was a line on the horizon, then a pattern of ships and buildings, and then they docked and the excited passengers surged down the gangplanks, to greet waiting mothers, sweethearts, brothers, friends. Sally collected her from the widow and escorted her down the gangplank and along the quay to a small square wooden building.

'This is Fay Knox,' she told the stern man sitting inside behind a desk. 'She hasn't anyone to meet her. The Embassy in Lisbon thought you might sort something out.'

'Did they, now? Fay Knox, you say. Well, Miss Knox,' the man said. He opened a drawer and taking out a form wrote out the date, 17 August 1944. 'Then we shall have to, won't we?'

*

Fay came to consciousness in soft darkness, her limbs still paralysed with sleep. Relief flowed through her. It had been only a dream. But what a dream, how vivid! She'd been a child again, lonely, unloved, unable to run or cry for help. She tried to remember the details, to make sense of it. Usually when she did this a dream would lose its power over her and retreat. This time though she could still picture everything clearly. There had been that image again of flying through the air and a woman crying 'Ups-a-daisy'; but surely what came next had been merely a dream. She'd been on a train that travelled on and on, winding its way up amongst mountains. The hull of a great ship had loomed above her. Then, she'd been on board and had watched its prow carving through an impatient sea, gasped as cold spray stung her face and, in a moment of rapture, had seen fish leaping from the water. She had with her a little canvas rucksack that contained all she had left in the world. The more she thought about it all, the more these pictures asserted themselves. They must have been locked away in some deep recess of her mind, and now she remembered. She had indeed been lost, as Nathalie Ramond told her: lost, silenced, and frightened of never being found.

She had been found though, hadn't she? She must have been. And she didn't know how or where or when.

Something had interrupted her dream. A noise outside perhaps, or simply the need to turn over. If she'd stayed asleep, would she have remembered the rest of it? Fay lay thinking about all the people who had helped her on her way to England. Thérèse, Cynthia, the man from the Embassy, the Portuguese boy with the violin, the pretty

Wren on board ship, the list went on, but what had happened to her back in England? Another image came to her then, the old familiar picture of a vast room full of children's voices. She sensed that she was close to the heart of the mystery now, but it wasn't quite in focus, not yet.

And she was going home today. She let out a long breath like a sigh. She'd see Adam, she hoped, but what else should she do? Mme Ramond had imparted all she knew about her, and she had learned much and regained certain memories. Yet the tale wasn't quite told. For that she'd need to go home and confront her mother. She yearned to do that now. But there was something else, too, something she'd tried several times to do – and that was to visit the curé at the church of Sainte Cécile.

She must have fallen into a deep sleep again, for the next time she woke the sun was shining through the curtains and, somewhere close by, church bells were ringing. It wasn't a frightening sound at all this time, not like at Notre Dame. These chimes were joyful, as for a celebration.

Chapter 35

Sunday

After breakfast, Fay finally managed to speak to the curé on the phone and arranged to see him at the church at noon, after the eleven o'clock service.

She had packed, and was waiting for the porter to store her luggage, and wondering vaguely if Adam would ring again when the front door of the hotel opened. She glanced up, thinking it might be Sandra returning, and her heart lifted, for it was Adam who entered. The lobby was busy and he didn't see her for a moment. She waved to catch his attention and he saw her and strode across.

'Fay. Thank heavens, I was worried I might miss you.' They regarded one another as if for reassurance, before he bent to kiss her cheek.

'What happened?' she whispered. 'I got your message and ... Is everything all right?'

'It is now, yes. I am so sorry,' he said. They were both conscious of others listening. 'Perhaps when you're ready – if you're not busy ...'

'I am ready, and I'm not busy till later. Thank you,' she said to the porter. 'You have locked the violin in the cupboard?'

'Yes, mademoiselle. It is quite safe.'

'Thank you. I'll collect everything early this afternoon.'

'How was the concert?' Adam asked once they were out on the street.

'Completely wonderful.'

'Damn. I mean damn that I missed it.'

She laughed. Though she had wanted him to feel guilty, she had said 'wonderful' with sincerity. 'Colin will be fed up that you won't have been able to review it.'

'Oh, I expect we'll manage a mention,' Adam said, with the mysterious air of a magician.

'How?' she wondered, surprised.

'Trade secret. Never mind that though, Fay. I am sorry I didn't come. Not least because I wanted to see you.'

'What happened? You haven't told me yet.'

'I will, but I want to show you something. Here we are, it's just down here.' They'd come to a narrow side street, and Adam steered her down it, past various local shops and restaurants. They came finally to a very ordinary-looking bar with a couple of tables outside where he stopped and took her arm, gently turning her to him.

'This is it. Before we go in, I ought to explain. There is somebody I want you to meet.'

'Somebody . . . here?' It was the ordinariness of the place that puzzled her. 'Who is it?'

'He's called Saïd.'

'Saïd? That doesn't sound very French.'

'It's not.' Adam hesitated, taking out his cigarettes as he waited for an arrogant old gentleman wearing a trilby and a fur collar to pass out of earshot. 'Saïd is an Algerian. I've been helping him.'

'Oh.' Then, 'Adam, it *was* you,' she breathed, suddenly seeing it all. A glimpse of a man's fair head in the crowd as the police dragged demonstrators away.

He looked at her enquiringly.

'I was there at the demonstration. I didn't mean to be. I was walking back to the hotel and was drawn to what was going on in the square. I saw General de Gaulle. He was going to present medals, didn't you say?'

'To soldiers who'd been stationed in Algeria, yes.'

Fay told him what she'd seen and what had happened to her, and Adam frowned as he concentrated on her story. 'I thought I saw you,' she finished, 'but I wasn't sure. Have you really been going to political meetings?'

'You know my interest in the issue. The continued subjugation of the Algerians is an injustice, and I try to get incidents like this reported in the *Chronicle*. Not that my editor thinks our readers are bothered by what's happening in a far-flung corner of the French Empire.'

'I'm afraid he's probably right. And what about your friend Saïd?'

'You'll still come in and say hello?' Adam looked eager.

'Would he mind?'

'Not at all. I've told him about you and he's keen to meet you.' He threw away his cigarette and she followed him inside.

The bar was empty of customers but for a moon-faced man sitting at a table reading a paper. The room stretched back, long and narrow, gloomy in its recesses. Adam greeted a spaniel-eyed youth tidying up behind the counter, introducing him to Fay as Armand Martin, and asking if they could speak to his father.

'*Mais oui*, of course,' the young man said, gesturing to the far end of the room. 'Go through and find him.'

They passed through a swing door into a small kitchen where a middle-aged man with the same sad look as Armand was frying thick slices of purple sausage in a spitting pan.

'*Ah, bonjour, m'sieur, m'mselle,*' Monsieur Martin greeted them, wiping his hands on the cloth at his waist and reaching for a plate of chopped mushroom. 'You've come to see our guest? Take yourselves up. You know where to go. The doctor has been, as you requested, m'sieur.'

Fay followed Adam up a flight of back stairs to a landing, dark and none too clean. Adam knocked on one of several doors, saying in a low voice, 'Saïd, it's Warner.'

The door was opened by an Arabic-looking man with a wiry build and a direct gaze. He was young, maybe thirty, and his unshaven face was horribly bruised and swollen; he wore a bandage over one eye. 'Please come in,' he said in French, and as he pulled the door wide, Fay saw that his right arm was in a sling.

They entered a small, sparsely furnished bedroom with a single window, across which a thin curtain was drawn. A folded newspaper lay on the untidy bed, its headlines shouting yesterday's violence. There was a sharp stink of disinfectant in the air.

'Saïd, this is my friend Miss Knox,' Adam said.

'Delighted to meet you.' Saïd was dressed in clean clothes that were so big they were obviously borrowed. He spoke in English and gave a polite bow rather than offering his hand.

Fay said a formal 'How do you do?' but couldn't help

adding, 'I'm sorry you're hurt. I was at the demonstration. It was terrifying.'

'*Oui*,' he said, feeling his jaw. 'The gendarmes were brutal. But you should have seen what I did to them.' He had the kind of quirky smile that made him easy to like.

'That's nonsense, of course,' Adam said quietly. 'Saïd didn't lift a finger against them, Fay – didn't even resist arrest.'

'The doctor tells me I'll survive.' Again, that smile. 'Maybe there is a rib cracked or two, but they'll mend. I won't be going out for a bit looking like this though.'

'I should hope not, you'd frighten the horses,' Adam said with a false cheerfulness. And when Saïd looked puzzled: 'It's something we say in England – never mind,' Adam added hastily. He turned to Fay. 'Saïd is my excuse for missing your concert. I was at the police station, trying to get him out of their clutches.'

'They wanted to charge me with, how do you say, disorder,' Saïd explained. She liked his expressive eyes and the way he spoke, with beautiful rolling Rs. 'But Adam here, and his friend the attorney, they helped me. I am most grateful.'

'It took some doing,' Adam put in with a laugh. 'Saïd will not keep quiet at the best of times.'

'Ach, well, they were accusing me of ridiculous things,' Saïd replied, trying to throw up his arms in horror. Instead he pressed his hand to his chest and grimaced. 'Would you mind if I sit down?' he said, and without waiting for a reply he sank onto the untidy bed with a grunt of pain. Fay sat in the only chair whilst Adam leaned against the doorjamb.

'We won't stay long. You should get some more rest. Also, it's Fay's last day in Paris and we have things to do.'

'I have not had much sleep,' Saïd agreed. 'Monsieur Martin has been very good. He says I can stay here for a few days, but I think if it is safe I will go home today.'

Shortly afterwards, they took their leave. Saïd looked exhausted, but his eyes burned with a passionate intensity when they said goodbye. '*Vive l'Algérie,*' he said quietly, shaking Adam's hand.

'*Vive l'Algérie, mon ami.*'

As they walked out into the sunshine, Fay pushed her arm through Adam's and squeezed it in a sudden rush of tenderness.

'What is it?' he asked. His expression was gentle, but there was amusement in it, too.

'I was thinking about you helping that poor man. And there was me, this stupid, narrow-minded English girl who should know better, thinking that people like him who make a stand bring everything upon themselves. Until I saw what happened yesterday.'

'You're not stupid,' he said, 'or narrow-minded. It's simply that you didn't know.'

'I *am* stupid. I never thought properly before, you see. About how you're not responsible for where and what you're born, but you can help what sort of person you are. Madame Ramond made me understand what a generous man my father was. You know, he and my mother needn't have stayed in Paris in 1940. Nobody would have thought the worse of him if he had taken her to America, or back to England. But he didn't go. He stayed and helped people. He didn't mind about their nationality or religion or anything like that. He just helped them.'

'He sounds a marvellous man,' Adam said quietly and Fay, imagining that he was thinking about his own father, chose her next words with care.

'You're doing the same thing, Adam, don't you see? By helping Saïd and his people.'

'I've been trying to report their side of things. Saïd, his wife and children, have to hide in a condemned house. It's so unjust, what's happening to these people.'

'I realize that now, but I didn't before.'

They had reached the main road and were waiting to cross the street. On an impulse she turned to him right there on the pavement, reached up, wound her arms round his neck and lifted her face to his, till their lips almost touched.

He bent towards her. 'You are wonderful,' he whispered, his breath mingling with hers.

'No, it's you who's wonderful,' she replied. 'I love you.'

'Oh Fay, I love you, too,' he just had time to say before their mouths met in a searching kiss.

Chapter 36

She and Adam didn't have much time left together in Paris, but there was one thing Fay had to do, and when she explained he agreed to accompany her.

The curé was waiting for them in the church as he'd promised, pottering about after the morning service, blowing out the candles. Fay introduced Adam to him and the older man shook his hand.

'We have but a small congregation on Sundays,' he said sorrowfully, 'now that the nuns have gone, but some still come. The old connection with the school means something to families in the neighbourhood, although it's a shame they can no longer rely on the convent for teachers.'

All the time he was speaking, Fay was looking about, thinking, Here is where it all happened. The place was so peaceful now, it was difficult to believe it had been the scene of such terror and violence. Perhaps it was the years of prayer that had overcome it.

She couldn't help noticing the grand piano, set proudly in its own space beneath the windows, and shrouded by a thick brown cover.

'Ah yes,' the curé said, seeing her interest. 'That is a fine instrument. Not played much now, which is sad, but it's kept in tune. Do you play, may I enquire? You said you were a musician, I believe.'

'I'm a violinist, but I do play the piano a little.'

'Please, will you try now? I should like to hear it again.' He went across and folded back the heavy cloth, then lifted the keyboard lid and set the piano bench in place.

She sat where her mother must once have sat, suddenly feeling unequal to the task. She glanced up, desperate, needing reassurance, and saw shafts of sunlight shining golden in the gloom. Adam was standing close by, watching her quietly, waiting, and she could tell he understood.

Now she knew what she needed to do. She arranged her fingers on the keyboard and after a false start or two, for she was nervous, she began to play the ethereal chords of the Moonlight Sonata.

She closed her eyes and it was as though the music played itself, at first haunting, then building to a passionate climax. And when she opened them again, behind the slim figure of Adam, she sensed there was somebody else, a burly man with a head of thick cropped fair hair, sitting on a chair in the front row, his hat beside him. She couldn't see his face clearly, but she knew who he was and somehow she knew that he was smiling.

The music quietened and the final chord faded away. There was silence in the church. She glanced across to where she'd seen the familiar presence, but the chair was empty. Had she really sensed her father, or had it been her imagination? It was strange, and yet instead of desolation she felt oddly comforted.

'Fay?' Adam was before her. She smiled at him and a wonderful sense of peace flowed through her as she reached up and gave him her hand.

Behind them came a sigh and the curé said quietly, 'Bravo, Mademoiselle Knox – that was sublime.'

'Thank you,' she said. 'It's a lovely instrument.'

'Tell me,' he said, as he helped her close the keyboard lid and let the cloth drop back into place. 'Was Madame Ramond of help to you? Did you find out anything more about your mother?'

'Yes, I did, thank you,' Fay said. 'She's been most helpful. It's rather a long story, but my mother lived here in the convent for a time, just before the war. She'd come to Paris to study the piano and didn't know anybody, so her guardian sent her here. It wasn't long afterwards that she met my father and they married.'

'Ah, so that is the connection with Sainte Cécile. And your father, what was his name?'

'Eugene, but everybody called him Gene.'

'Eugene Knox.' The curé gave a slow, satisfied nod.

'You said that there was something you wanted to show me?' Fay reminded him.

'Yes, there is,' he said. 'Come with me, please, both of you.'

They followed him out through a heavy door and into the passage that must lead to the convent. But instead of continuing to the far end, he stopped a short way along next to an unassuming-looking door in the side wall and started to draw back the bolts.

In the half-darkness, Adam's hand grasped hers and squeezed. The curé turned a key and shoved at the door until it suddenly unstuck. It opened onto a narrow yard. They stepped outside and followed the curé's black-cassocked figure along a flagstone path that took them to a small graveyard behind the church that nobody would ever guess was there. It was tightly packed with graves, some large and ornate, others more modest. Many of the stones were ancient and crumbling, the names on them no longer legible.

'Hardly anyone comes here now,' the curé said, his voice echoing against the walls that overshadowed this hidden place. He placed his hand almost fondly on a tall, leaning stone. 'Mère Clothilde here died at the time of the Prussian siege, 1871. Now, over here somewhere . . .' he set off to walk between the graves, eventually stopping at a small cross squeezed between two long coffin-shaped edifices, 'this is Sister Clare, who died during the Occupation. I believe she was the last nun to be buried here. There was no more room after that. Father Paul, my predecessor, he is buried in Montparnasse. We laid Mère Marie-François to rest there, too. That was a sad day.'

Fay listened to all this, wondering why he'd brought them here.

'This is beautiful.' Beside her, Adam was examining a stone statue of an angel, its wings sheltering the grave of a long-dead priest.

'Yes, though I would prefer something much plainer myself when my turn comes,' was the curé's dry comment, 'such as these over here – come, this is what I want to show you.' He picked his way across the cemetery until he came to an area in the middle where there were a dozen modestly labelled graves even more closely spaced than the others. His eye scanned the scattering of gravestones, then he stepped across to one marked only by a simple cross, like Sister Clare's. Another nun? wondered Fay, as she moved alongside. She stared down at it. In a vase before the cross was a single red rose, full blown, its petals starting to fall.

She crouched by the grave to examine the words cut deep into the stone, and as she read them a ripple of shock ran through her. She glanced up. 'Adam,' she whispered. She stared at the stone again, the words fixing themselves in her head. *Eugene Knox, 1912–1942*, and underneath, *In forever loving memory*.

'My father,' she breathed. Adam came to crouch beside her and laid his hand on her arm as he read the words.

'I thought this must be him, my child,' the curé said, coming to stand behind the stone. 'I am sorry I did not remember this the last time you visited, but I rarely come here. The name Knox, when you said it, was familiar to me – but the way you said it was different to the way I pronounced it in my head, so I did not make the connection. Still, there is a reason that I ought to have done.'

He pointed to the dying rose, its petals scattered on the ground. 'Every spring, one of those arrives. An early rose – I don't know where they find it. There's never any message, only the instruction to lay it on the grave. Mère Marie-François was very old when I came here a few years back and her mind was going, poor woman. She said the young man had been killed in the war, but she mixed up the story with others about airmen escaping and a girl she called Sofie. It made no sense to me.'

'Poor lady,' Fay said. 'She was right though about my father being killed in the war. I'm afraid that it was here in the church that it happened.'

'Was it?' the curé said, dismayed. 'I know that Father Paul used to hide people from the Nazis here. I found a letter from one of them in the drawer of his desk, thanking him.'

Briefly, Fay explained everything to him.

'What a very terrible story,' he said when she'd finished. 'And Madame Ramond told you this? I did not know about her past here as Sister Thérèse. Mère Marie-François's mind was very confused in her last days.'

'Did she know who sends the rose every year?' Adam asked.

'I don't remember us ever speaking about it,' the curé said sadly.

'I think I know who sends them,' Fay said with quiet confidence. There could only be one person in the whole of the world who would remember her father every year and who would send him one of the flowers she grew – a red rose, the symbol of passionate true love. Her mother.

Fay and Adam walked hand-in-hand back across the river towards Notre Dame, to where it had all begun for them. As they approached the magnificent façade with its air of lightness and grace, they exchanged smiles. 'Would you like to go in?' Adam asked, but Fay shook her head.

'It's beautiful, but I've had enough of gloomy places for the moment,' she said. 'I'd rather find somewhere to sit down in the open air.'

They found a café overlooking the river with tables scattered outside and soon Fay was warming her hands around a large cup of creamy white coffee, whilst Adam sipped a tiny espresso.

'I still can't believe it,' she said, 'that my father was buried there and my mother knew all the time. It's such a shock, and this might sound strange, but I feel I've found him properly now.'

'I'm glad,' Adam said sincerely. 'It must make such a difference to you.'

There was the slightest of catches in his voice, and he did not speak for a while. Fay wondered whether he was thinking about his own father, who was very much alive, but with whom his relationship was tainted. She wanted to say something to him, but couldn't think what. Perhaps it was something she could help him with in the future, to find his way back to him. Surely his father loved him and there must be hope.

She watched Adam, trying to absorb everything about him, so that she'd remember how he looked and carry the memory with her. Strands of his fine hair lifted in the breeze from the river, which blew away the ash from his cigarette. He gave her a lazy smile. 'What are you thinking?' he asked.

'That . . . I'll miss you,' she said, and at once he moved closer and took her hand, lacing his fingers with hers.

'I'll miss you, too,' he whispered. 'I can't bear the thought of you going. The week has passed so quickly. We've been together such a short time, yet I feel I've known you all my life.'

'Oh, Adam, it's the same for me.'

He leaned in and kissed her cheek by her ear so that she shivered with desire.

'Where shall we go, what shall we do? Now, I mean. I don't suppose we have time to go back to mine, do we?'

She smiled at his hopeful face and glanced at her watch. It was lunchtime nearly, but she wasn't hungry, not really. She thought about it and finally the loving look she gave him and the way she squeezed his hand told him the answer.

Chapter 37

Monday
Norfolk

The sun was low in the afternoon sky as Fay walked across the hospital garden towards her mother. It was little more than a week since she'd last been here, but already the weather was warmer, the air alive with the humming of bees. The tulip-like blooms of the magnolia tree were fully open now, and under its soft white canopy Kitty rested on a pillow on the arm of her bench, asleep. Fay pulled up a chair next to her, and Kitty's eyes fluttered open. She raised her head, sat up smiling and gave Fay her hand.

'Darling, you're back. I hoped you might come today. Dr Russell said you would be too tired after your journey, but I'm glad he was wrong.'

'I didn't have very much sleep last night,' Fay admitted, leaning to kiss her mother's cheek, 'but I wanted to come straight away. How are you?'

'Oh, much more my usual self, I think.' Fay thought her mother did indeed look better. Her eyes were bright, her expression alert, and she'd lost that fuzzy pallor that a stay in hospital can give people. 'It must be those delicious oranges you brought me.' Her eyes were full of mischief now.

'If so, they must be magic ones,' Fay told her and her mother laughed, but it wasn't yet her old, happy laugh and Fay detected wariness in her manner.

'How was your trip? Did the concerts go well? Tell me about it. You must have had a wonderful time.'

'Wonderful is the word,' Fay told her. 'The performances went really well. The sponsors were so generous. We had some marvellous dinners and Paris was ... well, beautiful. And, oh, I brought you a present.' She handed over the prettily wrapped parcel and her mother exclaimed over the blue scarf. They talked for a while about the music and how Colin had promised Fay a permanent place in the orchestra following Frank's departure.

Finally, it was as though a spell of quietness fell over them. Fay shuffled in her chair and said, 'I don't know where to begin. Mummy, you sent me a letter ...'

'Yes.' Kitty paused, then said quickly, 'Perhaps I overreacted. I'm sorry, Fay, it's just that when Dr Russell gave me your phone message, I was upset. Thérèse was the last person I thought you'd meet. I'd wanted you to find out ... everything – but not from her. I was hurt by—'

'*You* were hurt?' All Fay's pent-up frustration burst out. 'What about me? Why did you never tell me anything yourself?' Suddenly she was overwhelmed by it all over again. Last time she had sat here, a week ago, she had known almost nothing of her early childhood, had not even suspected that anything her mother had told her about herself had not been true. And now, after these dumbfounding revelations, Kitty was talking about her own shock, her own feelings. Fay turned her face away to hide her misery.

'Don't,' Kitty said in a fluttery voice. 'Oh, please don't.'

'Mummy . . .' Fay began, still not looking at her. 'I don't know what to say to you.'

'Tell me all about what *she* told you then,' Kitty said urgently. 'I need to know what I have to answer for.'

Fay met her mother's eyes now and read so much in them. Pain, yes, but also courage. Most of all there was a strong, steady love, the love that had been there for her all her childhood, when there had just been the two of them, Kitty and Fay, living together in Primrose Cottage, secure and happy. If this cosy picture hadn't been the whole truth then it was still part of the truth. Kitty had given Fay the life she had now.

'All right,' Fay said, and she related the story from the beginning, describing how, following the clue in the ruck-sack, she'd visited the convent and met the current curé, André Blanc.

When she broke it to her mother that Mère Marie-François was dead, Kitty cried out, 'Nobody told me! Oh, that's so sad.' She had known, however, that Sister Thérèse had left the convent after the war and married Serge and that the couple had gone to America.

'I wrote to the Reverend Mother once, soon after we moved to Primrose Cottage. I felt she should know that you'd been found and that we were all right. And she wrote back and told me. It was a surprise, I can tell you. Who would have thought it? A pair of dark horses. But don't let me interrupt. Go on, do.'

So Fay related everything that Mme Ramond had told her, from the time of Kitty's arrival in Paris and meeting Gene to the terrible scene in the church that had culmi-nated in Gene's death, and her journey down to Vittel with

Fay. Occasionally Kitty corrected some small error of timing or the nuance of a reported conversation, but largely she nodded in agreement as she concentrated on the story. Fay stumbled as she told the most awful part of all, and when she glanced up at her mother, saw that Kitty's eyes were squeezed shut, her mouth trembling as though she was trying not to cry.

'Then his hiding place was discovered when Hoff felt the shape of the ring beneath his boot, and turned back the carpet to reveal the trap door.'

Kitty's eyes flew open. 'Tell me that again.'

'Why? Is something wrong with what I said?'

'No, nothing. Just tell me exactly what she said about how Obersturmführer Hoff discovered the crypt.'

Fay repeated what she'd said, how the man had been pacing up and down on the carpet and must have felt beneath his foot the awkward shape of the ring lying in its recess in the flagstone.

'Didn't Thérèse say ...?' Then Kitty stopped. 'No, it doesn't matter.' She looked thoughtful for a moment, then much brighter. She said, 'Go on.'

The next bit was worst of all. As Fay repeated in broken phrases what Mme Ramond had told her of how Gene was shot, Kitty stared out across the garden, an exquisite pain etched into her face.

'She said you were taken away and sent to prison, Mummy. And then to an internment camp. She didn't know all the details, only what she learned from the letters you sent Mère Marie-François.'

'It's true what she told you,' Kitty sighed. 'They took me away from you.' She described how she'd been questioned by Herr Obersturmführer Hoff but that he'd had to let her go in the end. And how she'd been sent to Vittel and hadn't been allowed either to leave or felt able to have Fay with her. Hearing her mother say this to her face helped dispel some of the anger and confusion Fay felt. It wasn't that her mother hadn't wanted her, it was that she hadn't been allowed to come home to Fay. And, as Mme Ramond had said, Kitty had refused to put her daughter in danger by having her with her in the internment camp.

When Fay described how she and Thérèse had travelled down to Vittel and how Thérèse had put her on the train for Lisbon, her mother's anger was unmistakable.

'I have never forgiven her for that,' she snapped. 'The woman was an imbecile.'

'I don't believe she was. She had to make a difficult decision in a fraction of a moment.' Fay explained it to her mother as carefully as Nathalie had done to her. How the young nun's English had not been good enough to understand that the others on the train merely *thought* Kitty was on it too, rather than knowing for sure that she was. 'She had no time to look for you properly, the train was about to leave. What would have happened if you *had* been on it and I was left behind?'

'I simply dread to think,' her mother said. 'But I wouldn't have got on the train without you. She should have known that, the simpleton. She should have made the guard hold the train whilst they found out if I was on board.'

They were both quiet again, thinking of the might-have-beens.

'I've remembered it now,' Fay whispered. 'The train journey, I mean.'

'Have you really, darling?' Her mother appeared troubled. 'You were never able to tell me anything about what happened. I believed that you'd blocked it out along with everything else.'

'It came to me in a sort of dream the other night, but when I woke I found I did remember bits. At least, I think I did. There was a woman called Cynthia who looked after me. At some point I stayed in a house overlooking the sea. I didn't feel unhappy exactly in the dream, just very alone. There was a boy who taught me how to hold a violin and draw the bow across the strings. I remember how happy I was when I made it sound.'

'I didn't know that. How curious – that you became a violinist. You were nearly five in the summer of 1944, and most successful violinists begin that young.'

'I'd forgotten all about it, but now my memory has started to come back. I remember the ship, how gigantic it was. What I don't remember is what happened after we reached England. I can't seem to link everything up. There was a man with very bushy eyebrows, I know that much because I was frightened of those eyebrows.'

'I know who he was, Fay!' her mother cried. 'He was in the harbourmaster's office at Southampton – the first person I found in England who remembered seeing you!'

'How did you find me? What happened when you arrived back at Vittel and found that I'd gone?'

'It was an awful shock. Frankly, I wanted to kill Thérèse. She scurried back to Paris. It was the doctor at the camp who helped me. He went to see the camp Kommandant and managed to put me on a train for Portugal the following day. It was the most appalling journey.'

Kitty paused to collect her thoughts, then went on. 'The train stopped altogether at Lyon and there wasn't another one for days because of the fighting. After that there was a hold-up just before the Spanish border. I was the only English person on the train and a German soldier who was checking everyone's papers insisted mine weren't in order. I think he had some grudge towards the English. He kept talking about how an English soldier – well, "swine" was the word he used – had "murdered" his brother. I was still on your father's passport and there was some confusion as to whether I was English or American, and the ghastly man decided to make something of it. So there I was, tearing my hair out in a police cell at this little border town whilst they decided what to do with me. Finally they received instructions from someone further up and let me get on a train. But it was too late to catch you, far too late. By the time I reached Lisbon the *Marina* was a distant dot on the horizon.'

'How did you find out I was on it?'

'When I arrived at Lisbon I went straight to the British Embassy and besieged them with questions. Eventually they found a Major York, who told me he'd put you on board the boat himself. It had been on its way back from Egypt, he said. After that I didn't know what to do. He said the Wren he'd put in charge of you was expected to hand you to the local authorities at Southampton. It's difficult to explain what a muddle everything was. There were so many displaced people trying to get home, he was pulled every which way. He promised to try to get someone to radio the ship about you, but who knows whether this happened and if anything resulted from it.

'I was put on a Swedish cargo ship that was going home via Liverpool. I can remember a week later a fellow passenger pointing out the coast of Cornwall, and feeling I would die of frustration because we weren't stopping. Liverpool was so sad – the area round the docks had been flattened by bombs. It was a relief though, to be back in England. I took a train to London, then another down to Southampton. Southampton was in a terrible state, too. England seemed a different country to the one I'd left seven years before. Everyone looked so very drab and tired, yet there was this relentless cheerfulness, too. We were winning the war, you see.

'At what remained of Southampton docks I spoke to a great many people before I found your man with the eyebrows. He thought he remembered you, but only in the vaguest way. He had so many such cases to deal with, I think, and one more lost little girl didn't really register.

'He had a note that some woman had arrived at the office when he wasn't there and had collected you, but when I made enquiries no one could find any trace of who she was and where you'd been taken. I stayed in a guesthouse in Southampton whilst I searched, and Uncle Pepper's lawyer wired me some money, but it was a couple of months before the truth emerged.

'I went back to the Harbourmaster's Office twice in that period to ask further questions, and it was only after the second time that I noticed an untidy row of office buildings near the quay that I hadn't paid much attention to before. One of them had a battered sign up over the door on which was printed a name I recognized. The company was called something like Silver Stone Cruises, but it's the proprietor's name I'm talking about – John Stone.'

'I know that name.'

'He was our Flight Lieutenant Stone, who hid in our apartment in Paris. I remembered then that we'd talked about both coming from Hampshire and he'd told me about his family business. Well, I didn't know what to expect, but when I went across to see, I found the office open, and I could hardly believe it when there was our John Stone behind the desk working away, surrounded by stacks of paper. He was just the same as I remembered, poor man. His face was awfully scarred and, well, there was something not quite right about his posture. He didn't recognize me at first and was guarded, but when I told him who I was he was affability itself. We talked a for long time, and I learned that he hadn't passed his medical exam to return to flying, which had set him back badly. He was most upset to hear about your father, of course, but when I told him I was desperately looking for you, he promised to help. It was marvellous finding somebody who cared and who knew what to do. Such a brick. It turned out he was a local councillor. Eventually he discovered that your case had been muddled with another child's and that instead of waiting for me in Southampton you'd been sent to an orphanage. The only thing is, they didn't know which one. Several weeks more went by before there was news.'

'An orphanage,' Fay said slowly. She had a picture in her mind of a vast Victorian building full of skinny ragged children like something out of a history book. But perhaps it hadn't been like that.

'The woman from the charity who'd fetched you had thought you were an orphan. There was some plan that you might be adopted. Fay, it was so awful. I might have lost you to another family. I tore off to find you immediately. Blackdyke House, the place was called. It was in Derbyshire. *Derbyshire.* Miles away. Apparently it had been based in Kent but they'd had to move somewhere safer because of the bombs, you see. The place was probably perfectly well run, but I can remember the shock of seeing it: it looked, well, so bleak, like its name. Matron told me it had been requisitioned from a local industrialist. Not surprising. From the outside the house looked as dreary as a factory.'

'An orphanage,' Fay whispered again. A fog was clearing in her mind. There had been a vast room filled with the voices of children. She had used to dream about it. Could that have been Blackdyke House?

'The worst thing of all was that you didn't know me at first. And for a long time, weeks and weeks, you would not speak. When finally you did, you wouldn't talk about anything that had happened – and then I realized that you must have put it behind you, deliberately, that you'd locked away all your memories.'

'But what happened next? What about the things you've told me about, living in London and the deer?'

'That's all true, Fay. I rented a house in Richmond at the beginning of 1945 and brought Uncle Pepper's furniture out of storage to furnish it. I didn't want to go back to Hampshire, you see, it would have been too sad, and I thought, well, in London, I would be able to find some sort of job with my music.'

'And it was hit by a bomb?'

'Yes. Oh, those horrible Doodlebugs. It must have been one of the last that fell. Fortunately, it happened while we were out one day. We came back to find our house and the one next door completely destroyed. I was in despair after that, as we'd lost practically everything. Then I remembered dear Adele Dunne. She'd always said that I was welcome to go to stay with her in Norfolk, so I thought that perhaps we would for a while, just until we sorted ourselves out. Well, the trouble is, I couldn't remember where it was she said she lived. I only found it by poring over an old map in the local library until I found a name I recognized. Little Barton, near Norwich. I did recall that the house was Primrose Cottage and so I wrote to her there. And that's where we ended up. She wanted to move to her parents' holiday home near the sea, and suggested letting us have Primrose Cottage at a ridiculously low rent.'

So then had begun the life Fay knew. The life her mother wanted for her: a perfect, tranquil childhood with a perfect tranquil mother. If it hadn't always been quite perfect, nor her mother quite tranquil, it had been most of the time.

'I tried to make up for everything, Fay, all the bad things that had happened to us. When I realized that you didn't remember anything from before, I was actually relieved. It gave us the opportunity to start again. I could pretend that you hadn't ever felt abandoned and afraid. I still had that photograph of your father – I had carried it in my handbag always – but that was all there was left of our previous life.'

'There was a postcard of the ship,' Fay remembered, 'in the frame with the photograph.'

'Was there? I'd forgotten. Major York gave that to me in Lisbon. At the time it felt my only link to you.'

The sadness in her mother's face was almost too much for Fay to bear. She'd come here frustrated and angry, but all the accusations, all the anger had faded away. It was as though she realized for the first time the weight of the burden that her mother had had to bear. After all, Kitty had always remembered everything. She had endured it alone. There had only been Miss Dunne to speak to who would understand, but she had died a few years after the move to Little Barton.

'Did we see much of Miss Dunne?' Fay asked. 'I do remember her a bit. Didn't she come to tea occasionally?'

'Yes,' her mother said. 'But when she did, we were careful not to touch on the past. I think she was aware that I was trying to protect you. But I also sensed that she didn't wish to dwell on the bad things that had happened. She was like that, always very positive, full of what she was doing in her village, her work with the church, and she drew and painted a great deal. In fact, we have one of her pictures – that snowy landscape hanging above the sofa in the sitting room.'

'I didn't realize that was by her.' Fay had always been fond of the wintry scene with rosy-faced children throwing snowballs.

'The vicar at her funeral was very surprised when I told him how brave she'd been during the war. Nobody seemed to know about the refugees she'd helped, or how she was involved in saving Jews at the camp. She wasn't popular at Vittel because some people thought that by working at the Kommandant's office she was collaborating, but she actually used the opportunity to access internees' records. She would warn people who were about to be transferred, or put them in touch with local *résistants* who could help them to escape. And I do know that she hid a Jewish man in her room once. There was another woman from Vittel who came to the funeral, and she told me that. I dread to think what punishment Adele would have suffered if he had been discovered. And she never told anyone.'

Fay was moved beyond measure. Mme Ramond had certainly made Miss Dunne sound strong and high-principled, but she hadn't realized that the woman had put herself in quite such danger to help others.

'She was a modest person and would have been embarrassed if anybody had spoken about it or praised her,' Kitty explained. 'She was ill for some months before she died, but she hated anyone to fuss. "Worse things happen at sea," she'd say, even when she knew she was dying. She was a good friend to us, Fay, and helped us so much.'

'I wish I could remember her better.'

'She was very fond of you. It was so wonderful, that time in Paris when she arrived through the snow with milk for you. Did you say that you visited our apartment? You are resourceful. I wonder if it's changed much?'

'I think some of the furniture must be the same, though there's no piano. Oh Mum, I can't think how I forgot.' Fay reached for her bag and withdrew the letter that the boy Bertrand had given to her. With it came the photograph from Mme Ramond's album. The wooden zebra was in her case, left in the reception hall of the hospital. She'd show her mother another time.

Her mother almost wept over the photograph, then her eyes widened as Fay passed the letter to her. 'The woman who lives in our apartment now kept this for you. She said it arrived soon after they moved in, after the war ended, but she didn't know what to do with it.'

'I don't recognize the writing,' Kitty said, frowning. She turned it over and broke open the flap easily. The letter she slid out was written on two leaves of onion paper that rustled as she unfolded them.

Fay left her mother in peace to read the letter. She had noticed that a tea trolley had arrived in the garden room and went to collect tea for them both. When she returned, she was concerned to see that her mother was crying, the letter still open in her hand.

'Mum, what is it?' she asked, laying the tray down on the grass and going to her. Who could the letter be from?

Kitty was not able to speak for a moment. She took a handkerchief from her sleeve and blew her nose. 'I'd always thought it was her fault.'

'What do you mean?' Fay asked, misunderstanding. Surely the letter was nothing to do with Mme Ramond?

'It's from my old friend Lili Lambert,' Kitty said. 'Here.' She held it out to her daughter. Fay frowned as she studied it. It was written in French and the handwriting was still fresh and legible. The date at the top was 25 September 1944 – a month after Paris had been liberated, then. The first couple of sentences were easy to translate: *My dearest Kitty, I am leaving this with the concierge in case you return. You will be surprised* ... but Fay could not quite get the sense of what followed.

'It's something about her husband, isn't it?' she asked her mother, passing the letter back. 'My French isn't good enough. Tell me what it says.'

'I'll translate.' Kitty's finger traced the lines as she read.

I don't know where you are all living now, but perhaps you will come back, and I wanted you to know ...

After the last time I saw you, I did not like to come again. I felt that I had in some way betrayed you already and feared that I might bring you further trouble. Still, now that the war is over in Paris I would like to explain. You will remember how we spoke in the park about Jean-Pierre, my husband? Well, as I made my way home a man stopped me and said he knew I was worried about Jean-Pierre and wanted to help. He was French, and said that he was a policeman, but I do not know why he wore

no uniform. He said that he would be able to help Jean-
Pierre, but that I must do something for him. He said
that you were under suspicion of activities that would
damage the interests of Free France and that he'd like me
to visit you to see if you were harbouring anyone illegal
in your apartment.

I was terrified, Kitty. I did not know what was the right
thing to do, but when I visited you and saw that letter on
the table, the one beginning Mes chers parents, *which you*
tried to hide from me, I knew this policeman's suspicions
must be true. But I want you to know, I did not betray you.
When it came to it I simply could not, for you were my
friend – so I went and told him that I'd found nothing and
nobody. I don't know whether he believed me, but after that
he did not bother me again.

'Oh, Fay,' Kitty said, leaning back and closing her eyes
briefly. 'I can't tell you how good it is to hear this. To
know that Lili was my true friend, after all. It must have
been an awful decision she had to make. She might have
been putting Jean-Pierre in danger. How brave of her.'

'But what happened about Jean-Pierre?' Fay persisted.
'Does she say?'

'Yes.' Kitty returned to the letter. 'Here we are: *You can*
imagine my joy when a week after that, a card arrived from the
Red Cross to say that Jean-Pierre was alive and well. He had
merely been transferred to another factory and the records had
not been updated, which is why my letter had been returned. I
have heard from him several times since then and now my hope
grows every day that we shall soon be reunited.'

'Oh, I hope that they were! But what do you think the
whole thing meant? Who was the man with the gloves?'

'I don't know, Fay. Perhaps I never shall. Lili says here he was French, not German. Perhaps he had overheard our conversation in the park and used it to persuade Lili to do what he wanted. I wonder if he was connected to the Resistance? Or to Mrs van Haren? There is no doubt that Serge would have been in danger if he'd stayed in his lodgings – he had told me that the Jewish family he lived with had been taken away – but perhaps he was also in danger from someone else, someone who resented his visits to Mrs van Haren. So many odd things happened at that time, and some never made any sense.' Here Kitty sighed.

She's so much better, Fay thought suddenly. Her mother seemed like her old self again, lively and interested, though she still wore an air of sadness.

'There's more though – look, Fay, you read it. I can't, not without crying.'

Fay took the letter once again and slowly worked out the final paragraphs.

I hope one day, Kitty, that we will meet again as your friendship meant so much to me. I was so lonely in Paris without Jean-Pierre, and seeing you and little Fay used to be the highlight of my day. You were so kind to me and helped me be strong. We had such fun together, didn't we? I pray all the time that you are safe and well, you and your husband and Fay. What a lovely mother you are to that little girl. Never have I seen a child and her mother so close. One day I hope to give Jean-Pierre children, but in the meantime I still look after my Joséphine. She is five now and blossoming like a flower.

Avec toutes mes amitiés,
Lili xx

'That is a beautiful letter,' Fay said, folding it and returning it to her mother.

'I would like to see Lili again some day,' Kitty sniffed.

'Perhaps you should go to Paris and find her?'

'Oh, I wouldn't know where to start.'

'But you could try. And you could visit Serge and Nathalie.'

Her mother was quiet for a long moment then said slowly, 'I was wrong to tell you in my letter not to believe Nathalie Ramond. I . . . I did not know what she would say, whether she might come between us. But now . . . I think I might be ready to see her again.' And Fay felt a quiet happiness flow through her.

It was so peaceful out here in the garden. Difficult to believe that it belonged to a hospital. They finished their tea and an orderly came across to collect the empty cups. It was a different girl from the surly woman who had spoken to Fay last time and not allowed her time to say goodbye properly to her mother. This one was smiling and kind. She said that Dr Russell would be coming along shortly to see them, and then she left them alone again.

'If you did want to go to Paris,' Fay told her mother, 'I could go with you. I've a reason to return now, you see – not the music this time.' And she explained about Adam, how they'd agreed he would come to London in two weekends' time.

'He's someone special? Oh Fay, I am glad.'

'I'll take you to meet him when it feels right. I think you'll like him, Mum.'

'He is special, isn't he? I can see it in your face. You look so happy.'

'I always wanted someone I would love as much as you loved Dad.'

'Oh, Fay. I did love your father so much. No one else could ever measure up to him. But then I had you. It was such a lovely thing that Lili wrote, don't you think – that she had never seen a mother and child so close? I have looked after you, Fay, and loved you, haven't I?'

'You have,' Fay said gravely. 'Always.'

'I don't feel afraid any more, Fay. It's as though I've let go of something terribly difficult and heavy.'

Fay was moved to see her mother like this – free, for the first time. 'It sounds to me,' she said smiling, 'as if it won't be long before you'll come home.'

December 1944

One Sunday morning after church, Fay was sitting by herself in the refectory wearing her best dress that scratched and staring at a glass of milk. It wasn't the kind of milk she was used to, having horrid lumps of cream floating in it, but she'd been told to stay there until she'd drunk it, so when the youngest and kindest of the nurses came and said, 'Matron wishes to see you,' it was with relief that she got up from the bench and took the young woman's hand.

Had she visited Matron's office before? She didn't think so. Matron had hardly ever spoken to her. *Don't look at the dead animals*, the child told herself as they reached the hall. When the nurse knocked on Matron's door and propelled Fay into the room, the low winter sun coming through the window was so dazzling she hardly saw Matron's stout, corseted silhouette behind the desk. She was more interested in the other woman in the room, a slender, neatly dressed stranger with a gentle face, who rose from her chair with a soft cry.

'Well, Fay,' Matron pronounced. 'You must go and pack. It seems you'll be leaving us.'

She stood uncertain, peeping up at the stranger. Who crossed the floor and knelt before her with arms outstretched. 'Don't you remember me, darling?' the woman whispered in a voice that trembled with emotion.

Fay was noticing things about her more clearly now.

She was older than the lady in her dream and her face was tired and thin, her eyes purple-shadowed, but there was something about her Fay was trying to catch, like the words of a half-forgotten song. There, she could remember it now. She gave the tiniest sigh and the shard of ice in her heart began to melt.

She took an uncertain step forwards into the safety of her mother's arms.

Author's Note

The French invaded Algeria in 1830, but it took them many long and bloody years to subjugate the country and make it part of France. It subsequently became a destination for hundreds of thousands of French and other European immigrants who formed a colonial élite there, benefiting from the confiscation of land from local tribes. Dissatisfaction from the Muslim population, who were denied political and economic status, gave rise to demands for greater autonomy and finally independence from France. Tensions between the two populations led to violence and eventually the outbreak in 1954 of what became known as the Algerian War. This only came to an end in 1962 when the country was granted independence.

After a constitutional crisis in France over Algeria in 1958, President de Gaulle returned to power and instituted a sudden change of policy, deciding to work towards Algerian independence. Outraged, the OAS, an extreme pro-France group, used every means they could find to oppose this, and their clashes with the FLN, the main Algerian independence organization, brought the struggle to Paris. Repression by the French authorities was extremely harsh.

On 17 October 1961, six months after Adam rescued

Saïd from the incident described in this novel, the French police attacked a demonstration of some 30,000 pro-FLN Algerians. The resulting massacre in which seventy to two hundred people were killed – the true number remains uncertain – appears to have been ordered by the head of the Parisian police, Maurice Papon. Many demonstrators died when they were forcibly herded into the River Seine. Others were killed at the Paris police headquarters after they were arrested and delivered there in police buses. The events of that day remained hushed up for nearly forty years. In 1998 the French government finally acknowledged forty deaths. Papon was convicted in the same year on charges of crimes against humanity for his role under the Vichy collaborationist regime during World War Two.

On 17 October 2001, the Mayor of Paris set a memorial plaque on the Pont St-Michel that reads: *In memory of the many Algerians killed during the bloody repression of the peaceful demonstration of 17 October 1961.*

Acknowledgements

Whilst all my characters (saving the obvious ones) are fictional, it is impossible to write about the American Hospital and not to mention its real-life Chief Surgeon, Dr Sumner Jackson, who spent the wars years quietly aiding Allied servicemen to escape to Britain, and who died after being rescued from imprisonment for it. His story may be read in *Americans in Paris: Life and Death Under Nazi Occupation* by Charles Glass, one of a number of texts I consulted while researching this novel.

I should also like to acknowledge use of the following: *The Piano Shop on the Left Bank* by T.E. Carhart, *Murder in Memoriam* by Didier Daeninckx, *Curfew in Paris* by Ninette Jucker, *Red Princess* by Sofka Zinovieff and *Rosie's War* by Noel Holland and Rosemary Say. Clara's school trip in *Jerusalem the Golden* by Margaret Drabble inspired my imagining of Fay's first meeting with Adam. Agnès Humbert's *Resistance: Memoirs of Occupied France* with its vivid description of the Exodus from Paris in June 1940 was a starting point for this novel.

Another was a talk I attended at the Surrey Chapel in Norwich in January 2013 about Miss Elsie Tilney who, in Paris before the war, assisted Jews to escape abroad. Later she was confined in the Vittel internment camp where she worked in the Kommandant's office and hid a young Jewish man in her bathroom for a period to prevent his deportation to a death camp.

Many thanks to Christopher Jones at the University of East Anglia for advice on historical detail, to Victoria Hook for sharing her knowledge of music, to Dr Ann Stanley for medical information and to Louise Wormwell for suggesting the name Fay.

As ever, my grateful thanks are due to my agent Sheila Crowley and to all at Curtis Brown, to Suzanne Baboneau, Clare Hey, Sam Evans and all at Simon & Schuster, and to my copyeditor Joan Deitch. Lastly, love and thanks are due to my family, David, Felix, Benjy and Leo, who help in so many ways.

Discover France for yourself